PRAISE FOR MARY BURTON

THE SHARK
"This romantic thriller is tense, sexy, and pleasingly complex."
—*Publishers Weekly*

"Precise storytelling complete with strong conflict and heightened tension are the highlights of Burton's latest. With a tough, vulnerable heroine in Riley at the story's center, Burton's novel is a well-crafted, suspenseful mystery with a ruthless villain who would put any reader on edge. A thrilling read."
—*RT Book Reviews*, four stars

BEFORE SHE DIES
"Will keep readers sleeping with the lights on."
—*Publishers Weekly* starred review

MERCILESS
"Burton keeps getting better!"
—*RT Book Reviews*

YOU'RE NOT SAFE
"Burton once again demonstrates her romantic suspense chops with this taut novel. Burton plays cat and mouse with the reader through a tight plot, credible suspects, and romantic spice keeping it real."
—*Publishers Weekly*

BE AFRAID
"Mary Burton [is] the modern-day Queen of Romantic Suspense."
—Bookreporter.com

THE
DOLL
MAKER

ALSO BY MARY BURTON

The Forgotten Files
The Shark

Morgans of Nashville

Cover Your Eyes
Be Afraid
I'll Never Let You Go
Vulnerable

Texas Rangers

The Seventh Victim
No Escape
You're Not Safe

Alexandria Series

Senseless
Merciless
Before She Dies

Richmond Series

I'm Watching You
Dead Ringer
Dying Scream

MARY BURTON

THE DOLL MAKER

THE FORGOTTEN FILES BOOK 2

Published by Montlake Romance, Seattle

www.apub.com

Amazon, the Amazon logo, and Montlake Romance are trademarks of Amazon.com, Inc., or its affiliates.

ISBN-13: 9781503938441
ISBN-10: 1503938441

Cover design by Mecob Design Ltd.

Printed in the United States of America

THE
DOLL
MAKER

PROLOGUE

Sunday, October 2, 11:05 p.m.

The instructions were clear: Don't look inside the red trash bag. Meet the buyer, collect the money, and give him the goods. For God's sake, don't talk. Just leave. No one gets hurt. Everyone comes out a winner.

Simple. A moron could do it.

But Terrance Dillon was eighteen. And he was too curious, too fearless, and too naive for his own good.

Two hours ago, Terrance had been at the Quick Mart counting out the last of his rumpled bills and scattered coins to buy an energy drink and a bag of beef jerky. Terrance's thoughts had been centered on his girlfriend, who had spent the last couple of hours snuggling close to him and talking about the homecoming dance. As he'd dumped the last of his change on the counter, he worried about finding the money to pay for the big winter dance date and wondered how he'd tell his grandmother that he and Stephanie were dating again.

As Terrance had left the store and crossed the parking lot, his father pulled up in a new white Lexus, sporting a big grin. Fresh out of his latest stint in prison, Jimmy got out of the car and hugged his son, wishing him a happy birthday. The guy had been gone the last decade, and though they'd traded a few letters and phone calls, they weren't exactly what anyone would call close.

Still, Terrance had been stunned and kind of pleased by the in-person visit. He was flattered when Jimmy asked him if he wanted to go for a spin in the car and maybe help him tackle a big-paying job. Jimmy needed an extra hand for a couple of hours. Grab and go. Simple. Easy money.

Terrance found Jimmy's infectious laugh and smooth voice compelling. His old man made the plan sound foolproof. And despite all the shit between the two of them, he wanted his father's approval.

Now as Terrance stood in the alley, the half-moon glistening in a cloudless sky and shadows cloaking hidden nooks and corners, doubts whispered. The deeper the cold night air cut through his high school letterman jacket, the further his thoughts wandered from his father's guarantees of success to the contents of the bag gripped in his right hand.

Don't look in the bag. Better you don't know. Grab and go. Simple. Easy money.

He hadn't seen Jimmy in an hour, and his gut was telling him to bail on his old man. His grandmother had said Jimmy's get-rich-quick ideas always ended in disaster. She'd warned Terrance to stay away from the guy. Terrance wanted to love his old man, but he wasn't stupid. He knew Jimmy had gone to jail for selling drugs.

But Jimmy had seemed different at the Quick Mart. The ex-con acted like he really wanted to help his only son.

A freight train rumbled above on the triple trestle in Richmond's Shockoe Bottom district. The night chill oozed deeper, fueling his impatience and nerves. A small animal scurried in the dead end of the alley. A cat howled. Terrance shivered.

His phone chirped with a text. Hoping it was Jimmy, he fished out the two phones from his pocket, glancing at both displays. The message was on his personal phone, not the burner Jimmy had given him. The text was from Stephanie.

```
You home yet?
```

Terrance smiled, glad she was thinking about him. Jimmy had told him not to use his personal phone, but to communicate with the burner. Using the new phone, he texted back.

```
Terrance here. Almost done. Waiting on
my ride.
```

```
You okay? Where is your phone?
```

An unseen creature scratched in a darkened corner. He didn't enjoy lying to Stephanie, but she wouldn't like any of this.

```
I'm fine. My battery is dead. I'll call
in the morning.
```

```
Text me when your ride arrives.
```

```
Okay.
```

He shifted his feet and dropped the phones back in his pocket. He hated lying. This was bullshit. He was cold. Tired. Ready to go home.

He held the bag up to the moonlight, but thick plastic guarded its secrets. He shook the sack gently and heard the clink of glass. What the hell was in the bag? Jimmy had said it wasn't drugs, but why was it worth so much money? How much could one peek hurt? Just one.

Don't look inside.

He shooed away Jimmy's warnings and in the stillness unknotted the bag and looked inside. Moonlight shimmered off ten vials of drugs. The labels read "propofol."

Jimmy had lied. Terrance should have seen it coming. He should dump the bag. Run. But if he ran, there'd be no money. No "get rich quick."

He'd heard about the drug in the news. It was the kind rock stars took when they couldn't sleep. This kind of shit had killed some of those same stars. What the hell was someone going to do with this? His thoughts raced with unexpected excitement. Could it be for a famous singer? Someone he might know? It would be unbelievable to meet a pop star right here in the alley. Crazy. Maybe.

A slash of headlights approached and swiped across Terrance's face as a vehicle turned into the narrow lane. He quickly knotted the bag as a white van approached, slow and careful. The van was older. Clean. The kind of vehicle he drove when he worked on the lawn maintenance crew over the summer. The kind people didn't pay attention to. The kind he wouldn't drive when he got rich.

Heart pounding, he clutched the bag close to his side, doing his best to look like he knew what he was doing—like this wasn't his first drug deal. He pictured the way Jimmy stood, easy and relaxed. Always with a big grin.

Nerves fired with worry as he reminded himself Jimmy had promised the exchange would be easy. No questions.

Grab and go. Easy money.

He grabbed the burner and texted Stephanie, Terrance, again. My ride is here, I hope.

Who? Where are you?

In the city. White van here. Got to go.

Shoving the phone in his pocket, he stood straighter, heart pounding, his mind skipping beyond the next few minutes to the money he'd make. $2,000. Pocket change to famous singers, but it was a damn fortune to him. He'd already decided to buy his girl the necklace she liked. And put money toward a dryer for his grandmother so she didn't have to use the clothesline this winter.

The driver cut his headlights but kept the engine running as he stepped out of the car. Moonlight silhouetted the man's large frame. The stranger wore a hoodie and kept his head tilted down so shadows cloaked his face. Maybe that was for the best. No questions.

Just a little bit longer, and it would be over. He'd take the money and never look back.

Terrance held up the bag. "I have a delivery for you."

The driver didn't speak for a moment, then he moved forward, gravel crunching under his boot as he stepped into the alley.

The stranger didn't speak for what felt like forever before he reached in his jacket pocket. "Where's Jimmy?"

"Sick," Terrance lied, like Jimmy had told him.

For a moment the stranger stood still as stone. "Jimmy didn't contact me," he barely whispered.

"Said it was safer not to. Less said, the better."

A weighty silence lingered between them before the stranger spoke again. "Let me see in the bag."

"Do you have the money?"

The man pulled his hand from his pocket, a thick wad of bills clutched in his long fingers.

With trembling hands, Terrance untangled the hurriedly tied knot. He opened the bag so the man could see inside.

Approaching slowly, the man looked and nodded. He held out the roll of bills with one hand as he reached for the bag with the other. Eyeing the stranger, Terrance took the money and shoved it in his pocket. As much as he wanted to count it, he had no idea what he'd do if it were short.

The man turned, and for an instant, moonlight illuminated the side of his face. Terrance froze, transfixed as a memory elbowed free. Before he could rein in the question, he asked, "Hey, man. Do I know you?"

The buyer paused but didn't look up. A grin washed over stony features. "Do you?"

Don't talk. Grab and go. "Sure. Seen you around our town."

The man clutched the bag tighter. "That so?"

"No worries, dude. I'm no snitch," Terrance said, mustering false bravado. "As far as I'm concerned, this never happened."

"No, it did not."

Terrance patted the money in his pocket. "We're good. That's it?"

"Yeah. That's it."

Terrance stepped to the side, expecting to walk past the man and out of the alley. As he passed, the guy asked, "Your name is Terrance, right?"

Hearing his name sent a chill down his back. He didn't want anyone knowing he was here either. Shit. If his grandmother found out, she'd go nuts. And fuck, he was due to hear any day about the scholarship. He should have kept his mouth shut.

Terrance halted midstep. "Hey, man, I said I wouldn't tell."

"I know." He smiled.

Terrance's nerves eased.

The man moved with the blinding swiftness of a snake. Moonlight glinted briefly on a knife blade before he jabbed the sharp tip into Terrance's belly and twisted hard, then removed the cold metal quickly before stepping back. Terrance staggered. For a moment, he was stunned and simply stared at the hole in his jacket. Shit. A hole in his jacket.

With trembling fingers, he unzipped it to find a bloodstain blooming and growing wetter and warmer across his belly with each beat of his heart.

Terrance touched his stomach and pressed. Wincing, he studied his crimson-stained fingertips as if they belonged to someone else. Blood gushed from his gut. His head spun, and he dropped to his hands and knees. His fingers dug into the gritty cobblestones lining the alley.

Terrance looked up at the guy. "I said I wouldn't tell."

Long fingers clung to the blood-tipped knife. "I know, kid."

Terrance's body twitched. The heat raced from his limbs toward his torso. Somehow, he knew he was dying.

Carefully, the man knelt and slowly wiped the blade on his own pant leg before sheathing the weapon in a holster on his belt. Gently, he lowered Terrance to the ground.

"It'll be over soon. Close your eyes, Terrance. It's like going to sleep."

Terrance gripped the man's arm, his fingernails biting. "I don't want to die."

"We all die, kid."

He could feel his heart pumping hard, struggling now. "Not me. Not now."

"Death isn't terrible. Death is stillness. It's peace. I'll pray for you."

Terrance tried to sit up, but his body wasn't responding any longer. His skin had turned icy cold. He had no choice but to lie there listening to his killer's whispered prayers. He thought about his grandmother. His girlfriend.

"My grandmother's going to hear I got knifed in a drug deal," Terrance said.

"I'll see to it she doesn't know about this."

"Why me?"

"This isn't personal, kid."

"My old man told me not to talk."

"Jimmy was right."

How many times had his grandmother warned him about Jimmy? She was going to be so pissed and heartbroken.

Terrance's vision grayed, and his last image was of this man praying for him as his life bled out onto the dirty, gray cobblestones.

CHAPTER ONE

Monday, October 3, 9:00 a.m.

Agent Dakota Sharp with the Virginia State Police stood apart from the paltry gathering of mourners. Hands clasped. Feet braced. He wondered if guilt or loyalty had tipped the scales in favor of the twenty-mile drive north to this small town to attend his stepfather's funeral. They'd never been close, their relationship a study in toleration. And after Sharp's half sister died from an overdose, they rarely spoke again. And yet here he stood, carrying the banner for what remained of their family.

Roger Benson, RB to his friends, a talented artist and former chair of the local college's art department, would have been embarrassed by the low turnout at his final tribute. Two decades ago, when Roger was in his prime, he had been a showman who'd inhaled attention and devoured the limelight. He once joked his memorial would be a festive event. He'd envisioned hundreds in attendance, a New Orleans–style brass band, and an open bar. Or course, there'd be a proper prayer or two. Tears from the ladies. Bemused male laughter over past exploits. And, in the end, a fitting celebration of a life well lived.

Sharp scanned the cemetery's gray headstones, which skimmed the sloping hill toward a hedge and a stand of oaks ripe with orange and red leaves. The sky was a thick gray, and a southwesterly wind blew at ten knots.

A gleam of light glistening on a cross affixed to the coffin drew his attention to the four people behind the priest who stood at the head of the simple casket. To think so few had shown for the old man's closing performance; that had to sting for whatever incarnation of Roger hovered in the ether.

To the right of the funeral attendant stood Benson's former agent, Harvey Whitcomb, whose frequent cell phone checks undercut his bereaved expression. Benson's attorney, Donna Conner, wore a dignified black pants suit, a strand of pearls, and an expression that looked more bored than bereaved. Last was Douglas Knox, the town's former police chief, who'd shoehorned his expanded frame into a wrinkled gray suit.

Sharp had been ten when his mother, Adeline, a stunning woman with auburn hair and an infectious laugh, had been hired as Roger's office assistant. Four months later she was pregnant, she and Roger were married, and Sharp and his mother moved to Roger's lake house near the small college town north of Richmond.

From day one, Sharp and Roger had been at odds. Roger thought in shapes, sensations, and colors. Sharp clung to hard facts. Roger painted. Sharp shot empty bottles off a fence with a BB gun. Abstract versus linear lines. Joie de vivre met bull in a china shop.

As different as the two men were, they agreed on two things. They both loved Sharp's mother, and they both loved the baby she and Roger had together. Katherine Whitney Benson. Kara to friends and family. Because of Kara, Sharp and Benson did their best to get along.

Twelve years ago when Kara disappeared after a college party, Sharp had been deployed in Iraq as a marine sniper and was stationed miles outside Al Fallūjah. When word of Kara's death reached him, they'd been in the thick of some very nasty fighting. He wanted to leave immediately, but weeks would pass before the fighting eased enough so he could return home to his sister's grave and a family torn into fragments.

Neither his mother, Benson, nor Sharp could really accept that Kara had died of an overdose. It simply didn't fit the girl they'd loved so much. The devastating news had driven his mother to sedatives. Roger began harassing the police chief for any answer to explain why his only daughter was dead. And feeling helpless, Sharp had returned to Iraq.

His mother died a year after her daughter, and Roger grew more adamant about finding a reasonable explanation for why Kara was dead. No answers were ever unearthed, and the old man became more withdrawn and eccentric. When Sharp's contract with the marines ended, he'd wanted to protect his home turf, not a far-off desert, so he joined the Virginia State Police. After eight years as a trooper, he was promoted to agent two years ago.

Rain droplets leaked from thickening clouds as the priest read from the Book of Common Prayer, "I am the resurrection and the life, saith the Lord."

When the service ended, the priest made the sign of the cross, then picked up a handful of dirt, which he gently tossed on the casket. Sharp followed suit, scooping up some soil and letting it drop from his fist.

The priest said a final prayer, and Sharp turned toward the two headstones next to the empty grave soon to be Roger's final resting place.

He muscled off the heavy grief resettling on his shoulders as he stared at the stone-etched names of his mother and sister and the dates encapsulating their lives. Flexing his fingers, he suddenly realized he'd not brought flowers. Shit. It was a small failure but another in an endless succession.

His attention settled on Kara's headstone, and most specifically, on the day she died. The actual date was a guess. She had been missing five days before her body was found propped against a tree by a country road, so October 21 represented the medical examiner's best estimate. Her birthday was tomorrow. She'd have been thirty.

"Dakota Sharp."

Sharp braced and turned to see the old man in the gray suit approach. He walked with a slight limp and had bloodshot eyes. He'd been drinking.

"You're Dakota Sharp," the old man said.

A chill clung to the moist air and burrowed into his bones. "That's right. Chief Knox, correct?"

"I've not been chief for over ten years." His red tie, stained with a grease spot, was twisted in a large careless knot. "I became a private investigator after I left law enforcement. I worked for your father."

"Stepfather."

Knox reached in his pocket and pulled out a pack of gum. He offered a stick to Sharp, who declined. "Right. RB told me you two didn't get along."

At forty-one, Sharp could acknowledge he'd not been the easiest teen to rear. Roger, in his own way, had tried to be kind. "Your point?"

"Roger and I were friends for years. He knew I became a private investigator after I left the department, and he hired me to find out what happened to Kara."

"She died of an overdose."

"He never believed that."

Death and murder were a part of Sharp's job as an investigative agent for the state police. He'd dealt with families like his own who couldn't accept devastating loss.

Knox folded the gum wrapper in half and then into a triangle. "When did you see RB last?"

"We met for drinks in early summer."

They'd met in a run-down bar on Richmond's north side. Tense and feeling awkward, Sharp had nursed a beer as Roger drank gin and tonic and recalled how lovely Kara had been when she'd left for college. The old man's hand had trembled slightly when he summoned the waiter and ordered a second drink. "She had an artist's eye, like me," he'd said.

Sharp had let his stepfather reminisce until the conversation circled back to the same unanswered questions about Kara's last days. By the time Sharp had paid the tab and put the old man into a cab, he'd felt only pity.

"Roger never mentioned you two worked together," Sharp said.

Knox sharpened the folded edge of the wrapper with a yellowed thumbnail. "He talked about you a lot. He was proud of you."

Fat raindrops fell. Within minutes the skies would open, and they'd both be soaked. "What can I do for you, Mr. Knox?"

"Roger called me a couple of days ago. He said you'd be at his funeral."

"He died of a heart attack. How did he know there'd be a funeral?"

"I can't say for sure, but my guess is he sensed the end was close. RB said you were loyal to a fault. Best way for me to talk to you face-to-face was to wait for him to die. He knew you'd be here."

Unsettling to think the old man had pegged him. "You could have called me."

"Better to have this conversation in person."

"Why?"

"Roger wanted you to have all my files on Kara's case." The weary-looking old man shook his head. "I talked to so many people. There was a time or two when I thought I might have something, but none of my leads ever panned out."

"Why give me the files?"

"RB said you're one of the best at what you do. He said if anyone could find a hint of foul play, you could."

"Again, why dig into the case? The medical examiner ruled her death an accident. Overdose."

"You know RB never believed that."

"You were the chief of police then. You know there was no forensic data to back up Roger's suspicions of homicide."

"I'm not appealing to your logic, but your loyalty to RB. He wanted you to have one more look at the case."

These files were likely a rabbit hole. A goddamned blind alley destined to loop back to an unrecoverable loss that still bred anger and blame. Jesus, Kara would be alive now if Roger had been a more attentive father. Or, shit, if Sharp had stuck around, not joined the marines, and seen to it Kara lived a full life.

Sharp cleared his throat. "Do you have my address?"

"RB said you lived on Libby Avenue."

"That's the old place. I moved out about eight months ago." He pulled a business card from his pocket. "Send it to my work address. I'm there more than not."

Knox took the card, flicking the edge with a bent finger. "I looked into everyone who knew Kara, including you."

"Me?" Sharp had no secrets, so if Knox's comment was meant to put him on edge, it fell flat. "I was in Iraq when she died."

"She met people through you. I was interested in them."

"She also met people at school. At the lake. In the bars where she used her fake ID. You look into all those people as well?"

"I did. Funny you ended up marrying one of her friends. Tessa's her name, right?"

"We aren't together anymore." *Separated* was the legal term, but he wasn't keen to jab into more wounds today.

"I asked around. She's doing well. Hear she's overseas identifying the remains of lost US servicemen."

Sharp's patience snapped. "Make your point."

"When you're looking at my case files, keep an open mind. I think RB was right."

"What do you mean, right?"

Knox shoved his hands into his pants pockets as he turned. "Look at the files."

Sharp blocked the older man's attempt to leave. "You know who fed her the drugs?"

"I think if you look at the files, you'll see things I didn't."

The heaviness on Sharp's shoulders grew, but he didn't attempt to shrug it off this time. Kara's death was his burden to carry alone now.

Knox looked past Sharp toward the headstones. "I'd go to my grave willingly if this case were closed and I thought the person responsible for Kara's death were caught." He shook his head. "Maybe I spent too much time with RB. But I don't think the kid accidentally overdosed."

Sharp glanced back at the funeral attendant as he removed the flowers Knox had brought from Roger's casket. The man's gaze met Sharp's. When Sharp nodded, the attendant signaled two gravediggers to lower the casket into the vault and seal it.

"Send me the files."

CHAPTER TWO

Monday, October 3, 3:00 p.m.

The Dollmaker gently touched his newest creation's face, knowing it was still tender. The redness and swelling had faded, and the skin had shed the damaged cells, leaving healthy skin in its place. Still, her face would be sensitive to touch, and he didn't want to hurt her.

Her skin warmed his fingertips as he traced the outline of her thin dark eyebrow, then slowly along high cheekbones dotted with freckles, and finally over bright-red heart-shaped lips.

She was perfect.

A living doll.

Four weeks ago when they'd met again, her face had been lovely in an ordinary sort of way. She was in her late twenties with long limbs, a trim waist, and perky round breasts. But she'd reached her full potential, which was sadly destined to fade with age. So he'd intervened, rescued her from her predictable life, renamed her Destiny, and enhanced her beauty by painstakingly tattooing her face.

Experience taught him flawless tattoo art began with detailed prep work. And knowing Destiny deserved the best, he took his time, first sedating her, then cutting off her brown hair and shaving her scalp and eyebrows until the skin was as smooth as glass. Next he used alcohol pads to clean the skin so there'd be no risk of infection.

Only when the canvas was ready did he reach for the first tattoo gun loaded with the finest of needles. It took a full day of meticulous work to cover the key portions with the base coat of white ink. And though there were times when his hands ached and his back stiffened, he refused to rush. Finally, when all the base color had been applied and the tiny amount of blood wiped clean, he tattooed gracefully arching eyebrows. Next came the rosy blush of color on the cheeks. Stippled freckles. Heart-shaped lips. He saved the eyes for last, permanently lining the upper and lower lids with the steady hand of a seasoned artisan.

Toward the end of the transformation, she began to wake, so he injected a fresh syringe of sedative into her IV line. Very quickly she drifted off to sleep again. The transformation had taken more time and drugs than he'd planned, but the end result was worth the complication of restocking his drug cabinet.

After the job was complete, he wrapped her head and face, knowing the healing process was critical to the best tattoo work. Infection and neglect ruined tattoos. He changed her bandages four times daily, understanding his work at this stage was akin to an open wound.

For her safety, he kept her drugged and hydrated with an IV bag hanging over a special reclining chair. And as she slept, he spent hours embellishing and tailoring the clothes to match her flawless features. Again and again, he gently removed her bandages and carefully washed her face.

Ten days of healing had passed, and he now stood back and studied her. All the hours of labor and the extra days of recovering had been worth it. The colors on her face were vibrant and vivid, the lines clear and sharp.

He'd dressed her in a plaid skirt and a white top that was formfitting but not overly tight in a vulgar sort of way. He turned toward the collection of wigs and vacillated between blond and auburn. Finally, he chose the blond wig with long locks that curled gently at the ends. All the wigs were natural, the best on the market. He'd even taken extra care to trim the bangs on this particular model so delicate wisps of hair brushed the tops of her painted brows.

The Dollmaker carefully settled the wig on her head, centered it, and after brushing it, braided the strands into two thick ropes. He slowly rolled on knee socks, savoring the silky smoothness of her freshly waxed calf, and then folded the white cotton neatly at the top. He slid on patent-leather shoes and fastened the buckles so they were snug but not too tight.

Destiny's finishing touches included a small bracelet with a heart charm on her left wrist, and on her right hand, a delicate pinky ring. He painted her fingernails a pale pink, fastened delicate earrings, and dabbed hints of perfume behind her ears and on her wrists.

He stepped back, pleased. She was his living doll. A perfect mate.

He lifted her listless body and placed her on a red couch in front of a photographer's screen. He angled her face to the side and propped it up with a silk pillow. He arranged her braids on her shoulders and fluffed her skirt. Reaching for his camera, he snapped a couple of pictures as he did with all his dolls.

Glancing in the viewfinder, he frowned, not liking what he saw. Her eyes were closed. And to have the right effect, they needed to be open.

Time to wake up.

"Destiny," he whispered close to her ear. He ran his hand over her cheek, along the smocked edge of her blouse, and over the swell of her round breast. Drawn by her seductive lure, he squeezed her nipple. His body hardened, and unable to chase away temptation, he slid his hand under the skirt and caressed her.

She wasn't ready for him yet. But she soon would be. He needed to be patient.

"Time to rise and shine."

When she didn't stir, he pulled an ammonia caplet from his pocket, snapped it, and held it close to her nose. She inhaled sharply as the acrid smell chased away the haze.

His Destiny doll looked up at her creator with a lovely look of bewilderment. Yes, her open eyes completed the look.

He snapped his fingers. "Wake up, my sweet little doll."

She stirred and her eyes fluttered, but the sedatives still lingered. She was confused as she stared up at him. "Where am I?" she asked. "Am I getting better?"

"You're perfect."

She blinked, focused, and looked at her hands, now tattooed white like her face. She tried to rub off the ink, and when it didn't smudge, confusion turned to worry. She pushed off the couch, but her legs wobbled as her head no doubt spun.

"Not too fast, Destiny. It'll take time for the drugs to clear."

She staggered a step, crumpled to one knee. "What's happening? What have you done to me?"

"I've made you perfect."

She looked at her delicately painted fingernails, and as her gaze rose, she caught her reflection in a large mirror he kept in his studio. She froze, shocked. Tears mingled with disbelief. "What have you done?"

He didn't like the judgment in her voice. A perfect doll didn't judge. It didn't get angry. Look at you with disgust and horror. A perfect doll was still. Accepting.

"Shh," he said. He put his camera aside and reached for a drink cup with a straw. "It's okay. You're fine."

With a trembling hand, she touched the wig and then her bow lips. "I look like a freak!"

Worry crowded out his happiness. "Don't say that. I've made you perfect."

"I'm a monster!" Her hands trembled. Red-rimmed eyes spilled more tears.

He hated to see a woman cry. They used their tears to make him feel bad and to manipulate him. "Don't be ungrateful."

Shaking her head, she raised her hand to her head and felt the wig. "My hair?"

When she tried to tug the wig free, he brushed her hand away. "Don't do that," he said, trying to remain calm. "It took me a lot of time to get it right."

"It's not my hair. Not my skin." She forced herself to stagger toward the mirror. Her face inches from her reflection, she gawked.

"You must be pleased with the work. You're one of my best creations."

She rubbed the round blush on her checks and the dots of freckles. Worry ignited in her eyes. "What have you done to me?"

"I've made you beautiful." He snapped more pictures, enthralled by this instant of discovery. She might be shocked now, but she would be beholden to him when she realized the beauty of his work.

Her fingers curled into fists. "You've ruined me."

"I've made you a living doll."

With a yank, she pulled the wig off and smoothed her hand over her bald head. She screamed. The shrill sound cut through his head, shattering his calm.

She glanced wildly around at the large four-poster bed, the rocking chair, and the small table with the tea set. When she saw the door, she stumbled toward it. Her knees wobbled as her skirt skimmed the top of her shins.

She yanked on the knob, and realizing it was locked, screamed, "Let me go!"

"No one can hear you," he gently said.

She pounded her fist on the hard wood, crying for help and mercy. "This is a nightmare!"

"You need to calm down. It'll be all right. I have taken such good care of you."

Her eyes blazed with hate and disgust. "You fucking freak!"

Her harsh words belied the angelic features. "That's not necessary."

"Like hell it's not! Let me out of here! Let me go!"

As her raw words mingled with more weeping, he knew he had to silence her. Dolls were not supposed to speak, and Destiny was not supposed to cry.

He moved to his worktable and hurriedly dumped a powder into a glass. As she shrieked louder and pounded on the door, he added fruit-flavored water because he knew she'd like the taste.

Mixing the drink with a straw, he stood beside her. "Here, drink," he said, raising the straw to her lips.

She slapped at his hand. Red drink sloshed on her white skin. "Get away from me. I'm not drinking anything else."

"You have to drink," he coaxed. "It'll help you, and when you wake up, you'll be better than you were."

"How can I be who I was? This shit is all over me." Her hands clutched into fists, she slowly slid to the floor, her legs crumpling under her like a rag doll.

"I promise. Drink this and you'll be fine. You'll see." He pressed the tip of the straw to her lips that now were always smiling. "Please, drink."

"I don't want to drink." She tried to stand but couldn't rise. "I want to go home."

"And I want you to go home, too."

The Dollmaker wiped the tear from her cheek with his fingertip, pleased her face remained unspoiled. No smudged mascara or faded blush and lipstick. No one would undo his work.

She stared up at him, eyes large with fear and hope. Finally she sipped, her throat and mouth clearly parched.

When she finished, he pulled the straw away and dabbed the corners of her mouth. "You like the taste of cherry, don't you?"

She nodded.

"That's a good girl."

As she stared up at him, her breathing hitched, and she tried to suck in air. She drew a stuttering breath. "What's wrong?"

"It's okay. This is what's supposed to happen." The Dollmaker smoothed his hand over her bald head, already eager to put the wig back on her. "Soon your lungs won't work at all, and you'll stop breathing forever."

"What?" she gasped.

"Don't worry. I'll be right here with you. I would never leave you alone at a time like this."

"You're killing me?" Her tiny voice was now a hoarse whisper.

"No. I'm finishing the job."

Destiny tried to speak, to scream, but her lungs were paralyzed. He knew she was afraid, but her fear would soon fade. Gently, he tilted her back so he could peer into her eyes and watch the life drain from her body.

Her hand rose to his arm in one final attempt to cling to life. Her grip was surprisingly strong for someone who teetered so close to death.

He let her hold on to him, smiling and touching her cheek softly. "Shh. Let go."

Her fingers twitched and slackened a fraction. No more tears moistened her painted cheeks. Death pulled.

The Dollmaker leaned forward and kissed her warm, full lips. Slowly, her hand fell away as the remaining spirit faded from her body.

When her eyes closed, he removed a clean tissue from his pocket and wiped her face, marveling at the peaceful stillness settling over her.

God, she was a perfect creation. In all his years of practice, he'd never made anything so beautiful.

"Death has made you my permanent little Destiny doll."

He kissed her lips again, savoring the sweet tranquility. "I wish I could keep you forever, but we only have two or three hours. But don't worry, I'll be as careful as always. You'll see how much I love you."

CHAPTER THREE

Tuesday, October 4, 6:45 a.m.

Agent Sharp rolled up on the homicide scene, slowly drawing in a deep breath. Shutting off the engine of his unmarked police car, he stepped out, noting the half-dozen local police cruisers gathered, lights flashing, on the side of the rural road twenty miles northwest of Richmond. Tugging on his jacket, he moved across the open field toward the glare of floodlights, absorbing the morning chill hearkening an early winter.

Tall brittle grass brushed his pant legs as he made his way toward the uniformed trooper who stood guard at the edge of yellow crime scene tape. Sharp didn't need to ask for case details since he'd received them en route. The body had been found on the creek bank near Roger's hometown.

A local man checking on deer stands this morning had spotted the victim's white shirt as his flashlight's beam swept the creek's bank. The responding officer had secured the scene and found a driver's license lying on the victim's blood-soaked chest. The dead man was Terrance Dillon, age eighteen.

Sharp extended his hand to the officer, Trooper Riley Tatum, who along with her search-and-rescue canine, Cooper, patrolled along this section of the I-95 corridor. Sharp and Tatum had graduated in the same class at the police academy, and they'd both worked patrol together until two years ago when he transferred to the criminal investigations unit. "Riley."

Riley took his hand, her assessing gaze taking in his slightly damp hair, neatly shaved face, and black suit. "I think if I woke you up in the middle of the night, you'd be clean-shaven and wearing a suit."

He liked Riley. She worked hard and didn't pull any punches. "Don't hate me for being so *GQ*, Tatum."

"No, man, I just wonder if you ever let your hair down," she said.

He smoothed his hand over his closely cropped hair. "My hair's always down, Tatum."

Riley laughed. "You wouldn't know a good time if it bit you in the ass."

"I'm not that out of touch."

"You're aging exponentially, Pops."

At forty-one with a six-foot-one frame, he kept his body fit so Father Time's damage wasn't as apparent. He'd accepted the flecks of gray in his hair and deepening lines around his eyes as enviable marks of character. But, *Pops*? No.

"Where's Cooper?" he asked.

"In the car. We're about to wrap up the night shift and head home. I'd like to be there when Hanna takes off for school this morning."

"I remember my senior year of high school. Lots of fun."

She held up her hands in protest. "Don't tell me about your exploits. It'll give me more things to worry about."

He grimaced. "You're sounding like a mom."

Riley was only thirty but had slipped into the role of mother to an adopted daughter, who was almost eighteen. "I'm a fast learner."

When Kara was in high school, he'd been overseas, so their infrequent conversations were limited to the telephone. He'd enjoyed listening to her prattle on about her life, even if he didn't catch all the endless details about fashion and friends.

"Dakota!" Kara shouted. *"This is important! Are you listening?"*

"I'm listening."

"Okay, what's the color of the dress I'm wearing to prom?"

"Red."

"Oh, that's close. It's blue, Mr. Distracted!"

Sharp reached in his pocket and pulled out a packet of latex gloves pressed against a rumpled package of cigarettes. He tucked the cigarettes back in his pocket and, unsealing the gloves from a wrapper, tugged them on.

"They're going to kill you," Riley said.

"We all gotta die sometime." On a good day he pretty much avoided the cigarettes, but lately, there'd not been a lot of good days.

She shot him a look he was used to getting from her now—sisterly exasperation. She was dating Clay Bowman, the new chief operating officer at Shield Security, a firm based sixty miles north near Quantico. She didn't talk much about her personal life, but when Bowman's name came up, her demeanor softened.

"Do we have any county deputies on scene?" Sharp asked.

"They were called away to a fire in town. I told them I'd cover the scene and you'd update the sheriff later."

"I understand the victim has been identified," he said.

Riley shifted her stance and flipped open a small notebook. "Terrance Dillon. Age eighteen."

"Did you interview the man who found him?"

"I did a preliminary question and answer. His name is Mike Andreessen. He was scouting the land before hunting season opens. Inspecting deer stands."

"Where is he?"

"The local deputy talked to him and let him go. We've all the contact information, so it'll be easy enough to find him."

"Did he see anyone in the area about the time he found the body?"

"Didn't see a soul nor did he hear anything that was out of the ordinary. But he was pretty upset."

Extreme stress could narrow vision and shut down the other senses. "Is this his land?"

"No. Belongs to a friend, but he showed me a note he has from the owner. He has the right to hunt the land, a fact I've also verified with a phone call."

"Did he touch the body or move anything?"

"No, he did not."

Good. The less outsider interference there was contaminating his crime scene, the better. "Right."

State police didn't have automatic jurisdiction in this homicide, but Terrance Dillon had been found in a rural locality with limited forensic resources. There was also evidence the body had been moved from a primary scene, indicating multiple jurisdictions could be involved.

"Didn't you grow up in this area?" Riley asked.

"Yeah. About five miles east of here."

"Somewhere near the college, right?"

"Stepfather was chairman of the art department. His house was on the lake."

"Art department? I can't picture you around a bunch of artists."

"It wasn't pretty," he said. "Let's have a look at the body. Lead the way."

The sun peeked over the horizon, guiding them across the frosted field that crunched under their boots. Riley, an experienced search-and-rescue tracker, cut through the brush easily, forcing him to match her quick pace. Closer to the creek's embankment roped off by crime scene tape, a halogen light running on a generator glowed unnaturally bright on the water's rippling edge.

He lifted the yellow tape for her.

"Stop, you're spoiling me," she said.

"Only the best for you." He waited for her to pass, then ducked under himself.

The victim lay on his back, arms crossed over his chest. The boy's body was long and lean and had yet to gain the muscle mass many boys developed at this age. He wore jeans, boots, and a muddied letterman jacket.

Hands on hips, Sharp tapped his index finger on his belt. Needles pricked at the base of his skull, just as they had when he'd been a sniper and had his eye poised millimeters from the scope, finger on the trigger. "When was he last seen?"

"According to the missing persons report, when Terrance didn't come home on Sunday night, his grandmother got worried and went looking for him. She visited his regular haunts, including the Quick Mart on Route 1. The manager told her he saw Terrance about nine p.m. getting into a fancy white Lexus."

His gaze remained on the kid as he absorbed details: faint thin whiskers on a smooth chin, a small diamond stud in his left ear, a shiny high school class ring on his right ring finger. "Did he get in willingly?"

"Manager told the grandmother the kid was grinning when he opened the car's front passenger door."

"Has anyone been to the store to get surveillance footage?"

"Not yet."

"I'll take care of it." Sharp squatted by the boy's body. The creek's waters lapped against the victim's shoes.

A sensible man avoided this kind of violence and death. The horror was too much to process for the rational mind. But he had a knack for dealing with it. His ability to lock his feelings away into a box allowed him to narrow his focus to the target or objective. Later, sometimes weeks after a grim death scene, the emotions might stir. They wanted to be acknowledged. But he never let them loose. When it became too much, he went to the gym and pounded on a punching bag until his body was drenched in sweat and he was huffing for air.

Fellow officers said he was made of ice. They called it a blessing. The shrinks called it *compartmentalization*. The second term warned of consequences, but good or bad, he couldn't turn off this innate skill, which at times he considered a curse.

Sharp thought about the pack of cigarettes in his pocket. He'd light up after he left the crime scene. "Who's doing the forensic work-up?"

"Martin Thompson."

"Good. Where is he?"

She glanced around and pointed. "Shooting pictures." She raised her hand and caught Martin's attention. "He's headed this way."

The victim's hair looked as if it'd been cut recently. The jeans were new. The kid's clothing suggested he'd taken time with his appearance, as if he'd expected to be out with friends or maybe on a date.

"Why the hell did he get in the car?" he asked, more to himself.

Riley shook her head. "Why do teenagers do half the stupid-ass things they do? Your guess is as good as mine."

He'd been one hell of a daredevil as a teenager and at times run wild. If fate had shifted a fraction, maybe he'd have died young like this kid. But by some miracle he'd lived long enough for the marines to get ahold of him and channel his energy. Fortune had cut him a break, but it had cheated Kara and this kid.

"I preach to Hanna all the time about danger," Riley said. "Her time on the streets and kidnapping taught her how bad it can be, so she thinks she has all the answers. I know she's tuning me out when I'm on one of my rants about safety."

He'd always figured Kara for smart. "Just keep reminding Hanna. You can't do it enough."

Sharp studied the fingers on the boy's hand and noted the nails were crusted with dirt. His date-night-like attire didn't fit with dirty nails. "When is the medical examiner's office coming?"

"Soon. They're short staffed," Riley said.

"Aren't we all?" The rejoinder came from Martin Thompson as he stepped forward. In his midforties, Martin was a slim man who wore a blue Windbreaker that read "State Police" on the back, khakis, and black boots. Martin ran the police forensic team in this part of the state.

"Can I inspect the body?" Sharp asked. "I want to look at the wound."

"Sure, I've processed the evidence," Martin said.

Sharp laid his hand on one of the victim's before he lifted the folds of the jacket and searched the pockets. He found a rumpled bill, fifty-two cents in change, and a receipt from a convenience store. He also noted the blood staining the boy's fingers. "Martin, do you have an approximate time of death?"

"Hard to say. It was thirty-one degrees the last two nights, so rigor mortis would have taken longer. If I had to give a rough guess, I'd say thirty-six hours at most."

Sharp pushed up the bloodied T-shirt and inspected the knife wound cutting directly into the midsection. The wound was small, clean, and made with one neat jab. Judging by the injury and the dark blood, the blade had damaged the liver. There appeared to be no other marks or bruises on the kid.

He noticed the kid's belt buckle had been dusted with black fingerprint powder. "Martin, you pulled the print?"

"It was only a partial, but it's something."

Sharp pushed up the sleeves but didn't see signs of needle marks, and a check of the teeth found no signs of meth use.

"And the wallet was found on the body?"

"It was under the hands lying across his chest," Riley said. "Makes me think the killer wanted the kid identified easily."

"Any money in the wallet?"

"One dollar. According to the missing persons report, he'd received twenty dollars from his grandmother for his birthday," Riley said. "He must have spent the rest before he died, but I've seen people killed for less."

What the hell did you do, kid?

Sharp rolled the body on its side. "There's no blood under or around the body."

"He definitely wasn't stabbed here," Martin said. "If he had been, the bank and the surrounding soil would have been stained with his blood. He was dumped here."

"Not dumped, but placed near water," Sharp said more to himself.

"That's my theory," Martin said. "Wherever he was stabbed, he bled out and died within a minute. There's a crime scene out there somewhere soaked in blood and hard to miss."

"I've walked the area with Cooper, and we didn't find anything associated with the victim," Riley said. "He wasn't stabbed in the immediate area."

"What about tire tracks near the road?" Sharp asked.

"I found two that I've marked," Martin said. "There are traces of blood near the tire marks. They've been flagged and photographed and are ready for casting."

"Good."

The sun inched farther above the horizon, casting a brighter orange-red light on the creek. If the killer had tossed anything in the water, it could be miles from here by now.

His jaw tightened. "Thanks, Martin. Riley."

"Glad to be of service," Martin said.

"Cooper and I can make another pass in the area," Riley offered.

"No, you clock out. Go home. See your daughter off to school." Sharp searched the boy's pockets a second time. Double-checking behind his comrades and himself had been a habit he'd developed in the marines. He found nothing new. "If I need you and the dog, I know where to find you."

"I've the next three days off, but that's never stopped me from working a case," she said. "You have my cell."

Martin shook his head as he tucked a pencil in his pocket. "You two are workaholics. Do you ever stop and smell the roses?"

Riley shrugged. "Clay's in Houston on a job until late tomorrow or Thursday, and Hanna is obsessed with decorating the school gym for the homecoming dance. I won't see them until the end of the week."

"You and Clay are still an item?" Martin teased. "What's it been, five weeks?"

The comment startled a nervous laugh from Riley. "Six weeks and going strong."

"Hard to picture you domesticated," Martin said. "Are marriage bells ringing?"

"Too soon to tell. But if I ever go down the aisle, it'll only be once." She glanced at Sharp as if she realized what she'd said. "Sorry. Second time will be the charm for you."

The first had been the one. But he'd screwed it up.

When he didn't respond to her quip, Riley navigated back to the safer waters of murder. "Keep me posted on this case. I want to know why shit like this happens to young kids."

"I'll call the medical examiner and see when she's scheduled an autopsy." Sharp stared at the young boy a long moment. Dead at eighteen like Kara. "Is it true Shield Security is offering its expertise to law enforcement working on unsolved cold cases?"

"They are," she said, swinging her full, and clearly curious, attention to him. "I hear the applications are pouring in."

Absently, he pulled the victim's jacket closed and laid his hand on the kid's shoulder for a moment. "Could I get a case in the queue?"

A frown wrinkled her brow. "Clay would bump yours to the front of the line."

He was silent for a second as he took one last look at the boy. "At this stage, I'm not sure a girl's death was a homicide. The medical examiner tagged it as an accidental overdose, but the family never really accepted the ruling." He rose, stepping back onto the firmer ground of the bank. "I'm too close to the family to work the case."

"Who was the girl?"

"Kara Benson. Found dead on the side of the road not too far from here twelve years ago. Like I said, the medical examiner said it was a drug overdose, but Kara had no history of drug use, and again, her family never believed she took the drugs willingly." He hesitated before saying, "She was my half sister."

"Damn, Sharp," Riley whispered. "I'm so sorry."

Martin's expression darkened as he shook his head.

Sharp shifted and locked his focus on Riley. "Now's not the time for a blow-by-blow, but I'll soon be receiving case files that need reviewing. Like I said, I'm not the man to do the job since I have no objectivity."

"I'll call Clay today and give him a heads-up." Riley's low and steady voice was tight with emotion.

He wouldn't allow her sympathy to penetrate his guard. "Thanks."

Back at his car, Sharp slid behind the wheel and turned on the engine. He clicked the heater to high, anxious to drive the bone-deep chill from his body. He sat in the silence, watching as the body-removal team arrived and worked their stretcher through the tall grass toward the creek.

He reached for his phone to check messages. The first two were on existing cases. A witness had called the station and wanted to talk. Another was from the commonwealth's attorney regarding another case.

And the third—for a moment he sat still, staring at the name. Tessa McGowan. His wife, or more accurately, his estranged wife, had called a half hour ago. No doubt she was finally ready to file papers.

He fished out a cigarette and a silver lighter from his pocket. He lit the tip. Scents of tobacco mingled with trepidation. He inhaled twice before he played back the message.

"Dakota, this is Tessa. Hey, I'm back in Richmond, and I'd like to see you. Maybe we could meet for coffee. You've got my number. Thanks."

Her tone held a tentative edge, betraying a nervousness that told him she was uncomfortable making the call. Shit, in the early days of their relationship, they'd been totally at ease with each other. Back then, if either was restless, it was because they wanted to get the other naked and into bed.

But the detachment that enabled him to deal with death had made him a shitty husband. When he withdrew, Tessa had tried to talk to him, but he never could bring himself to open up. Toward the end, she was all but begging him to communicate.

He stared at the glowing tip of his cigarette, suddenly irritated by the strain and distance in her voice. He listened to the message again as he opened his car door and stubbed the cigarette into the dirt.

At least she had called rather than texted. Anyone who texted tough conversations was a chickenshit.

Drawing in a breath, he called her. On the third ring, his call landed in her voice mail. *"This is Tessa. Leave a message and I'll get back to you."*

Bubbly, upbeat, and no signs of stress in the recording. That tone fit the memories of the woman he'd once loved. Hell, still loved. He missed that voice. *That* Tessa.

At the beep he spoke succinctly. "Tessa. It's Dakota. I can meet you today at the coffeehouse next to the station. Two o'clock."

He ended the call giving her no room to negotiate. If she really wanted to talk to him about filing divorce papers—the only reason he attributed to the call—she would do it at his convenience. He'd made it easy for her to leave him, but right now he didn't feel like making this easy.

He started the car and was backing out onto the road when his phone pinged with a text. It was from Tessa. See you then.

The typed response must underscore her dread. She'd known that this time when she called, the probability of him answering was high. She needed to communicate, but she wasn't eager to talk.

As much as Sharp wanted to bust Tessa for the text, he couldn't, because he didn't want to discuss the final stages of their marriage either.

He put the car in drive and texted: Understood.

CHAPTER FOUR

Tuesday, October 4, 9:00 a.m.

Dr. Tessa McGowan sat in her car, staring at the one-word text from Dakota. Establishing their first meeting in eight months, a task she'd been avoiding since her return to Richmond days ago, was done. What little relief she'd hoped to feel was fleeting and quickly knuckled under to anxiety.

"I will fix this mess," she whispered.

She glanced up at the tall building located in Richmond's city center. The building housed the state medical examiner's office, where in a half hour, she had a job interview for a yearlong fellowship as a forensic pathologist with Dr. Addison Kincaid.

For the last eight months Tessa had worked with the United States military's Project Identify in Vietnam to identify the remains of lost American soldiers. She'd been navigating the jungle paths and partly paved roads of the northern rural province, growing adept at slicing through jungle or dodging cows and widow-maker potholes.

The months away had left her out of practice with maneuvering rush-hour traffic and scouting parking spots. She'd allowed nearly an hour for the five-mile drive from her cousin's Manchester apartment just south of the James River. Thanks to green lights and a prime parking spot opening up, she still had thirty minutes to kill.

Doing her best to shove Dakota from her thoughts and unknot a tangled stomach, she got out of her car and steadied herself on low heels. Straightening her pencil skirt, she squared her shoulders as she tucked her purse under her arm. Her plan was to walk around the block a couple of times, burning through the remaining minutes and calming her mind. She'd hiked hundreds of miles in the jungle and loved the steady rhythmic pace of walking. But the new heels negated whatever relief she'd expected when they quickly pinched and promised blisters.

With Plan A looking less viable with each step, she switched to Plan B, which was to sit in the medical examiner's lobby and wait for her appointment. She walked toward the gray building and opened the front door. A rush of cool air greeted her as she approached a thick plate-glass window shielding the lobby receptionist.

Tessa leaned toward the circular opening and said, "Good morning."

An African American woman in her fifties wearing a blue security guard uniform looked up over pink half glasses. "May I help you?"

"I'm Dr. Tessa McGowan. I have a job interview with Dr. Addison Kincaid. But I'm a half hour early."

The woman studied her, as if reconciling Tessa's words with the image of a too-petite, too-young woman with long black hair who did not fit the image of a pathologist. "Have a seat. I'll call down."

"Thank you." Tessa turned and crossed the lobby, her heels clacking on the tiled floor. She sat on the edge of her seat, tightening her hand on the leather strap of her purse.

She'd applied for this job online two weeks ago on impulse, making the filing deadline by hours. When she'd received a call for an interview last week, second-guessing had kicked into high gear as it always did when she rushed without thinking. It wasn't that she thought she couldn't do the job. She could. What nagged her was the idea of establishing yearlong roots in a city filled with complications.

The elevator chimed open, and a tall, slim woman in her midthirties stepped into the lobby. She wore long dark pants, a white silk blouse, and thick brown hair coiled into a twist. Small hoops dangled from her ears, and around her neck a chain was threaded through a gold band. Green eyes scanned and settled on Tessa. The woman smiled. "Dr. Tessa McGowan?"

Hand extended, Tessa crossed to Dr. Kincaid. "Yes. I'm Dr. McGowan."

Dr. Kincaid's handshake was firm, her gaze direct. "It's a pleasure to meet you."

"I've heard great things about your department."

Perceptive eyes sparked with curiosity. "Really?"

"I asked around about you." She drew in a breath and reminded herself her rash candor had gotten her into trouble before. "When I was in Southeast Asia, we had several Virginia doctors attached to our group. They knew you by reputation. All spoke highly of your department."

"Good to know." A subtle smile tipped the edge of her lips. "Come on down. I want to hear all about what you've been doing this last year."

"Great."

The elevator doors opened, and they both stepped inside. Dr. Kincaid pushed the basement floor button.

"Tell me about the work you did in Vietnam."

"The directive of Project Identify is to find the remains of US servicemen. We spent most of our time working with our guide and the village elders, who were trying to remember back fifty years ago when an air force F-III crashed. Once we narrowed our search, we confirmed the actual site with ground-penetrating radar. From there it became a struggle to clear the jungle and excavate twelve feet of earth to find the remains of the two crewmen."

Dr. Kincaid arched a brow. "Twelve feet?"

"The jungle grows fast and doesn't like people reclaiming what it's taken."

"I understand you were able to make an identification."

She was proud they'd reunited the lost soldiers' remains with their families. "You're well informed."

"It's a project I also feel strongly about. And of course, I've asked around about you as well." The doors opened, and they walked the tiled hallway to her corner office.

Dr. Kincaid's space was small, but the walls were covered with a dozen degrees and awards. Along a credenza behind her desk hung pictures of the doctor with several governors, a couple of senators, and a tall man dressed in fatigues. Neatly stacked papers were piled on her desk beside a University of Texas mug filled with sharpened pencils.

"Tell me about Johns Hopkins," Dr. Kincaid said.

Tessa detailed her rotations and her interests being pulled away from surgery toward pathology. She also spoke about her residency at Virginia Commonwealth University here in the city and her familiarity with the state system.

"I realized the dead have a story to tell," Tessa said finally. "And I want to be their translator."

Dr. Kincaid absently tapped her finger on the still-blank notepad. "Not everyone is comfortable with death."

"It's the end stage of life." She briefly considered a joke about having issues with the living but caught herself. This was a job interview, not a social call.

"Many of our autopsies confirm natural causes of death, but we do get our share of violent deaths. Not always easy to see, especially when dealing with the young."

"I worked part-time in the Baltimore area hospitals' emergency rooms while at Hopkins. I've seen my share of traumatic death. And when I did my residency here in Richmond, I was exposed to quite a bit in the emergency room."

Nodding, Dr. Kincaid sat back, regarding Tessa. "I understand the hospital here offered you a full-time job in the pathology department last year, but at the last minute you withdrew your name and opted to work abroad."

Tessa smiled. "It was an incredible opportunity I couldn't pass up."

And it had been. But she'd put her name into the hat for the overseas assignment as a rash wake-up call to Dakota. *Commit to the marriage, or I leave.* When he'd called her bluff, she'd taken the job.

However, rethinking her answer now made it sound as if she thought the job with the state had not been a great opportunity, which it had been. She could explain about her marriage, but that was a rabbit hole she did not want to explore.

"After working in the jungle," she hurried to say, "I think I can tackle anything you throw at me."

Dr. Kincaid waited a beat, and then, "Let's have a look around the place."

"I'd like that."

"Excellent." Dr. Kincaid moved into the hallway at a fast pace and pushed open the swinging door to an autopsy suite.

The room was outfitted with a long stainless-steel sink and counter, instrument carts, and several empty gurneys. To the right was a bank of refrigerators. Dr. Kincaid gave her what she described as the ten-cent tour, stopping to show her the afternoon logbook of what they would be doing. "We have a stabbing case coming in as we speak. Eighteen-year-old. I'd ask you to stick around, but I can't have anyone here who's not on the payroll during official business." She then said with a wry smile, "The investigating officer can scare the best of people away."

"I don't scare easily."

"Then you haven't met Agent Dakota Sharp."

Her smile froze. "Dakota Sharp."

Dr. Kincaid stood by an instrument table equipped with a tray of wrapped sterile instruments. "You know of him?"

What had she expected? Of course their paths would cross. "I know Dakota Sharp."

A dark brow rose. "Really?"

She did her best to look calm, marveling how worlds always grew smaller at the worst times. "We're married. Separated."

Dr. Kincaid studied her a long moment. "Really?"

"I can assure you," Tessa rushed to say, "that our relationship will not be an issue. We're both professionals and dedicated to our jobs. I'm sure he's still one of the best agents in the state."

"He is that. And as long as you think you can work with him, I won't worry about it. Do you have any other questions for me?"

Tessa rattled off several practiced questions based on her research of the facility, hoping they made her look well prepared. Finally after another twenty minutes, Dr. Kincaid extended her hand. "Dr. McGowan, thank you for coming today. I'll be in touch."

Dr. Kincaid's expression was impossible to read, and Tessa's hopes deflated as the doctor shook her hand and wished her a good day. She suspected her relationship with Dakota had complicated her chances of landing the job.

***

It was early afternoon when Sharp pulled off the interstate into a small town just a few miles from the cemetery where they'd buried Roger yesterday. The town, north of Richmond, had roots dating back 150 years and links to the RF&P Railroad. Its center featured pre–Civil War architecture, historic Victorian homes, and a main street boasting dozens of shops and restaurants.

His mother had brought him to this area when he was eight and then she married RB, and for almost a decade he'd lived here, attending high school, raising hell with his friend Jacob McLean, and generally champing at the bit until he left for Quantico. Since the day Kara died, he'd never looked back at this place with any fondness.

Winding through town, he found the small side street canopied with orange and yellow trees anxious to drop their leaves. At the end of the block, he parked in front of the one-story white brick house listed as Terrance Dillon's address. Leaves had been raked into piles at the curb, and the thick green lawn was cut. Mums filled twin planters flanking the front entrance.

He dreaded death notifications, and this one weighed especially heavily on him as he got out of the car and strode along the sidewalk to the front door. Cool air blew across his shoulders, burrowing deep into his bones. He knocked hard on the front door.

Seconds later the thud of footsteps sounded inside the house before the door snapped open. Standing on the other side of the screen was a young man in his midthirties. Dark hair, gray eyes, and a square jaw mirrored Terrance's motionless pale face.

"I'm Agent Sharp with the Virginia State Police." He pulled his badge from his breast pocket and held it up for the man to see. "I'm here to see Terrance's grandmother. She filed a missing persons report on her grandson."

The man hesitated, his frown intensifying into a scowl. "Have you found him?"

He tucked the badge back in his pocket. "I need to speak with Terrance's grandmother before I can comment."

The man pushed open the screened door. "My grandmother is in the kitchen. I'm Henry Jones. I'm Terrance's older cousin. All the grandchildren have been taking turns with my grandmother since Sunday, trying to keep her spirits up while we waited on news about Terrance."

Sharp noted the white walls decked with framed pictures featuring dozens of different children over the last few decades. Several looked like school pictures taken of a younger Terrance.

"Grandma's been raising Terrance since his mother died eight years ago. His father is in prison mostly. Terrance is a good kid. Grandma expects the sports scholarship to come through and for him to go to college next fall."

"It's a nice collection of pictures."

They entered the small kitchen outfitted with a narrow Formica countertop, a vintage 1950s stove and refrigerator, and an oval-shaped table rimmed with a dull stainless-steel ribbon and encircled by four matching chairs.

An older woman sat at the table with a steaming cup of tea in front of her. Graying hair, which hung loose around her round face, drained her of color and aged her by another decade. She looked up from the stoneware cup, and when she saw Sharp's face, tears filled her eyes. She rose and faced him. "Where is Terrance?"

"This is my grandmother," Henry said. "Edith Jones. Grandma, this is Agent Sharp."

"Mrs. Jones," he said, softening his voice. "We found Terrance dead about five miles from here." He never delayed this kind of information. Better to get it out and end the agony of not knowing. "I am very sorry."

Her chin trembled as she dropped back into her seat. She pressed wrinkled hands to her mouth and for a moment closed her eyes. "Are you sure it's my Terry? Are you sure? He only went to the Quick Mart to get candy and an energy drink. He called me and told me he was coming right home."

"Yes, ma'am, we're sure. He was carrying his driver's license." Moments like this, Sharp wished he had the words to ease the gut punch he understood too well.

Mrs. Jones shook her head. "You must have made a mistake. He came to church with me on Sunday. It was his birthday."

"Yes, ma'am, we're sure." He cleared his throat. "I'm sorry. There's no mistake."

Tears spilled, and for a long moment, she didn't speak as Henry stood beside her, his arm draped over her shoulders as she sobbed. Finally, she raised red-rimmed eyes. "Did my boy die quick? Did he suffer?" Mrs. Jones asked.

Sharp didn't need a medical examiner to tell him the knife wound had been devastatingly efficient and had ended his life swiftly. "He did not suffer."

She folded her face into her hands and wept. "My poor baby. How did he die?"

"The medical examiner will make the final determination."

Henry glanced up at Sharp, his gaze full of fury. "Who did this?"

"That's what I'm trying to find out." Sharp stood still. "I know this isn't a good time, but I need to ask you some questions about Terrance."

Henry's gaze darkened. "Can you just leave her be? Shit, she's crushed."

Mrs. Jones shook her head and looked up with tears in her eyes. "It's okay. I owe it to Terry to tell what I can. Agent Sharp, go ahead and ask me any question."

Sharp took the seat beside her. "I understand you filed a missing persons report on Monday morning."

"We were expecting him home by eleven on Sunday. He'd been out with friends and said he was on his way home when he got a line on a job with the maintenance company that gives him work from time to time. We needed the money, so I let him stay out longer."

"What was the job?"

"I just assumed it was Mr. Ralph Dobbins. He owns Dobbins Maintenance. Terry worked there part-time last summer. Had to quit for football practice and school."

Sharp scribbled down the information. "Do you know where he was calling from?"

"He said he was outside the Quick Mart on Route 1."

"What time was that?"

"Just after nine on Sunday night." Her voice cracked, and more tears pooled in her eyes. "I thought the job was cleaning out an office building or hauling trash. I should have known it was trouble. Who offers a boy a job on a Sunday night? I should have told him to come home."

Henry raised his chin. "Terry was a good kid. Straight arrow. He worked for a friend of mine last summer, and I heard he was a hard worker."

"When's the last time you saw Terrance?"

Henry shrugged. "It's been about a week. I owned a lawn business in Nashville, and I didn't get up here much. I only just moved back a couple of months ago."

"Why'd you move back?" Sharp asked.

"The work dried up in Nashville. Hoping to get more here."

"I have twenty-six grandchildren," Mrs. Jones said. "It's getting harder and harder to get them together."

Henry shook his head. "Grandma raised him right despite his no-account daddy, but I should've helped more."

"Mrs. Jones, I understand he'd just gotten money from you for his birthday," Sharp coaxed.

Henry nodded. "Twenty dollars."

"Was my boy robbed and killed for twenty dollars?" Mrs. Jones asked.

"I don't know. You said his father was in and out of prison? Is he currently incarcerated?"

"Jimmy's out," Henry said. "He's been out over a month."

Mrs. Jones's jaw tightened. "He should be rotting in jail."

"What's his father's full name?" Sharp asked.

Henry glanced at his grandmother. "James Tyler Dillon. Jimmy to everyone."

"Have either of you seen him at all since his release?"

"No," Mrs. Jones said. "He knows I'd get my double-barreled shot-gun handy, and I will shoot him if he shows up on my property."

Henry shook his head. "I saw him on Saturday in town. He came by my new shop looking for Terrance."

"You never told me," she said.

"I didn't want to upset you. I know how you feel about him. I told him Terrance had missed having him around all these years."

Mrs. Jones wiped a tear from her cheek. "You should have told me. I'd have tracked him down and run him out of town."

"Grandma don't mean that," Henry said to Sharp.

"Did you tell Terrance about the visit?" Sharp asked.

"I didn't want to, but I knew Terry had always wanted to know his daddy better. I shouldn't have, but I called and told him."

"And what did the boy do?" Sharp asked.

"Jimmy left a number for Terry to call him, and I gave it to Terry. I don't know what he did with the number."

"Henry!" Mrs. Jones said. "What the hell were you thinking? Jimmy is the devil!"

Henry nodded, his face tight with grief. "Yes, ma'am."

"Where is Jimmy Dillon now?" Sharp interjected.

"I don't know," Henry said. "He took off again. I called him when we couldn't find Terrance, but he never called back. He does that. Comes and goes like a cat."

"He runs from trouble," Mrs. Jones said.

"Do you know if Terrance called his father?"

"I don't know," Henry said. "What about the job Terry told Grandma about?" Henry challenged. "Whoever offered him a job might have hurt him."

"I'll go to the Quick Mart after I leave here and see if they have Terrance on surveillance tape. Do you know if Jimmy Dillon has a job?"

Edith shook her head, her eyes filling with fresh tears. "Selling drugs, no doubt. He was in prison for dealing."

"Jimmy wasn't a great father," Henry said. "But I know he loved that boy."

"The people Jimmy hangs out with wouldn't care a bit about Terry," Mrs. Jones said. "Jimmy has no sense. Always thinks every situation will work out."

"Do you know the name of any of Jimmy's associates?" Sharp asked.

Both shook their heads, but Mrs. Jones was the first to speak. "We try and stay clear of any dealings to do with Jimmy."

"What about Terrance's friends? What were they like?"

"All good boys. Ronnie and Garcia were his best friends. All three of 'em would rather play football than eat." She rattled off their full names.

Sharp noted the names. "Do you know where I can find these kids?"

"In school, no doubt," Mrs. Jones said. "And after school the football field for practice." The old woman leaned forward, pinning Sharp with a surprisingly piercing gaze. "You're going to find out who killed my boy."

"I'm going to do my best, ma'am." As much as he wanted to promise justice, cases like this didn't always end in arrest. He handed Mrs. Jones and Henry cards with his contact information. "If you think of anything else, call me. And I'll call you if any new information comes up."

Mrs. Jones clutched his card tightly in her hand. "Thank you, Agent Sharp. I know you're going to find out."

Tension banded Sharp's lower back. "Yes, ma'am."

"I need to know why," she said. "Why would someone hurt such a good boy?"

"I want to know that, too," Sharp said. "I want this killer caught."

Her eyes narrowed. "Don't disappoint me."

"No, ma'am."

Henry walked him to the door, and he passed another collection of pictures featuring Terrance smiling and holding a football. "Is it smart for Grandma to get her hopes up? I know how it goes. The killer isn't always found."

The screen door squeaked as Sharp pushed it open. He imagined this same scene playing out twelve years ago with Roger and his mother.

There wasn't a hole deep enough for this killer to crawl into. "I'm going to turn this place upside down looking for an answer."

Henry flexed tense fingers at his side. "That would be real good."

Sharp shook hands with the man and moved to his car. Once inside, he reached for a cigarette. He fumbled with the rumpled package, cursing when he realized it was empty. Crushing it, he tossed the packet onto the passenger seat and started the engine. He promised to give the damn habit up before it killed him. Soon.

He drove across the small town to the Quick Mart on Route 1. The store appeared to have been a part of a larger chain store at one point and then converted into a local business. A couple of cars filled the small parking lot.

Inside, Sharp moved to the register and showed his badge to a tall gawky kid. "I need to see the manager."

"Yeah, sure." The kid rushed around the counter toward the back of the store. Seconds later a heavyset man in his late forties ambled out. He wore a short-sleeved shirt emphasizing arms covered in tattoos.

As the kid returned to the register, Sharp again showed his badge. "I'm Agent Sharp with the Virginia State Police. I'm investigating a murder, and I was hoping you have surveillance footage from Sunday night at about eleven."

The manager gave Sharp a long, pondering look as he slowly shook his head. "Tell me it ain't Miss Edith's grandson. She's been looking for Terrance since Sunday."

"We found him. He's dead."

The manager jabbed thick fingers through thinning hair. "Shit."

"The surveillance tape?"

"Yeah, sure. We keep the recordings backed up to a hard drive for thirty days. Come on back in the office."

The office was piled high with boxed inventory. In the corner was a small desk covered with papers huddled around a computer screen. The manager sat and typed a few keys. Black-and-white images appeared on the screen. The time stamp was 9:00 p.m. He tapped the screen as Terrance entered from the right of the computer screen. "That's Terrance. And I'm working the register."

The two watched as the boy, who was wearing the same jeans, white T-shirt, and school jacket as when Sharp saw his body, made his way into the store, chose two items near the counter, and paid for them with coins and rumpled bills.

After sharing a laugh with the clerk, Terrance left and crossed the lot as a white sedan drove up. Terrance leaned toward the passenger-side window and spoke to the driver. At first his face was blank, almost stoic, but soon he was laughing. The driver got out and hugged Terrance, who nervously glanced around. Sharp thought about the boy's father, Jimmy, fresh out of prison and lurking around town.

As the car pulled away, the camera caught a partial shot of the license plate. "Can you freeze that and enlarge it?"

"Yeah, sure."

Sharp removed a small notebook and recorded the four visible plate numbers. "Thanks. Can I get a copy?"

"I can e-mail the video."

Sharp gave him his card. "Thanks. That would be a help."

After the manager copied and sent the footage, he turned back toward Sharp. "Still can't believe the kid is dead."

Death of a youth always struck the core. "Know anyone who didn't like Terrance?"

"No. He was in here a lot, like most of the locals. Nice kid. Never made a fuss."

"Seen the boy's father around?"

The manager looked surprised. "I didn't know he had a father. Lived with his grandmother. Mother's dead. He's got a lot of cousins in town. It's a big family."

"Right. Thanks. If you think of anything, call."

The manager blinked nervously. "Sure. Will do."

On his way out, Sharp bought a packet of cigarettes and got in his car. As he opened the packet, he dug out his phone, found the number of his DMV contact, and dialed. She picked up on the second ring.

"Samantha Davis," she said.

"Samantha, this is Agent Sharp, VSP. How's my favorite lady?" He leaned back in his seat.

Soft laughter trailed through the phone. "I'm doing just fine. Been a long time since you called. I miss you."

"Sorry about that." He closed his eyes and pinched the bridge of his nose. They'd gone out a couple of times before he'd met Tessa. "It's been crazy."

"Who are you kidding? It's always crazy for you. You live to work, Agent Sharp. One day they'll find you hunched over your desk, a withered old man with a case file in your cold dead hands."

The lighthearted comment hit a nerve. "Let's hope the case is solved. I'd hate to leave this world hanging."

He could imagine her curling her dark hair around her index finger like he'd seen her do before. "Anybody tell you that you're a workaholic?" she said.

He traced a scratch in his steering wheel with his index finger. "Once or twice."

"So why're you calling? It's been two years, so this can't be a date."

He leaned back. "I need a partial plate run."

"You didn't call to see how your favorite lady was doing?" Her tone echoed a mock pout.

"I could have called someone else, but I called you."

"Because no one works the magic like I do." She sighed as paper rustled in the background. "Let me have it."

He read off the partial plate as well as the car's make and model.

"What am I looking for?"

"I need the name of the car's owner. He's wanted for questioning in a homicide investigation."

The tap of computer keys clicked in the background. "I have a car that matches your description and the partial plate. That car was stolen," she said. "Six months ago."

That wasn't a surprise. He scribbled down the owner's name and the entire license plate. "Thanks. I owe you."

She laughed. "Yes, you do."

After he hung up, he put out a BOLO on the stolen car and the boy's father.

He checked his watch, knowing he had until three to catch Terrance's friends in school before sports practice began. He put a call into the parole board and got hold of Jimmy Dillon's parole officer.

"This is Jeff Taggart," a gruff voice barked over the line.

"Agent Sharp, Virginia State Police. What can you tell me about Jimmy Dillon?"

"What's he done?"

"He's broken no laws that I know of yet. But his son was murdered sometime over the weekend."

A heavy sigh huffed over the line. "Jimmy Dillon is a career criminal, and it's a matter of time before he finds trouble."

"Has he kept his meetings with you?"

Keys tapped in the background. "Yes. He's made the first three. The fourth was supposed to be yesterday, but he missed it."

"Does he have a job?"

"He said he interviewed for a janitorial job, but he hasn't told me if it worked out."

"Do you know where he was trying to get this job?"

"Dobbins Maintenance."

The same place where Terrance worked.

The parole officer rattled off the information as Sharp noted the name and address of the local maintenance company.

"Have you tried to track Jimmy down?" Sharp asked.

"I've made a few calls. I'll issue a warrant for his arrest now."

"Did he give you a phone number or address?"

"Gave his mother's home address and phone."

"She's not seen him since his release."

"Great." A pause. "If I get any fresh tips or he's picked up, I'll call you."

"Thanks."

Sharp put the car in gear and pulled up to Route 1, waited for the road to clear, and turned left toward the sign reading "Richmond." He called the maintenance company's service number where Jimmy Dillon was supposed to be interviewing for a job. He landed in voice mail and left his name and number.

The thrill of the hunt burned through him. He wouldn't rest until he had tagged Jimmy Dillon.

CHAPTER FIVE

Tuesday, October 4, 2:00 p.m.

After her interview with Dr. Kincaid, Tessa drove back to her cousin's apartment, where she crashed for a few hours. She'd been back in the States nearly a week, but jet lag still dogged her. However, sleeping wasn't as easy as she'd expected. Thoughts of Dakota troubled her until finally she gave up on sleeping and got up. To burn restless energy, she went for a run. Afterward, she showered and changed into jeans, a blouse, and boots before heading to the coffee shop. Once again, she was early.

She ordered an espresso, not because she needed another hit of caffeine, but because she needed an activity to keep her hands busy while she waited for Dakota.

As the young man behind the counter made her espresso, her phone buzzed. It was Dr. Kincaid. She drew in a breath and answered, "Dr. Kincaid."

"Good, I caught you." No chitchat. "The job is yours if you want it."

She blinked, ducking her head as she moved away from the counter. She lowered her voice. "Really?" The job locked her into Richmond for a year. No avoiding or running away for twelve months. "That's wonderful. I accept."

"You don't want to think about it?"

"No. I want this job."

"All right, then. Can you start tomorrow? The sooner the better."

"Yes."

"Good. I'll see you in the morning at seven. I'll e-mail you details."

"Great. See you then."

She ended the call. When she paid the clerk and reached for her cup, her hand trembled just a little. Damn. She was taking the next step in her life. This was good news, right?

She dumped her extra change in the tip jar and chose a seat that put her back against the wall just as Sharp had shown her when they were dating. *"Know your exits,"* he'd said during one of his many safety lectures. At first she'd found the lectures endearing, but in the end she began to think he just didn't trust her to stay safe. *"I'm not a child, Dakota."*

She traced the rim of her cup, and then, fishing out her phone, replayed Dakota's voice-mail message, hoping to glean any hints from his tone. As his terse voice rumbled in her ear, the bells on the front door jingled.

She looked up. Dakota stood in the door, the bright afternoon sun at his back. He wore his trademark dark glasses that hid what little emotion he projected, a black suit that skimmed broad shoulders, a crisp white shirt, and a conservative red tie she'd given to him for Christmas two years ago, though she doubted he remembered where he'd gotten it. He was leaner, and if possible, more rigid.

She shut off her phone and nervously tucked a strand of hair behind her ear. She moistened her lips and prayed her heart would stop beating against her ribs.

He pulled off the glasses, letting his eyes adjust to the room as they swept left to right. She thought for a moment he didn't see her, but the gray eyes swung around like the barrel of a gun and landed on her. A muscle pulsed in his jaw as he moved toward her with a determined, if not grim, stride.

She shoved her phone back in her pocket before smoothing her hands over her jeans. She rose, bumping the table, jostling her coffee and sloshing it over the rim. Automatically she snagged a couple of napkins from a dispenser and mopped up the wet mess as it dripped over the edge of the table. By the time she looked up, he was standing next to her, staring, studying the soggy mush of napkins in her hand like one of his crime scenes.

Shit. So much for smooth. She pushed aside the coffee-soaked napkins, now a crumpled wet ball, and straightened. Coffee had splashed her jeans and dampened her fingertips, which she quickly wiped against the denim. Should she extend her hand or hug him? He made no attempt to break the ice or make this moment easy. She'd called the meeting, and he was letting her run the show.

"Thanks for coming," she said. "I know it was last-minute."

"No problem, Tessa."

"Can I get you a coffee?" she asked.

"No. Thank you."

She muzzled the urge to prattle on and sat back down, fairly certain her legs might give way if she kept standing.

He pulled out a seat, moving it to the side so he had the front door in his peripheral vision.

"I can trade seats," she said. "I know you like your back to the wall."

"Not necessary." Slowly he folded up his sunglasses and tucked them in his pocket.

"Right."

When she didn't expound, he raised a brow. "Why the meeting, Tessa?"

"I wanted to let you know I'm back in Richmond. I've applied for a yearlong fellowship at the medical examiner's office. In fact, Dr. Kincaid just offered me the job. I start in the morning."

That muscle twitched again in his jaw. "She's smart. Manages a good shop. Why tell me?"

Ice coated each word. He wasn't attempting cordial. But then it had never been easy with him. "We're going to run into each other. In fact, the medical examiner's office has one of your cases on the docket for tomorrow."

"You could have told me all this in a text."

"I know you don't like texts."

As he sat back, his jacket opened a fraction, offering a glimpse of his badge clipped to his belt, inches from the grip of his weapon. He waited.

She tucked another strand of hair behind her ear. "I understand this victim is young."

He impatiently tugged at the edge of his jacket. "When you officially start, we'll talk about it."

Old frustrations stirred, and she remembered he could be abrupt, his tone blunt when he was upset. She knew he was angry with her. She'd blasted out of his life on a rush of emotion and little thought.

Now, when she wanted to say the right words to mend a once-strong connection shattered into so many pieces, words alone felt inadequate.

Dakota's question was as piercing as a honed blade. "So that's it? You wanted to give me a heads-up?"

"That was part of the reason."

He didn't speak. Barely seemed to breathe.

"I wanted to see you. To see for myself you're doing okay."

He shook his head, as if he were bracing for a second shoe to drop.

"I also wanted you to know I remembered today is Kara's birthday. I haven't forgotten."

He didn't blink. "Okay."

"She was my friend, too. What happened to her changed my life as well." Her thumb rubbed the underside of her ring finger as if expecting to feel her wedding band.

"Happened?"

"Yes." She'd hoped mentioning Kara would chip away at the wall between them, but it only added more bricks. "Sorry, I didn't mean to rub salt."

A weary sigh leaked from his lips. "I assume you're now making small talk and screwing up the courage to talk about a divorce."

Their broken marriage dangled between them like glass shards. Hardly anyone would have noticed any hope glinting around the jagged edges. "No, I'm not."

"No, you're not what?"

This was the moment she'd rehearsed a hundred times on the long plane ride home. "I'm not filing the papers."

His gray eyes narrowed. "You want me to?"

"No," she blurted.

Wariness flashed as his eyes narrowed. "Why not? A clean break means you can get on with your life."

If this had been a tug-of-war game, she'd have been digging in her heels. "Is that what you want?"

Staring. Silent. Still. He was giving her no glimpse of his thoughts. She'd have to work for every inch of progress.

"I've done everything I can think of to get free of you. I was sure ten thousand miles would do the trick. But no luck." As the words rushed over her lips, she regretted them immediately.

Challenge sharpened already keen features.

A cold chill swept over her and threatened to scatter whatever hopes she'd painstakingly collected over the last weeks as she continued, "I thought eight months apart would mellow us both."

"I haven't changed and neither has my job, Tessa. It never will. I don't know why you imagined I'd change."

"I've changed."

Shaking his head, he rose as if he could no longer stay still. "Do yourself a favor and move on with your life. File the fucking papers, and I'll sign them."

She stood quickly, again bumping the table, sloshing more coffee. As he turned away, she fired back, "I never figured you for a chickenshit, Sharp."

He might recognize her outburst as one of the investigative techniques he used interviewing a hostile witness, but that didn't mean he was immune when the tables were turned. "Provoking my temper won't work, Tessa."

"Figured you were more of a fighter," she pressed. What the hell did she have to lose now? "Never pegged you for a quitter."

Unruffled, he reached for his sunglasses. "I'm a realist. We are not suited for each other. I know. You know it."

She moved a step closer to him, knowing the sunglasses were one of his tells. He put them on when he was rattled. She'd hit her target. "I'm not filing papers."

"And then what? We remain in limbo?"

"No. We figure it out. We make our marriage work."

"There's nothing to figure, nothing to fix."

She'd met him years ago through his sister, Kara, when Tessa was seventeen. More than a decade would pass before they reconnected and, after a quick, electric courtship, rushed into a marriage that had lasted eight months. It hadn't taken long before the demands of his job bled into their marriage and she realized being married to a cop wasn't easy. He worked long, hard hours and was dedicated to the work. The eleven-year age difference also began to widen the cracks forming between them. She wasn't sure what she could have done, but darting halfway around the world hadn't been the answer. Now she was back, determined to fight for a second chance.

She took his hand in hers, savoring the rough edges of his fingertips she'd once welcomed on her body. It had been so long since they'd touched. Kissed.

She expected him to pull away, but he didn't. Her bravery growing, she moved closer to him, sensing his gray eyes studying her.

Bolder now, she slid her hand up his arm and behind his neck. He watched her closely as she pulled him toward her. She pressed her lips to his mouth. Instinctively, he kissed her back.

The kiss sent a ripple of desire through her body, making nerve endings fire and muscles grow weak. Anger and resistance hummed under his touch, even as his hand came reluctantly to her side. She leaned in a fraction, skimming her breasts against his chest. She relished his scent. His taste. As heat rose up in her, she made no move to douse it.

"I haven't been able to forget you," she whispered.

Dakota lingered a beat before the fingers on her hip curled into a fist and he broke the connection. "Sex was never an issue with us."

"The bedroom wasn't the only place we connected," she said.

"You're wrong. Out of the bedroom was our issue. Still is. Like I said, I've not changed, Tessa," he said, his voice strained. "And I mean it when I say I'll never change."

"Maybe I'm kidding myself."

"You are."

She shook her head. "But I'm willing to risk that I'm not."

"Like I said, I am a realist, Tessa. I know when to cut my losses."

He wasn't ready to talk. Fair enough. What had she expected? That he'd greet her with open arms? There was always a challenge with Dakota.

But Tessa would embrace this damned second chance no matter what he said. "I'll see you in the autopsy suite tomorrow, Agent Sharp."

With measured movements, he turned and left without another word.

She dragged a shaking hand through her hair, glancing around to see who had witnessed the kiss. This was a hangout for cops, and several people were staring. No one said a word, but news would spread. Fine. Let 'em talk. She wasn't going anywhere.

***

Sharp had been braced for Tessa's one-two punch of divorce, but reconciliation had been an unexpected left hook.

There'd been no drama. No gushing words. But that was Tessa. She was always reasonable. Calm. Even when she'd told him she was leaving him, she'd been in control. He'd been the one who'd been pissed. Instead of listening to her plans to leave the country, and her desire to return to him after a sabbatical, he'd slammed the door to their house and left.

And now she was back. For a yearlong fellowship. And when it was over? And when she figured out he'd meant what he'd said and she realized he'd not changed, what would she do? She'd leave. Again.

Those thoughts chased Sharp twenty miles north on I-95 toward the high school Terrance Dillon had attended. He parked in the visitor lot and made his way to the office and the long counter that portioned students off from administration. Showing his badge, he asked to speak to the principal.

A short, fit man in his midfifties came out immediately and introduced himself as Principal Woodrow Tucker. "This must be about Terrance."

"Yes, it is. There somewhere we can talk?"

"Of course. My office."

Sharp followed the principal to his office and took a seat in a gray chair. "Have you ever met the boy's father?"

"No. But one of my teachers met him years ago when she was teaching elementary school. Mr. Dillon wasn't in prison then, and he came to one of Terrance's class concerts. He was inebriated and by intermission was asked to leave school property. He wasn't happy with the administration, but he did finally leave. We've never seen him again on our campus."

"Terrance ever talk about his father with you or any of his teachers?"

"Not to me, but if he did talk, it would have been to his coach." He reached for the phone on his desk. "This is Coach Wagner's planning break. He should be able to join us." A quick call and the principal arranged for the coach to come straight to the office.

While they waited, Sharp couldn't help but remember his days in this school. He'd been an average student, but his interest had not been in the books, which he'd considered a necessary evil until he could enlist in the marines. It wasn't until his midtwenties that he'd started taking online college classes. It had taken him nearly a decade of taking classes part-time before he could cobble together enough credits for a degree.

A knock sounded at the door, and he rose to see a sturdy man with a short haircut at the threshold. He wore a golf shirt in the school's trademark burgundy along with khakis and athletic shoes.

Sharp shook his hand and introductions were made. "Did anyone carry a grudge toward Terrance?"

"The kid had no enemies. Easygoing. One of the kids I pictured with a real future, despite the fact his father wasn't worth much."

"What do you know about Jimmy Dillon?"

"That Terrance wanted to please him. The kid loved his father and wrote to him while he was in prison. He was excited that Mr. Dillon was about to get out of prison. The kid thought they could be more like father and son."

"You sound skeptical," Sharp said.

"The man made promises in his letters that he'd come to the kid's games, but he never showed as far as I know. Hard to see a good kid spurned by his father."

"Would Mr. Dillon have killed his own son?"

"I don't know. But I know the guy's been in prison and wouldn't be surprised if he introduced the kid to someone who did kill him."

"Any names?"

"None. Sorry."

"What about Terrance's friends?"

"He hung out with Ronnie and Garcia," the coach said.

"Either of them here?"

The principal entered the names into the computer. "I can pull them from class if that will help."

"It would. Thanks," Sharp said.

The principal made calls to the boys' classrooms, and minutes later they appeared. Both looked worried, nervous.

Sharp rose as the principal introduced him. "I'm here to ask you about Terrance."

The boy on the left—tall, lean, and well muscled, with pale skin and red hair—spoke first. "We still can't believe it."

"And your name?" Sharp asked.

"I'm Ronnie. Ronnie Tolley."

"Okay, Ronnie. Did Terrance hang out with anyone who might have wanted to hurt him?"

The kid shifted his stance. "No, he was clean. He was easygoing. Never pissed anyone off."

The other kid, shorter, thicker, had raven-dark hair and large brown eyes. He had to be Garcia. "Everyone liked him."

"Garcia, right?" Sharp asked.

"Joey Garcia. I've known Terrance since the sixth grade."

"Did you ever see Terrance with his father?"

"I never saw him, but I know they talked on the phone. Jimmy started calling Terrance a couple of weeks ago."

"Do you know what they talked about?"

"Terrance never would say," Garcia said. "He was a little nervous about talking to Jimmy. He was afraid his grandmother would be upset."

"Did Terrance have a girlfriend?" Sharp asked.

"He did," Garcia said. "But they broke up six months ago. Terrance's grandmother didn't want him dating anybody. She wanted him focused on school and football."

"You sure about that?" Sharp asked. "When he was found, he was dressed nice. Did he always dress up?"

"He liked to look nice," Garcia said.

"Did he have a date?" Sharp asked.

The boys looked at each other, then back at Sharp. It was Ronnie that said, "He never told us."

They spent the next fifteen minutes talking about Terrance. He learned the kid often went to a diner in town named Bessie's with the other players. Nothing else the coach, kids, or principal had to offer amounted to a lead.

"Thank you for your time," Sharp said. "Call me if you hear anything."

Outside in the bright sunshine, he put on his sunglasses. He couldn't do much to fix his personal life, but he sure as hell could find justice for Terrance.

CHAPTER SIX

Tuesday, October 4, 10:00 p.m.

Sharp had spent the rest of the afternoon visiting with Terrance's neighbors. The door-to-door visits took time and energy, but he'd learned as a cop that there was no substitute for the footwork. Forensic science might sway television juries, but in reality, knocking on doors solved more cases.

In the end he only confirmed what he'd heard so far. Terrance was a good kid, who not only had played football but also had been one of the stars in the region. He'd had a shot at a scholarship to an NCAA Division II school—not the big leagues, but it would have been a full ride and likely his only ticket to a better life. Terrance, or Terry as his neighbors called him, had dated a girl named Stephanie earlier this year, but as his friends had indicated, they'd broken up in mid-February. He had a host of friends and all liked the kid. Everyone was shocked he'd been stabbed.

A few old-timers remembered Jimmy Dillon, and they all agreed he had been a deadbeat before he went to jail. For a time Jimmy, his wife, and Terrance lived with Mrs. Jones, and once or twice the cops had been called when neighbors heard screams. The neighbors said it was flat-out domestic abuse, but when Sharp returned to the office and checked Jimmy's arrest record, he found no charges of domestic abuse had been filed.

Jimmy had still not checked in with his parole officer, and so far there'd been no sightings of him. Sooner or later, rats like Jimmy had to crawl out from under their rocks.

By the time Sharp arrived at his town house, he was tired and in a foul mood. As he dug out his keys, he spotted several boxes piled in front of his door. He reached for the lid of the top box. A glance at several pages told him they were Kara's files. Douglas Knox had found his personal address. Once a cop, always a cop.

Sharp rolled his head from side to side as he closed the lid. The knot in his gut tightened.

He wanted all the questions around Kara's death answered, but he wasn't the man to find them. His lack of objectivity coiled around too much emotion meant he could easily screw it all up.

He pulled his cell from his pocket and dialed Clay Bowman's number.

Bowman picked up on the second ring. "Sharp."

He wasn't any good at calling in favors. Rather chew on broken glass. "I hear Shield is organizing a cold case group."

"It's in the works."

"I have a case."

"Riley told me."

"I've a half-dozen boxes full of files."

"Good. I've already spoken to Garrett Andrews, our tech guy. He's ready for them."

No quibbling. No questioning. Just a pledge that now shouldered some of the burden. "Thank you."

"Riley is on patrol tonight, and she's wrapping up her shift. Let me call her."

"I can bring in the boxes."

"If she's close, it makes sense to send her. Stand by."

Bowman hung up. Sharp opened his front door and readied to haul in the first box when his phone dinged with a text from Riley. Five minutes away.

He texted back. Thanks.

He loosened his tie and shrugged off his jacket, which he draped on the back of a chair by the door. He rolled up his sleeves and waited only a few minutes before a Virginia State Police K-9 SUV pulled up in front of the town house.

Riley got out of her vehicle, her black Lab watching from his window. She glanced from side to side before moving forward. State troopers worked alone on the road most of the time and quickly became accustomed to checking their surroundings, a habit most carried to the grave. As she moved away from the car, the dog's focus never left Riley.

"I hear you have some boxes for me," she said.

"I do."

"Let's load them in the front seat."

"Great."

She picked up a container and walked back toward the vehicle with even, steady strides. "Bowman's putting Andrews on your case."

"He told me. I haven't met him." Sharp picked up the three remaining boxes and followed.

She placed the first box on the floor. "Computer geek. Very smart. He's a good man to have."

Sharp stacked his boxes on the front seat.

Riley slammed the door closed. Her leather duty belt creaked as she shifted her weight. "I've volunteered to help with your cold case on my days off."

Gratitude warmed his voice. "You don't have to do that."

"But I will." After his nod of thanks, she added, "If anyone can find new evidence, it'll be Andrews."

He shoved his hands in his pockets. "I should be the one investigating this case."

Riley shook her head. "You're the last guy who should be doing this work."

Sharp felt like he was failing Kara again.

As if she'd read his thoughts, her voice softened as she said, "You're going to be the guy who gets to the bottom of what happened."

Like Henry Jones, he feared promises of closure. At best, they were hopeful but misguided. "Thanks, Tatum."

She jokingly jostled him in the shoulder. "You've got friends willing to help."

He watched as she slid behind the wheel of her SUV and drove off. Her words echoed what Tessa had said a thousand times before. "Easier said, Tatum. Easier said."

***

It was two in the morning, and the barest sliver of moon hung in the sky as the Dollmaker cut his headlights and parked in the lot butting against the county park. The lights from the condo complex were dark, and the woods around it, silent. Out of the van, he crossed to the side door, opened it, and lifted his doll in his arms. He cradled her close before making his way along the path he'd traveled dozens of times before. He had learned where every root, rut, and twist in the path was located as he'd scouted this location over the last few weeks.

With Destiny in his arms, he made his way toward the playground, relishing these final moments together. A cool breeze coaxed a rusty swing back and forth. Its hinges squeaked. A cold snap had sent temperatures dipping. It was peaceful.

He hated giving up his creation, but he reminded himself that he'd known all along their time together would be fleeting. She was never intended to remain in her physical state forever. Their journey together would continue in the videos and photographs he'd taken. She was now a work of art, deserving to be seen and admired.

He'd grown accustomed to having her strapped in his chair. Refashioning her face. Touching her. Lying beside her in bed. Kissing her. Being inside her and savoring the utter stillness wrapped around them both.

The Dollmaker had chosen this resting place for her carefully. Destiny was a doll. And it made perfect sense he would leave his doll where children played. And where the cops were certain to find her.

He lowered her to sit at the base of a tall oak tree and rested her head against the rough bark. He took his time, positioning her curls around her shoulders, straightening her head so she faced outward, fluffing her skirt, and then carefully crossing her feet at her ankles. As he stood back, he studied her face with an artist's critical eye. She was perfect, except for one small detail. The eyes. They were closed. They needed to be open. She needed to see him.

Reaching in his pocket, he pulled out a needle and thread, then crouched beside her. Carefully, he raised one lid and with practiced ease, stitched it open. The skin had grown brittle, making it easy for the needle to puncture. He tacked up the second lid.

In the distance, a dog barked and leaves crunched. He needed to move quickly. The last complication he wanted was a random person stumbling on this scene before he was finished. But as he stared into her clouded, dull eyes, he knew he must do one more thing.

Replacing the needle and thread, he tugged a contact lens case from his pocket. He removed the first oversize lens and carefully laid it over her eyeball. The lens created a wide-eyed doll look so perfect he wondered why he hadn't put it on her while she was alive. He positioned the second lens and leaned back, smiling at his baby doll. So, so perfect.

"Beautiful." He kissed her on the lips, lingering several beats, before he drew back. "I will miss you so much."

Quickly, he snapped several dozen pictures using only the moonlight. He studied each image carefully and took a couple more. He'd always been diligent about taking pictures of his girls. He never wanted to forget any of them.

With a stab of regret, he kissed her gently one last time on the cheek, hovering close as he inhaled the perfume he'd sprayed on her earlier. He rubbed his knuckles against the sharp cut of her cheekbones. Traced her lips. With another pang of regret, he stepped back.

After a long last look, he turned toward the parking lot and walked to his van. As much as he wanted to stay, it wasn't safe. He'd taken precautions, but there was no telling who might see him. He started his engine, the headlights catching his baby doll's sightless eyes. So pretty. When she was found, all would marvel at his work.

CHAPTER SEVEN

Wednesday, October 5, 6:30 a.m.

In Sharp's mind, every aspect of the autopsy suite was unnatural. The air was heavy, and it smelled of antiseptic and death. Fluorescent light robbed the living of color, and the hollow sound of the basement hallway reminded him of a horror movie.

His mother and Roger had traveled to a morgue like this to see Kara. His mother had told Sharp how she'd wept as she stared at her daughter on the metal table. The doctor's kind words had not chased the chill from her. So cold. His mother had been convinced Death followed her from that day forth.

He rolled his head to the side, waiting for the small pop in his neck to relieve some of the persistent stiffness from an IED explosion that had sent him flying fifteen feet across a street in Iraq. It had been eleven years since that explosion, but the smell of fire on flesh, screams, and pain still stalked him. This damn place always jarred those memories free of their cage.

"Shit," he whispered.

The past was gunning for him. First Roger. Kara's files. Iraq. Tessa.

Tessa.

Why the hell had she kissed him? She'd said she couldn't forget him. She wasn't willing to file papers. He wasn't sure where she'd dreamed up the idea of embracing second chances. If he had to bet, he'd put his money on guilt and pent-up sexual tension.

He shouldn't have allowed the kiss. He should have stepped back. Refused contact. But the kiss had been Eden's forbidden fruit.

Touching her hadn't silenced any of his demons. In fact, the kiss had antagonized the monsters within and had rewarded him with a night of tossing, turning, and enduring a shitload of his own sexual tension.

A reunion with Tessa was seductive but impossible. She might be naive enough to believe a second try would work, but he wasn't so foolish.

He pushed through the suite doors and found Tessa standing at the instrument table. A frown furrowed her brow as she studied the instruments. She'd tied her black hair back into a neat bun and tucked it under a surgical cap. She wore green scrubs and paper booties over her tennis shoes.

She looked up at him. A smile flickered, then scurried away. "Dr. Kincaid is on her way, and the lab technician is bringing up Mr. Dillon."

"Thanks."

He turned and moved toward a small set of lockers, where he shrugged off his jacket, carefully unfastened the cuffs of his shirt, and rolled up his sleeves. He knew damn well the extra care he took was buying time until Dr. Kincaid arrived. The last thing he wanted was conversation. Grabbing a surgical gown, he slipped it on as a lab technician rolled in the gurney carrying the sheet-clad body of Terrance Dillon.

The tech positioned the body under a lamp hanging from above, and Tessa pushed the instruments closer to the exam table.

The tech was in his early twenties with muscled arms. He grinned at Tessa and winked. "That's my job."

Smiling, Tessa flexed gloved fingers. "I know, Jerry. Just trying to get the lay of the land." She held up her hands in surrender. "I leave it all to you."

"I'm not fussing at you," Jerry said. "Just know, you'll have your hands full soon enough."

"Great," she said. "I can't wait."

Sharp didn't mind the way Tessa smiled at Jerry. He recognized it as her polite smile, the one saved for strangers. There was no charge lingering behind her gaze when she looked at Jerry. No undercurrent. Just simple. The exact opposite of what they shared.

He envied her ability to shrug off anxiety and at least look calm and happy. If one of them had a chance at getting out of this marriage whole and healthy, it was Tessa. And he'd see to it she got that chance.

Run while you can, Tessa.

The doors opened to Dr. Kincaid, whose gaze swept to him and briefly to Tessa. "Agent Sharp. How are you this fine day?"

"Can't complain." The doctor's body language revealed what he suspected. Tessa had been up front about their relationship. She was like that. Straightforward. What you saw was what you got. *I haven't been able to forget you.*

Dr. Kincaid pulled the microphone toward her lips. She moved closer to the table. Her gaze dropped to the body, and all traces of lightness vanished. "Shall we get started?"

"Let's do this," Sharp said.

Jerry pulled back the sheet, folding it, leaving it just below the feet. He clicked on the overhead light, and Dr. Kincaid flipped on the microphone. "This is Dr. Addison Kincaid, and with me today are Dr. Tessa McGowan, lab technician Jerry Taylor, and Agent Dakota Sharp with the Virginia State Police."

Terrance Dillon's body had been stripped and cleaned. The dried blood and mud were gone, and his ebony hair was brushed back from his face. His body was lean and fit.

The kid had it all going for him. And yet here he lay, perfect except for the neat knife wound puncturing his midsection. Because cool weather had preserved his body, he looked as if his eyes would open and he could hop off the table.

Dr. Kincaid began with the external exam, detailing a tattoo of a football flanked by wings on his chest as well as an old scar on his knee. She took a reading of his liver temperature and estimated his time of death was between midnight and 2:00 a.m. of Monday morning. The medical examiner's tone grew heavier as she talked about the knife wound. "This wound is efficient. Either the killer was lucky, or he knew exactly where to jab the knife. I'll get a better look at the damage when I open him up."

A review of the X-rays revealed the kid had cracked a rib and his right index finger. Both breaks had long healed, and according to Terrance's medical records, they had been sustained in a football game. After studying the body's exterior one last time, she reached for the scalpel and pressed it to the top right of his chest under the collarbone. With practiced ease, she made a Y incision into his chest. Bone cutters snapped the edges of the rib cage, enabling her to remove the breastplate.

The body cavity was mostly void of blood, and after the doctor suctioned what little was left, she was able to point to where the knife's jab had shredded the kid's liver, one of the body's most vascular organs.

"The blade hit its mark," Dr. Kincaid said. "The victim bled out very quickly."

"The killer would have had to get close to inflict a wound like that," Sharp said. Did the kid know his killer, or was he just too damn trusting?

Tessa's gaze dropped to the boy's hand. She picked it up and studied it closely. "There's foreign matter under his fingernail." Jerry handed her tweezers, and she gently plucked what looked like a small hair strand from under the nail bed.

"Good eye," Dr. Kincaid said.

Jerry bagged the hair strand, labeling it for the lab. "Can't believe I missed it."

The rest of the exam revealed healthy organs. No sign of any other trauma. Dr. Kincaid looked at Tessa. "Dr. McGowan, go ahead and close."

Tessa nodded.

As Tessa moved around the table and closer to Dakota, he caught the whiff of a soft jasmine soap, but no frilly perfume. That was Tessa.

She positioned the breastplate back in place and closed the large flaps of skin. Threading a large needle with practiced ease, she sewed up the body.

As he watched her work, he realized she was wearing her wedding band on her ring finger under her gloves. She'd not been wearing it yesterday.

They'd eloped alone to Las Vegas. He'd not had a ring for the ceremony but had insisted they drive to a jewelry store and buy one. She'd wanted a simple band, saying a stone was too fussy for her. Six months into their marriage he had ordered an engagement ring for her as a birthday surprise, but by the time it had been made, she was gone. It remained in a drawer in his bedside table. They'd officially been married sixteen months, but half that time had been spent apart.

His phone buzzed, and he glanced at the text. It was the station. Another body had been found in a park twenty miles north of the city. "All right, Doc. Thanks. Let me know if toxicology comes back with any interesting results. I've received a homicide call that I have to deal with now."

"Never a dull moment," Dr. Kincaid said.

"I wish to hell it were," he said.

He stripped off his gown. "Jerry and Dr. McGowan, thank you for your time."

"Of course, Agent," Jerry said.

Tessa looked up from her stitching. "Have a nice day, Agent."

Right. A nice day.

He reached for his jacket and left through the swinging doors without a look back. Outside, he was steps away from the building before he reached for a cigarette. As he lit up and inhaled, he was annoyed with himself on multiple fronts. Whatever promises he'd made about the smoking sure as shit had gone by the wayside, and whatever vows he'd made about staying clear of Tessa McGowan were officially on shaky ground.

His phone rang as he slid behind the wheel of his car. "Sharp."

"Jacob McLean," the caller said.

Sharp stubbed out the cigarette in the ashtray. "I thought you were dead."

A deep chuckle rumbled through the receiver. "I get that a lot."

Jacob and Sharp had been buddies in high school and both served together in the marines. Sharp had been a sniper. McLean had been a medic attached to a Special Forces unit. When Kara had died, McLean had been reassigned for specialized training at Quantico and had driven down for her funeral dressed in his marine uniform.

"Where are you?" Sharp asked.

"I returned to Virginia about a week ago. I'm prepping for a job interview with an old college buddy who works with an outfit called Shield Security."

"I've dealt with them. Smart. Dedicated. Cowboys," Sharp said.

"Sounds like my kind of people."

Sharp started the engine. "You might be right. Need a place to bunk?"

"Been crashing at my mother's old place. Getting it ready to sell, but that's wearing thin."

"I'll text you my address. There's a key hidden above the front door in a small crack on the left. I'm on my way to a homicide, so no telling when I'll be home." It would be nice to have a friend around who might distract him from thinking about Tessa.

"Don't worry about me."

Sharp drove to the small suburban park northwest of Richmond, not far from where Terrance Dillon's body had been found. This was his third visit to the area in as many days. What the hell was it with this place?

When he arrived, a collection of local cop cars blocked the park's entrance. He paused at the checkpoint, showed his ID, and made his way back along the narrow winding road that butted into a playground complete with swing sets, a carousel, and an elaborate jungle gym. A buzz of activity by a picnic table drew his attention, and he could see a local forensic team was on hand. Again, a ring of yellow tape enclosed the area, blocking any random visitor who might stumble onto the scene.

A thin woman in her early thirties approached him. She was dressed in jeans, a loose T-shirt, leather jacket, and booted heels. Ink-black hair skimmed her shoulders, a delicate cross on a chain hung around her neck, and a detective's shield was clipped to her belt. Her lips were fixed into a grim line.

He recognized her. She was new to the Richmond division of the Virginia State Police, having transferred in from the Tidewater area where she'd worked undercover.

Sharp pulled his badge from his breast pocket, held it up for her to see, and attached it to his belt. "Agent Dakota Sharp."

She extended her hand. "Agent Julia Vargas. Thanks for coming so quickly." Her handshake was firm, her gaze direct.

"What do you have?"

Agent Vargas rubbed the back of her neck as she glanced back toward the body. "I received a call from the local deputy because this scene is so odd. One look and I knew I needed a second set of eyes."

"Male or female?"

"Body of a young female. I've seen a lot of heinous acts, but this one takes the cake."

"What's different about her?"

She shook her head. "You're going to have to see it for yourself."

"Okay." He tugged a set of black latex gloves from his pocket and slid them on over his hands. "Lead the way." She turned toward the yellow tape, raising it to allow him to pass first. A ring of officers and forensic technicians parted as he approached.

For a moment, he simply stared at the scene. His brain didn't quite process what he saw until he brushed away the shock and refocused.

Leaning against the tree was the body of a woman, dressed like a doll. White billowy dress, knee socks, shiny patent-leather shoes. However, it was her face and eyes that took his breath away. Her eyes were tacked open, revealing unnaturally large pupils staring sightlessly at him. Her face was painted white, cheeks tinted a blush red, with eyebrows arched in a thin line. The hair, twisted into twin braids, was a wig.

His gut clenched. When he spoke, his voice sounded ragged, rough. "It's paint?"

"No, it's not paint," Agent Vargas said. "It's ink. All tattoos."

He cleared his throat. "What?"

"Every bit of her face, scalp, and hands is covered. Must have taken weeks to do the work."

"Cause of death?"

"We don't know. There're no signs of trauma on the body other than the eyes, and the forensic team thinks the stitch job was done postmortem."

"Have you searched the area?"

"We have officers fanned out searching a half-mile radius right now."

Sharp stared off into the thicket of woods and spotted several uniforms canvassing the area. Beyond the woods he saw the outline of what looked like condos or apartments. "Who found the body?"

"An early-morning jogger. He came running through about five a.m. along the path from the condos and spotted the victim. He called 9-1-1, and the responding officer immediately closed off the area."

"Where's the jogger?"

"I interviewed him and let him leave for work. I've his name and number if you want it."

"Uniforms find any evidence?"

"So far, nothing. The front gates on the park weren't locked, so whoever left her here could have driven her in that way, parked in the lot, and carried her the thirty feet to this spot. There are no cameras in the park or at the entrance. I think he or she could have been in and out of here in ten or fifteen minutes."

"Assuming she was driven in."

"Correct." She nodded toward a graveled path angling into the woods. "That leads to a condo complex with plenty of parking. It's about ten yards to the parking lot. The association has an after-five-p.m. towing policy, which the killer may or may not have realized. I checked with the towing company, but they weren't patrolling the area between one and four in the morning. The flatbed was already full, and they were taking their bounty to the impound lot."

"Unless our killer lives in the condos."

"Possible. We've called the management office. Got voice mail and hoping for a callback soon."

He squatted and studied the garish face. "The tattoos are healed. That takes a couple of weeks."

His gaze dropped to her hands placed so demurely in her lap. Carefully, he touched the arm and found it was locked in place by rigor mortis.

"For the killer to position her like that would require that she still have flexibility in her limbs," Vargas said.

Sharp studied the wide, vacant eyes. "Twenty-four hours for rigor mortis to set the muscles, so she would have been dead at least fifteen hours before he brought her here and posed her."

"Jesus, what was he doing with her for fifteen hours?"

He had an idea but didn't want to voice it yet. Instead, he focused on her pale arms. "There's one needle mark. Any signs of trauma?"

"Other than the needle mark, no. The medical examiner will be able to tell us how she died. I'm betting asphyxiation or overdose."

"What about fingerprints?"

"We were able to pull prints. We've sent them to AFIS." AFIS was the Automatic Fingerprinting Identification System managed by the Virginia State Police.

Sharp studied the tattooed heart-shaped lips. "This tattoo work took a lot of time and planning. You think she consented to all the tattooing?"

"Any scenario is possible," Vargas said. "She could be a working girl who attracts fetish customers."

"I'm not so sure. She wasn't dumped. She was posed. And whoever put her here wanted her found. A panicked john wouldn't take the time."

"So what are you saying?"

"Whoever left her here was a careful planner," Sharp said.

"It's not his first time?" Agent Vargas asked.

"My guess is no, but if it is, he's been fantasizing about doing this for a long time."

"I'm going to input the case into the FBI's violent crimes database and see if I get any hits," Vargas said.

"Not a bad idea." Sharp studied the intricate detail work on the victim's face. "Whoever worked on her face is one hell of a talented artist. The fine lines under her eyes are perfectly smooth."

"Amazing in a very creepy sort of way," she said.

Sharp rose and took a step back. He'd thought he'd seen it all. He was wrong. "I'd like to follow this case with you."

She studied him. "I'm glad you said that. I think this one is going to take a hell of a lot of detective work."

"Understood." He turned away from the body, knowing his expression was hard. The stone-face mask, as Tessa had once said.

"I've put a call in to the medical examiner," she said.

"Dr. Kincaid's one of the best."

"She's in a meeting now but will return my call soon. I've requested her to be on scene."

"Good idea."

He looked again at the dead woman's wide-fixed eyes. Jesus. What kind of sick fuck did this? He started walking, needing a moment away so he could calm the fury smoldering and threatening to erupt.

Agent Vargas followed, her long legs matching his strides as he ducked under the yellow tape and pulled the cigarette pack from his pocket. He lit one and inhaled.

"That will kill you," she said. "Fast track."

"So I've heard."

"Black lung. COPD. All that shit is linked to those sticks."

A trail of smoke drifted up and coiled above his head as he studied the parking lot, trying to imagine the killer driving in here late last night. With only the condos to the west, it would have been easy to come in unnoticed. There was a strip mall south of the entrance, which meant there was a chance a security camera caught an image of a passing car between one and four in the morning. "Send out a few uniforms to check the area stores. See which vehicles came up on camera last night."

Her tone was matter-of-fact without a trace of defensiveness. "It's on my list. What else could I have missed?"

"Tattoo parlors. Whoever did the work on her face is very good. Had to get training somewhere, or one of the artists might have a theory about the style or level of detail."

As he moved to toss what remained of his cigarette, she snapped her fingers and motioned for it. He handed it to her. She took a drag on the end of the butt, savoring the taste before she dropped it to the asphalt and ground it with her boot.

"I hear that stuff can kill you," Sharp said.

"Yeah, I tell it to myself at least ten times a week as I talk myself out of the next pack. I've not had one in thirty days until now."

"Sorry to be the one to break your streak."

"If you hadn't been smoking, I'd have bought a pack today. It's going to be hard to shake the images of this case. If those tattoos weren't her idea, then he would have needed to have worked on her for weeks."

He shook his head. "You really think those tattoos could have been her idea?"

"I worked undercover vice in the beach area. Most johns are looking for straight sex, but there are some who like the kink. She could have cornered a niche in the doll market. Fetish and fantasy pay good money, with a lot of repeat business."

"The tattoos appear new."

"She could have just decided to rebrand herself on the streets."

It wasn't that Vargas couldn't be right, but he still didn't think the theory would pan out. Something about the entire scene suggested planning and thought. Still, he had to follow the evidence. "If she were hooking, she likely will have a record."

"That's what I'm hoping for. The sooner we can ID her, the better." Vargas grabbed hold of the small cross around her neck and absently moved it back and forth on its chain. "Why did he stitch open her eyes?"

"Makes her look more doll-like. Let's say she was a prostitute. She might have been playing a role he took far more seriously than she did.

Or maybe, it was an ego trip. He wanted her to have a good long look at the person who transformed her, then took her life."

"Do you really think she was dead when he stitched open her eyes?" she asked.

"God, I hope so."

"Jesus. Fucking. Christ." Vargas pushed a strand of hair from her eyes. "Why?"

"I'll worry about the whys when we catch this guy." Sharp offered her another cigarette. "Seeing as you fell off the wagon."

Vargas accepted the cigarette and the lighter. When the cigarette's end glowed, she inhaled as she handed him back his lighter. "Yeah, nobody likes a quitter."

CHAPTER EIGHT

Wednesday, October 5, 3:30 p.m.

After the Terrance Dillon exam, Tessa and Dr. Kincaid autopsied a man who'd died in a car accident. By the time they'd closed up the third case, a heart attack, it was after three and Tessa's feet and back were aching. Dr. Kincaid looked nonplussed as she stripped off her gloves and gown and tossed them into the waste bin.

"You did well today," Dr. Kincaid said. "It's not normally this hectic, but you held your own."

Tessa pulled off her cap. "Keeping up with you will be a challenge."

"You'll get used to it."

Jerry poked his head in the door. "Don't get too comfortable, ladies. Agent Vargas called. She'd like you to visit one of her death scenes." He glanced at a note. "Woman found in park. Covered in tattoos and no signs of trauma on the body. She's working with Agent Sharp on the case."

Two murder investigations on Dakota's plate. He would be in overdrive now, his attention focused like a laser on work.

"What makes the case unique?" Dr. Kincaid asked.

"Vargas said you'd need to see it to believe it."

"Thanks, Jerry." Dr. Kincaid checked her wristwatch. "Looks like our day isn't over yet."

"I'll get changed," Tessa said.

Dr. Kincaid stopped, as if she'd caught herself. "You both were so professional this morning, it was easy to forget you two know each other."

"I'll take that as a compliment."

Dr. Kincaid rubbed the side of her neck. "Why accept this job here? You knew you'd bump into him sooner or later."

"It's my hometown, too. And it's not like I hate the guy. He's one hell of a cop."

"He's intense. I like him, but I'd hate to cross him."

"Not a good idea when he's on a mission to solve murder cases. He's possessed."

"Because of his sister?"

She'd never heard Dakota talk about his sister to anyone. "You know about Kara?"

"He asked me to review her autopsy file a couple of years ago. I went over it with a close eye but didn't discover anything that made me think the cause of death wasn't an accidental overdose."

"I'm sorry to hear that. I'm not sure he'll ever know any peace."

"Did you know his sister?"

"As a matter of fact, I did. Both of us were local girls, and we ended up at the college here together. We had a lot in common. And we got along well until that last night." Tessa drew in a breath, knowing she was opening a door that had been so hard to close.

"Look, I don't mean to intrude."

"It's okay. Might as well tell you. Kara and I and a couple of our friends went to a fraternity Halloween party together. It was a warm Friday night, midterms had just ended, and we were ready to have a good time. I left the festivities early. I ended up getting hit by a car blocks from the party. I don't really remember the accident or the days surrounding it. My aunt told me later friends visited me in the hospital and told me Kara's mother was looking for her. My aunt said my cousins were there, and they offered to call around, but they all agreed what could be done to find Kara was being done. I was released on a Wednesday, the same day she was found dead."

"I'm sorry," Dr. Kincaid said.

She balled up her cap and tossed it in the trash. "The whole family fell to pieces. I was on pain meds, so I really don't remember. My cousins tell me the funeral was one of the saddest moments of their lives. It was a blur to me. Dakota couldn't get home until a month after the funeral, and by then I was in rehab. Dakota and I didn't meet up again until about two years ago."

"Ah."

Talking about this felt oddly disloyal to Dakota, but she wanted it out in the open. Life was full of enough drama without secrets. "We fell for each other, rushed into a marriage that imploded all in the course of one year."

Dr. Kincaid didn't comment, but she was listening.

"As you know, Dakota is totally dedicated to the job. He doesn't rest when he has an open murder case, especially when it's a young person. I understand somewhat where he's coming from, but there came a point when it drove a wedge between us. When I learned about the opening on Project Identify, I took it. Now I'm back."

Dr. Kincaid shook her head. "He's not changed."

"I know. But I have."

***

As Garrett Andrews considered taking a very late lunch, weighing the merits of Chinese versus Italian, he caught Clay Bowman's reflection in his computer screen. Andrews turned toward the doorway, the scars from an IED explosion along his back and arms tightening as he rose.

"Agent Dakota Sharp has sent us files," Bowman said. "You said you wanted the first cold case Shield tackled."

"I thought there was going to be a review process. We've already received a couple dozen requests for assists."

"Sharp gets bumped to the front of the line."

Logical. He'd proved himself to be a good cop, and he'd helped close the Shark case last month. Still, Andrews liked protocol. "What's the case he wants us to review?"

"His half sister's. A dozen years ago, she went missing from her college campus and five days later was found dead. The medical examiner ruled it an overdose."

Sharp's emotions would understandably be running high on this case. "A tragic case, but how does it relate to us?"

"I'm not sure it does. And if it weren't Sharp, I'd have said no."

"What do you have?"

"Sharp received case files from the former police chief who originally investigated the case. I said we'd go through the files."

"There's a high probability I'll confirm his sister made a terrible mistake that killed her."

"Maybe, but I'd still like you to work your magic."

"Not magic. Science."

A smile warmed Bowman's face. "Have a look at the case."

Andrews was still not convinced the files deserved a second look. "The original plan for the cold cases was for me to work closely with the submitting law enforcement officer. Not possible this time. Sharp's objectivity is compromised."

"Exactly why he wants us to look at the case. Is that a problem?"

"No. Not a problem. But as you might have noticed, I'm not the best at dealing with emotional messes."

Bowman arched a brow. "Really? I'd always pegged you as the warm and fuzzy type."

That almost prompted a smile. "You have a skewed sense of warm and fuzzy."

"You might be the perfect person to handle this for Sharp. He'll need someone who's completely detached and sees the facts for what they are."

"Assuming there's any new evidence to be found."

"Are you telling me you aren't up to the job?"

A tactical challenge lurked behind the comment. Management 101. Despite recognizing this classic maneuver, he wasn't immune to the ploy. Challenges and puzzles kept his mind engaged on the present and away from troubling replays of the past. "I'm very capable and willing."

"Good."

A half hour later, pasta in his belly and a double espresso in hand, Andrews returned to his office to find four dusty boxes on his desk. Sipping his coffee, Andrews moved to the first box and flipped off the lid. He'd barely thumbed through the first box, filled with handwritten notes of the police chief's interviews, when Bowman reappeared.

Without turning, Andrews set down his cup and said, "No filing system, only clumps of papers, some of which are rumpled and stained with what looks like pizza sauce. No organization. No patterns established."

"Making sense out of chaos is what you do best."

Absently, Andrews scratched fingertips over well-mapped rough scars on his left hand. "I do."

"If you need any assistance, ask," Bowman said. "I want this case resolved as soon as possible."

"I'll get started on this straightaway."

"Great."

Alone, Andrews opened the next box and found stacks of photos. Some had been identified on the back and others left blank. As he shifted through the pictures, he found an image of four young girls dressed in jeans and sweaters in front of what looked like a college dorm. They all grinned, and interlocked arms suggested they were close. On the back there were four scrawled names. *Diane, Kara, Tessa, Elena.*

He dug deeper into the files and found an image of a much younger Sharp with the girl who closely resembled him. He wasn't more than early twenties, and she must have been about twelve. He was young and slim, and the smile on his face exhibited an exuberance Andrews suspected had long since been tempered by life.

The remaining boxes were filled with an odd mix of police files, which he suspected had been copied without permission. Cops made duplicates of case files that mattered, and clearly the case had meant something to the former police chief.

Andrews's first order of business was to sort all the papers into stacks. Organization would need to be forged from the chaos. He began to work, grateful to let time pass and the outside world fade.

***

The Dollmaker sat in the dimly lit basement room, staring at the pictures he had taken of Destiny in the very early hours of the morning. Then he scrolled back more frames to pictures snapped in this room. He'd posed her in a variety of ways. Sitting. Lying down. Poised on the bed in a seductive manner.

Remembering their time together, he scrolled through the snapshots, stopping on one that captured her perfect face. He'd not used his flash for this picture, and moody shadows crossed her high cheekbones. But her eyes had been closed, and he'd felt cheated that she couldn't see him.

"Still, such a pretty girl, Destiny. I already miss you." He enlarged the picture and studied the fine detailing around her eyes and her mouth.

He'd worked hard to perfect his art, practicing first on himself, marking up his thighs until they were covered in ink, and then on the random whores who worked the streets. They'd been easy to drug, easy to keep for days because no one missed them. No one cared about them.

Some of the whores he dumped back onto the street, drugged and dazed. Others he'd practiced on too long and ruined their faces. Letting them go would have brought the wrong kind of attention to himself, so it had been easy to overdose each with a lethal hit of heroine before disposing of their bodies.

He scrolled through more pictures to another woman's face. This picture he'd snapped at the mall today. She'd been buying cosmetics. Her long dark hair framed her round face and drew attention to large eyes. Her skin was pale and flawless. A high slash of cheekbones.

Pretty enough that he'd grown hard while he'd been following her and taking pictures. But the longer he watched her, the more flaws he noticed. Pretty but not perfect.

She would be his new doll. She would be his new work of art. And he'd already picked out a name for her.

"Harmony. Harmony. Harmony." He said the name out loud several more times, liking the way it rolled off his tongue.

It wasn't really wise to make a new doll so soon, but he could feel the pressure of loneliness building inside him. In the past he'd wait months, even years before creating a new doll.

But waiting was too hard when he remembered Destiny. He didn't want to be alone. He wanted someone to love. To taste. He needed to wait, but he could not.

He reached for a packet of matches and lit one, watching as the flame danced and swayed. A fire would calm him. It had when he was a boy. He'd not set any fires in town in over three years, so one small one now would likely go unnoticed.

Holding the match until the flame died, he smiled. One small fire. And then he'd bring his Harmony home to live with him for a long, long time.

"I'm going to make you perfect, Harmony."

CHAPTER NINE

Wednesday, October 5, 5:00 p.m.

Under the glare of a portable lamp, the forensic crew worked the doll victim as Sharp walked through the woods to the condos adjacent to the park and knocked on the doors of the units facing the woods. No one had seen or heard anything last night. Retracing his steps, he stood at the edge of the crime scene, watching as the forensic technician photographed the body.

Judging by the victim's bone structure and build, she'd been a beautiful woman in the prime of her life. But the garish tattooing had disfigured and perverted her features.

The medical examiner's van arrived. Dr. Kincaid and Tessa got out with somber expressions, taking time to gather their gear. Tessa's long black hair was pulled into a thick ponytail, and she was dressed in khakis, well-worn boots, and like Dr. Kincaid, a dark-blue slicker that read "Medical Examiner" on the back. Sharp stood straighter, watching as she and Kincaid removed the stretcher from the back of the van. He thought he could handle working around Tessa, but he realized it was going to be harder than he'd first thought.

Julia Vargas approached Dr. Kincaid and Tessa. They listened to the agent give her report on the body before moving toward the crime scene tape. When they ducked under it, he followed.

Dr. Kincaid extended her hand to Martin Thompson and smiled as she introduced Tessa. "Dr. McGowan is a forensic pathologist. You'll be seeing more of her."

Martin shook her hand and only tossed a quick questioning glance at Sharp. "Welcome."

If Tessa read Martin's questioning gaze, she gave no sign of it. "Thanks."

The older man's normally banal expression actually softened, and he held her hand an extra beat. "Glad to have you on the team."

"Good to be on it," Tessa said.

Sharp caught a couple of young officers looking at Tessa. Their gazes weren't curious, but lewd. They didn't realize Tessa was his wife. A primitive impulse demanded he punch each guy in the face.

"Who found the body, Agent Vargas?" Tessa asked.

"An early-morning jogger. He said he didn't touch her. Thought she might have been a mannequin at first. He called the cops right away, and we had a first responder here within five minutes to secure the scene."

"May I touch the body, Martin?" Dr. Kincaid asked.

"Yes. I've collected every bit of evidence I can find, so the body is ready to remove," Martin said.

Dr. Kincaid knelt and with a gloved hand touched the victim's face, circling her finger around the red circle, a cartoon version of a blushing cheek.

"It's a tattoo," she said, hints of surprise in her tone. "And judging by its color and skin texture, it's recent. I'd say she only finished healing days ago."

"Have either of you ever seen anyone with this kind of tattooing?" Julia asked.

"I've seen facial tattoos within the gangs," Dr. Kincaid said.

"Some of the cultures in Asia tattoo the females' faces, but that's dying out," Tessa said.

"I've seen women who've had permanent makeup applied to their faces. Eyeliner, blush, even lip color," Dr. Kincaid said. "Even had a woman on my table who had her boyfriend's name inked on her forehead. But a doll face is a new one."

"It's fine workmanship," Tessa said. Her expression telegraphed a mixture of fascination and sadness.

Tessa pushed up the sleeve of the oversize doll dress. "The white stippling tattoo work that's on her face also extends from her fingertips to her wrists. Her eyes are expertly lined in a dark ink, and very precise freckles dot her cheeks." She touched the victim's mouth. "The red heart-shape tattoo here redefines the shape of her lips."

"She'd have to be out cold, otherwise the work couldn't have been done to her face," Vargas said.

"The injection site isn't infected, and there's no bruising, suggesting whoever inserted a needle in her arm knew what they were doing," Tessa said.

Sharp folded his arms, trying to envision the woman before this work was done, but he couldn't see past the ink.

Tessa pulled the sleeve back over the victim's arm. "Look at the detail around her eyes," she said. "It's hard enough to do with pen and ink, let alone with a tattoo needle."

"Only a monster would do this to an unwilling woman," Vargas said.

"I didn't say the person who did this was sane," Tessa said. "I was simply commenting on the skill."

He watched as Tessa absently rested her hand on the victim's arm as if assuring her it would be okay, and she was now in good hands. He suspected if he weren't standing there, Tessa would have spoken to the victim, issuing words of reassurance.

He cleared his throat. "Dr. Kincaid, do you have any idea how she died?"

Dr. Kincaid checked the victim's neck for signs of strangulation and tipped her body forward to look at her back. "Dr. McGowan, what's your opinion?"

Frowning, Tessa studied the body. "There are no signs of trauma on the body. We'll have to check her blood levels for signs of asphyxiation and drug overdose."

"Why the frown, Dr. McGowan?" Vargas asked.

"Her shoulder blades and the backs of her hands are discolored."

"What does that suggest, Dr. McGowan?" Dr. Kincaid asked.

"After her heart stopped pumping, the blood settled in the lowest part of her body, which was her back." She rolled down the knee socks and inspected the back of the victim's calves. They were also bruised. "If she'd died here, her shoulder blades would not be discolored."

"Correct," Dr. Kincaid said.

"On her back," Vargas said, shifting as if uncomfortable with the idea. "I don't want to think what that suggests."

"We'll determine if there was sexual activity," Dr. Kincaid said. "Though I might not be able to determine whether it was pre- or postmortem."

"Jesus," Vargas muttered.

Dr. Kincaid ran her hands over the dead woman's arm. "The skin is smooth, and there are no signs of hair on her arms or legs. She's been waxed recently."

"Do you think it's murder?" Tessa asked.

"She didn't die here," Dr. Kincaid said. "But that doesn't mean she was murdered. She could have overdosed."

"The second party panicked," Vargas said. "She could have been into some kind of weird shit, and it went sideways. Whoever she was partying with dumped her here."

"She wasn't dumped," Sharp said. "She was carefully posed."

"A final sign of respect?" Vargas asked.

Sharp shook his head. "Or a final statement from the killer. Right now, I don't know. We'll let the evidence lead us."

"How long would it take to tattoo her face and arms?" Vargas asked.

"I can't speak to how long the tattoo work took," Dr. Kincaid said. "There are no signs that infection ever set in. That means the wounds would have to be washed, there would have been extensive bandaging of her face and arms, and the dressings would have to have been changed daily to avoid infection."

"We're looking for someone who could have gone missing a month ago?" Sharp asked.

"I'd say so," Dr. Kincaid said.

"Thanks."

Tessa studied the back hem of the victim's doll dress. "This appears to be a bloodstain," she said.

Martin nodded. "I saw that. Don't know if it's her blood, but it's marked for DNA testing."

Needing a moment, Sharp turned from the scene and walked back to his car. He dug his cigarettes out of his pocket. As he shook loose a cigarette from the pack, he felt Tessa's gaze on him. He let the pack fall back in his pocket. "What is it, Tessa?"

For a beat she didn't speak, and then in a voice that was both tender and harsh, "You're thinking about Kara."

He flinched at the sound of his sister's name. Their last big fight was over Kara. He'd been so angry when she'd tried to talk to him about letting his sister go. He'd blown up at her, dumping all his anger for his lost sister on her. Tessa had absorbed his pain to a point, and then she'd gotten angry. Two days later she was on a plane to Southeast Asia.

"So you're psychic now?" he asked.

"I don't need to read your mind." An edge honed the words, telling him she would not tolerate his temper. "I know you. She's never far away when you're investigating a case."

"Really?" He patted his pockets for his lighter and lit the tip of his cigarette. He sensed her disapproval, which only made him inhale deeper. It didn't help that she was right. If their marriage hadn't gone sour, he might have tried to free some of those compartmentalized emotions and talk.

"It was her birthday yesterday, Dakota. And your victim is a young woman who would have been about Kara's age now."

"Shit, Tessa. It's been twelve years." He said it as if the passing years had dulled his sense of failure.

She arched a brow. "Don't give me that bullshit," she said, lowering her voice. "For you, no time at all has passed."

A sigh shuddered through him as he opened the car door. "I'm assuming you're doing the autopsy."

Her eyes narrowed. "I'm assisting Dr. Kincaid."

"Call me when you have this victim on the table. I want to be there."

***

Tessa arrived back at the medical examiner's office with Dr. Kincaid and the body just after ten that night. She checked the victim in as Dr. Kincaid scheduled the autopsy for the morning. After the body had been stripped and placed in cold storage, the women opted to call it a night.

It was close to midnight when she made the drive through Richmond and over the Mayo Bridge into the Manchester section of the city. The drive took less than ten minutes. As she pushed through the front door of her cousin's converted warehouse apartment, relief shuddered through her. She had six hours' break before returning to the office for the autopsy.

For a moment she stood, staring out the large windows overlooking the James River and the city. As she had done since she began her rotations on the hospital floor in medical school, she stripped off her work clothes and turned on a hot shower. When the steam rose, she stepped into the spray and allowed the heat to wash over her skin and rinse away her day.

As the water pulsed over her face, her thoughts turned back to the kiss she'd given Sharp yesterday. Loving him would never, ever be easy. And still, touching him had felt right. "God, Dakota, let me help us figure this out."

When she'd dried and changed into sweats and a T-shirt, she went into the living room. The furniture in the apartment was eclectic, minimalist, and highlighted her cousin Rebecca's travels. The rugs were from Morocco, a vase filled with fresh tulips was from Paris, and the collection of black-and-white photos featured many of the places she and her late husband had visited.

When Tessa and Sharp had been together, she'd made an effort to create a nice home. But when she'd left him, she left all they'd acquired behind. Soon, she'd have to find her own place and start collecting secondhand and discount furniture. For most of the last year, she'd all but lived out of a tent, so in her mind, any furniture was a step up. The only piece she was determined to invest in was a quality mattress and bedding. No more sleeping on hard, lumpy surfaces.

One of the keepsakes she'd held on to after her departure was a collection of pictures framed in white distressed wood. She'd kept her wedding picture, though it was in storage. What was displayed on her dresser was a picture of Tessa, her mother, and her aunt at Inner Harbor in Baltimore sixteen years ago, right before her mother died. As she stared at her mother's pallid, sunken features, it was obvious she was gravely ill. But at the time as an idealistic fourteen-year-old, she'd remained hopeful her mother would beat the illness. Another picture showcased four young girls fresh to college. Kara, Diane, Elena, and Tessa. The image was taken at the fall festival several days before that last Halloween party. They stood at the apple-bobbing tent. They were all smiling, but she was the only one with wet hair. The only one who'd dared ruin her makeup to catch a bobbing piece of fruit in her teeth.

She lifted the image and studied their faces. Twelve years was an eternity. Kara, as always, stared boldly at the camera, her hands crossed in a playful way, a breeze catching her dark hair and gently blowing it from her face. Sadness tightened Tessa's throat. "Happy belated birthday, Kara."

The front door opened, and she turned to see Rebecca dressed in her scrubs and holding a pizza. Rebecca was a nurse practitioner at the hospital. "So you survived your first day on the new job?"

"Barely."

"When did you get in?"

"About twenty minutes ago."

"Long day."

Rebecca dropped her purse on the couch and slipped off her shoes. "I thought you were expecting regular hours."

"For the most part, I am."

Rebecca handed the pizza to Tessa. "Let me shower and change, and then we can visit before I drink my wine and crash into bed."

"Sounds great."

Minutes later Rebecca joined Tessa in the kitchen dressed in a very oversize T-shirt, with her damp hair draping her shoulders. She dug one wineglass from the cabinet and a half-full bottle of white chilling in the refrigerator. Rebecca pulled the wine cork and filled her glass while Tessa grabbed a soda can and popped the top.

Rebecca raised her glass and toasted. "To my day off tomorrow. Your new job. And to a jungle-free, civilized life."

Tessa clinked. "Thanks."

"How did it go today?"

"We responded to a very grisly crime scene. I saw Dakota there."

Rebecca stilled the glass inches from her lips. "And?"

Tessa knew him well enough to know that under the still waters circled anger as alive and all-consuming as a shark in the ocean. In the coming days, eating would happen on the fly and speaking would whittle to the basics until his case was solved. "Not bad."

Rebecca raised a brow. "It's me you're talking to. How was he?"

Tessa flipped open the pizza box and took a slice. "The same."

"So what's the deal with you and Sharp? Married or divorced?"

"Married, technically."

Rebecca's eyes narrowed. "What else aren't you telling me?"

"Nothing really."

"So it is strictly business?"

Tessa pulled a piece of cheese from the top and coiled it around her finger. "Basically."

"Have you forgotten what it was like when you were married to him? I respect the hell out of the guy as a cop, but you weren't happy with him."

"You make him sound like a monster. He isn't."

"I didn't say that. But he got so wrapped up in his work that he wouldn't come home for days, and when he did, he would hardly speak."

"There's no way you can see what he sees on a day-to-day basis and not be affected."

"I know Dakota is doing good work, but he's not an easy man. God knows, I saw what his sister's death did to the family. We were both at the funeral."

Silent, Tessa swirled her soda. "I miss him."

"Then sleep with him and get it out of your system. He's not the kind of guy you want to spend your life with. Time is only going to make him worse."

"Why do you say that?"

"As the years pass, he'll see more death, and Kara's murder will only continue to fester."

"You don't know that." She rose to Dakota's defense even though she doubted her own words.

"Look, Tessa, I'm not a fan of fixer-upper projects. I can say that because I'm a work in progress myself. Any man foolish enough to get close to me is asking for trouble."

Tessa studied her cousin's face. "Why do you say that?"

"Never mind. Just know some of us are just meant to be alone. I never liked Sharp because I see a lot of myself in him."

Despite the wisdom, she still couldn't accept it. But for her cousin's sake, she said, "I'm not in the counseling business. I'm focused on my job now. I respect the people I work with, and I won't screw it up over a man."

"In all seriousness, do me a favor: fuck the guy, file divorce papers, and move on with your life."

***

It was past 1:00 a.m. when Sharp pulled into his apartment complex. His hope was to catch a couple of hours' sleep, shower, and be ready to roll in the morning when Dr. Kincaid did the autopsy on his Jane Doe. Right now he had little to go on. Uniforms had searched the area around the body but found no additional evidence. No ID on the victim.

He shoved his key in the lock and noticed the apartment felt off the instant he stepped inside. His hand went to his weapon before he remembered Jacob McLean was here.

"Don't shoot me"—the deep voice sounded from the dark—"and I won't shoot you."

Sharp flipped on the lights and found McLean lying on the couch. One hand was flung over his eyes; the other lay on the grip of a Beretta lying on his chest.

Letting go of his weapon, Sharp shrugged off his coat. "You made it."

"A few hours ago. Thanks for the shelter."

"You still fixing up your mom's place to sell?"

"That's the plan." McLean had hated living with his mother as a kid. She'd struggled with alcoholism for years until it killed her five years ago.

"I'd have welcomed you with a steak dinner, but I've been at a murder scene."

McLean swung his long legs over the side of the couch and sat up. He ran his fingers through lengthy hair that brushed the tops of his shoulders. "Beer?"

"Love one."

Sharp removed his shoulder holster and placed it on a rented dining room table, which like the rest of the furniture had been chosen in less than five minutes online.

McLean opened the fridge and grabbed a couple of longnecks as well as a few packages of freshly cut luncheon meat and bread. "You look like shit."

Sharp accepted the beer, twisted off the top, and drank, savoring the cold liquid. "You didn't come all this way to talk about my pretty face."

"I wasn't going to launch into a Q and A session on Shield Security right off the bat."

He loosened his tie. "Catch me while you can. There's no telling when I'll get home again. What kind of job are you interviewing for?"

"Security. They've got contracts all around the world." McLean absently tugged on the beer bottle's label.

Sharp slapped cheese and roast beef on fresh bread. He was hungrier than he realized and quickly consumed it. "That will be a good fit for you. Means putting down roots."

"Maybe it's about time." McLean tipped the neck of his beer toward the living room. "Speaking of roots, there's no sign any woman has had any influence on the decorating," he said. "Classic postmarriage pad."

"Tessa and I are separated." Sharp drained the last of his beer, unwilling to travel this stretch of memory lane.

McLean walked to the mantel and studied a picture featuring a group of ten marines dressed in full battle gear. He gaze shifted to the picture of Kara. "Sorry to hear it."

"Thanks for the beer and sandwich. I've got to get some sleep. Keep me posted on the job?"

"Will do."

***

An hour before dawn, the Dollmaker fingered the red tips of the matches as he saw her returning to her apartment, running through the cold. She was dressed in jogging shorts, a top, athletic shoes, and a hoodie. Her dark hair was swept into a ponytail, and she carried a water bottle. She returned from the gym every morning at this time. She was dedicated to keeping her body as hard and fit as it had been when she was a teenager.

She always spent about an hour inside her apartment dressing, then left for work by seven fifteen. He never liked her choice of clothes, which were often peasant tops, jeans, and heels. He understood trends, but his tastes always ran to the classics.

As she fumbled with her keys at the front entryway, he was so tempted to approach her. The more he watched, the greater his desire to own her. He imagined her strapped in his chair and transforming her from beautiful to absolutely perfect.

The process wouldn't take long. Maybe a few weeks. He'd honed his skills over the years and knew exactly how long the deconstruction and reconstruction process took.

His design for Harmony would be different from Destiny's. This one would be his dark exotic beauty. He'd been sketching geisha designs as well as Russian nesting dolls for days. He'd yet to decide and knew final choices would be made when he could touch her face with his fingertips.

She would be his little exotic beauty.

Simple. Obedient. Pliable. Perfect.

As he thought about touching Destiny's cool pale skin, he grew hard. Already he missed Destiny and was sorry now he hadn't kept her a little longer. Why had he been in such a rush to show her to the world? He should have kept her longer. He ached for her.

The Dollmaker was anxious to begin again. But he had to wait one more day, when this doll was scheduled to take a week at the beach. She'd blocked time away from friends and family. He couldn't ask for better timing. Just one more day.

He'd be patient, and he'd wait until she'd closed up her apartment and told her friends good-bye, and then he would take her.

And after her week off, it would simply be a matter of sending texts explaining that she was extending her vacation. Some might question. But if he were calm, the texts would buy him precious time. People were easy to fool if you fed them believable lies.

He would not rush this transformation process. He would take exquisite care with Harmony. And he just might keep this doll for a good long time.

CHAPTER TEN

Thursday, October 6, 6:00 a.m.

Andrews glanced up from his computer screen when Bowman appeared with two cups of fresh coffee. "If I had to bet money, I'd say you were here all night," Bowman said.

Andrews glanced at his watch. "I took a break about three a.m. Went home and grabbed a couple hours of sleep."

He stood and straightened, unkinking stiff and protesting muscles impaired by scars and nerve damage, which were a constant source of "irritation," as he called it.

Andrews accepted one of the coffees. "Tastes good."

"How's it looking?" Bowman asked.

Andrews glanced at the two dozen stacks of paper piled on the floor around the room. "I'm still sorting. Mr. Knox amassed a great deal of information, but as I said before, he didn't organize it at all. The man's mind must be chaos."

"Any items jump out at you?"

"I've not had a chance to read all the interviews closely yet. There are at least fifty witness statements taken from people who either went to school with Kara Benson or who lived near the Benson house. Knox also spoke to several of Roger Benson's business associates as well as friends of both his wife and Sharp. I'm hoping some kind of pattern materializes."

"Can you give me the short version of what happened to Kara Benson?"

"She went to a Friday-night Halloween party, and sometime around midnight got into an argument with a female friend and left shortly afterward." He detailed the search and finally the grim discovery of her body five days later.

Bowman's fingers tightened around his mug. "How long had she been dead by then?"

"About a day."

"For four days she was alive and unaccounted for."

"Correct."

"What was the condition of the body?"

"When found, she was fully clothed, and there were no signs of trauma on the body."

"Do you have pictures?"

"I do." He shoved out a sigh. "These were taken by the officer on the scene. They aren't the best quality and don't document the scene adequately, but I can see why Sharp can't look at these. They would be disturbing for anyone attached to the deceased."

The photos of Kara Benson showed her lying on her side by the road, wearing a short red dress. Her feet were bare. Many of the pictures were out of focus, but the ones that were readable showed her face turned from the camera.

"You said she was last seen at a Halloween party?" Bowman asked.

"That's right."

"Explains the outfit. Were there signs of rape?"

"There were indications of intercourse. Though there was no vaginal bruising or tearing to suggest force."

"Was semen found?"

"Yes, and it was tested. But when the sample reached the lab, technicians determined it was compromised, so a full DNA panel couldn't be obtained."

Bowman stared at his pale face. "Hell of a tragedy for Sharp to deal with."

Andrews was silent for a moment. "I still don't want to discuss this case with him right now. I want to have specific questions before we talk."

Bowman nodded toward a pile of handwritten papers. "These are the notes Knox made during his interviews?"

"Yes. He talked to dozens of people about Kara. Each time he focused on any stranger who might have been spotted with her. Nobody saw her leave with anyone."

"Anything else?"

"There are still receipts to be catalogued, pictures to be examined, including a copy of her autopsy report, which I've yet to read."

"I can read the witness files. You can read the autopsy report, and we can compare notes."

"Not necessary. Better I process it all and give you a report. It won't take much more time."

"Understood," Bowman said. "Knox gave these files to Sharp for a reason. Said he thought if there were any new clues to find, Sharp would uncover them."

"The case might have been solved twelve years ago if Knox and his department hadn't done such substandard work at Kara Benson's crime scene."

"Maybe that explains why he never let the case go. He felt guilty."

"It's been my experience that the real intentions are usually hidden under the surface."

"You think Knox is hiding something?"

"Perhaps."

"Knox lives close by. Talk to him."

"As soon as I read the files today, he's first on my list."

"Keep me posted."

"Always."

***

When Tessa's alarm went off at six in the morning, she hit "Snooze." She was still struggling with jet lag, and it had been a long time since she'd been this tired. The late night at the crime scene hadn't helped. To compound the situation, she'd dreamed again about Dakota, the man who was never far from her even if she put thousands of miles between them.

In the dream she'd had so many times, she was standing at the stove of their Libby Avenue apartment and stirring tomato sauce for their dinner. Pasta boiled on a back burner.

Dakota always moved so quietly, she often didn't hear him approach. And when he wrapped strong arms around her waist, she'd started. "Damn it, Dakota. I'll spill the sauce."

A deep chuckle rumbled in his throat as he kissed the crook of her neck. His hands slid along the sides of her sundress and then up under the thin cotton, caressing her thighs' bare skin.

Her breath hissed through clenched teeth as she tried to focus on her task. His hand skimmed her belly to the front of her panties and teased the nest of curls. Hot energy raced through her blood, and her appetite for food vanished. Letting the wooden spoon drop into the pot, she shut off the stove and pressed her bottom against his erection.

"That's my girl," he whispered close to her ear.

"You make me crazy." From the beginning, he'd known how to touch her body and make it react in ways she'd never imagined.

He pulled her away from the stove and lifted her up onto the kitchen table they'd just bought a couple of weeks ago. As he stared at her, he pushed her legs open, then freed himself from his jogging shorts. He shoved her moist panties aside and pulled her close to the table's edge. With one thrust he was deep inside her, moving both her and the table with determined lunges.

She arched her back to take the full penetration, and he leaned forward and sucked her breast through the dress fabric. Her fingers balled into tight fists as the tempo built. He liked taking her to the brink and then easing up. She whimpered his name, begged him to continue, and then he licked her until she came.

Finally, when the last spasm shuddered through her body, he slid inside her moist center. "Watching you lose control makes me so hot," he whispered against her ear. He was never in a rush as he thrust in and out of her, holding her face in his hands as he growled her name until he came.

Tessa's alarm went off a second time, and this time she sat up and swung her legs over the side of the bed, cradling her head in her hands. She glanced at the empty side of her bed, feeling hungry for him and aware she was alone.

She'd wanted to kiss him for weeks and had hoped for more of a reaction from him. She could feel he wanted her, but Dakota had held himself in check and detached as stone. "I'm not finished with you, Dakota Sharp."

She placed one foot in front of the other until she reached the shower. Turning on the hot spray, she let the water rush over her and wash away some of the fatigue. A half hour later, she was out of the shower, her damp hair curled into a knot, and wearing clean scrubs. She made herself coffee and poured it in a travel mug before grabbing her purse, backpack, and keys.

Tessa arrived at the medical examiner's office twenty minutes later. The morning traffic had already fallen into a somewhat predicable routine, and she was grateful for this one consistency in her life.

After stowing her backpack in her desk, she and Dr. Kincaid moved to the bank of refrigerated shelves to make morning rounds of the pending cases. The first case appeared to be a heart attack, but an autopsy would confirm it. The second, a fall. And the third was the Jane Doe from last night.

Dr. Kincaid pulled out the tray. Lying on the cool table was the body of the young woman. Her body had been shaved of hair, and her face and hands were perfectly covered in tattoos.

"I've no doubt she was sedated during the process. Her arms, legs, and muscles have atrophied, suggesting she moved very little in the last month," Dr. Kincaid said.

There was a familiarity in the woman's features that still bothered Tessa, but without hair and a clear view of the woman's face, she couldn't place her. "Where are her clothes?"

"With the forensic department. They're testing the blood sample."

In the stark light, the garish doll-like features looked all the more shocking and gruesome. The classic red cheeks, freckles, and bow lips lost all their charm and innocence in this brash context.

She stared at the eyes still open. "You removed the contacts?"

"I didn't want them fusing with the eye. But there's no closing the lids."

Tessa shifted her right leg, which was aching more than usual today. She chalked it up to too much time on her feet and not enough stretching.

"When will Agents Sharp and Vargas be here?"

"The autopsy is scheduled for ten," Dr. Kincaid said.

Dr. Kincaid nodded toward her leg. "Your leg bothering you?"

"I'm a little tired."

"Is it painful?"

"Just stiff." Even after a dozen years, long days still irritated the bone that had been nearly shattered by the car. "It'll pass."

At nine forty-five she moved into the autopsy suite, where she found Jerry setting up the instrument tray Dr. Kincaid would use.

"You're an early bird," Jerry said as he placed a sterile pack of instruments on a small worktable.

"It's the newbie in me. Once I get this place figured out, I'm sure I'll be cutting it closer."

He laughed. "When you get this place figured out, would you send me the cheat sheet?"

"I'll be sure to copy you."

He nodded toward the bank of cold storage compartments in the other room, where they kept the bodies. "Help me get the next case ready?"

They transferred Jane Doe's sheet-clad body to the autopsy room.

She raised the sheet and studied the woman's face. "Have you seen any disfiguration like that here?" she asked.

"I've seen some crazy stuff over the years," Jerry said. "Piercings, body modification, tattoos, but I have never seen anything like that."

CHAPTER ELEVEN

Thursday, October 6, 10:00 a.m.

Tessa turned as the doors to the autopsy suite whooshed open to admit Agent Julia Vargas. The agent had pinned up her ink-black hair in a ponytail, which accentuated an angled face and a faint splash of freckles peppering her skin. She wore a black T-shirt and blazer over dark jeans, ankle-high boots, and her badge dangling from a chain around her neck. She cradled a cup of coffee close. "I'm Agent Vargas. The victim with the doll face is mine."

Her voice sounded rough and heavy with fatigue. Tessa knew she wouldn't get much rest until the case broke. Cops worked nonstop in the first two to three days of a homicide, knowing there was a golden window to find a killer before the case went cold.

Jerry raised his hand first. "Hey, Julia. This is our newest recruit, Dr. McGowan. Second day on the job."

"We met last night at the crime scene," Tessa said.

"I remember," Vargas said as she sipped the last of her to-go coffee and dumped it in the trash. "It was a bit of a zoo. We had a dozen cops and deputies show up to steal a look. Like herding cats." She rubbed the back of her neck as she turned to change. "I'll get gowned up."

Barely seconds passed before the doors opened again, this time to Dakota. He had showered and was clean-shaven, his shirt crisp, and he moved with quick steps, his heels striking like a man on a mission. Her heart beat faster as he shrugged off his jacket and slipped on a gown.

"Sharp, you look too chipper," Vargas said.

Ignoring the attempt at camaraderie, he asked, "Did you find any evidence in the park associated with the victim?"

Vargas's eyebrow went up, and her eyes sparked with challenge. "We combed the perimeter for hours. We found nothing. Not even a tire track."

"What about security cameras near the park?"

She rolled her shoulders. "My guys pulled video from three gas stations and a convenience store, and they're waiting for a couple of stores in a strip mall facing the park entrance to open. We'll have it all researched by the end of today."

"And AFIS?"

"No hits yet."

He tied off his gown and grabbed a set of latex gloves. "Maybe there's something on the body that'll tell us more."

"That's the hope," Julia said.

Tessa noted that when he talked to Julia, his shoulders weren't as rigid, and the snap in his voice, though not relaxed, didn't crack quite as hard. But he'd always been able to get along with his coworkers. The cases they worked bonded them in ways that, during the investigation, crowded out the rest of the world.

She resented her outlier status when Dakota worked a case. She wanted the easy banter she'd once shared with Dakota back again. One way or the other, they had to muscle past the demands of his job, the failures of the past, and move forward as a couple.

Dr. Kincaid entered, and Tessa took her place across from the doctor. The detectives gathered at the foot of the table. Whereas Vargas absently fingered the thin fabric of her gown, Dakota clasped his hands behind his back and stood at attention.

Dr. Kincaid uncovered the victim's face.

Vargas automatically shifted her gaze to the victim's eyes, then quickly looked away. "Forensics captured hair samples from her clothes. Seeing as she doesn't have any, I'm hoping it belongs to whoever she last saw." She shook her head. "Jesus. I hope to hell she was medicated during the process."

Dr. Kincaid studied the body. "That I can't tell you with certainty. I can tell you she has had cosmetic surgery before. I suspect she's had a nose job, and she has breast implants," she said as she palpated the taut breast tissue. "If the fingerprints don't pan out, I can pull the serial number from the implant and run it through the manufacturer."

Dakota gave no hint of what he was thinking as he watched the doctor catalogue the victim's exterior physical landmarks. She had a scar on her forehead, two moles on her right breast, and two older tattoos, a filigree at the base of her spine and a heart on the inside of her right ankle. There was also an appendectomy scar. All these markings offered glimpses into a woman who cared about her appearance.

The doctor leaned toward the victim's face, pulling a magnifying glass closer to study the tattoo work as she continued to give her report. "We did a full X-ray work-up on her this morning, and there were no broken bones. She does appear to have suffered a fracture in her right wrist, but that would have been at least a decade ago. I checked her eyes and nasal passages for signs of asphyxiation, but found none. I also ran a full tox screen. I put a rush on the test results, so we should have some details back in the next forty-eight hours."

"How old is she?" Dakota asked.

"I'd say between twenty-five and thirty. Her skin is in great shape, though it's clear she liked tanning, as evidenced by the faded lines around her breasts and groin."

"Tan lines take a couple of weeks to fade," Vargas said. "That might help with fixing a timeline."

"They fade anywhere between a week to six weeks," Dr. Kincaid said.

"She's thin," Dakota said.

"She's underweight by about ten pounds," Dr. Kincaid said. "But if you look at her biceps and quads, you'll see some muscle definition. At one point she worked out regularly."

"A woman who cares this much about her looks suddenly decides to disfigure her face? Makes no sense," Vargas said, more to herself than anyone else in the room.

"I can tell you she had intercourse right about the time of her death," Dr. Kincaid said. "No signs of vaginal tearing, and I was able to swab a satisfactory DNA sample from the semen that her partner left behind. If this guy is in any kind of DNA database, you'll find him."

"Let's hope only one DNA signature is present. Narrows the field," Vargas said.

"Agreed," Dr. Kincaid said.

"This kind of detailed tattoo work, if done against her will, takes planning," Vargas said. "Why plan so carefully and then leave a DNA sample behind?"

"He might not be that smart, but I doubt it. He could have gotten sloppy, but after all the time and effort he took to change her and pose her, that makes no sense either," Dakota said. "If I had to guess, I'd say he is simply arrogant and knows he isn't in a database."

"This doesn't look like the work of a first-time offender," Vargas said.

"No," Dakota said. "He's never been caught before."

The internal exam lasted an hour and proved that the victim had been healthy. Her lungs were clear and her other internal organs in top shape. Her heart was a normal weight and size. Stomach contents revealed what appeared to be oatmeal. There were no signs of a pregnancy in the uterus.

When the entire exam was complete, Tessa began to suture the victim's chest. Dakota backed away from the table and tugged off his gown, clearly anxious to be away from the room, and most especially, her. The body had been a barrier between them and had been a neutral subject to discuss.

"Vargas, let me know if anyone shows on the surveillance tapes or there are hits with DNA," Dakota said, depositing his gown in the trash.

The agent joined him and tossed her wadded-up gown in the disposal bin. "You'll be the first to know if we spot anyone."

"Good."

Vargas reached for her jacket and pulled it on. "Keep those lines of communication open on your end, Agent Sharp. I want to know what you know."

"Right."

Vargas turned toward Tessa, who was using the classic baseball stitch to close. "As soon as the tox screens arrive, Doc, you'll call me?"

"You two will be the first to know," Tessa said.

Dakota tossed a look toward Tessa and held her gaze for a beat. Heat rose up inside, making her cheeks burn.

"Thank you, Dr. McGowan," Sharp said.

He'd never called her Dr. McGowan when they'd been together. Until their relationship was settled, working with him was going to be maddening.

"Right, thanks, Dr. McGowan," Vargas said.

"Certainly, Agents. Call me with any questions."

***

Sharp had too much work on his plate to be sidetracked by Tessa. The sooner one of them filed papers, the better for both of them.

As he slid into the car, he checked his voice-mail messages. An officer in the city of Richmond had an eyewitness who'd seen Terrance Dillon about 11:00 p.m. on Sunday. He redialed the officer's number. "This is Sharp. Got your call regarding Terrance Dillon."

"Yes, sir. We have a bartender who thinks he saw your murder victim with an older guy on Sunday night."

Sharp cradled the phone under his chin as he pulled a notebook and pencil from his breast pocket. "Do you have a number of the bar?"

"Sure do."

Sharp scribbled the name and number, thanked the officer, and dialed. The bar manager answered and told Sharp to come in about four when the Sunday-night bartender arrived for his shift.

He drove the twenty miles north toward Terrance Dillon's town, parked, and walked down the street toward the diner called Bessie's. He remembered as a teenager how he'd hated hanging around town. It had felt so small and confining, and he was always angling for any reason to leave. He'd left, anxious to chase the thrill of battle and conflict. Finding both had given him a new appreciation for large lawns with old oaks; historic, slow-paced charm; and the tedium of everyday life.

He pushed through the front door of the diner he'd eaten at dozens of times as a teenager. The 1950s decor and the smell of coffee and burgers brought back memories as he sat at the counter. Back in the day, he sat here dreaming of better places. Excitement. Now he wondered why he'd hated the place so much.

The waitress, a redhead in her late thirties, set a menu in front of him. Sharp ordered coffee and the number six without looking at the menu.

"You know what the number six is?" she asked as she set a coffee mug in front of him.

"I've eaten here before."

She filled his cup and studied his face. "You're the Benson boy."

"Roger Benson was my stepfather. I'm Dakota Sharp."

She set a creamer pitcher within reach. "You were a couple of years ahead of me in school. Weren't you the one who set off those fireworks in the center of town when we were in high school?"

A smile edged up the corner of his lips. He and Jacob McLean had gotten ahold of extra fireworks left over from the Fourth of July celebration and decided to re-create the show with what they had left. It did not go over well that it was the middle of August and two in the morning.

"That would be me."

"I'm Ellie Duncan. You're a cop now, right?"

He nodded. "Karma's a bitch."

"I heard folks talking at breakfast this morning. You're here to ask about the Dillon kid, aren't you?"

He sipped his coffee as the flicker of nostalgia vanished. "That's right."

"Damn shame about him. Terrance was a good boy. Always looking for odd jobs and ways to make extra money. He wanted to go to college."

He set his cup down. "How well did you know him?"

She rested her hand on her hip. "Knew the family better than the boy. Father was bad news, but the kid was on the straight and narrow thanks to his grandmother."

The front doorbells jangled and she glanced up, grinning. "Hey, Norman."

His answer sounded warm. "Ellie. How are you today?"

Sharp tossed a glance toward the baritone voice as the man settled at the counter several places to his left. Tall, fit. He was the funeral director who'd overseen Roger's graveside service.

Ellie set a cup in front of him and filled it with coffee. "Norm, this is Agent Sharp. He's working that dead boy's case, like you."

Sharp extended his hand. "DeLuca, right?"

His grasp was firm, his gaze direct. "That's right."

Ellie tapped her fingers on the counter. "Norm, let me get your to-go order."

As she vanished into the kitchen, Sharp faced the man. "You will be handling Terrance's funeral service?"

"I am. I spoke to his grandmother this morning. Sad, sad thing to happen. They are a good family, and the kid had so much promise."

"You know the family well."

"Know them well enough to say hi. Henry has the maintenance contract with the cemetery, and I see him often. The guy works hard, and I know he was proud of his cousin's football career."

"What about Jimmy Dillon? Do you know much about him?"

"He's been in prison for at least nine or ten years. I think his last conviction was related to drugs. He was in prison when his wife, Terrance's mother, died."

"Did Terrance have any contact with his father?"

"I did see Jimmy at Terrance's football game a couple of weeks ago. He was off to the side, I think, trying to go unnoticed."

"Why do you say that?"

Intelligence burned in DeLuca's stare. "He stayed close to the bleachers and close to the exit. Thirteen years of running funerals and you get a knack for reading people."

"Why were you there?"

"DeLuca's was a sponsor. We were being recognized that night by the boosters."

Ellie reappeared with a large brown bag stapled closed with a ticket on it.

"Thanks, honey."

The waitress grinned as she ripped off the ticket and rang up the order. "You're not working too hard, are you, Norm?"

He smiled, his face warming. "No."

She winked at him. "See you tonight."

"Count on it." He paid her a twenty, collected his change, and winked back at her before she moved around the counter to wait on another patron.

Sharp tapped his finger on the side of his cup. "Was there any talk in town about the boy using or dealing drugs?"

"No. Never."

"What about the people he was hanging out with?"

"One of his teammates was arrested last year for dealing, but I couldn't say how close Terrance was to the boy."

Sharp pulled out a notebook from his pocket. "Does that kid have a name?"

"Jake Wheeler."

He scribbled down the name. "Thanks."

DeLuca checked his watch and pulled a card from his pocket. "I've got a family coming by in a half hour. But if you need anything, call me. I'll do whatever I can to help."

"Appreciate that."

DeLuca picked up his order. "Good luck to you."

"I'll take all I can get."

After Sharp ate his meal, he made a call and discovered Jake Wheeler was still incarcerated. His next call was to the maintenance company that had hired Terrance last summer. "This is Agent Dakota Sharp with the Virginia State Police. I'm looking for the owner of Dobbins Maintenance."

"You found him. I'm Ralph Dobbins," the man said. "You've called me a couple of times. Sorry I haven't been able to get back to you. It's been crazy."

"Yes, sir."

"Terry's death was a terrible loss. Just saw the kid last week at his football game."

"How long had he worked for you?"

"On and off all summer whenever we had work for him. He was a good worker and had a great attitude. Wish I could have found more kids like him."

"His grandmother said he was offered a job last Sunday. Was that you?"

"No, it wasn't me. I haven't had Terrance on a job since August."

"What businesses do you clean?"

"Well, we clean banks, a couple of insurance agencies, two salons—and we also do move-out cleanups."

"Did his father apply for a job with you?"

"Jimmy Dillon. Yeah, he did. He worked a couple of jobs, but he wasn't a great worker."

"What jobs did Jimmy's crew clean?"

"Medical offices. We got a cluster of them near Mechanicsville."

Doctors' offices meant drugs in stock. And Jimmy Dillon had done time for drugs.

"Can you get me a list of the places where Jimmy Dillon cleaned?"

"Sure. But what's that have to do with Terrance?"

"Maybe nothing. I'm re-creating his last couple of weeks as well as his father's. I'm just trying to figure out who might have killed him."

"I'm on a job now, but I can send you the list."

"I'll text you my contact information."

"As soon as I get back to my office, I'll get it to you as quick as I can."

"Thanks."

"You got any ideas who would have done this to that boy?" Dobbins asked.

"I don't know much yet. But I'm working on it."

"Damn shame."

"Did he make any friends on the crew? Was there anyone he hung out with?"

"Not really. Most of the guys on the crews are older. Forties or fifties. He was always talking about his buddies from high school."

"He mention anyone in particular?"

"Talked about Ronnie and Garcia, but I never met them."

Sharp had spoken to them both. "He ever give you a reason to think twice about him?"

"No. He never said a word that gave me pause about him. Loved his grandmother and said he wanted to give her a new dryer for Christmas."

"Okay, thanks."

Sharp hung up. His priority now was to find Terrance's father. He suspected his old man was at the center of the shit storm that got Terrance killed.

***

The abduction was the hardest part of the Dollmaker's job. It was the moment when the entire operation could go sideways. Discovery and arrest were always imminent.

So to control the variables, he spent time watching and taking notes weeks in advance. He detailed the doll's schedule. When she slept, got up in the morning, ate, went to work, the gym. He noted her friends and family. Who paid attention and had the greatest reason to sound an alarm bell when she went missing. Favorite dress shops, restaurants, hobbies. The profile was designed with one objective: to find out when she was most vulnerable.

He checked his watch. He was minutes away from reaching this doll's most vulnerable moment.

Nervous energy buzzed, making his muscles tense and tight. He felt fear, but also excitement and anticipation. Soon they would be alone together.

Her red car pulled into the parking lot two spaces from her regular spot. He'd placed orange cones in her usual spots so they appeared unavailable, forcing her to park in the shadows and out of the surveillance camera's view.

Her headlights went dark and the engine died. Seconds later, she slid out of her car, grabbing two plastic bags of groceries as well as a gym bag. She locked the car with her key fob and started up the sidewalk. He watched from the passenger-side mirror of the white van. Seconds before she neared his door, he opened it. It swung wide, blocking her path, as it should. He got out, dropping a pack of cigarettes, fumbling for it and then a lighter that he also dropped close to her feet.

She stopped, tried to sidestep as he rose, and held out a hand. "I'm so sorry." He grinned, knowing when he smiled he could catch a woman's eye. "I didn't see you coming."

Her smile was tight and nervous. Her natural inborn fear receptors were telling her to run. *Danger! You don't know this stranger!* But like most women, she overruled any natural fight-or-flight alarms because she didn't want to appear rude. He'd seen it so many times. Like most women, she was too polite to give in to the natural impulse. "That's okay."

"I scared you, didn't I?" He leaned a little closer, studying her wide brown eyes. "I'm so sorry. I'm clumsy, and I've startled you."

"No, no, it's okay."

He smiled, careful not to hold eye contact too long. "You are too nice. Here, let me get my stuff and be out of your way." He fumbled for the lighter. "So sorry."

"It's okay. I just wasn't expecting you."

He started to step aside. Her smile brightened. "Have a good night," she said.

"You, too." As she moved, he pressed the remote entry to the van's side door, and it opened. The noise startled her rattled nerves, and she looked toward him a second time, likely to get his reassurance.

Instead, he pulled a stun gun from his pocket and jabbed it in her side. Her head jerked back, and her knees buckled. He caught her a split second before she hit the ground and easily laid her in the bed of the van. He scooped up her bags and set them beside her as he got inside. A click of the button and the door closed. They were alone in the dark.

"Please," she muttered. "Please don't hurt me."

Straddling her and pinning her hands flat with his knees, he stroked her hair back with one hand as he pulled a loaded syringe from his pocket. "I'm not going to hurt you. I love you."

Her body still trembled from the electric shock force. "Please. Let me go. I won't tell. I won't say a word. Just let me go."

Tears filled her eyes as she stared up at him through the streak of moonlight beaming through the windshield into the back. With tenderness, he brushed the tear from her cheek. "Shh, I don't want you to be afraid. I'm not going to hurt you. I'm going to transform you into the most perfect woman. A living doll."

She shook her head. The fear in her eyes was heartbreaking, and he didn't like seeing it. Dolls weren't supposed to be afraid. They were a source of comfort.

She drew in a deep breath, but he drove his knee into her belly and forced the air from her lungs before she could scream. God, but he hated hurting her.

"Be quiet. Be a good girl, and I won't hurt you again. I don't like hurting you."

She shook her head from side to side. "No, no, no."

He held up the syringe and flicked the sides and squeezed the plunger a fraction, sending serum and bubbles out the tip. He drove the needle into her thigh. She struggled, but it was easy enough to hold her in place as he pushed the drug into her system.

Slowly her muffled cries quieted, and her body stilled. When she was asleep, he straightened, his heart racing. He smoothed his hand again over her face, then captured a lock of hair between his fingers, savoring the silky feel. Pity he'd be cutting off all her hair. But as lovely as it was, it didn't fit his vision of who she was about to become.

The transformation would take weeks. And though it was painstaking work, the sacrifice of his time would be worth it. Harmony deserved it. He'd made a critical mistake with Destiny. He'd been in too much of a rush for the total stillness of death, which in the end had robbed him of more time with her.

He wouldn't make the same mistake twice. There were other ways to mimic the stillness, and though it wasn't as perfect as death, it meant he could keep her much, much longer. He wanted to play with his doll for a while. Savor her. Taste her. Perhaps even find her a friend who would keep her company.

Drawn now by her calming stillness, he traced his hand over her soft hair and her full bright lips. So pretty. A doll. He leaned forward and pressed his lips to hers, unable to resist a kiss. His hand slid to the swell of her breast, and he gently squeezed. He grew hard imagining what it would feel like to be in his new doll, Harmony.

Outside, a car's headlights drove past the van, its lights sweeping inside the empty front cab. He pressed his body against her, holding his breath as the car's brake lights turned the shadows bloodred. Finally, the car sped up and left.

Her eyes grew glassy and her stare fixed as the drugs took hold.

"It's going to be okay, Harmony. I'm going to get you safely out of here and transform you. You'll be my perfect doll by the time you and I are finished."

CHAPTER TWELVE

Friday, October 7, 8:00 a.m.

Sharp had been at his desk nearly two hours when he received Terrance Dillon's financial statement. He was surprised to see the kid had two new credit cards.

According to the records, the kid had filed an application for the cards four weeks ago and received the new cards last week. He surveyed the purchases, and immediately red flags popped out at him. The kid had been buying items during the school day. Beer, wine, steaks. A tattoo parlor.

The principal said the kid didn't miss school, so there'd have been no way he could have made these purchases thirty minutes from his school without someone noticing. He'd also have needed a fake ID to buy the booze.

He'd bet money Jimmy, freshly out of prison with no job, had stolen his son's identity to get the credit cards. "Piece of work."

His phone rang; it was Dr. Kincaid. "Doc, tell me you have news."

"I don't know if the news is good, but I have information. Blood work came back positive for high levels of barbiturates in your tattooed Jane Doe. There are also traces of propofol. She overdosed."

His chair squeaked as he leaned back and processed the information. "Overdose." The word always reminded him of Kara. And then he asked the question plaguing Roger, his mother, and him since his sister was found dead. "Propofol is administered by IV, so she couldn't have given it to herself, correct?"

"That is right. There were no pills in her stomach, so the drugs had to have been delivered via an IV bag, thus the mark on her arm. I'm calling it a homicide, because even if it were some kind of game, whoever administered the drugs to her was the one responsible for her death." Homicide literally meant the death of a human by another human's hand. The ruling didn't speak to premeditation or intent. The woman had died at another's hands, but the homicide still could have been accidental.

"You said there might be a serial number on her breast implant."

"There was, and I just got off the phone with the plastic surgeon's office. Your Jane Doe has a name. Diane Richardson. According to her doctor, she had breast augmentation two years ago. He listed her address in the city's Fan District on Monument Avenue." She rattled off the house number.

Sharp pulled his notebook from his breast pocket and wrote down the address. "Doc, that's great. Now that I have a name, I have a prayer of figuring this out. What about Julia Vargas? Have you notified her?"

"I have. She'll be calling you to set up a meet today at the victim's home."

A critical piece of the puzzle had fallen into place. "Doc, you're the best."

"So I keep telling my staff, but no one seems to believe me."

When he ended the call, he quickly rang Vargas, and the two agreed to meet at the Monument Avenue address as soon as he arranged for a search warrant. By ten he had a judge willing to review his case.

Knowing the review process could take a couple of hours, he decided to visit the tattoo shop where someone had bought a tattoo in Terrance's name last week.

Less than a half hour later, Sharp entered the tattoo salon Ink Plus, located on Broad Street, a thoroughfare in the center of the urban campus of Virginia Commonwealth University. The school took up most of this section of Richmond and added to the hip vibe of the area.

The windows of the salon were covered with a collection of pictures showcasing the artists standing beside their customers sporting new ink.

Sharp had gotten four tattoos while in the marines. None of them were fancy or ornate like these. One was a simple saying, I WIN WHERE I FIGHT. The second read DUTY. HONOR. COURAGE. And the third, MY TIME IS AT HAND. And the last was a list of the five good men he'd lost in battle.

He moved through the front door. Bells overhead jingled. Jazz music played softly.

"Can I help you?"

The question came from a young woman behind the front counter. Thick dark hair skimmed her shoulders. She wore a gray tank top that left exposed sinewy arms and an ornate tattooed cuff ringing her right bicep.

"I hope so," he said.

She eyed him, already had him figured for a cop. But her smile was genuine. "What can I do for you?"

He pulled out his badge and introduced himself. "And your name?"

If he hadn't been paying attention, he'd have missed the micro hesitation and the wave of tension rippling through her. "Shay Profit. I'm the girl Friday here. If I'm not tattooing, I'm answering phones or working the front desk."

"How long have you worked here?" he asked.

"About two months."

He wasn't interested in whatever she might be hiding. "I'm trying to track a guy who might have been through here about a month ago."

Relief chased away the unease. "That's a long time."

"I have a credit card receipt if that will help."

"Sure." He showed her Terrance's and Jimmy's pictures as well as the printout of the credit card purchase. He didn't say more, wanting her to fill in the gaps.

She took both pictures and studied them. She turned Terrance's picture around. "That's the kid who was killed. I saw his picture on the news this morning."

"Good memory."

Black nails tapped the edge of the photo. "I have a memory for faces."

"What about the other guy?"

"He does look familiar. I want to say he got a tiger tattoo." She keyed the date on the credit card receipt into her computer. "Yeah, he was here just as you said, but he got a tattoo of a lion on his right shoulder blade. I didn't do the work, but Reggie did."

"So the kid didn't get the tattoo?"

"The kid was never here. Just the older guy." She studied the pictures of the two. "They look like father and son."

"They are. Can I talk to Reggie?"

"Sure." She raised a section of the counter and nodded for him to follow her into the back. They moved between burgundy curtains and along a long hallway with three doors on each side.

Shay knocked on the first. "Reggie, can we come in? Five-oh is here to ask a couple of questions."

After a moment's hesitation, a gruff voice fired back, "Sure, come on in."

They found Reggie, a tall muscled man with ink covering his arms and chest. He was leaning over a woman's exposed back with a tattoo gun gripped in large gloved hands and filling in the red shading of a rose. Half glasses perched on his nose.

Sharp introduced himself, prompting the woman on the table to turn her head and study him with open curiosity. "Reggie, do you mind stepping into the hall?"

"Sure." The big man set aside the tattoo gun and stripped off his latex gloves. He patted the woman on the arm. "Be right back, doll. Just chill."

The woman nodded. "Sure, Reggie, but remember, I got to be out of here in an hour. I've got a new business presentation this afternoon."

"I got you covered." In the hallway, Reggie closed the door. "So what do you need?"

Sharp pulled out Terrance's and Jimmy's pictures. "I'm trying to piece together the last days of this kid's life. He was last seen with his father, who was here a month ago getting ink. I think the kid's old man used his son's identity to get a credit card."

Reggie studied the pictures and nodded. "I remember the guy. He was covered in ink, and judging by the quality, it was done in prison. Did a lion's face on his back shoulder. Took me about six hours. After I did the work, I had him wait in the back room like I do for all my clients so I could make sure he wasn't having a reaction to the ink. After that he left, and we haven't seen him since."

"What did the guy talk about for six hours?"

"Damn, man, I don't know. Some folks lie on the table and don't say much. Others talk like I'm their therapist. I tune them all out and focus on the work. I do remember he had a high tolerance for pain. The needle didn't bother him at all."

Shay snapped her fingers. "Didn't he mention his kid? Said he'd wanted to take the boy out for ice cream when he saw him last month but when he did, he realized his kid was all grown up. Seeing the kid reminded the guy of how long he'd been in prison."

Reggie nodded. "That's right. Went on and on about how he and the kid were going to start fresh. He saw them as a team." He shook his head. "That's when I really tuned him out."

"When the guy was in the back room, he was chatting with another customer while he was waiting," Shay said. "When I looked in to check on them, they were in deep conversation. That guy paid cash. I haven't seen him before."

Sharp scrolled through the images on his phone until he reached the face of the newly identified Diane Richardson. "Mind if I ask one more question?"

Shay glanced back at the clock. "Sure, my next appointment won't be here for another five or ten minutes."

"Make it quick," Reggie said. "Molly hates to be kept waiting."

Sharp glanced at the victim's face. "We came across this woman, and it's clear she had quite a bit of specialty ink done to her face."

Shay looked at the picture and enlarged it with a swipe of her fingers. "The detail is amazing. Some of the best work I've ever seen." She handed the phone to Reggie.

Reggie adjusted his glasses, and the instant he saw the picture, his annoyance vanished. "Damn."

"Any idea whose work this might be?" Sharp asked.

"I'm good, but Shay's better," Reggie said. "She's the only one in the shop who could come close."

"I worked in a beauty salon doing permanent makeup for a while." As she traced the imprint of the victim's right eye, her brow furrowed. "I've not seen this much facial detailing before." She pulled dark-rimmed glasses from her pocket and slid them on before raising the image closer. "You're right about the attention to detail. It's hard to get this kind of facial coverage and still make it look natural."

"Natural?" Sharp challenged. "What's natural about it?"

"I'm referring to the subtlety of the colors. Easy to cover the skin in a heavy patch of white, but it's not so easy to stipple in other softer colors to create a more realistic—for lack of a better word—look. Her face looks like porcelain. That's not easy to do. I've only done two facial tattoos. They were simple tribal markings. I've had no requests for this fine a detail. This guy is a true artisan."

"How long would a job like that take?" Sharp asked.

"Days," Shay said. "And she'd either have to have a high tolerance for pain or be taking sedatives, but you have to be careful with those. Some drugs cause excess bleeding. It's critical she not move at all while the work is being done." She returned the phone to Sharp. "Why are you asking about her? Did she know the kid?"

Sharp tucked the phone back in his pocket. "No. She was found dead in a park recently."

"Who is she?" Shay asked. "Some kind of performance artist?"

"I'm not really sure." He wasn't ready to share case details at this point.

Reggie shrugged. "We make no judgments here. Art has different meanings to each individual. Look, if you have more questions, send Shay in to get me, but I'm on the clock and have to get this job done."

Sharp nodded to Reggie. "Sure, thanks. You've been a big help."

Sharp followed Shay to the front. "What about the other guy hanging out with Jimmy in the back room. Does he have a name?"

"I can look up the name in the appointment book," Shay said.

She pulled up the day Jimmy Dillon had visited the salon. "There were three guys in here about then. But I think the one you're looking for was named David. Like I said, he paid in cash. Most of our customers pay cash. Reggie charges 20 percent more for credit cards."

"What kind of tattoo did David get?"

"I do remember that. It was a woman's face."

"Did he happen to mention who the woman was?"

"Said it was his girlfriend. People get their significant other inked on their skin all the time. Half the time they're back a year later getting it covered or removed."

"And the other two men?"

She pulled up their names and read them off to Sharp. One got his baby's name inked on his arm, and the other client had SHE'S WITH STUPID stenciled on his left breast.

He noted the first client's information. "You stared at the picture of the woman on my phone long and hard. Did you see any detail you didn't want to mention in front of Reggie?"

She hesitated. "Like I said, the work is just incredibly detailed. I doubt there are more than a handful of artists in the region able to create such fine work."

"You have any names?"

She met his gaze briefly but couldn't hold it. "Not off the top of my head, but I can ask around."

He wasn't sure if she was nervous by nature or hiding something. He took a risk and fed her a detail. "The woman in the picture is dead. And the work on her face was done in the last month. I'm trying to piece together her last weeks."

Her face paled. "I never met her, if that's what you're asking."

"But you have an idea who might have done the work?"

"No. I really don't. But I can ask around. This guy has an obsession with dolls?"

"I believe so." He handed her a business card. "Please call me if you hear of any helpful information."

"Sure." She studied the card a beat. "How does the work done on her face relate to her death?"

He had already tossed her a couple of morsels of information, but no more. "Can't say. Keep in touch. Thanks."

***

Sharp and Vargas arrived at Diane Richardson's Monument Avenue house just after two. The historic redbrick town house had been built circa 1912 and had floor-to-ceiling front windows as well as a wide front porch stretching the length of the house. A large planter on the porch was filled with dried and withered marigolds.

Vargas touched a brittle blossom. "My plants look like this, though I'll bet she didn't forget to water hers."

"How long does it take for a plant like this to die?" Sharp asked.

"Under a covered porch like this in mild weather? A couple of weeks."

Sharp nodded. "Did you speak to Diane Richardson's parents?"

"I did as soon as the doctor identified her. They're shattered. They couldn't talk and asked that I come back. They're expecting me this afternoon."

"I'll come with you," Sharp said.

"Sure."

Sharp studied the building's brick exterior and looked inside the brass mail slot centered in the front door. "There are no signs of forced entry on the lock. A month's worth of mail is scattered on the floor inside. No newspapers."

"Not too many people get the newspaper delivered anymore."

Sharp checked his watch. "When is the leasing agent going to be here?"

"Any second."

The sound of high heels clicking on the sidewalk had them both turning to find a neatly dressed woman in a dark A-line skirt, white blouse, and red heels. Her blond hair was twisted into a knot, and gold hoop earrings dangled. Keys jangled in her hand as she hurried up the brick front steps.

"You must be with the police," she said. Expensive perfume wafted as she brushed bangs from her eyes.

"I'm Agent Sharp with the Virginia State Police, and this is Agent Vargas. We're here to see Diane Richardson's place."

"I'm Gina Heath, the property manager." She thumbed through a ring of keys. "I understand you have a search warrant."

Sharp reached in his notebook and pulled it out. "Would you like to read it?"

"Yes. I need to justify your entry just in case I have an issue with Ms. Richardson or her family."

"Ms. Richardson is dead," Vargas said.

Frowning, the woman scanned the paper. "My maintenance man said her mother called him a couple of hours ago and wanted to get into the apartment. He said she sounded upset."

Ms. Heath found the right key and handed the search warrant back to Sharp. "What happened?"

"Can't say right now," Sharp said.

Her gaze held his for a beat, and then she shoved the key in the lock. It didn't work. After a couple more tries, she discovered the right key and the dead bolt clicked open. "Sorry, I haven't been on this property in the three years since Ms. Richardson rented it. She is—*was*—a model tenant."

Ms. Heath pushed open the door and knelt to carefully collect the mail, piling the envelopes into a neat stack and setting them on a small entryway table. She clicked on the light.

The house had ten-foot ceilings, and from the front entry, Sharp could see through to the kitchen. A stairway to his left climbed to the second floor, and to the right were two large rooms. The first was a living room and the second a dining room. His footsteps echoed through the house as he made his way toward the kitchen. The room was bright with granite countertops and modern light fixtures. A large window looked out on a narrow grassy yard with a small table on a slate patio.

"I checked her records," Ms. Heath said. "According to her rental application, she was a marketing director for a chain of restaurants in the central Virginia area. I don't know if the employment information is still correct, but I made a copy of her application." She removed the photocopy and handed it to Vargas. "Now you know all I know about her."

Sharp glanced at the application. "What's the rent here?"

"Thirty-five hundred a month plus utilities."

"That's kind of tough to swing on a fifty-thousand-dollar annual salary," Vargas said as she looked up from the application.

"She had a trust fund." The woman's gaze swept the front living room. "One look at the furniture and you can see there had to be money in her family."

"Or she had more creative ways to make her money," Vargas said.

Ms. Heath frowned. "I doubt that. She didn't strike me as the type."

"What's the type look like?" Vargas challenged.

"I've been in property management for a long time, Agent. I know trouble when I see it."

Vargas moved to the hallway and picked up the stacked mail. "You would be surprised, Ms. Heath, how people make their money or what trouble really looks like."

"She had a real job."

"It didn't cover the rent. And a real job doesn't mean she wasn't moonlighting. Drugs and prostitution are both great ways to make some sizable cash on the side."

The woman tugged at the hem of her shirt. "I approved her application. She gave me the bank account information confirming a sizable amount of money she told me was a trust fund payment."

"And you were able to verify the money's source?" Vargas asked.

"No. But you're wrong about her," Ms. Heath said.

"We're trying to find out how she died, Ms. Heath," Sharp said. "That means we have to ask some unpleasant questions."

"Diane wasn't trouble," Ms. Heath said.

"Did you do regular maintenance on the apartment?" Sharp asked.

"Sure. We come in every six months to change the filters and check for issues, such as damage to floors or walls, as well as pets. This is a no-pet property."

"Did maintenance ever find anything out of the ordinary?" Sharp asked.

"Not that I'm aware of, but I've contacted our man and he should be here soon."

Sharp walked up the polished front stairs to the second floor. The first room on the left was a guest room and office combination. All neat. Nicely decorated. Again, screamed *money*. The next room was a renovated bathroom fitted with white marble tile and a walk-in shower and claw-foot tub. When he and Tessa were first married, she had moved into the small place he'd rented on Libby Avenue. Bathroom counter space had been nil. There was no tub and only a small shower just big enough for the two of them. How many times had he stepped into that shower and rubbed against her?

Shaking off the memory, he opened the medicine cabinet and found a collection of pill bottles. By their looks, they were for anxiety and depression. He took a picture with his phone and moved to the bedroom. Dominating the center was a mahogany bed with a canopy. Nothing about the room struck him as off.

Vargas appeared at the door. "Ms. Heath said the maintenance man is here."

"Okay."

Downstairs, Ms. Heath ended her call and nodded toward a beat-up red truck. "That's my superintendent of properties, Mike Bauer."

A midsize man wearing jeans, heavy work boots, and a green T-shirt got out of the truck. Graying thick hair was brushed back off a lean face. His muscles were taut, and he had the look of a body builder.

Sharp extended his hand to the man and made introductions.

Bauer's grip was strong. "Yes, sir, what can I do for you?"

Sharp repeated the questions he'd asked Ms. Heath. "The place was always clean and well kept," Bauer said. "No pets. I changed the filters. Her place was always nice. I was here a week ago, and I noticed the dead plants. That's not like her, so I took extra time walking the property."

"And?" Sharp prompted.

"In the back alley, I found a doll shoved in her trash bin. The can was already full, so the doll was sitting on top. It seemed odd. Garbage hadn't been picked up the week before, so it was lucky I saw it."

"What kind of doll was it?" Sharp's gaze locked on Vargas, who looked up when he said *doll*.

"One of those old-fashioned types. White face. Heart-shaped lips. Frilly dress. If you saw one, you'd recognize it."

Sharp's muscles snapped with interest. "What did you do with the doll?"

Bauer shrugged. "It was in the trash."

"That's not what I asked," Sharp said.

Bauer hesitated. "I took it. It was in perfectly good shape, and it seemed a shame to waste it."

"Do you still have the doll?"

"I was going to give it to my daughter."

"We need to see it," Vargas said. "It might be evidence."

"But it was in the trash."

"It's evidence. I need you to bring it to the station, or I can send a patrolman to your house for it."

"I get off in a few hours. Send someone by the house." Bauer rattled off his address. "Can I get it back?"

Sharp shook his head. "If it's linked to a case as evidence, not until the case has been settled."

"How long is that?"

"Years," Vargas shot back.

"Why are you all so worried about a doll?" Ms. Heath asked.

"I can't say," Sharp said.

Bauer tossed a glance at Sharp, then headed back to his truck. "I'll get you the doll."

Sharp followed and handed him his card. "Thanks."

As Bauer drove off and Ms. Heath locked the home, Sharp and Vargas moved several paces away before Sharp said, "Recent medication in the cabinet tells me she was being treated for anxiety within the last couple of months."

"So what was stressing her out?"

"I don't know if she was having other issues or perhaps figured out someone was watching her and sending her little keepsakes that made her uncomfortable."

Vargas's cell phone chimed with a text message. She checked and nodded. "Department of Motor Vehicles just sent over a picture of Diane Richardson without all the crap on her face. Despite it being a DMV photo, she really was a stunning woman. I'd have killed for those cheekbones."

He accepted the phone and studied the black-and-white photo. Memories stirred in the shadows. "Diane E. Richardson." He said the name hoping to jostle free a memory.

Vargas checked her notes. "Diane Emery Richardson. Richardson was her married name. She has been divorced four years."

"Diane Emery?"

"You say her name like you know her."

Where had he heard the name? And then it clicked. "My sister had a friend in high school and college by the name of Diane Emery." There'd been four girls that first semester at college who'd all been friends in high school and then in college.

Kara, Diane, Elena, and Tessa.

"Your sister died, right?"

"She died of an overdose. Twelve years ago." The back of his skull burned with a warning. He'd learned quickly never to ignore the feeling. He dialed Andrews's number. He answered on the second ring.

"Loading your files into my computer."

"Andrews, I just identified a murder victim we found in a local park. Her name was Diane Emery Richardson. She was a good friend of my sister, Kara, at the time of her death."

"I came across her name in several of Knox's files. He interviewed her twice."

"Cause of death was a high amount of narcotics in her system via an IV. Her face was tattooed to look like a doll's."

Andrews didn't speak, but Sharp knew he had his full attention.

"Kara had been missing for days before she was found. The crime scene photos I saw were either blurred or didn't show her face. I'm hoping Knox had other pictures."

"Witness statements report your sister had been to a Halloween party, and she and several of her friends went dressed as dolls, but your sister was wearing a red dress. One of those friends was Diane Emery."

Sharp's heart hammered in his chest. What were the chances Kara and a good friend of hers had died in the same manner? Drug overdoses weren't unheard of, but his instincts, which had never failed him, said otherwise. And in both cases, there'd been a link to dolls.

"My sister hated dolls," Sharp said. "Everyone knew she couldn't stand them. That explains why she wasn't dressed as one."

"There was no evidence of tattooing on your sister's face, nor was there any makeup from what I can see."

Emotions Sharp had struggled to keep locked away for years clamored for freedom. He shoved them all back into their dark recess and forced his mind to focus. "The cases could be connected."

After a pause, "Feed me what details you can on your active case. I'll analyze both cases separately and see if evidence connects."

"Understood." The call disconnected. Sharp checked his watch and shoved his phone in his pocket.

"So what was that all about?" Vargas asked.

"I don't know. I'm going to find Tessa. She knew my sister and Diane Emery."

CHAPTER THIRTEEN

Friday, October 7, 4:00 p.m.

Tessa was finishing the last of a stack of HR forms when she felt him. The familiar tightening in her gut told her Sharp was close. Setting her pen aside, she looked up. He was standing in her doorway, studying her.

Slowly she rose, sensing this was the moment he was going to insist she file the papers and be done with their marriage. "Is everything all right?"

He walked into her office, his tall frame dominating the space. Boxes filled with medical books and unhanged framed diplomas lined the wall behind her desk. His gaze settled on a picture resting on the top box. It was taken of her in the jungle six months ago.

He frowned. "What can you tell me about Diane Emery?"

What had prompted that question? "Diane was one of our friends from town. There were four of us from town who went to the college."

"I remember Kara mentioning her, but not much else." At her desk, he picked up a paperweight given to her when she'd made the honor society in medical school. Slowly he turned it over in his hand. "I remember you. But not Diane, or Elena."

"We all knew each other in high school, but we didn't get together much outside of school. We four roomed side by side on the same freshman hallway, but you were in Iraq then. I was Kara's roommate, and Diane and Elena stayed in the room next to ours."

"She never mentioned Diane to me." How many times had he tried to recall their last conversations together, she wondered. "But then there were always other things to talk about. Mom. Roger. College applications. She did say she had friends from high school going to college with her."

"Why the questions about Diane?"

He looked at her with no hints of emotion. "Diane Emery was the Jane Doe on your table yesterday."

The familiar name of an old friend was the last she'd have expected to hear. Her memories of Diane dated back twelve years to college, when they'd been so excited about striking out on their own. A cold knot settled in her gut. "Diane Emery is our Jane Doe? That victim's last name is Richardson."

"Richardson was her married name."

"God, I thought there was something familiar about her, but I didn't make the connection." Sadness strangled her heart. "Are you sure? The Diane I knew just wouldn't end up like this."

"How long has it been since you've seen Diane?"

She was irritated and disappointed with herself for not knowing the woman on the table had been a friend.

"I haven't seen her in twelve years."

"What do you know about her?" He studied the paperweight.

"Clearly not much. I didn't know she'd gotten married. We both went our separate ways after my accident. I had to take the rest of the semester off, and by spring I really started to focus on the sciences. I also moved back in with my aunt to save money because the accident ate into most of my savings for college. Diane stayed in the art department, and I think she spent her sophomore year in Paris."

"She married a guy named Nathan Richardson five years ago and they divorced a year later. I'm tracking her ex-husband now, and I'll be talking to him soon enough. I remember Kara ran with a few other girls that first few months in college. One was you. Was Diane one of the others?"

"Yes."

"I want to know more about her relationship with Kara." A razor-sharp edge had crept into his voice.

"Diane was from town, just like Kara and me. Kara and Diane were school friends. They were both on the cheer squad in high school. They had a lot in common, and I know even by mid-October they were already talking about being roommates during their sophomore year. Both of them were art majors. They went to the frat parties together. They even went out with the same guy."

"What guy?"

"Stanford Madison."

"Where can I find him?"

"I don't know, but I have a phone number for him. You can try that."

"You've kept in touch with him?"

"He came to visit me in the hospital after my accident. Helped me with my rehab. I haven't seen him in a couple of years. I'm still digging out eight months' worth of e-mails, but I did notice he e-mailed me about an upcoming art show here in Richmond. I think he's also teaching at the university."

"He's in Richmond now?"

"Yeah."

"Send me his number."

"Sure." She pulled her phone from her lab coat pocket and forwarded the contact.

His gaze darkened. "Dig into your memory and find every connection you can between Diane and Kara and Madison."

"I don't understand. Kara's death was different than Diane's. She didn't have tattoos or any kind of doll getup."

"She died of an overdose, which Dr. Kincaid believes is Diane's cause of death. She was missing for five days before she was found. And witness statements put her at a Halloween party with friends dressed as dolls. I'm assuming one of those 'dolls' was Diane."

"Yes. Diane, Elena, and I were wearing the doll costumes," Tessa said, more to herself. "All four of us had gone to a Halloween party, and I thought it would be fun if we dressed alike."

"Kara went for that? She hated dolls."

"She didn't like the idea at all," she said. "Diane tried to talk her into it, but she wore a red dress. She thought we looked ridiculous. She kept making cracks about how she was trying to look like a grown-up and not a kid."

He shook his head. "Jesus," he said, so quietly she almost didn't hear. "Roger might have been right all these years."

Tears tightened her throat. It pained her to see him twisted in knots. "Dakota, you're suggesting the same person is responsible for two deaths separated by a dozen years."

"Killers evolve, Tessa. They learn and they practice, and even though they go dark for years, they don't stop thinking about the killing."

She wasn't buying his theory. "Facial tattooing is a major evolution."

"The killer could have taken Kara on impulse. She might have been his first kill. Fast-forward a dozen years, and this same killer is now thinking and planning his next kill. He now isn't satisfied with a doll costume but wants to completely change her. Whoever killed Diane put a lot of thought into it."

"Why her? It can't be as simple as a Halloween party that happened twelve years ago."

"I don't know. Not yet, anyway. Maybe he targeted her because he knew her from college. Or because she was Kara's friend. I don't know the connection yet, but it's there. It's one of the first questions I'll be asking Madison."

"God, I can't believe this. I think you're getting ahead of yourself."

He rubbed the back of his head with a grimace. "Believe it. There's one thing I know. Coincidences are rare things."

She recognized the look in his eyes. He was a dog with a bone. And he wouldn't rest until he had answers. How many times had they argued over his work, his distance, or his inability to let go? A year ago, she'd have tried to talk him out of this. Now she took solace in the fact that they were working together. "I hope you're wrong, but I'll do whatever I can to help."

He smacked the paperweight on her desk, but when he looked into her worried eyes, he inhaled. "I know you think I'm going to obsess about this case like I have the others I've worked. And you know what? I am." He shoved out a ragged sigh. "I know I wasn't easy to live with. I know I get lost in my work. But it's going to take someone as driven as me to catch Kara and Diane's killer."

She blinked back tears. "I want to help, but I don't know what to do."

"All I need from you are any pictures taken when you four girls were together. I want you to make lists of all the people you girls knew. Please think back. Was there anyone lurking around, watching you?"

"Okay. I'll do it."

"Call me when you have information. This killer has murdered one woman you know, maybe two. Until I know what his agenda is, keep your eyes open and be careful."

"Sure."

***

The Dollmaker laid Harmony carefully on the chair he'd modified especially for his work. Though she could sit up, there were armrests with straps as well as lower straps for her legs. She would be sedated for the duration of her transformation, but he would bind her just as he did Destiny because he couldn't run the risk of her moving while he was doing some of his most delicate work.

He straightened her head in the headrest and took a moment to trace his finger across the fine bone structure of her face. High cheekbones. Pale skin. Arched eyebrows. She was pretty now and soon would be perfect.

Turning to his computer, he switched on soothing music and hummed as he strapped her arms to the chair and then her legs. He plugged in the hot wax machine, and as the hard material melted, he moved to his workbench and reached for a comb and a pair of sharp scissors.

Slowly he ran his hand through her hair. Thick. Lovely. But wrong. He gathered it at the top of her head, and with his shears, cut through the thickness until the long ponytail was free. Her hair fell around her face. Setting the ponytail aside, he cut away at the remaining locks until they weren't more than a half inch from her scalp.

Next came hot wax. With a flat edge, he picked up a dollop of wax and smeared it over her scalp. Quickly he laid a strip of cloth on the wax and pressed it into her hair and skin. Then with a quick practiced jerk, he pulled back the cloth, ripping the hair from her scalp. She moaned, still drugged but unable to completely escape pain.

"Shh," he said gently. "You have to suffer a little to be beautiful."

***

Sharp called Stanford Madison but landed in voice mail. Instead of leaving him a message, he decided to pay him a visit in person. He drove to the man's Hanover Avenue address, located a few blocks from the Virginia Museum of Fine Arts.

Many of the older homes built in the early twentieth century had been renovated and now went for good money. Wrought iron framed the windows, and porches made each home as distinctive as the massive old trees that lined the streets.

Stanford Madison's corner-lot art studio and second-floor apartment was located in an old converted grocery. Its facade included a red door paired with a large plate-glass window. The window displayed the portrait of a woman with dark hair, rich mocha skin, and green eyes.

Sharp got out of his vehicle and walked up to the building. He peered through the large front window.

Inside, the structure's historical details had been gutted to create a long simple space with whitewashed walls and tiled ceiling. Hanging on the walls was a collection of portraits of women. Each exhibited the same extreme detail.

He knocked on the door and waited. When there was no response, he knocked again. Still silence. "I will be back."

As he headed back to his car, he received a call from the Sunday-night bartender who'd rung up the credit card of "Terrance Dillon." The man introduced himself as Liam Hunter, also the bar owner, and said he was working tonight.

The bar was less than five miles from his current location, so he made the detour south to speak with Liam Hunter.

Traffic was light, and he easily cut through the side streets until he spotted the bar. He pushed through the front doors into the darkness as a cue ball smacked against a freshly racked stack of balls. He noticed the early-evening crowd was light as he strode up to the bar, where a tall, thin man stood polishing bar glasses.

Sharp reached for his badge. "Agent Sharp. Virginia State Police."

The man glanced up from his glass, studied the badge, and nodded. "I'm Liam Hunter. I own the place."

He tucked his badge back in his breast pocket. "Thank you for getting back to me."

"Sorry I missed your call. I was called away on a family matter. Normally I'm always here. You said something about a credit card receipt. Terrance Dillon, right?"

"Yes. I'm looking for the guy that used the card." Sharp pulled his notebook from his pocket and flipped through a couple of pages. "According to the time stamp on his credit card, the card was used about eight on Sunday night."

Liam flipped the towel over his right shoulder. "I don't remember the transaction, but you're in luck—we haven't scrubbed the security footage yet." He nodded his head toward a camera pointing toward the bar and cash register.

"Best news I've had all day."

The bartender asked a waitress to take his place before he led Sharp past a collection of well-worn pool tables that smelled faintly of beer and cigarettes to a backroom office. A small desk was crammed in the corner and piled high with invoices and papers. Above the desk on a shelf were three monitors for the security cameras. The first camera captured the store's entrance, the second covered the bar, and the last an exit door from the outside.

Despite the clutter on the desk, Sharp could see the surveillance was high-tech. "Nice setup."

Liam pulled dark-rimmed glasses from his pocket and slid them on. "We had a few robberies last year and then a waitress who was skimming the till. I decided to beef up the surveillance." He pushed aside a stack of papers, revealing a laptop. He opened it, selected the cameras, and typed in the date and time.

Sharp leaned in as nighttime footage from Sunday emerged on the screen.

"This is the camera covering the bar," Liam said.

The color image showed Liam at the bar, ringing up a purchase and handing a credit card to Jimmy Dillon. As Dillon was turning from the bar, he fished his cell phone from his pocket. Dillon's face melted into a frown. He glanced around the bar and moved quickly to the back exit.

"Where does that door go?"

"Back alley."

"And you said you have a camera outside there?"

"Yeah." Liam pressed more keystrokes, and the back alley materialized. Dillon moved in the alley, the phone pressed to his ear as he paced back and forth. He pressed a fist to his forehead and scowled. He ended the call and continued to pace before heading along the alley to the parking lot. The time stamp read 8:25 p.m. That would have given Jimmy Dillon just enough time to make the twenty-five-minute drive north to meet Terrance at the parking lot. So who the hell had Jimmy been talking to on the phone? Agitated body language suggested he'd encountered a problem.

"Can you send me a copy of that?" He handed the man his business card.

"Sure."

"Anything about him strike you as odd?"

"Now that I see the tape, I remember him. He drank a few beers. Kept to himself. A couple of the ladies hit on him, but he didn't seem too interested. He looked impatient."

"Did he say he was expecting a meeting?"

"It was a busy night. My barback was late getting to work, so I didn't have a lot of time to chat."

The medical examiner had put Terrance's death between midnight and 2:00 a.m. on Monday.

Liam stared at the screen, now frozen on Jimmy's face. "So you think this guy killed that kid?"

"I don't know. But finding him is a top priority."

Seconds later the DVD copy popped out, and Liam handed it to Sharp. "Good hunting."

***

It was nearly eight in the evening when Sharp received a call from Vargas. The Emerys were willing to meet with them now.

Vargas told him that the home of Diane Richardson's parents was located at the end of a cul-de-sac in the gated community on the James River. The Emery family was from Sharp's small town but had moved closer to Richmond ten years ago when Mr. Emery was named senior partner in his law firm. Mrs. Emery was a public relations professional who worked mainly for nonprofits. Diane was their only child and the sole beneficiary of a generous trust fund from her grandmother.

Sharp got out of the car, jangling his keys in his hand as he stared at the ivy-covered home with its wide front double doors. A dark mourning wreath with a silk bow hung on the door.

Vargas pulled up in a plain white vehicle and took a sip from a to-go cup. He watched as she rubbed her eyes and stifled a yawn before she got out of her car.

The pace during the first forty-eight hours of a homicide investigation was often nonstop and brutal. With two cases on his plate now, he'd be lucky if he got more than two or three hours of sleep a night in the coming days.

"Not the kind of place a cop will ever own," she said.

"Who needs a fancy address when the job is so glamorous?"

"Right." Vargas's gaze settled on the dark bow on the front door. Her frown deepened. "Who has time to do arts and crafts at a time like this? I just talked to her a few hours ago. When my mother died, it was all I could do to push a vacuum before the minister came by the house."

"I don't know." His mother had all but shut down after Kara's death. The family doctor prescribed tranquilizers to get her through the worst of it. Unfortunately, the drugs created a habit that chased her to the grave a year later.

Approaching the door with Vargas, he rang the bell. Footsteps sounded inside and the double doors opened to an older man. He was midsize, distinguished, with neatly groomed hair brushed back to accentuate a tanned face. Deep lines creased the corners of his eyes and around his mouth.

Sharp held up his badge. "I'm Agent Dakota Sharp and this is Agent Julia Vargas. We've come to talk to you about your daughter."

The old man cleared his throat. "I'm Stephen Emery. I'm Diane's father."

"Thank you for seeing us," Vargas said. "May we come inside?"

Mr. Emery stepped back, his outstretched hand beckoning them inside. "Please come inside."

Emery led them into a sunroom, where an older version of Diane's DMV photo sat in a chair by the window. Dressed in black, she'd pulled her white hair back into a neat ponytail. Her makeup was expertly applied, and she was wearing a fruity perfume.

"This is my wife, Cassandra."

Cassandra Emery stood and met Vargas's gaze. "Thank you for returning. I know it must be an inconvenience."

"Again, let me say how sorry we are for your loss," Vargas said.

Mrs. Emery nodded. "Thank you."

The four sat around a large glass table outfitted with a huge display of irises in a crystal vase. Sharp set his notebook on the table and opened it.

"When was the last time you saw Diane?" he asked.

"It had been a month," Mrs. Emery said. "We were traveling. She's in sales for her job, so she travels quite a bit as well. When your children get older, they have their own lives to lead."

"Did anyone call you from her office and let you know she was missing?" Vargas asked.

"No one called," Mrs. Emery said. Her lips flattened into a hard line. "And I didn't call them because Diane didn't need her mother chasing after her at work. I wish now I had hovered over her more."

"I spoke to my daughter's boss this morning and asked why he hadn't contacted us earlier," Mr. Emery interjected. "He said Diane quit her job three weeks ago."

"Did Diane give you any indication she wanted to leave her job?"

"No," he said. "She loved it. And it's not her style to quit with a text message and not offer a proper notice. She was a professional and would have at least had the courtesy to face her boss in person."

"Was there anyone in her life she had a romantic relationship with?"

"No," Mrs. Emery said. "She divorced four years ago, and then last year she started dating a painter, but she broke it off."

"Where is her ex-husband?"

"Nathan is stationed in California," Mrs. Emery said.

"Was the divorce mutual?" Sharp asked.

"No," Mr. Emery said. "Nathan left Diane. She was very upset, and I think that's why she ended up with the painter."

"Do you have Nathan Richardson's contact information?" Sharp asked.

"I have a phone number," Mr. Emery said. "You might have trouble reaching him. He's in the navy, and his ship is out to sea for a couple more months."

Emery found the number and gave it to Sharp. It would be easy enough to verify the ex-husband's alibi if he was stationed on a ship.

"Diane's husband divorces her, she rebounds with a painter, who she leaves. Do you know why?" Vargas asked.

"Stanford's a lovely man but does not have a strong work ethic," Mrs. Emery said. "He's the kind of man a woman dates until someone better comes along."

"His name is Stanford Madison?" Sharp asked.

"Yes. He teaches classes in the city and is prepping for an exhibit on Hanover Avenue," Mr. Emery added. "I have a few of his paintings in the study if you'd like to see them."

Whoever had done the work on Diane's face had been a skilled artist. "I'd love to see them."

"Do you think he did it?" Mr. Emery demanded.

"I don't know who's responsible yet," Sharp offered. "We're still piecing together the evidence. Did Diane meet Stanford in college?"

"They did know each other then. How did you know?"

"Came up in another interview."

Mrs. Emery led them into a study where three small oil paintings hung. There were paintings of Diane done in such vivid detail, Sharp found himself leaning in to capture all the nuances.

"He gave those to us last Christmas," Mrs. Emery said. "We were thrilled, of course. They're so beautiful." A phone rang, and Mrs. Emery turned to check the display. "That's my sister. I need to take this—please excuse me."

"Of course," Vargas said.

When his wife left the room, Richardson kept his gaze on the pictures. "I asked to see my daughter, but so far the medical examiner isn't granting us access."

"There are certain details the police are trying to keep under wraps right now," Sharp said.

"I'm not asking for sensitive case information. I just want to see Diane. To know that this is all real and not some kind of mistake."

Sharp pulled in a breath, knowing difficult details were best told directly. "Did Diane ever talk to you about tattooing?"

"I know she has two. She told her mother, who then told me. I wasn't thrilled about the idea, but she's a grown woman."

"Did she express interest in having work done on her face?" Vargas asked.

The question sparked surprise, which gave way to anguish. "No! Why would she cover her face? She's beautiful."

"What happened to her face?" Mrs. Emery asked from the doorway.

Sharp waited until she reached her husband's side. "It was tattooed. The ink was designed to look like a doll's face."

Mrs. Emery raised a trembling manicured hand to her lips. "I can't believe this."

"We're trying to find out if the tattooing might have been a choice she made," Vargas said. "We found antidepressant prescriptions in her apartment."

"I don't know what you're trying to suggest," Mrs. Emery said.

"We're just trying to fill in the gaps of the last three weeks so we can bring you closure," Vargas offered.

"She didn't disfigure herself," Mrs. Emery said. "She was a smart, bright young woman who was mentally balanced."

"How do you know she would not have tattooed her face?" Sharp asked gently.

"Diane was vain," Mrs. Emery said, her eyes watering with fresh tears. "She would never damage her face. She likes—liked—to look her best. You make her sound sick."

Mrs. Emery's cool demeanor cracked, and she sobbed. She reached for a tissue in her pocket and pressed it under her eyes to catch the spilling tears.

"We're not trying to put your daughter in a bad light," Sharp said. "I'm trying to create a picture of the woman she was." These same questions had been leveled at Sharp's stepfather, mother, and even him after Kara died. He remembered feeling offended and angry by the assumptions his sister had been a drug addict. "I can only catch this killer if I fully understand Diane."

A breath shuddered through Mr. Emery as if the anger had drained the last of his reserves. No doubt today had been a living hell since Vargas had made the death announcement. "I know you're trying to help, Agent Sharp. This just isn't easy."

"I know that, sir." He asked more questions. Did she have a history of drug use? Did she exhibit any erratic behavior? *No* followed all the questions.

When Sharp and Vargas left the house, he pictured Diane as a rising star in her career. She had taken excellent care of herself, and if she had any vice, it was that she had been vain. She painted in her spare time. Her work hadn't been Rembrandt, but her parents saved her art pieces because they'd loved her. She was definitely not the kind of woman to disfigure her face.

"So who in her life hated her so much that he wanted to permanently mess up her face?" Vargas asked.

"Why do you assume it was done in hate?"

"He fucked up her face," Vargas hissed. "It doesn't get much more personal than that."

"This work was done with great care and precision. An angry person would not have gone to this length. Remember, there were no signs of infection, and she had been eating. This guy cared very much about Diane."

Vargas dug in her pocket and pulled out a packet of unopened cigarettes. "You're shitting me."

"I wish I were," Sharp said.

"We need to talk to the boyfriend," she said, tapping the packet against her thigh.

"I went by his place earlier. There's no sign of him."

"This killer isn't a stranger. Women, more often than not, are killed by someone they know or perhaps by someone who loved them at one time."

"Tessa said Stanford Madison knew Diane in college. She said they dated."

"Oh, really," Vargas muttered as she opened the pack and put a cigarette to her lips.

Sharp pulled his lighter from his pocket and lit the tip of her cigarette. "He has the artistic chops, and she did break up with him."

She inhaled, shaking her head. "Could it be that simple?"

"I don't know. But I want to pay him another visit tonight."

"Count me in."

CHAPTER FOURTEEN

Friday, October 7, 9:00 p.m.

Sharp and Vargas parked their cars on Hanover Avenue. A full moon glistened over a sidewalk flanked by tall trees clinging hopelessly to their orange and red leaves.

This time there were lights on in the art studio. Sharp and Vargas walked up to the front door. He tried it and discovered it was unlocked. They entered a room filled with the portraits of women painted with exquisite detail. The only furniture was a simple white desk.

"Hello," Sharp said. "Anyone here?"

From a back staircase came the sound of footsteps, and a muscled man stepped out from around the partition. He was wearing a gray V-neck sweater, jeans, and black boots. "We don't officially open for a couple more days."

Sharp pulled his badge and identified Vargas and himself. "We're looking for Stanford Madison."

The man twisted a ring on his index finger. "That's me. What can I do for you?"

Sharp sensed the man's unease. "We came to ask you a couple of questions about Diane Richardson."

Madison lifted a brow and folded his arms over his chest. "I don't know what she's been telling you, but I can guarantee it's not true."

"What would she be telling us?" Sharp asked.

Madison sighed. "We dated, and the breakup didn't go well. She sat for several portraits for me, and she wanted them back after she left. They were nudes and some of the best work I'd ever done. I said no. She said she'd sue."

"She didn't mention the paintings to us," Vargas said, testing for a reaction.

"What's she saying about me?"

Sharp shook his head, picking up on Vargas's lead. "She was upset."

Madison held his hands up in surrender. "You know how women can be. Emotional. Difficult."

Vargas raised a brow. "Really?"

Madison looked at her, his gaze imploring. "She and I had a relationship, and it was intense and amazing. She was a muse to me. I created some of my best work when we were together."

"How's the work been going since she left?" Sharp asked.

"I'm holding my own."

"But it's a struggle," Sharp offered. "Not eating. Not sleeping. Generally in a foul mood."

"Sure. You understand."

"I surely do," Sharp said honestly.

"When people saw the work I'd done with her, I started to get more commissions, so I didn't have as much time for her. She didn't like being ignored, and she became demanding. She got clingy. Then I was told she was stepping out on me."

"Who was the other guy?" Sharp asked.

"Another artist, I heard. At that point I didn't care, so I broke it off."

"Someone told us she broke it off with you," Vargas said.

Madison laughed as his gaze settled on Sharp. "She's a woman. You know how it goes. They don't want anyone to know they've been left. What's this all about?"

Vargas rested her hand on her hip, her index finger tapping her gun holster. "When did you break up?"

Madison's smile faded. "About four months ago. Why do you care?"

"Bear with us. When's the last time you saw her?" Sharp asked.

"Six weeks, give or take." His fingernails were cut short and neat, though there was a hint of paint still embedded in the cuticle of his right thumb.

"Was she into drugs?" Vargas asked.

"No. She's always saying her body is a temple. The occasional white wine, but that was it."

"What do you know about tattooing?" Sharp asked.

"I have several, if that's what you're asking."

"And Diane?"

"Two, as I remember. She had a filigree at the base of her spine and a heart on the inside of her right ankle."

"No tattoos on her face?" Sharp asked.

"No. What's all this about?"

Sharp watched him very carefully. "Diane's body was found in a park a couple of days ago."

His eyes widened, and he leaned in a fraction. "That makes no sense. I just saw her."

"Six weeks ago, right?" Vargas asked.

"Yeah."

"Where was that?"

"Here. Like I said, she came by to try and get the paintings I'd done of her." He shook his head. "Are you sure you found Diane? None of this makes sense."

"We're sure." The guy had paled. He looked upset, but skilled liars always played their part well. "Did you sell or give her any of the paintings?"

Madison ran a trembling hand through his hair. He drew in a breath. "No. Several were going to be the centerpiece of my show next week."

"May we see the paintings?"

"Why?"

"Curious," Sharp said.

Madison shook his head as he fisted his right hand. He appeared to be struggling to hold on to control. "I don't understand how seeing my paintings will help you find out who killed Diane."

"We never said it was murder," Sharp said. "But I'm looking to piece together her life."

"Fine. Sure. If you think it'll help." Madison guided them into another exhibit room. Centered on the back wall was a three-by-three-foot painting of Diane. She was nude and draped over a red velvet couch, the long fingers of her right hand clutching a strand of pearls.

Sharp walked up to the portrait. The attention to detail was stunning, and he found himself drawn in by her dark eyes and the slight smile on her lips that suggested she knew a secret. Madison was a hell of an artist.

"How did she die?" Madison asked.

"We don't know yet," Vargas replied.

"How could you not know?" Madison's tone held a new sharpness. "Don't you have people to figure that out?"

Sharp turned from the painting. "I'm the guy that figures stuff like that out. Do you have a basement in this building?"

"Sure. Why?"

"May I see it?"

Madison folded his arms. "Why do you want to see it?"

"Curious."

Madison hesitated before saying, "These questions are making me feel like a suspect."

Vargas shrugged and managed an innocuous smile. "Everyone is a suspect during the initial stages of an investigation."

"Should I have a lawyer?" Madison asked.

"This is simply fact-finding, Mr. Madison," Sharp said. "I just want to see the basement."

Madison drew in a breath. "I guess I don't have a choice."

"You always have a choice," Vargas said.

"Right," Madison said. He moved to a side door and unlocked it. He flipped on a light, and as he descended the stairs, Vargas glanced at Sharp.

She raised a brow. "What's his deal?" she mouthed.

"Wait and see," he whispered.

The two detectives descended the old set of wooden stairs leading to a dank basement with a low ceiling. The lighting was poor, but Sharp could see the space was crammed full of boxes, easels, and props. There were no signs anyone had been held here.

"You own any other properties?" Sharp asked.

"No."

"Would you mind if we searched this room?" Sharp asked.

"For what?" Madison demanded.

Sharp shrugged. "Just want a look around."

Madison shook his head, his mouth tightening into a grim line. "Get a warrant. I've been patient with you long enough."

"I'll do that," Sharp said.

"Get out of here now."

Sharp and Vargas climbed the stairs. When Madison came up behind them and locked the door, Vargas tossed Sharp a glance that told him the artist topped her suspect list.

Once Sharp had his warrant, he would be back to search the premises as well as dig deep into Madison's finances. "Thank you for your time, Mr. Madison."

***

Thoughts of Diane stalked Tessa the better part of the day, so as soon as she left work, she went to the storage shed she'd rented before leaving the country. It held what she'd taken from their apartment, along with her medical books. She opened the small roll-top door and clicked on a light. Inside was basically her entire past crammed into a couple dozen boxes. When her mother had died, she'd moved in with her aunt Grace and cousins, Rebecca and Holly. Because their house was small, she'd not been able to keep much. Pictures, selected keepsakes, and her mother's desk had been all she really wanted. By the time she left Dakota, she'd not really accumulated all that much more. More pictures. Some clothes. Books. A painting. Enough to fit in this small unit.

She moved the boxes marked "Winter Clothes" and "Medical Books," then grabbed another box labeled "Pictures." It had been a long time since she'd gone through the images from college, but talk of Kara had turned her thoughts back to then.

Tessa dug into the box and worked her way through the years, first looking at when she and Dakota had been together. To her surprise, she didn't have many printed pictures. What she did have was mostly on her phone.

Going back further, she found photos documenting the medical school years. More memories bubbled up from those days and brought a smile.

And then she reached the pictures capturing her college memories. One of the first pictures she touched was of herself and her three friends from freshman year. Kara, Diane, and Elena.

The photo that caught her eye was taken the first day she'd moved into her dorm. Kara was front and center, grinning, her arms wrapped around Diane and Elena while Tessa leaned in by Diane's left shoulder, close but still separate from the group. They'd all been girls from town, and because of that connection, they grew close as a foursome quickly.

And now two of the four girls were dead.

She searched the box for the pictures she knew she'd taken the night of the Halloween party. Not finding them, she realized they must still be at her aunt's house.

"Damn it," she muttered. She quickly replaced the lid on the box and locked up the shed.

The drive across the city took Tessa twenty minutes. By the time she arrived at her aunt's house, she was determined to track down the photos. If anyone had saved the pictures, it had been her aunt.

Knowing her aunt was on vacation and her cousin was house-sitting, she used her key to push through the front door of their home. The large brick colonial was located on the steep side of a hill overlooking the James River. Keys jangled in her hands as the hum of the television echoed from the den. "Holly!"

"In the den!"

She found Rebecca's sister, Holly, sprawled on an overstuffed couch, dressed in sweats and a T-shirt. The wide sliding windows overlooked the hill sloping sharply toward to the river. A large leather sofa backed up to the window and faced a couple of club chairs upholstered in bright floral prints. A glass coffee table was covered with magazines, spilled popcorn, and empty diet soda cans.

"Aunt Grace will kill you if she sees this mess," Tessa said.

Holly sat up and muted the television. An old T-shirt brushed past her knees, and her long hair hung wild around her shoulders. Grinning, she said, "She won't know if you don't snitch."

"When is she due back?"

"Cruise ship docks in Miami next Tuesday, and then I think she's visiting friends in Tampa. Home by next weekend. Plenty of time to clean."

Tessa picked up a couple of Holly's rumpled shirts from one of the club chairs and sat. "How's school?"

"Third-year law isn't taxing. Mostly clerking for the judge these days."

"Anything of interest?"

Holly yawned. "No."

Holly was five years younger than Tessa and would graduate law school in the spring. She was near the top in her class and the "not so interesting job" she referenced was a prestigious clerkship with a federal judge. Her mother fully expected her to be running the world one day.

"Hey, do you know where your mom stowed all my junk from college?"

"She was threatening a major purge last year, so not sure if it survived."

"She's been threatening to toss my stuff for years. What did she do with all my boxes when she had my room remodeled?"

"They're in the room over the garage. I know because she made me haul all your crap up there when she had the painters come through."

"Great."

"What are you looking for?"

"Some photos that I took right before my accident. I know I took pictures and Aunt Grace developed them, but they aren't in my storage bin."

Holly yawned. "And why the walk down memory lane?"

"Just want to have a look."

Holly rose. "I'll give you a tour of the junk piles. If Mom hasn't done another purge, I can find your boxes."

"Thanks."

Holly shoved her feet into slippers. Outside, they crossed to the garage and entered by the side door. A short flight of stairs took them to the second floor. Holly clicked on the light, which illuminated a collection of random items no one likely wanted to deal with, including holiday decorations, clothes, furniture, and boxes from college.

Holly picked her way through a narrow trail toward the back of the room. She searched a couple of boxes and said, "Here it is. All the college crap you saved that you should have thrown out years ago."

Tessa knelt and opened the first box filled with textbooks.

"So why do you care about the photos?"

"I'm looking for pictures of the girls in my freshman hall."

"Why?"

"One was murdered this week."

"Shit."

"Yeah." Finding nothing of use, Tessa closed up the first box and dove into the second and then a third. It was at the bottom of the third box where she found an album covered in red cloth. She lifted it out, half amazed it still existed.

When she opened the album, the first pictures she saw were taken before her mother died. For a moment she sat, silently staring at her mother hugging her in an apple orchard. "I miss her."

"Yeah. She was pretty great."

Clearing her throat, she turned the page. The album's spine creaked in protest.

"Why don't we look at this in the kitchen? It's a little bit of a mess in here."

"Sure." Tessa closed the album, grateful for the pause. She straightened and backed out the narrow path. Holly followed and shut off the lights.

Back in her mom's kitchen, Holly pulled a couple of mugs out of the cabinet and set the coffeemaker to brew. Tessa sat at the counter and opened the album, unleashing scents of popcorn and lavender, which had once permeated her freshman dorm room. A pressed daisy lay in the crook of the middle pages.

"It's not like you to travel down memory lane," Holly said.

"I've been thinking a lot about Kara lately."

Holly's gaze sharpened. "What brought her up? Her birthday?"

"We had a case in the medical examiner's office. I didn't recognize the patient during the autopsy and only found out from one of the agents that she was on my freshman hall. The victim's name was Diane Emery."

"Wow. I remember her. I was in middle school when you two were seniors in high school."

"That's right."

"I also remember her from the time Mom and I visited you in your dorm room. She was kind of stuck-up."

Diane had had no interest in making nice with the thirteen-year-old Holly. "You never forget a detail, do you?"

"That's what happens when your astrology sign is Cancer and you have an eidetic memory," she joked. The coffeepot gurgled, so she turned to pour some coffee in a couple of mugs. She pushed a mug toward Tessa and set a carton of milk beside it. "Why couldn't you recognize her?"

"Her face was covered in tattoos. Which isn't to be shared. The cops haven't released the details, so keep it quiet."

"Understood." Holly sipped her black coffee. "How does this relate to college pictures?"

"Dakota thinks her death shares similarities with Kara's death."

"Dakota. As in Dakota Sharp." She shook her head. "I'll be sure to double back to that prickly topic."

Tessa knew Holly didn't approve of Dakota any more than Rebecca did. "What do you remember about the time Kara was found dead?"

"She was missing for five days. Found on the side of a country road. Drug overdose. She was wearing a red dress and lots of makeup, but she'd been last seen at a Halloween party."

"You said she was wearing makeup? I don't remember much from that time."

"Head injury and heavy-duty pain meds will do that."

"But how would you know about the makeup?"

Holly shrugged. "Elena mentioned it at her funeral. Elena and her sister found Kara's body."

Tessa searched through the scrambled memories of the funeral. Her aunt had not wanted her to attend, but she'd insisted on leaving the hospital to be there. Tessa picked up the pressed daisy.

"I remember you had a fight with Kara the night she vanished. You called Mom while you were walking home from the party, and you complained to her about the argument. Mom said you were pretty upset."

"Kara and I had a fight?"

"You barely ended that call with Mom when you were hit by the car."

"How do you know that?"

"Mom put the timing together when she was talking to the responding deputy who followed your ambulance to the hospital."

"Why was I fighting with Kara?"

"You were crushing on a boy who was only being nice to you so you'd introduce him to Kara. Wounded pride."

She flipped through the pictures but found none that were taken the night of the Halloween party.

"Kids get upset over stupid things," Holly said.

"Yeah. Maybe if we hadn't fought, she wouldn't be dead."

"You can't play that game."

"I suppose."

Tessa turned the page, staring at a picture of herself with Stanford. His thick dark hair skimmed his shoulders, and he looked wild and dangerous. He'd been the boy she'd had a crush on. It was a lifetime ago. The past.

"You're staring pretty hard at Stanford," Holly said.

"I guess. I wonder what I ever saw in him."

"He's nothing like Sharp," Holly said.

"That's a good thing."

"Is it?" Holly asked. "He's a different person now. We both know Dakota's a little crazy when he's got a murder case, and that's almost all the time."

"It's what he does for a living. He'll always have a murder case on his desk. And after seeing Diane's body and this other kid I autopsied the other day, I can see why he does get a little obsessed."

The pages creaked as they turned. A packet of photos fell out. They were still in the drugstore envelope. "I don't remember these," Tessa said.

"They might have been the ones Mom found after you were hit. She was so scared you wouldn't wake up that first night. She couldn't sleep, and when she found the camera and film in your backpack, she drove them straight to the drugstore just to keep busy. When she came back to the hospital, you were awake. She tried to give them to you later, but you didn't want to see them," Holly said.

Tessa folded back the flap and pulled out the pictures. For a moment, she didn't speak.

It was an image of Kara, Diane, Elena, and herself, taken by a girl from their dorm hall as they left for the Halloween party. Three of them were dressed as dolls. Kara was wearing her red dress.

"Kara's not wearing makeup," Tessa said, more to herself.

"Elena said she was wearing a lot when they found her. Find her. Ask her. I bet that is something she never forgot."

She looked at Diane's face and outfit. Her cheeks were stained with a bright blush. Painted freckles dotted her face. And her lips were painted in a bright red.

Her breath caught in her throat as she stared at the image. Dear God. She looked the same as she had days ago in the park.

***

When Sharp arrived back at his apartment, jazz music echoed from inside.

He glanced into the kitchen and saw the back door was propped open; McLean was standing by a grill. He crossed the room and grabbed a beer from the fridge. Twisting the top off, he took a long pull. "McLean."

"Heard you pull up," he said as he drank from his beer and flipped the second of two steaks. "Tossed one on the grill for you. Figured with the case, you aren't eating."

The air was cool and the sky so clear, the stars shone bright and crisp.

McLean swigged his beer as he flipped a steak. "You like your steak rare, as I remember."

"Good memory." He swirled his bottle as a cold breeze cut across the small fenced-in backyard. "How'd the job interview go today at Shield Security?"

"I bet I have a job offer in a day or two."

"Always confident."

"Of course." McLean turned the steaks again. "Any luck with your tattooed victim?"

"Spoke to the victim's parents and her ex-boyfriend. Everyone is shocked. No one really picked up on the fact she was missing for weeks."

"What about friends? Or coworkers?"

"She sent a text to her boss three weeks ago and quit her job."

"She sent a text? No one spoke to her?"

"Correct. The text did come from her phone, which is no longer pinging off any cell tower, so the battery is either dead or the chip smashed."

"Whoever this guy is, he thought it out carefully."

"Yeah. A lot of time and effort."

The front bell rang. Sharp shook off his frustration, moved to the door, and opened it. To Tessa.

For a split second he stood frozen, questioning, wondering why she was here. He'd left it badly between them today. Pissed, irritated, tired, hurting. All the shit he could handle most days. But it percolated to the surface when she was close. She had a way of shredding his nerves with the slightest look.

Tessa was dressed in jeans, a sweater, and boots. Her hair hung loose around her shoulders. Damn. He wanted to touch her.

"I have pictures." Her tone was flat, guarded. "You asked for pictures."

His hand gripped the side of the door. "Right."

She handed him the packet. "These were developed while I was in the hospital after my accident. I didn't remember them, but found them when I went to my aunt's house. As you go through them, let me know if you have any questions. I'll fill in the gaps."

He set his beer aside and took the envelope. When she turned to leave, he asked, "How about now?"

"What?"

"Fill in the gaps now. My buddy McLean is here. Grilling steaks." He stepped aside. "Come on in. Maybe you'll recall some details that will be of use. And I bet you haven't eaten."

She tightened her hand on the strap of her purse. "Sure. I'll stay for a few minutes."

He released the door and stepped aside so she could pass. As she walked past him, he caught the jasmine scent. "Can I get you a drink?"

"Thanks, but no, I'm fine."

"Steaks are done," McLean said. He froze midstep when he saw Tessa. He set the sizzling platter of steaks on the kitchen counter.

Seeing him, she smiled. "Hi, I'm Tessa."

"Tessa, as in Sharp's wife."

She stilled and kept her gaze on McLean. "That's right."

"Jacob McLean," he said, extending his hand as his grin widened.

"McLean interviewed with Shield Security," Sharp said.

"That's great," she said.

McLean clapped his hands. "Tessa doesn't want to hear about my career. But she looks hungry."

"No, I really can't stay," she said.

"Won't take no for an answer," McLean said.

She looked at Sharp, clearly unsure.

"Stay," Sharp said.

Her fingers tightened again on the purse strap. "Sure."

McLean turned to Sharp. "Get the lovely lady a beer."

"Right," Sharp said.

As he moved into the kitchen to get a beer, he heard McLean say, "Sharp doesn't bite. At least I don't think he does."

CHAPTER FIFTEEN

Friday, October 7, 9:45 p.m.

"What pictures did you bring?" Dakota asked.

Leave it to him to keep the target in his sights. Work came first. But she wasn't angry. He was who he was. "They're all taken the night of the Halloween party."

"What can you recall about that night?" Dakota asked.

"I don't remember anything. My memory was wiped for the few days leading up to the accident. I wasn't even sure these pictures still existed until I found them at my aunt's house tonight." She dug her fingernail into the label on her beer bottle. "I saw my cousin Holly, and she remembers that Kara and I had a fight. She said I was walking back to the dorm early. A few minutes later, I was tagged by a car."

He laid his fork and knife down. "I always wondered how you could just step into traffic. You're one of the most alert people I know."

"Everyone gets tired, I suppose. And I must have been distracted by the fight."

"I always assumed you were drunk," Dakota challenged.

"Thanks a lot."

"It was college, Tessa. Kids do stupid things."

"I never got that stupid."

"Do you think your drink could have been drugged?" McLean asked.

"I never considered that."

"Why not?" Dakota asked.

"I don't know. I was at a party with friends. I thought I was in a safe place."

"Not friends. Acquaintances," Dakota said. "Were you drinking draft beer?"

"I assume so. But I was never a big drinker." She and Dakota had talked about the accident before, but never in great detail.

McLean groaned. "It makes sense. I'd bet money someone slipped a roofie in her drink."

She'd always attributed the car accident to her own distracted thinking. But what if she'd been drugged?

Dakota balled up his napkin and tossed it on the table beside his plate. "Do you remember what Kara was drinking?"

"Beer, I suppose. Like I've told you before, I have no memory of the night. The concussion wiped out about three days' worth of memories."

"Who gave the party?" Dakota asked.

"My aunt told me later it was at someone's house near the cemetery. I did go back later when my leg was healing. It was near the graveyard. I suppose that made sense for a Halloween party."

"Who owned the house?"

"I don't know. I never asked. But I do remember where it was. It won't be hard to trace."

He tapped his finger on the table. When they'd been together and he'd worn his wedding band, the clink, clink of the ring on the table meant a case bothered him. She could tell by the speed and rhythm of the clinks if the case was going well or not.

"I saw Stanford Madison tonight," he said. "Did you know he was dating Diane Richardson?"

"I did not know that."

"Tell me about Madison," Dakota said.

"I had kind of a crush on him in college. I told Kara. She thought it was sweet." A memory rose out of the shadows. "I remember them at the Halloween party. They were kissing." She frowned. "That must be why I left."

Dakota studied her a beat. "Why didn't you ever talk about him to me?"

"Because he was a college crush and a friend after my accident. He visited me a few times that semester I had to drop out, and then we lost touch."

McLean rose and moved to the envelope Tessa brought. "Tell us about the pictures?" he asked.

Relieved to look away, she rose and laid the pictures out like playing cards. "They were all taken the night of the Halloween party. Kara wore a red dress. The rest of us were dressed as dolls."

"Dolls," Dakota said.

"Yes. It was kind of a lark at the time, but now that I look at them, I get chills."

Dakota leaned forward and for a long moment stared at the images. "Did you run into anyone that night that you thought might be trouble? Was there anyone interested in Kara, you, or the other girls?"

"I don't know."

"Did Knox ever interview you?" Dakota asked. "He said he talked to everyone who knew Kara."

"He did. It was later, though. I was a junior in college, and he caught up to me as I was coming out of the library."

"What did he ask you about?"

"He wanted to know about that night Kara vanished. I couldn't tell him anything."

"What else?"

"Did I notice if anyone was hanging around the dorm in the weeks before the party."

"And?"

"No one that I remembered. But . . ." A detail long forgotten focused. "Someone did send her flowers."

"When?"

"A couple of weeks before the party."

"Who sent them?"

"There wasn't a card on the flowers. I remember they were purple irises and were in a pretty vase by our dorm room door."

"How do you know they were for Kara?" McLean asked.

"I just assumed. I didn't know anyone that would send me flowers."

Dakota tapped his finger on the pictures, clearly struggling to control his anger over Kara's unsolved murder.

"The point I need to make, Dakota, is that Holly remembers Elena Hayes at Kara's funeral. Holly says that Elena and her sister found Kara on the road. They said when they found her, she had makeup on her face."

"She remembers that specific detail?" Dakota challenged.

"She has a photographic memory. If Holly remembers, it happened."

Dakota stared at her, his face an unreadable mask.

"If you want more details, talk to Elena Hayes. She was the fourth girl in the picture. She was living abroad for a couple of years, but I saw in one of the alumni magazines that she was back in Richmond. I know the cops interviewed her after Kara was found, as they did me. She might have been afraid to talk more candidly then. Her father was strict and would have punished her if he'd known she'd been at a party drinking with a bunch of strangers."

"I'll talk to Vargas, and we'll go see her," Dakota said. "Anyone strike you as odd at the funeral or in the days leading up to the party?"

"At the funeral, I was on pain meds and couldn't stay long. I spoke to your mother. She was sweet but so overwhelmed. Your stepfather was also a mess."

Dakota tapped his index finger on the table, and she sensed he was struggling to remain objective. "Diane's mother said she was vain. She was convinced she'd never ruin her face."

"She wasn't stuck-up about her looks in college, but she was conscious of them. And I agree, unless there was a really drastic change in her mental makeup, she wouldn't have disfigured herself."

Tessa stared at the pictures of Kara, Diane, Elena, and herself. Pathologists, like cops, could distance themselves from death so they could effectively analyze the chain of evidence. But she found it nearly impossible now.

Dakota reached for his phone, took snapshots of the images, and sent them off.

"What are you doing?" she asked.

"Sending them to Garrett Andrews at Shield Security. If anyone can pull a detail out of these, it's him."

Fatigue had seeped deep into Tessa's bones. She'd be no good at work tomorrow if she didn't get some sleep. "I've got to get going," Tessa said. "I've an early call in the morning. Let me know if I can help."

"Would you be willing to meet with Andrews at Shield?" Dakota asked.

She rose, hitching her purse on her shoulder. "Sure. Whatever you want."

He followed her to the door, which he reached before her. He gripped the knob but didn't open it. "Thank you."

"Sure."

So close, and yet the distance between them felt endless.

"Why did you kiss me the other day?" he asked suddenly.

"Why?" Good, he'd been thinking about the kiss. "Because I've dreamed about it for months. I wanted to see if you tasted like I remembered."

"Nothing's changed, Tessa," he warned. "I can promise you we'd be great in the sack and terrible out of it."

"Maybe. Maybe not. I'm not going to chase you, Dakota. If you want this marriage, you'll have to meet me halfway. But I'm not going anywhere this time."

A frown wrinkled his brow. She sensed he wanted her. The marriage. She leaned slightly toward him to make it easier for him to touch her.

Instead, he opened the door with a snap. "I'll think about it."

She straightened as the night air chilled her skin. "Right."

"Tessa?"

"Yes."

"Be careful. Keep your eyes open."

"Don't worry about me, Dakota. I can take care of myself."

***

The woman woke up in stages. It took time to shake off the smothering fatigue weighing on her like bricks pressing against her chest. When she opened her eyes, her vision was clouded, and she had to blink several times for it to clear. Finally, a white ceiling. She blinked again, pushing away another wave of tiredness ready to pull her back to sleep. She shook her head, grimacing at the dull headache behind her left eye. *Think.* What happened?

She remembered walking home. She'd been tired and ready to call it a night. And then, there'd been the man on the sidewalk. Smiling. Charming. She thought she might know him. And then a sting of electricity before her mind went blank.

Her heart beat a little faster as she thought about the memory, hoping it was a dream. Gathering her tattered energy, she tried to sit up. Her head spun, and for a moment she closed her eyes and waited for the world to settle. Finally, she glanced at her chest and the white cotton nightdress with fine lace and wondered where it came from. It wasn't hers.

Searching the room, she saw only simple white walls. There was the chair where she lay but no other furniture. No window. Only a door. She pushed off her covers and swung her feet to the cold tile floor. She tried to stand, but her legs wobbled. Seconds passed as she steadied herself. And then, straightening her shoulders, she shuffled to the door, tottering much like a novice sailor trying to find her sea legs.

She tried the door handle and discovered it was locked. She twisted it again. And again. It didn't open. Her panic growing, she called out, "Help! Where am I?"

She strained to hear an answer, but she heard only the silence and the beat of her thudding heart. Keys jangled on the other side of the door.

"Help me, please!" A key rattled in the lock, and she automatically ran a trembling hand over her head. Instead of hair, she felt only smooth skin. Both hands shot to her scalp and eyebrows, and she realized not one wisp of hair remained.

Frantic, she stared at her arms and legs and realized in horror there was no hair. She grabbed the folds of the nightgown and saw her pubic hair was gone. There wasn't one strand of hair on her body.

The door handle twisted, and she staggered in fear. As much as she prayed a savior had arrived, she knew whoever was there was evil.

Hinges swung silently open to reveal a man carrying a tray of soup and crackers. "Good, you're awake, Harmony. I need for you to eat."

Anger mingled with fear. "My name isn't Harmony."

"It is now, Harmony."

"No."

"It's time to eat," he said. The matter was closed.

"I don't want to eat. I want to get out of here."

"You have to eat," he said gently. "If not, I'll have to force-feed you, and you won't like it."

She touched her bald head with trembling fingers. "What happened to my hair?"

He set the tray on the edge of her bed. "I removed it all, of course, Harmony."

Tears pooled in her eyes as an overwhelming sense of loss and hopelessness washed over her. "Why?"

He twisted his lips into what he must have imagined was a friendly smile. "I need a blank canvas to work with."

"What do you mean?" She teetered, her head spinning from standing.

He placed his hand under her elbow, catching her before she stumbled. With care, he walked her back to the bed and helped her sit. He smoothed his hand over her lips. "You need to eat and take care of yourself."

Her stomach grumbled and her vision blurred again. The smell of the soup was making her hungry. She ignored the hunger pangs, fearing more drugs. "I'm not eating."

"You've not eaten in two days. You need your energy."

"Two days?" Heart racing from fatigue, she scanned the plain white room, knowing without a clock or a window she had only him to rely on to mark the time. "People will miss me. They'll call the police."

"Shh. Don't worry. I used your phone and texted all the right people. No one is fretting about you. When they do start to look, our work will be finished. Your transition will be complete."

Transition. She glanced at her arms and hands. "Why did you remove my hair?" Tears spilled down her cheeks, and she prayed this was all a terrible dream. *Please, let me just wake up.*

He gently took her hand in his and raised it to his lips. "I know you miss it now, but soon you won't. Soon you'll understand, and it'll all be worth it."

"Worth what?" If she had the energy, she'd snatch her hands free and hit him. Run. Do something.

He held up the bowl of soup and coaxed her lips open with the spoon. "My art will dazzle you."

She swallowed the soup, savoring the warmth and taste. He fed her another spoonful and another, and soon the bowl was empty.

"You're such a good girl," he said.

Her eyes felt heavy, and her vision slipped out of focus. She felt the darkness creeping closer.

"It's okay," he said. He set the bowl aside and carefully lowered her against the headrest.

"Please don't do this."

"Shh. It's going to be fine. Complete beauty doesn't happen overnight, but the next time you wake up, you'll thank me."

Tears welled in her eyes and then fell. "What are you doing to me?"

He kissed her softly on the lips. "I'm making you perfect."

CHAPTER SIXTEEN

Saturday, October 8, 6:00 a.m.

After Tessa left, Sharp was too restless to sleep. He'd called Vargas and told her about Elena Hayes. She'd promised to follow up. Finally, he was able to grab a couple of hours of restless sleep but then gave up and went into the office. He spent time watching the surveillance tape of the park entrance where Diane Richardson's body had been found.

He was reviewing footage from a nursing home across the street from the park when he spotted the white van pull up to the park entrance at two in the morning. The van moved slowly past the "Closed at Sunset" sign. Five minutes later, the driver circled back and drove into the park, vanishing.

Sharp paused the picture and magnified the image only to discover the Virginia license plate had been obscured by splashes of mud. He sat back in his chair and replayed the footage dozens of times, searching for any scrap of evidence that would tell him who owned or drove the van. There was a two-second portion of the video when the driver's side of the van slid under the light. The driver was male, but a black skullcap and an upturned collar hid his face. The splay of light on the vehicle revealed no markings on the van, though there were faint shadows of past lettering. The windows were tinted, and the back fender was dented.

The van remained in the park for ten minutes and thirty-two seconds, and when it left, the driver kept his face turned from the cameras. The vehicle drove southeast away from the park.

Sharp pulled up satellite maps of the area and discovered there were no stores or gas stations equipped with cameras in that direction.

"You've thought this through carefully, you son of a bitch," he whispered.

He then flipped through the discs collected from the homes around Diane Richardson's house and searched for signs of the white van. He plowed through several weeks of footage. He was hoping the tapes covered more time but quickly discovered the cameras had storage-capacity constraints.

One camera across the street captured footage of Stanford Madison going up Diane's front steps twice, bearing flowers. The first time had been eight weeks ago. Madison rang her doorbell several times, and when she didn't answer, he pounded on her door. Finally, when she didn't appear, he threw the flowers at the front door and left. Six weeks ago, Madison visited Diane a second time. This time she answered the door, but she didn't come outside. He shouted. Raised a fist. She slammed the door.

From the camera mounted on the house next to Diane's, the recording caught footage of parked cars and houses across the street. On the far west corner of the block, he spotted a white van. The resolution was too blurred for him to see the driver or get a plate, but the white van sat there for over an hour before it slowly drove off.

The killer had been stalking her.

Sharp called Vargas and updated her on his findings. She promised to meet him at the artist's studio right away.

He drove to Madison's studio and parked across the street. As he crossed, Vargas pulled in behind his car. A few quick steps and she caught up to him.

"Thanks for the heads-up," she said. Dark under-eye smudges told him she'd not been sleeping much either. "Doesn't look like there are any signs of Madison."

There were no lights on. The display windows had been shuttered from the inside, and the front entrance was locked.

"He's gone."

"Think our visit spooked him?"

"Maybe." Irritated, Sharp nodded toward the narrow side alley that led around the building.

"He could be distraught over Diane's death. You said the footage suggested he was trying to give her flowers. Men give flowers when they're trying to get out of the doghouse."

"That's the only reason?"

"Basically."

He'd never given Tessa flowers. Never brought them to his mother's or sister's graves. "Flowers are an empty gesture."

Vargas shook her head. "Spoken like a man."

Would Tessa have liked flowers? She'd never struck him as the flowers type. But then he'd consistently read her wrong from the outset. He could recall dozens of details about her. The way she sang in the shower. How his T-shirts skimmed the top of her thighs as she was cooking breakfast. The feel of her rubbing the tension from his neck. She could make him so damn hard with just the simplest of touches. But did she like flowers?

"You like to receive flowers?" Sharp challenged.

"Sure."

"Even if the guy is in the doghouse?"

"In that case, he would be required to give a very expensive bouquet."

"I don't get it."

"I see that. It's a wonder you got out of your marriage alive. I'd have killed you."

"I've no doubt."

Large green trash cans lined the back of the building, and each was piled high with rubbish. Removing latex gloves from his pocket, Sharp opened the first of three cans. The first trash can held dozens of rags covered in paint, thinner, balled-up newspapers, and brushes. They needed a search warrant for the inside of the building, but the garbage placed outside was fair game.

"I love it when people throw out evidence." Vargas pulled on latex gloves.

"Maybe he doesn't care or he assumed the trash man would carry it all away before we got here."

"Figured wrong, didn't he? By the way, I received the doll from Mike Bauer. Very creepy doll if you ask me. It looks like Diane Richardson. I've asked the forensic guys to go over it. But I'm not holding out hope. Bauer wiped it clean so he could give it to his daughter."

"Doesn't hurt to check."

Vargas lifted a broken paintbrush from the can. "A man who has given up on his art?" she asked.

"Maybe."

The second can was filled with blank canvases, unopened paints, and drop cloths. The last can was packed full of frameless canvases twisted into tight rolls. Sharp pulled out several and unrolled them.

"They're all of Diane," Vargas said.

The paintings contained exquisite detail and created an eerily life-like rendering. In each, she stared at the artist with a direct, almost amused gaze. Diane had been a stunning woman.

Vargas dug deeper into the can, pulling out several canvases that had been shredded with a knife.

"He's upset about something," Sharp said.

"Losing her is too painful? He can't bear to look at her anymore?"

"Maybe." Sharp thought about the surveillance footage of Madison at Diane's front door. "Or he was angry and aggravated with her and wanted to permanently mark her as his own."

Frustration deepened her frown. "I'm having his cell records pulled as well as his credit card purchases."

He glared at the pictures. *What the hell was going on with this son of a bitch?* "Right."

"You look like you could eat nails," she said.

Sharp met Vargas's gaze. He reached in his pocket and pulled out a Halloween picture of Kara, Diane, Elena, and Tessa.

The extra focus on Kara this last week had torn open a lot of pent-up emotion. He drew in a breath and handed her the picture. "My sister is the one on the far left."

Vargas dropped her gaze to the picture and studied it. "She looks like you. I bet she ran that gang."

The image coaxed a small smile. "She was bossing everyone in the house from the day she could sit up."

"Who are the girls?"

"Look closely at the brunette to her right. She's only eighteen, but she didn't change too much."

"Diane Richardson."

"Diane Emery then, but it looks like her. And the woman to her right is Elena Hayes."

"Who I haven't been able to speak directly to on the phone," Vargas said. "She responded to my voice mail with a text, but she's yet to call me back." Vargas tapped Tessa's face. "And the other woman is Tessa McGowan?"

"Yes."

Vargas shook her head as she dropped her gaze back to the picture. "Ah, Tessa. The wife. Hence the flower discussion?"

"No."

She laughed. "So you think Tessa might have had a grudge against these ladies?"

"What? No. That's not what I'm saying at all."

Vargas didn't look convinced. "She knew the two victims. When's the last time Tessa saw your sister?"

She was analyzing the case as he would have if he were on the outside. But he wasn't on the outside. Sharp was dialed in completely. "The night Kara vanished. She tells me the two fought. Over Madison."

"This Madison?" she said jabbing her thumb back at his building.

"Yes."

"Was it some kind of love triangle? Do I smell motive?"

"No. You do not." He ground out each word.

"Hey man, don't shoot the messenger. I have to look at this from all angles."

"Understood," he said, cooling his anger. "A car hit Tessa shortly after she left that Halloween party. Her leg was badly broken, and she suffered a concussion. She was in the hospital for days. She couldn't have hurt anyone."

"Maybe she was hit after she stashed Kara?" Vargas said. "Maybe her thoughts were distracted by a terrible secret and she didn't see the car."

"You're stretching a lot."

Vargas shrugged. "Tessa could have been working with someone else, like Stanford."

"No."

"All I know is Tessa was around when your sister vanished, and now Tessa shows back up and Diane Richardson is found dead. And let's not forget, whoever held Diane knew how to use an IV, like a trained doctor would."

"*Not* Tessa."

"You rise to her defense too quickly." Vargas slid off her latex gloves. "You still love Tessa, don't you?"

"That's not relevant."

"It is, if it clouds your judgment."

"My judgment is crystal clear."

"You've got a reputation for laser focus. But I bet this is the first time your ex has been involved in a case. Or your deceased sister has been mentioned in connection to a case."

"You're missing the point." He tapped the image with his index finger. "Look at what the girls in the photo are wearing. They were headed to a Halloween party, and three were dressed as dolls."

Vargas studied the picture again. "So you think whoever took your sister overdosed her, and is now back and killed Diane, one of the girls in this picture."

"I do. Tessa also spoke to her cousin, who was at Kara's funeral. According to the cousin, Elena was the one that found Kara, and Kara had a lot of makeup on her face."

"What kind of makeup?"

"I don't know. The pictures taken at the crime scene were poorly done. I have no clear view of Kara's face."

Vargas tapped her finger against her hip. "So, assuming that is all true, we have a guy who likes to make dolls out of living women?"

"A dollmaker. Yeah, that's exactly what I'm saying."

"Or are you trying to find a reason for your sister's death other than the fact she took a walk on the wild side and took too many drugs?"

"Goddamn it, Kara didn't take drugs," he said, louder than intended.

Nonplussed, she pulled the picture from his fingers. "I'm not trying to trash your sister. I really am not. But I'm asking all the tough questions I would of any family member."

He drew in a breath, locking down his frustration. "I get that. I do."

"But you hate it. And believe me, I know how it hurts to have family questioned."

How many times had he played the role of devil's advocate to solve a case? "My sister didn't use."

"Okay. I'll take you at your word on Tessa, your sister, and the cousin who remembers something Elena Hayes said twelve years ago. But," she added more softly, "I will not ignore any evidence pointing me in a different direction, even if what I find ends up pissing you off. I'd be doing a disservice to your sister and Diane if I did."

He released his breath. "Fair enough."

"In the meantime, we need to get ahold of Elena Hayes."

"Agreed."

She studied the picture again. Reached for her phone and dialed. Phone to her ear, she said, "Calling Elena now." After a pause, she held out her phone and they both listened to the voice-mail greeting. At the beep, "Elena, this is Agent Julia Vargas with the Virginia State Police. I need you to call me immediately." She left her number and ended the call.

"Keep me posted," Sharp said.

"Will do."

"And Vargas, thanks. I appreciate the good work."

The corner of her lip tilted into a grin. "I have a talent for irritating people."

"Keep it that way."

As she got in her car, he slid back behind the wheel of his car. He reached for the coffee in his cup holder and took a sip. It was stone-cold. His cell rang.

"Agent Sharp," he said.

"Deputy Mathew Ryan. I hear you're looking for Jimmy Dillon."

"I sure as hell am."

"One of my deputies stopped him on I-64 driving west about twenty minutes ago. He was driving nearly one hundred miles an hour and gave the officer one hell of a chase. We got him now. He's all yours if you want him."

"I do. I'll be there within the hour."

He maneuvered onto the interstate, and twenty-five minutes later he walked through the front doors of the small brick building housing the sheriff's department.

Inside the sheriff's office an officer glanced up, standing when Sharp entered.

"I'm Agent Dakota Sharp. Deputy Mathew Ryan called and said you've got Jimmy Dillon in a cell."

"I'm Ryan. Your suspect, Dillon, gave us quite a chase. He's in holding and waiting for you."

"Thanks."

"He's hungover, but he should be clearheaded enough to answer your questions. I'll bring him to the interrogation room."

"Thanks."

Sharp settled in the small room with grayish walls, a simple desk, and two chairs. There were no windows in the room, but a camera nestled in the upper-right corner shot down at him.

The door opened, and the deputy escorted in a wiry man with a crew cut. He wore a white shirt spoiled with sweat, jeans, and flip-flops. He looked at Sharp with bloodshot eyes. Sharp immediately recognized the man from surveillance footage as Jimmy Dillon.

Sharp sat back in his chair, opened his notebook, and clicked his pen several times as Dillon took a seat across from him. Dillon's pale face made the unshaved stubble on his chin all the darker. The deputy remained in the corner, arms folded across his chest.

"Mr. Dillon," Sharp said. "I'm Agent Sharp with the Virginia State Police."

Dillon yawned, and as he rubbed his eyes, the handcuffs around his wrists clinked softly. "Why does state police care about me speeding? Ain't you got real criminals to catch?"

"I was hoping you could tell me about Terrance Dillon."

"I don't know a Terrance Dillon."

Squashing a jolt of anger, Sharp reached in the side pocket of his notebook and pulled out a surveillance picture of Terrance Dillon laughing beside his father at the gas station. "Is that you with your son, Terrance Dillon?"

Dillon didn't bother to look. "I haven't seen my kid in ten years."

Sharp tapped the picture. "So this isn't you in the picture?"

"Nope."

Sharp leaned forward. A muscle in his jaw twitched. He understood playing it nice often earned him more information from a suspect, but right now it was all he could do not to break this man in half. His voice dropped to a low growl. "Take a second look at the picture, Mr. Dillon. Are you sure this isn't you and your son?"

Dillon shifted in his seat. "So what if he's my son? Why do you care?"

He watched Dillon carefully. "Terrance was found dead on Monday morning. He was stabbed, and the medical examiner estimates his time of death sometime between midnight and two a.m."

Dillon shook his head as he rubbed cuffed hands under his chin. "Terrance is dead? What kind of bullshit is that? Why would you say that?"

"You don't believe me?"

"I sure as shit don't. Cops like you play games."

"I don't play games like this."

"Bullshit. You lie, hoping I'll admit to some other crime also not my fault."

The old man's shock and outrage rang true, but then the best con artists could sound as innocent as a child at the drop of a dime. "The kid is dead. I witnessed his autopsy a couple of days ago."

"Bullshit."

Sharp removed another picture without saying a word. It was the boy lying dead on the medical examiner's table.

Dillon stared at the picture a long moment. He blinked. And then he leaned back in his chair. "That picture is fake. I don't believe you."

"Believe me or not. I don't care. But know this, I'm filing murder charges as soon as I can get the commonwealth's attorney on the phone."

Dillon's eyes widened. "Murder. What the hell are you talking about?"

"Murder. As in the next twenty to thirty years in prison." He tapped the pictures again.

Dillon shook his head, careful not to look at the pictures. "I didn't fucking kill the kid. He was my son."

"You picked him up at the convenience store at nine on Sunday night. What happened to Terrance after he got in your car?"

"I don't know."

"Look at the picture. Look at your dead son and tell me you didn't know what happened to him."

Dillon shifted in his chair.

"Look at it!"

Dillon's gaze dropped to the picture. "Could I get a soda? I'm not feeling so well."

Sharp wanted to grab the man by the scruff of the neck, but he didn't. He would back off, knowing the short reprieve might get him what he wanted faster. "Deputy, would you have someone bring Mr. Dillon a soda?" He raised a brow. "Would you like a cup and crushed ice?"

Dillon looked at Sharp closely. The man had been in the system long enough to know when the thin ice under him was cracking. And he rightly sensed there wasn't an ounce of goodwill behind Sharp's smile.

When another deputy returned a minute later with a cold soda and a cup, Sharp popped the top and slowly filled the plastic cup. He set it carefully in front of Dillon.

The older man drank, paused to take in a breath, and then drank more. When finished, he burped and wiped his mouth with the back of his hand. "Hit the spot."

Sharp poured the remainder of the soda in the cup. Images of Terrance on the autopsy table flooded his thoughts. This kid deserved

Sharp's best. "Talk to me about Terrance. What happened after you two left the Quick Mart?"

"I don't know exactly."

"Jimmy, you're not stupid. In fact, I think you're smart. We both know you did time for drugs. Did you use the kid for a buy?"

"I might have had a bag of goods that needed to be dropped off."

"What was in the bag?"

"I don't know."

"You're really starting to irritate me."

"I didn't know because I didn't want to know what was in the bag. I've always found it safer to know as little as possible during a transaction." He drummed his fingers on the side of the cup.

"When you sell drugs?"

He tapped one finger some more. "When I sell any item. The dumber the better."

"Who put the drugs in the bag?"

"I didn't say drugs."

Sharp rose, crushing the soda can in his hand. "You are now wasting my time. Better get a good lawyer."

"Wait. Don't rush out of here." Dillon's cuffed hands trembled as he dug his fingernail into the cup. "Some woman who works in the medical building. She said her name was Frances, but I think she was lying. She acted like she'd done this before. She told me she had some goods for me to deliver."

"How'd she find you?"

Dillon dug his thumbnail into the cup's rim. "We're from a small town. It didn't take long for word to get around I was out and back in town, holding court in my favorite bar. Everyone in town knew why I'd been sent away."

"How did Terrance get looped into this?"

"While I was away—"

"Away in prison," Sharp interjected.

"Yeah. Away. Terrance wrote to me. It's natural for a boy to write his father, right? I wrote to him. It's always good to have contacts on the outside. Anyway, Terrance and I reconnected. When I got out, I looked him up a couple of weeks ago just after I met with Frances."

"When did you decide to get the kid to do the delivery?"

"I don't know."

Sharp sat back in his chair, setting the crushed can in front of him. "So you tell your kid that you have a job for him. He can make a quick buck and no one gets hurt."

"Yeah, basically. I told him he'd make more in one night than he did working a month at that crappy maintenance job he'd worked over the summer." Dillon turned and looked at the camera and then the deputy. "Do I need my attorney?"

"I'm not here to bust you on drug charges, Mr. Dillon," Sharp said softly. "Or for stealing your son's identity and taking out credit cards in his name. I'm looking for your son's killer."

Dillon stared at the now-tattered edge of the cup, his expression tightening. "Is my boy really dead? This isn't some kind of con?"

"Like I said, I don't play those kind of games. Who was your buyer?"

Dillon frowned, clearly weighing the potential consequences of his son's murder. "I really don't know. That's the point. Nobody knows nobody."

Sharp drummed his pen against his pad. "How did you contact this mystery buyer?"

Dillon blew out a breath and glanced again at the camera beaming on them. "I didn't. Frances left me a burner phone. I was supposed to get a call and get a drop location."

Sharp leaned forward, producing a smile he suspected was more feral than friendly. "If I find out this is bullshit, I'll make it my personal mission to put you in prison for the rest of your life."

Dillon held up his hands. "Don't tense up. I'm being straight with you."

Sharp sat very still.

"Okay, I called the seller. I told her I wanted more money. I figured I had her by the short hairs, so to speak, and she'd have no other choice than to pay more."

"What did she say?"

Dillon's cuffs clinked as he sat back and rested his hands in his lap. "She was pissed. But she knows how business like this goes. There's always a surprise. She said she'd call me back. Five minutes later she said the buyer was willing to pay more."

"You looked in the bag, didn't you?"

"Yeah. I did."

"What kind of drugs were they?"

"I don't know. I don't ask."

"You had an idea. A guy like you is smart enough to know what he's dealing so he knows the value. What kind of drug was it?"

"It was enough to keep someone under for a long time."

"You're not helping, Jimmy. We both know a lot of drugs can do that."

"You need an IV to make it work."

"Okay. Now we are getting somewhere. How much did you sell?"

"A month's worth, maybe. I don't know."

Weeks? Diane Richardson had been drugged for weeks via IV. Could a connection to Diane Richardson's killer be this easy? "Are you talking about propofol?"

"Yeah. That sounds right."

Propofol could put a patient into a deep state of sleep and render the recipient totally immobile. Diane's killer would have needed it or a similar drug to work on her face.

"Why did you decide to use Terrance for the transaction?"

"Seemed safer that way. All the kid knew was he was selling a bag. I told him to make the exchange and bring me the money. It was an easy job."

"The kid didn't question you?"

"It took a little convincing at first, but I got him to agree."

"You had no idea who was on the other end of this deal?"

"I only communicated directly with him once."

Sharp simply waited.

Dillon tugged at his collar. "By phone. Frances gave me a number to call after our renegotiation. I called and we spoke. He was okay with the new price, and we set up the meet."

"So you sent Terrance because you got a bad vibe about the caller, right?"

"It's a vibe I get. I've learned not to ignore it."

"So you sent your son."

Dillon shook his head. "I really thought it would go down fine."

"No, you didn't. You sensed trouble and sent your kid to take the heat."

Dillon held up his finger. "That's not fair. You make it sound cold-blooded. The kid wanted to go. He wanted to make money so he could buy his grandmother a dryer." Dillon ran his fingers through his dark hair and smiled. "He loved that old bitch."

"She loved him."

"No, she didn't. Taking him into her home was another way she was sticking it to me. She never thought I was good enough for her daughter."

Sharp didn't respond.

"I really figured the worst that could happen was an arrest, maybe a night in jail, and then it would be like nothing happened."

"Terrance would have lost his scholarship."

"He didn't need college filling his head with stuck-up ideas."

"Where was Terrance supposed to meet the buyer?"

"An alley near Seventeenth Street in Richmond."

"I want an exact location."

"Why do you care where the meeting took place?"

He'd bet money that was the spot where Terrance had been knifed to death. "I care."

"In Shockoe Bottom near the train tracks."

"Why would this guy turn on Terrance?"

"Terrance can be a talker. He never knows when to shut up. I told him to keep his mouth shut. Shit, I must have told him twenty times. Don't talk. Grab and go."

"When Terrance didn't show up with the money, what did you think?"

"At first I thought he was stiffing me. I called him a couple of times, and when he didn't answer, I drove by his grandmother's house. I didn't see him."

"That didn't set off any alarm bells?"

"Yeah. A few. I decided to lie low for a while. I figured today I was in the clear, so I decided to head west. Then a cop did a U-turn and came after me. I wasn't speeding, so I knew they were after something else."

"Terrance's body wasn't found in the city. It was dumped close to his home, which strikes me as a real coincidence. How could this buyer know where Terrance lived? He couldn't have followed the kid home, because Terrance was counting on you to give him a ride back home."

"Lucky guess?"

Sharp didn't speak for a moment as fury surged in him. "Or maybe the kid said something that spooked the guy."

"How would I know? I wasn't there."

"Anything about this buyer's voice on the phone that reminded you of anyone you know?"

"How could I know him? I've been gone ten years."

"Maybe it was someone from your past."

"No, I didn't recognize his voice. I just know I didn't like the sound of it." He barely spoke above a whisper. "Freaky."

Time to find Frances. "What's the address of the building where you picked up the bag?"

"I don't know the exact address. It's off Route 360 a couple of miles north of I-295. There's a fast-food restaurant and a bike shop right by it."

"Jimmy, I'll be in touch. And if I find out you're lying to me, you're smart enough to know what I'll do next."

Dillon leaned forward, his fingers fisted. "I told you what I know."

Sharp rose. "I believe you."

"So that's it? I'm off the hook."

"No, you're not."

"You said you wouldn't charge me."

"The deputies in this county aren't ready to let you go yet. Reckless driving is a parole violation. And I'm betting you don't own the white Lexus you were driving."

Sharp left, not bothering to look back. This wasn't the first person he'd met who was willing to sacrifice his kid, but it never failed to piss him off.

CHAPTER SEVENTEEN

Saturday, October 8, 11:00 a.m.

As Sharp slid behind the wheel of his car, he dug out his phone and called Dr. Kincaid. When he reached her office, the administrative assistant on the weekend crew said Kincaid wasn't available, but Dr. McGowan could come to the phone. "Fine, put her on."

Seconds ticked before he heard, "This is Dr. McGowan."

"It's Dakota," he said quickly. "I need a favor from Dr. Kincaid, but she isn't available."

"I can help," she offered. "What do you need?"

"This is regarding the Terrance Dillon case. You found trace hair fibers on his body."

"Correct."

"I need that DNA cross-checked against any foreign DNA found on Diane Richardson."

"Dillon and Diane? How are the two cases related?"

"I'm still working on that. Can you check?"

"Sure. I'll take care of it myself."

"Thanks."

He hung up, before he was tempted to say more. His phone rang again. Julia Vargas. "Sharp," he said.

"I called Elena Hayes's office. They said she was on vacation, and she's supposed to be checking in with the office daily because of an upcoming deal. But no one has spoken to her in two days. Boss received a text saying she was sick, but when he called, she didn't answer."

Sharp started his engine. He did not want to be right about this, but he already knew he wasn't. "Where are you now?"

"I'm on my way to her apartment. I've contacted the landlord, and he's willing to let me have a quick look inside the apartment. Care to come with?"

"I would."

"Great. Sending you the address now."

"Thanks." His phone buzzed with the text, and he was en route immediately. A half hour later he was standing in front of Elena Hayes's address. It was a converted warehouse near the train tracks cutting across the Shockoe Bottom district of the city. He stared at the street signs intersecting Main Street. He was at the corner of Sixteenth and Main. The Seventeenth Street location Jimmy Dillon had mentioned was a block away. Coincidences like this were rarely accidental.

Her sunglasses catching the sun, Vargas leaned against the brick building, her arms folded. She looked relaxed, but he smelled the tension sizzling around her.

"Taking a nap?" he asked.

"Waiting for your sluggish self. I've spoken to the apartment manager, and he's ready to show us the apartment."

"What about a search warrant?"

"I have the go-ahead from a judge to ascertain the status of Elena Hayes. If we see any evidence of trouble, we'll back out and request the warrant."

Inside the building they took the elevator to the fifth floor and rounded a long corner where a skinny guy with a pockmarked face stood. He wore tattered jeans, a black T-shirt, and boots. In his hand was a ring of keys.

Sharp showed him his badge and introduced himself.

"I'm Max Quentin. Haven't seen Ms. Hayes in a couple of days," he said as he searched the ring of keys. "She was headed out for a vacation."

"Is it unusual for you not to see her for days at a time?"

"Yes. She had an obsession for schedules. Gym, work, and then out with her friends at night. She's always coming and going."

"Do you pay this close attention to all your tenants?" Vargas asked.

"No. Just the hot ones." The manager grinned as he found the right key and turned the lock. The door opened to an airy one-bedroom apartment with a large picture window overlooking the train tracks and the river. Her place was simply decorated with an overstuffed couch and a white shag area rug. A glass coffee table held a television remote and a neat stack of magazines.

Vargas rattled keys in her hands. "I confirmed with Elena's colleague, Miranda, who said Elena had a huge presentation at work in two weeks. Part of her getting away was to have a quiet place to prepare."

"Where did she go?"

"Miranda thought she may have gone to her parents' lake house so no one from work would drop in on her."

Sharp nodded to a laptop on the kitchen counter. "Think she would have needed that if she were going to work on her vacation?"

"Absolutely," Vargas said. "Miranda said she was dedicated and had her eye on a promotion."

"Has anyone checked with the hospitals?" Sharp asked.

Vargas flipped open a small notebook. "I called the local ones, and no one has heard of Elena Hayes or admitted anyone matching her description."

"What about a boyfriend?"

More notebook pages flipped. "She had one a couple of years ago. He left her and married someone else. She's been single since. Really into fitness. Loves yoga. Was talking last week about what she'd do if she closed this upcoming deal."

The living area connected to a galley kitchen, which was clean and tidy. A small hallway led to a bedroom. The shades were drawn up, bathing the room in sunlight. Lying in the center of a neatly made king-size bed was a doll.

"Damn," Vargas muttered behind Sharp.

"We need to get a search warrant and seal this apartment," he said.

Sharp moved closer to the bed, tugging on latex gloves. The doll had dark hair and wide bright-blue eyes and wore a red dress. He wasn't an expert, but he could see the doll's face was shaped exactly like the one given to Diane. The detailed painting around the eyes and the lips was perfect.

Sharp took a couple of snapshots of the doll before he and Vargas walked out of the apartment. The manager locked the door.

Sharp called for a uniform to stand guard in front of the door until the warrant and forensic team arrived. Only when a uniformed officer had secured the room did the two detectives take the elevator to the first floor.

When they were alone, he said, "We have at least an hour before we can get back in there, and I have a possible crime scene just a couple of blocks from here. Walk with me, and let's take a look at an alley a block away."

"Man, I got a full caseload. I don't have time for strolls."

"Humor me, Vargas," he said. He moved to his car and from the trunk collected a flashlight.

"It's the middle of the day," Vargas said.

He clicked it on, confirmed it worked, and turned it off. "Stick with me on this."

Vargas matched Sharp's quick pace as the two traveled the brick sidewalk. He found the alley Jimmy had described and paused at the entrance. The narrow lane sandwiched between two old brick buildings was empty except for a dumpster at the dead end. One way in. One way out. The perfect death trap.

"Heard about Terrance Dillon, the kid stabbed and dumped north of the city?" Sharp asked.

"I did. Word is he was a good kid with no record. What does this alley have to do with him?"

Sharp reached in his pocket and pulled out latex gloves. "According to Terrance's father, the kid came to this alley to make a delivery."

She arched a brow as she also fished out gloves. "You mean drugs?"

"I do."

"Drug deals go bad all the time," Vargas challenged.

"According to the kid's father, the drug in question might have been propofol stolen from a doctor's office."

"The kid's father set up the deal?"

"He did."

"Keep it in the family. Nice."

"Jimmy said the drugs were enough to keep a person out for weeks."

Her frown deepening, she shifted her gaze to the alley. "A month. That's about the amount of time Diane Richardson's killer needed to keep her immobilized."

Sharp clicked on his light, which cast an infrared beam. Hunters used this light to track the blood trail of shot game. He was hunting for human blood. "I asked Dr. McGowan to test the foreign DNA found on Richardson's and Dillon's bodies."

"You think they could be a match?"

"Right now, I wouldn't bet against it."

Sharp slowly moved into the alley, inspecting the worn cobblestones. At first, he saw only the gray. "If this deal occurred last Sunday, then the drugs wouldn't have been for Diane. The work on her was already done at that point."

"You think this guy is planning to take someone else? Maybe someone like Elena?"

"I'd like to be wrong." If Elena was in danger, that meant Tessa could be as well. Sharp kept his gaze on the cobblestones. "There was no blood at the spot where we found the kid's body. His stab wound did maximum damage, and Kincaid thinks he bled out quickly."

"So wherever he died, he bled."

"Yes."

"It hasn't rained since Monday, so we have a good chance of finding it if it's here." Vargas cocked her head. "So this kid's father might have been in touch with Diane's killer?"

"He talked with a woman looking to sell prescription medications."

She shook her head. "Does this lovely woman have a name?"

"Frances, he thinks."

"That's it?"

"Afraid so. But she most likely works out of one of the medical buildings off Route 360 near Mechanicsville. Based on what he told me, it won't take long to find the building."

Sharp was halfway into the alley when his light skimmed over a large dark patch. The air carried hints of a coppery scent. "Look."

Vargas knelt and studied the stain. "I'll be damned."

Sharp fished a small blood-testing kit from his side pocket. It came with a cotton swab and a glass vial with chemicals that reacted to blood. He dabbed the stain and pushed the swab into the vial, breaking the seal and releasing a chemical. He shook the bottle. Within seconds the clear liquid changed to a bright blue. "The blood is human."

She took the vial and held it up to the light. "So now we need to prove it belonged to Terrance and then find this mystery woman named Frances. She might have seen our killer."

Sharp reached for his phone. "Let's roll."

***

Tessa relayed Sharp's request to Dr. Kincaid, who ordered the tests on the blood samples taken from Terrance Dillon. After a brief discussion of the day's pending cases, they moved to the autopsy suite. Their first case was a man in his fifties who'd suffered a massive heart attack last night while watching his favorite variety show on television. Next on deck was an autopsy of a sixty-five-year-old woman who'd consumed twice the legal limit of alcohol and stumbled down a flight of stairs. She'd hit her head at the bottom and broken her neck.

Dr. Kincaid shook her head. "Stay in shape, watch the booze and drugs, avoid dark alleys at night, and look both ways before you cross the street, and your chances of making it to a ripe old age increase exponentially."

"The Diane Richardsons of the world are rare."

"And thank God."

When the cases had been cleared, Tessa stripped off her gown and grabbed her purse. She headed outside for some fresh air and a walk. As the sun warmed her face, she realized she was hungry. She'd not eaten much at Sharp's last night, and now she was starving. She stopped at a taco truck parked on Main Street and ordered a burrito. As she moved back up toward her office and took a bite, her cell chimed with a text. Benson file on your desk.

Benson. Kara Benson. This morning she'd arrived early at work and, troubled by Holly's mention of makeup on Kara's body, requested the autopsy file. She'd asked the records clerk to text her when she found it, not expecting to see it for several days.

Her appetite for her burrito instantly vanished, and she hurried back to her office. A yellow interoffice envelope resting on her desk greeted her. Putting her purse in her bottom desk drawer, she opened the envelope to Kara's old autopsy file. Her heart beat fast as she sat at her desk and pulled on her reading glasses. She slowly opened the file, wondering if she would ever be able to forget what was in it.

The first page was a diagram of the victim's body. There were a couple of scrapes on the knees and palms, suggesting a fall, but other than those minor injuries, there were no other signs of trauma to the body. She flipped the page to her first look at Kara's body lying on the autopsy table. Kara's thick dark hair was brushed away from her freshly scrubbed pale face, which was splotched with decomposition stippling. Her jaw was slack and her eyes half-open. The image took her breath away.

She sat back in her chair and took off her glasses as she raised her hand to her mouth. She thought about the argument Holly had remembered Tessa having with Kara. "It had to have been so petty and stupid."

Shaking herself mentally, she drew back her emotions and focused on the facts. The victim had been missing for five days but had only been dead thirty to forty hours when found. The temperatures had been unseasonably high, and decomposition had been rapid. By the time the body had been found, gasses from decomposition had bloated the corpse. When the crews moved her, she'd popped and deflated.

Tessa had seen this before and accepted this process as natural. But she'd also watched seasoned detectives when she'd been in Baltimore wilt and run to the nearest bathroom or bush to be sick. Death was inevitable, but it wasn't pretty.

The inventory of the victim's organs found them healthy. Her heart was of normal size, as was her liver. Stomach contents were minimal. There'd been traces of crackers and some broth. Wherever she'd been during those missing days, she'd been eating.

The medical examiner had conducted a vaginal examination and found traces of seminal fluid, but no signs of vaginal tearing or bruising, which suggested she'd not resisted intercourse. The fluids had been sent off for DNA, but when the results came back six months later, there'd been no match.

She flipped through the photos taken right after Kara's body had been brought to the medical examiner's office. In these images, her face hadn't been scrubbed by the technician yet. Though at first glance the face was clean, as she looked closer, she could see definite traces of pale makeup around her hairline and ears. Shadows of bright-red lipstick colored her lips, and hints of a pale blue shaded her eyelids. Though it appeared her face had been wiped clean, she'd clearly been heavily made up.

Kara had never been a big fan of makeup, and the night of the Halloween party had been no exception. Whereas Diane, Elena, and Tessa had had fun exaggerating their doll features, Kara had not warmed to the garish look. *"I'm a natural doll,"* she'd quipped as she straightened her red dress. And yet there were traces of makeup on her face five days after she vanished.

Where had the makeup come from? And why had it been wiped from her face before she arrived at the medical examiner's office? She'd been missing five days, but according to liver temperature readings taken in the medical examiner's office, she'd only been dead about thirty hours. There were no signs of exposure, so presumably she'd been inside. So if there had been makeup, one night in the elements, even if it rained, would not have been enough to erase the makeup so completely.

Tessa checked the inventory of the patient's belongings. She'd been wearing a simple red dress, black high heels, and a bow in her hair. The description matched the pictures Tessa had taken the night of the party. The only discrepancy was the bow. Kara had not been wearing a bow.

No one would have thought twice about the makeup or bow given Kara had been at a Halloween party before she vanished.

Kara's toxicology report revealed lethal levels of barbiturates. The drugs had caused her breathing to depress and finally her heart to stop. The drugs also explained the lack of vaginal tearing. If the sex had not been consensual, she'd have been too drugged to resist anyone.

Tessa checked the files and discovered there was still DNA logged in the evidence lockers that were kept refrigerated. Knowing how much science had advanced in the last dozen years, she ordered new DNA testing on the seminal fluids found in Kara as well as a cross-check with the DNA found in Diane and on Terrance Dillon. Two women made up, one with tattoos and the other presumably with makeup. Both deaths also involved high levels of drugs that led to overdose, and there was evidence both women had had intercourse near time of death.

Terrance Dillon was still the outlier, but if he had been killed in a drug deal involving propofol, then that was a solid link to Diane, who'd died from the drug. Yes, a dozen years separated the first death and the most recent two, but the otherwise unique cases showed too many signs of interconnection to be ignored.

A couple of days ago, everyone would have considered the tests too speculative and wouldn't have ordered them. Now she wasn't so sure this was a long shot.

She might get flak for the expedited tests and their costs, but as Sharp once said, it was easier to seek forgiveness than ask permission.

***

In the park, the laughter of children swirled around Sharp as he stood in front of the spot where Diane Richardson had been found three days ago. Though most of the crime scene tape was now gone, a trace of it was tangled in a bush and drifted in the fall breeze.

He tried to imagine the possible paths the killer would have taken to get her body here. The forensic team had found faint tire tracks and taken impressions. There'd also been one partial boot print found near the body.

He walked back toward the parking lot counting the steps. Diane Richardson had not been a big woman, but carrying a dead body was unwieldy, even for the fittest killer. This guy had stamina. He walked to his car and looked back toward the tree. What was it about this place? Why bring her here?

He lives close by.

The words whispered in his head. The killer knew this small town located twenty miles north of Richmond well. From this spot, Terrance Dillon lived 3.5 miles away. Kara had been found 4.6 miles from here. The small private college where all the girls had attended was 6.2 miles away.

Killers, like everyday people, were creatures of habit. They had their routines, too. They chose to dispose of their victims in familiar areas. Easy in, easy out, and no one was the wiser.

Sharp reached for a cigarette and lit it. He inhaled and thought about the thousands of homes in this area. This guy had held Diane for weeks, so he would have needed privacy.

Houses with basements and large lots came to mind, but Sharp knew if the killer were careful and kept his victim sedated, he might be able to keep her in close quarters. Keep your grass cut and say a nice word or two to your neighbors, and for the most part, people left you the hell alone.

As he stared at the glowing tip of his cigarette, he thought about Vargas's comments about Tessa. Vargas hadn't ruled her out as a person of interest, but no matter how compelling the argument, he could never imagine Tessa killing anyone. Ever.

He thought back to when he and Tessa had bumped into each other two years ago. He'd had one of his infrequent visits with Roger, who had said Tessa was back in Richmond working as a resident at the state hospital. Sharp had always been attracted to Tessa, but the decade difference in age and the awkward timing had kept him at a distance. Now the years didn't matter as much, and the timing was about as good as it would ever get.

He'd found out she hung out with friends who lived on Monument Avenue and made a point to just happen by one day. It was during his third "happen by" that he'd spotted her with some friends playing croquet in the wide grassy median strip dividing the historic avenue.

Her long black hair was pulled into a tight ponytail, and a sweat-stained tank top clung to her breasts. Shorts showed off long athletic legs and a great ass. He noted the scar on her right leg, the reminder from the car accident suffered the night Kara vanished. Still, she moved well.

The sun had given her skin a warm glow, accentuating her fit, toned body. Half the guys playing had been stealing glances of her as she bent forward to make a shot.

He'd leaned against a tree, watching the game. Watching her. Enjoying every moment of it.

She'd not recognized him, but when other players had broken for a break, she'd glanced over at him a couple of times.

"Tessa?" he asked.

"Yes?" She shielded her eyes from the sun, squinting as she tried to place him.

He pushed off from the tree and moved toward her. "Dakota Sharp." Automatically, he stuck out his hand, though he could see she'd still not connected the dots. "Tessa McGowan, right?"

"Yeah." Her head cocked to the side as she took his hand in a firm grip. Her hand was soft, smooth. She smelled of jasmine.

After another beat, her memory seemed to shake loose the connection. "Kara's brother?"

"Right." The association with his sister deflated some of his good mood as he reluctantly released her hand.

"I'm with the Virginia State Police now."

She tucked a strand of loose hair behind her ear. "Do you live around here?" she asked.

"No. Just getting in a run. Fresh air. I don't get enough of either. Saw the game and then you."

A delicate pink warmed her cheeks. "Oh."

"What are you doing these days?"

"Pathology residency."

He already knew the answers to these basic questions because he'd done a fair amount of digging before making contact. But he liked hearing her talk. Liked being close to her. "Sounds interesting."

"It is." She drank her water, and his gaze was drawn to the long line of her neck and her slender fingers wrapped around the bottle.

"Hey, Tessa, the game is about to start back up," one of the male players shouted.

"Well, I didn't want to interrupt," he lied. "I just wanted to say hi."

"Oh, no worries. Really. Sorry, it just took me a second. It's been, what, nine or ten years?"

"Give or take." He maintained eye contact and smiled.

"Hey, McGowan," one of the guys shouted. "Get your butt in gear."

She looked over her shoulder at the group, now grinning. "Let me buy you a drink. Be nice to catch up."

"You sure? I didn't mean to bust into your afternoon," he said.

"I'd like it." She tossed her towel over her shoulder and picked up her backpack. "If you're up for a little walk, there's a bar a block from here. It's cheap. And the burgers are good."

He grinned. "Sure."

All traces of hesitation melted from her green gaze. "Great."

Eight months later it was a hasty Las Vegas wedding, and eight months after that they separated.

He tossed the half-used cigarette into the dirt and ground it out with the tip of his shoe. Hearing the children's laughter, he picked up the butt and threw it in the garbage.

He'd shoved his way into Tessa's life, and she'd welcomed him. For a time, he'd been happier than he could remember. He'd never bothered to consider their age difference or that his world-weary, cynical view of life would clash with her youthful impulsiveness.

Sharp had almost convinced himself the past was dead and buried, forever. That he'd somehow made a shaky peace with Kara's death. But he'd been so wrong. All along the demons of the past had lurked. Hid. Stalked.

The case that had shattered their marriage had been the murder of an eighteen-year-old girl. She'd been a freshman in college, and after vanishing for two days, she was found strangled and sexually abused. He'd not slept or eaten much for weeks as he interviewed dozens of people. Tessa had been as patient as a saint. She'd pushed power bars in his pockets so he could eat. She'd not complained when he missed dinners. And then the killer had been caught. Their life should have returned back to what it had been. But the switch Sharp flipped had stayed on. Tessa had tried to talk to him. But he only grew frustrated.

Now he wondered if the switch could be turned off or if this was simply the way he'd remain.

***

Sharp had visited almost all the offices in the medical building fitting Jimmy Dillon's description. As the time neared 2:00 p.m., he entered the second to last on his list. This medical practice belonged to Dr. Bailey, an oral surgeon who'd been practicing in the area for twenty years.

He showed his ID to a plump young receptionist. "Is Frances here?"

"We don't have anyone here by that name."

He'd received a similar response at the other offices he'd visited in the building. "Can I see the doctor in charge?"

"Sure." She made a call. Minutes later a nurse escorted him to a corner office. A glance at the diplomas on the wall told Sharp the good doctor had an impressive résumé. But Sharp had crossed paths with many talented, smart people who took shortcuts when it came to making money. It wouldn't be hard for a doctor to skim narcotics and sell them on the side.

A short man wearing a white lab coat entered the room. Neat black hair was brushed away from a friendly face free of worries. He extended his hand. "Agent Sharp, I'm Dr. Bailey. What can I do for you?"

"I'm looking for a woman named Frances."

"Who?"

"She works in this office," he bluffed. Even if the name weren't real, hearing it spoken by a cop would rattle cages.

"The name doesn't ring a bell, but let me check with my office manager." The doctor moved to his desk and pressed a button. "Dana, can you come in here? Great." As he set down the receiver, he faced Sharp. "She's the brains of the outfit. In fact, sometimes I feel like I work for her."

"You don't know the names of all your employees?"

"I'm a surgeon. I arrive at five a.m. and I work nonstop most of the day. I hired Dana because she's efficient and knows how to run a tight ship."

"What kind of surgeries do you do?"

"Dental work. Pull teeth. Root canals. Gum surgery."

"So you've a full surgical setup here?"

"We have three suites that I move between in the mornings. Our patients are transferred to a recovery suite where we can keep an eye on them until they're ready to leave."

"You keep all your meds on-site?"

The doctor's eyes narrowed. "Is this about drugs? Did this Frances take drugs from me?"

"We don't know."

A soft knock on the door and an average-height woman with full brown hair, glasses, and bright-red lips entered. "You wanted to see me?"

"Dana Coggin, this is Agent Sharp with the Virginia State Police. Do you know a woman named Frances who works here?"

She adjusted her glasses. "No. Should I?"

"A confidential informant identified Frances as a source for illegally traded prescription drugs," Sharp said. He watched her closely for any body language cue that would tip her hand.

Dana adjusted her glasses again. "Why should I know this woman?"

"I believe Frances is an alias. Anyone in this office give you cause for concern when it came to the administration of narcotics?"

"No. Never." She shifted her stance.

"According to one of my sources, Terrance Dillon, age eighteen, was given a bag containing these narcotics and told to deliver them to a specific address. He was killed in a city alley."

"Were the narcotics found?" Dana asked.

"No."

Dana's gaze grew steady, as if she were doing her best not to look too upset. "That's terrible, but how would I know about the kid's death?"

Sharp noted how she tightly gripped a pen in her right hand. "We think someone in one of the offices in this building sold those drugs to Terrance's father, Jimmy Dillon. There are only two other businesses in this building other than this one that fit the profile."

Dana's smile was quick, forced. "I don't know what you're talking about."

He smelled the lie. "Who is Frances?"

She stood straighter. "I don't know."

The hair on his neck rose, just as it did when he had been deployed. "So if I ordered an audit of your controlled drug supplies, there'd be no issue?"

She glanced at the doctor. "There would be no problem."

"Good," Sharp said, reaching for his phone. "I'll have agents here within the hour along with the Virginia Board of Pharmacy."

The doctor shook his head. "I cannot have state agents coming into my office like this. It's not good for business."

"I suspect someone is using the drugs taken from this office to administer to and then kill women. So if I can track the supplier, then I'll find the buyer, who I believe is the killer."

Dr. Bailey slid his hands into his pockets. "I didn't realize it was that complicated. Dana, are you sure there's no issue with the inventory?"

She looked at him like he'd slapped her. "No, there's no issue. I haven't sold drugs to anyone."

"I never said it was you," Sharp said.

She leaned toward the doctor, locking her gaze on him and lowering her voice. "Dr. Bailey, I've worked for you for twelve years. You know me."

"I've already requested all the security footage around this building," Sharp said. "If someone in this office is culpable, I'll know soon."

Dana removed her glasses and glanced at the lenses before wiping them with the edge of her shirt. "I don't like your tone."

Dr. Bailey stared at his office manager. "Dana, you need to tell the officer what you know."

Dana stared at her employer, her eyes narrowing. "I think I better call my attorney."

CHAPTER EIGHTEEN

Sunday, October 9, 6:00 a.m.

Tessa came to Sharp often in his dreams. Most nights, she was dressed only in one of his white dress shirts. Her hair hung loose around her shoulders, sleeves pushed recklessly above her elbows, and only a single button was fastened, offering a generous peek at the full swell of her breasts. Firm legs, but so soft to the touch.

Sharp awoke and glanced at the empty side of his bed. He was thinking about her too much during the day, and now she was in his dreams.

Groaning, he got out of bed and went straight for the shower. He didn't bother with hot water. Ice-cold water was what he needed.

When he came into the kitchen, Sharp was grateful for the full pot of coffee waiting for him. He had only gotten a couple hours of sleep last night, and the cold shower hadn't quite cut through his fatigue. He filled a mug and found McLean sitting on the back patio, staring at a chessboard that looked to be in midgame.

"What are you looking at?"

"I find sometimes chess allows me to focus and identify patterns." He put his fingertips on a bishop, hesitated, but in the end, didn't move the piece.

"Patterns." Sharp shook his head. "I keep forgetting there's a philosophy minor lurking behind your math major. If a tree falls in the woods, and no one hears it fall, does it make a sound? All bullshit to me."

McLean sipped his coffee before moving a chess piece. "You would be surprised what secrets the universe will reveal if you're simply quiet."

Sharp took a sip of coffee. "Right."

McLean's eyes darkened with unspoken thoughts. "Even in chaos, there are paths. What's on your agenda today?"

"I'm headed into the office. More surveillance footage waiting for me."

"On the Diane Richardson case?"

"Indirectly. I'm working on the case of a kid knifed in a Richmond alley. I think the kid was killed because he recognized his killer."

McLean's lips curled. "So who did the boy know? What were his daily patterns?"

"I'm working on that. He came from a small town where most of the locals know each other."

"Your killer is a local?"

"I think he was either local or in the area often. The kid's neighborhood is right off I-95, which broadens the possible list of suspects."

"If you need help, shout."

"Will do."

McLean checked his watch. "Now, I've got to go. Headed to meet with the Shield people."

Sharp checked his own watch. "At this time of day?"

"They work nonstop, like you." He placed his coffee cup in the sink and, offering a quick salute to Sharp, snatched up his keys and left.

As Sharp sipped coffee, he mentally ran through the surveillance tapes he'd reviewed, until his phone rang. It was Martin. "Working on Sunday?"

Martin's chair squeaked through the phone. "A good excuse to skip brunch with my mother-in-law."

"You two don't get along?"

Without any malice in his tone, he said, "We're polite, but she could live the rest of her life without seeing me again, and I could do the same."

"Tessa's mother died before I met her. She has a cousin who never liked me. The cousin knows me better than I know myself."

"How so?"

"The cousin is a workaholic. She recognized the traits in me that I didn't see." He refilled his cup.

"She wasn't charmed by your witty dialogue?"

Sharp grunted. "I'm incapable of small talk."

"No kidding, really?"

Sharp ignored the sarcasm. "The blood in the Richmond city alley belongs to Terrance Dillon."

"No doubts?"

"None. The kid was AB negative and the blood is a DNA match to the evidence collected by the medical examiner at autopsy. Terrance Dillon was definitely killed in the alley."

"Any other evidence from either of the two crime scenes that are attached to this case?"

"As you might remember, there's a partial fingerprint on Terrance Dillon's belt buckle, which doesn't belong to the victim. We're running it through AFIS. Must have been transferred when the killer lifted the body. Judging by the blood trail, the killer pulled the body toward Cary Street. The trail ended abruptly two feet inside the alley."

He thought about the white van circling Diane's block. "He put him in a vehicle."

"Which has to have traces of blood in it. The kid lost a tremendous amount of blood, and even if he died in the alley, he was still spilling blood."

He remembered the faint bloodstain on Diane's doll dress. "What about the blood on our doll victim? Has that been tested?"

"It's in the works now."

"Compare it to Terrance Dillon's blood."

Martin hesitated. "Sure."

"What about the kid's cell phone? Did you find any numbers out of the ordinary?"

"All the numbers on the kid's phone can be confirmed. The father's phone is a different story. When he was arrested, he had three phones in his possession. One had not been used. The other two were used to make calls to another burner phone. I checked with the cell towers to see if I could get a location, but the phone is currently inactive. If the killer reactivates the phone, then there might be a chance to find him."

"If he's smart, he'll smash it and toss it in the river."

"You give him too much credit."

He wished that were true. This killer could possibly have been killing for a dozen years. "Can you send me a printout of the numbers?"

"Sure, why?"

"A man at Shield Security might be able to track the cells and see if one reactivates."

"Sure."

"What about the dolls found at the Richardson home and the Hayes apartment?"

"I was only able to pull a partial print from the Hayes doll. The Richardson doll was wiped clean. Both of the dolls' heads, arms, and feet are porcelain. Neither was manufactured, so I'm guessing the parts were ordered from a craft supply store and then assembled. The clothes are also not manufactured but hand-sewn. Finding the seller of any of these materials is a tricky matter."

With the Internet, this supplier could be anywhere in the world. "Are there similarities between the partial print on Terrance Dillon's belt buckle and the partial on the Hayes doll?"

"I have a thumbprint on the buckle and a right index finger on the doll. The thumbprint is a fairly good sample, but the index finger shows signs of scarring, perhaps a burn. I had no matches on the index finger and was able to match one, maybe two points on the thumbprint, but as you know, I need at least six for a solid identification."

"Thanks. Word is you were also on the team in Elena Hayes's apartment? Find anything?"

"Lots of prints, but no telling which ones, if any, belong to our killer. It's a matter of sorting through the hundreds we collected and matching them to either the thumbprint or the AFIS system."

"We're looking for a needle in a haystack, but at least we have a haystack now."

"I'll forward what I have."

"Thanks."

As Sharp ended the call, he heard a car door close and looked out his front window. He saw Tessa approaching the door. His first thought was there had to be a problem for her to come to his house this early. He set his coffee cup aside and moved to the door, snapping it open before she could knock.

"Tessa," he said.

She smiled. "Just the man I need to see. I have information for you."

He stepped aside. "Come in."

Closing the door behind her, he felt a familiar tightening in his gut when he watched her walk. Damn. When would he get over wanting her? She moved into the living room, and he motioned for her to sit. She chose the sofa.

He remained standing. "What do you have?"

She scooted to the edge of the couch, clutching a file in her hands. "I pulled Kara's autopsy file."

His insides turned brittle. "Why'd you do that?"

"The comment my cousin Holly said bothered me."

"About the makeup?" A calm tone hid the fire burning in his gut. "The Kara I knew didn't wear makeup."

"She wasn't wearing it that night. The picture proved it. I know my cousin remembers everything, but I thought she might have heard wrong. So I pulled Kara's medical examiner case files and looked at the pictures taken of her when she arrived at the medical examiner's office. Have you seen them?"

He paused to shore up his defenses. "No."

"I know this is painful, Dakota, which is why I did the looking without talking to you first."

He cleared his throat. "What did you find?"

"The photos show remnants of heavy makeup. The remaining coloring reminds me of a doll. Pale skin, red lips. The pictures prove Kara didn't wear any makeup to the party. The fact that makeup was on her face makes no sense. Especially considering she'd been missing five days."

Puzzle pieces snapped into place. "Someone else applied it."

"That's what I think." Her fingers gripped the edges of the file tighter. "I think someone kept her drugged and sedated her like Diane."

"The killer wasn't planning to take her," he said, letting the theory take shape. "He used what he had at the time. Barbiturates and face paint. And he overdosed either by accident or intentionally." The end result was the same. His sister was dead.

She opened the file and rustled through the papers. "I also discovered the medical examiner found DNA on her. At the time, it didn't match anyone in the system, but that was twelve years ago. The science is more refined now. Long story short, I've requested retesting, and I've also asked the DNA be cross-checked against the DNA found on Diane Richardson and Terrance Dillon."

Sharp rose and paced the room. He stared at her, not trusting himself to speak. Answers dangled just out of reach.

She stood, set the file aside, and moved toward him. "Have you found Elena?"

"Not yet." He flexed his fingers. "Madison dated Kara, Diane, and you."

"He did not date me. I kind of had a crush on him, and he came by to see me several times after my accident. It was never romantic."

"For you. You can't speak to what he was thinking."

"He never gave me any indication he was interested."

"It's a connection to all four of you. And until he's found, I don't want you going anywhere alone."

"Anywhere? That's kind of ridiculous. I mean, this is Stanford. The guy played cards and watched old movies with me while I was in a leg cast."

"I don't care if the fucker read bedtime stories to you every night. He knew all three victims, has professional artistic skill, and now has dumped all his work in the trash and vanished. We have no samples of his DNA yet, and until we do and can prove his innocence, you need to be on high alert."

"Dakota—"

He captured her wrist with his hand. "You did a great job, Tessa. I listened to every word you said. Now it's time for you to listen and let me do my job."

She looked at his hand on her wrist. Laying her hand over his, she pulled his fingers free and took his other hand in hers. Her touch was warm. Soft. Somewhere inside him, he felt locks tumble free and a door open. Emotions raced toward the light.

"I'm going to solve this." His voice sounded distant, hoarse.

"And then what?" she challenged.

"What do you mean?"

"Don't play dumb. After this case, *we* figure *us* out."

How could he make a promise to her he didn't know he could keep? He was far from perfect, but he'd never lied to her. "None of our problems will be fixed by solving this case."

"I don't believe that. Kara's case is the root of it all."

"And what if it isn't?"

She shook her head. "Did I ever tell you I had a little crush on you when I saw you that last Christmas? I tried to get your attention, but you didn't see me."

"I saw you."

That prompted a nervous smile. "You did a good impression of pretending you didn't."

"You were seventeen. Underage. And I was home on leave. And it's not acceptable to mess with your sister's friend."

"It was bad timing all around." The words carried more meaning than they should have.

"We never really got the timing right."

"No." He tried to pull free of her touch, but her fingers tightened around him. How much of the past would have to be exorcised for them to now have a chance?

"After seeing Diane and her face destroyed, I understand better why you're so driven. It's one thing to believe in monsters, but entirely another to cross paths with a real one. It's hard to know that someone is getting away with such cruelty."

Anger burned in his chest. He broke their connection, his fingers flexing involuntarily. "This killer isn't getting away with it."

She took his fist and slowly uncurled his fingers. She traced the scar slashing across his lifeline on his palm. "Despite all our differences, I know you're good at what you do. Without you, a lot of evil would be walking free."

He looked at her long finger with its neat, trimmed nail circling the scar. She'd been so young when they first met, but each time he saw her, he was more drawn to her. He'd never made a single pass at her. And later, after they were married and mired in turmoil, when she told him she had to leave, he'd again taken that damned high road. Didn't fight. Didn't argue. Accepting. Alone.

At this moment, he was tired of walking the same lonely, shitty road. Righteousness didn't welcome him home at night or warm his bed.

He wanted her. Wanted to feel like she once made him feel. Whole.

Moving his hand over hers, he wrapped his fingers around hers, savoring the warmth. He waited for her to pull free, for any sign she didn't want his touch. She didn't move. Didn't breathe. She simply stared into his eyes.

Sharp leaned his head forward and kissed her softly on the lips. She closed her eyes, leaning into the kiss. The sex had always been great between them, but it hadn't been enough. Temporary glue that couldn't withstand the storms.

But temporary was good enough right now. An urgency hummed in his veins. God, but she tasted sweet. This moment felt like a homecoming.

He released one hand, letting it roam over her shoulders and to the small of her back. He pulled her against him. He wanted her to feel him. To know just how damn much he wanted her.

Given a choice right now, he'd pull her into the bedroom, shut off the world outside, and thrust inside her until he'd exorcised all the pent-up pain begging for release.

But when his other hand slid from her hair over her neck to her breasts, she tensed. Reining in his desire, he waited.

"Don't stop," she said. "I want this."

He felt the thrust of her breast into his hand. Need elbowed past worry and any kind of resolve to keep his distance, and he gently brushed her nipple, feeling it harden through her sweater.

Months and too many issues had separated them, but he remembered her body and what pressure points made her forsake common sense and drop her guard.

As he kissed her, he continued to tease the tip of her nipple with his thumb and forefinger, all the while feeling her body melting into him. She moaned his name, her breath brushing against his skin.

God, he craved her.

"Are you sure?" he asked, wondering what the hell he'd do if she said no.

"Don't stop." The hoarse words traveled on a whisper.

He clasped her breast, and then glided his hand along her flat belly to the top of her jeans. He slid fingers under the waistband, taking pleasure when she sucked in her breath. He opened the snap with the flick of his fingers. He traced the top line of her panties, and her belly convulsed slightly as her breath hitched.

"I've dreamed about this," she whispered in his ear seconds before she nipped it with her teeth.

Screw the high road. Without another word, he pulled her toward his bedroom and backed her up toward the bed until her legs bumped against the edge. She sat and then lay back. Emotions pent up for too long raged and rushed the gates as he straddled her and pinned her arms above her head. He kissed her again, opening her lips with his tongue. She arched up toward him and captured his bottom lip gently in her teeth.

He grabbed the hem of her sweater and pulled it over her head, exposing full breasts peeking over the edge of a lace bra. He cupped each breast, kissed them, and sucked the tender skin.

A small whimper escaped her lips. "Best bad idea we've ever had."

He pushed down her pants, kneeling as he slowly slid them toward her ankles. She worked out one foot as he leaned forward and kissed her at her center before sliding her panties along her legs. He ran his calloused hands up her thighs. She hissed, and he felt the urgency tightening the muscles of her legs.

He unbuckled his belt as he kicked off his shoes and then shoved off his pants. He climbed back on top of her, his erection pressing against her belly. He leaned forward and kissed her stomach, her breasts, and then her lips as he pressed the tip of his erection against her moist center. She tilted her hips, beckoning him in. Desperate to claim her, he thrust inside her. She was so damn tight.

"You okay?" he rasped as he hesitated and waited for her to adjust to him.

"Yes."

For a moment, neither moved. He kissed her mouth and neck as her breasts rubbed against his chest. Slowly he moved in and out. Each time he thrust his hips, she opened more for him, growing wetter with each thrust.

She slid her hands to his ass and squeezed. "Harder," she whispered as she closed her eyes and tipped her head back.

"Look at me." His voice was sandpaper as he grabbed a handful of her long hair and pulled her head forward. This time he pushed harder, with greater urgency. "Look at me."

She opened her eyes and held his gaze.

He moved faster and faster, and she gripped him tighter, locking her legs around his waist. The desire rushed through them both, and as her moans grew louder, he felt the shudder of her orgasm. As much as he wanted to give into the pulsing need to release, he wanted to make this moment last. He didn't want it to end quickly. With an effort, he pulled out of her, savoring her whimper.

"Don't stop," she whispered.

"That's the last thought on my mind."

She moistened her lips, staring at him with doe eyes hazy with desire. He pushed her legs open, baring her before him, and took her clitoris in his mouth. She arched, threading her fingers in his hair.

He knew every spot on her body. Knew where to lick, kiss, or press to take her to the brink and then pull back. He teased her. Listened as her breath quickened, and when he thought she'd come, he raised his head to her breast and sucked. Again she whimpered, and he took a devilish pleasure in knowing he could make her so hot.

She smoothed her hands up his thighs and reached for his cock. She also hadn't forgotten how to push his buttons. When she wrapped her hands around his erection, his control slipped from his fingers.

He pulled free of her touch and pushed her legs wider. He drove into her again, this time not hesitating but pumping in and out with increasing speed. She arched, reached for her clit, and rubbed with one hand while she grabbed his ass with the other.

Jesus, she was so hot.

He rammed into her faster and faster. Her breathing grew quick and urgent until finally her body stiffened and her fingernails dug into his back as she orgasmed. He let go and came inside her, the wave shuddering violently through him.

For a moment he collapsed against her, burying his face in the crook of her neck. His heart hammered. Still inside her, he allowed the weight of his body to press her into the mattress. He'd fantasized about this for too long to let it go quickly. He didn't want this to end.

Finally, she smoothed a hand over him. Her gentle touch, no doubt meant as a dreamy kindness, burned along his skin as a reminder that this moment would soon be over. They'd dress. Leave this room. And the tension and distance would return. That was something he wasn't sure he could bear.

"Are you okay?" he asked, needing to hear her voice.

"Yes." She moistened her lips, her expression a mixture of satiety and embarrassment. "We should talk."

The talk. They'd used thousands of miles and silent reserve to fend it off for eight months. He sat up. "Sure. Talk."

She scooted up into a sitting position. She looked around for her clothes and hurried across the room to retrieve them. While he sat and watched her, she scooped her sweater up off the floor and pulled it on over her head. She tugged on her pants. "We've got to figure it out between us."

"What's there to figure?" He ran a hand over his short hair.

She pushed a long lock of hair from her eyes and wound her hair into a knot that fell around her shoulders as soon as she released it. He knew she hated wearing her hair loose, but he loved touching it when it hung free around her shoulders or skimmed the top of her breasts.

"I want the stuff that happens outside this room to work," she said.

"Why now? You didn't want it eight months ago."

She shook her head. "You're getting angry."

"I'm not." He shoved out a breath. He at least owed her the truth. "I am angry. At myself. I rushed us into this marriage, and that was a mistake."

"You didn't drag me kicking and screaming. I wanted it also."

"And you left it."

She fisted her fingers. "Because you shut me out."

He shoved his hands in his pockets. "I never pretended to be anything I wasn't."

"You were different in the beginning. We were happy. The Anderson case changed you."

He shook his head, knowing he couldn't blame all this on one case. "It brought to the surface what was always there. I've always been driven. I like catching bad guys. And as much as I'd like to tell you I want to be different, the truth is, I like my job. I'm good at it, and I hope to be locking up scum until my last days on this earth."

"I don't mind the long hours, the dedication it takes, but you made me feel like a stranger in my own home." Her voice cracked.

Her raw pain jabbed at him more than any anger she could hurl his way. He rose and crossed to his pants, yanking them over his legs. "That's on you, not me."

Her head dropped as if the fight abandoned her. "God, you're so damn hard to love. Why won't you let me just love you?"

Hearing the worry and shame in her voice stoked his frustration. He didn't know how to be anyone else. He didn't know how to be the person she needed. "What happened here doesn't change who I am. You need to hear that."

Tessa looked at him, her eyes filled with unspoken determination. "I don't buy that. I'm convinced we're good for each other."

He could still taste her on his lips. Smell that damn jasmine soap on her skin. And he wanted her more now than he did minutes ago. "You might be good for me, but I'm not good for you."

"That isn't true. And I'll prove it to you." She grabbed the rest of her clothes. "This isn't over, Dakota Sharp."

She made it to the doorway as she scooped up her purse, then she left the front door open and the file behind.

Sharp had followed her out of the bedroom and watched as she walked with a determined gait to her car and slid behind the wheel. He waited until her engine roared, her headlights clicked on, and her car left the curb.

He slammed the door. *"Shit."*

Grabbing his phone, he dialed. On the second ring a gruff trooper answered.

"This is Agent Sharp. I need you to keep an eye on a potential witness for me."

"Who?"

"Dr. Tessa McGowan. Can you put extra patrols around her work and home if I text you addresses?"

"Consider it done, Sharp."

"Thanks." He hung up and immediately sent Green the addresses. He might not be able to be the man she needed, but he sure as hell could keep her safe.

***

Elena swam through the haze, rising from the deep end of nothingness. Above, sunlight glistened, and she sensed if she kept pulling herself up, she would reach the surface and be able to take a deep breath. Just keep swimming. Keep pulling.

As the light grew brighter, she became aware of pain burning her face. The closer she moved toward the surface, the worse it became.

When Elena broke free, she could barely move her head because her face was so tender. Her lips and eyes were swollen, her cheeks stung, and her forehead and neck felt as if they had been scraped with sandpaper.

She tried to raise her hand but couldn't make her arms move. What the hell? She forced her eyes to focus on her fingers, only to realize her hands were strapped to the arms of the chair.

Lifting her head slightly, she felt the pull and crinkle of bandages on her face. God, what had happened to her?

Elena's gaze darted around the room, and she took in the simple white chair by her bed and the matching table across the room. No pictures. No windows. No sounds. No clue that told her where she'd been brought.

She tried to sit forward, but the movement sent agony slicing through her skull. She lowered gently back against the headrest. Panic rose inside her as bile crawled up her throat.

"Please," she whispered. "Someone, please help me?"

Had she been in an accident? Was she in a hospital? What had happened to her? Even as her mind cleared, her memory of what happened danced just out of reach. Tears welled in her eyes. It even hurt to cry.

Heart pounding, she twisted her hands in an attempt to free them from the bindings. The leather straps rubbed hard against her wrists. The left side didn't budge, but the right yielded slightly. If she could keep working on it, maybe she could get her hand free and find out what had happened.

On the other side of the door, footsteps sounded. Panic rising, she froze. Eyes wide open, she waited desperately to see who had restrained her.

When the door opened, the man smiled at her with an expression of surprise to find her awake. "I thought you'd be asleep at least another hour."

She paused, her lips protesting any movement. "What happened to me?"

He set down a small tray with what looked like soup and a smoothie. "You're fine," he said. "I don't want you to worry one bit."

Her vision was clearer now. And she could see that this man was tall and broad shouldered. "What happened?"

Brown eyes filled with genuine tenderness. "All that matters is you're going to be perfect."

Time folded in on itself. She couldn't remember what had brought her here. "Was I in an accident?"

He came beside her and took her left hand in his. Gently, he raised it to his lips and kissed her fingertips. "I don't want you to worry about what happened. Just know you're going to be fine. I'll see to it. I swear."

Her battered body and fogged mind succumbed to trusting him. He didn't look deranged. He sounded kind. His touch was gentle. "I can't remember anything."

"I know, sweetie. I know. It's the drugs. They often wipe the memory. Which in your case is for the best. Transitions aren't easy, and some experiences are best not remembered."

"Transition? Have I changed?"

He patted her hand. "You're fretting, and there's no need for it. I'm here. Let me feed you some of this soup. I made it just for you."

Despite the tug to trust, a dark fear curled in the pit of her stomach. Cradling the soup bowl, he ladled a spoon. "Be a good girl and open wide."

CHAPTER NINETEEN

Sunday, October 9, 1:00 p.m.

It took Andrews an hour in traffic to drive out to Douglas Knox's house located in the small town where Roger Benson had lived. This time of year, the tree-lined roads were exploding with yellow and orange, making this some of the prettiest country he'd seen in years.

He drove past million-dollar homes in gated communities sporting massive windows that took full advantage of the crystal waters of the lake.

Douglas Knox, former police chief and investigator on the Kara Benson case, had retired to a small brick rancher in an old lakefront neighborhood close to where Kara Benson's body had been found twelve years ago.

Andrews parked his Jeep behind an old red truck and took a moment to survey his surroundings before getting out of the car. He moved past the truck, noting the front seat was filled with a dozen fast-food wrappers and discarded paper coffee cups.

He made his way along an overgrown path to Knox's front door. The once-white paint trimming the windows had grayed and was peeling and popping in several places. He pressed the doorbell, but there was no chime or the approaching thud of footsteps. He then knocked on the door. From inside the house a television blared. He knocked again.

Finally, he heard footsteps and what sounded like a plate hitting the floor and a burst of curses. The door creaked open to a man well into his sixties. Thinning white hair hung over a rumpled plaid collar and framed a wan face. Stained pants and old athletic shoes finished off the look.

Andrews pulled off his sunglasses. "Douglas Knox?"

"That's right."

"I'm Garrett Andrews. I'm looking into the Kara Benson case for Agent Sharp."

The mention of the girl's name made the old man cringe. His right hand trembled as he raised it to rub his chin. "I gave the files to Sharp, hoping I could make it to my grave without hearing her name again."

"Why's that? I'd think you'd be willing to talk about the case and help us solve it."

He shook his head, his gaze growing distant. "I spent more hours than I want to remember thinking about that poor girl."

"I've read the files you gave Agent Sharp, and he has unearthed new details. Do you have a moment to discuss them?"

Knox curled arthritic fingers into a fist. Bloodshot eyes and the heavy scent of whiskey suggested the man had already had a few. "That case consumed me. I put everything I know in those files. You have the files, so you know what I do. I can't help you."

"Don't be so sure about that. I have questions. Let me ask them, and we'll see what you know."

Knox shook his head. "I'm tired of talking. And I don't see what good it'll do."

"You wouldn't have given the files to Agent Sharp unless you wanted the case solved."

"My memory isn't any good."

Deflecting the excuse, Andrews said, "I've spent the last couple of days going through every page in the boxes you provided, so I'm very familiar with the facts. I can jog your memory."

"All I know is in those files," Knox said as he wrapped gnarled hands around the doorknob and moved to close the door.

Andrews easily blocked the door with his foot. "I'm sure you can spare a little time." He attempted a smile, knowing there wasn't anything really friendly about it. "You did a hell of a job with all those notes. Don't quit on Kara Benson now."

Old eyes narrowed. "Who are you?"

"Garrett Andrews," he repeated. "I work for Shield Security."

A frown deepened the lines on Knox's face, but finally his shoulders slumped. He turned and moved into the house.

Andrews followed. The house was dimly lit. The center hallway dividing the long house in two was crammed with magazines and newspapers piled almost to the ceiling. Off the hallway was a larger room decorated in mauves and grays. A strong scent of mold permeated the room. The house would have been a total loss except for a large set of sliding glass doors that looked out onto a deck overlooking the lake. Andrews noticed the old man's recliner faced away from the view and toward a television.

Knox sat in the recliner and lowered the volume with a remote he clutched close to his chest. "Hurry up and ask your questions, young man. I got my television shows to get back to."

Andrews understood the psychology of interviewing. He knew he should sit. Try to build a rapport with Knox. But he'd never cared about playing nice. "Sharp said you attended Roger Benson's funeral on Monday."

Knox twisted a button on his shirt. "Seemed the least I could do."

"You two were friends before she died?"

Mary Burton

"We knew each other well enough to say hello on the street. But that was about it."

"And yet you spent years helping him with her case."

"Benson was devastated after Kara's death. Heartbreaking to see the tall and mighty brought to their knees."

Andrews pulled up a chair covered in magazines, which he set on the floor. He positioned the chair in front of Knox so they'd be eye level. He wanted to see the man's facial expression clearly. Ninety percent of communication was nonverbal. "You were one of the first officers at Kara's crime scene, correct?"

"Yeah. I was on duty. The scene still gives me nightmares."

"Was Kara Benson wearing makeup when you found her?"

The old man did a double take. "What?"

"Makeup."

"Why would you ask a question like that? Her crime scene pictures are in the files. What did you see?"

"The images are inconclusive. The photos are either out of focus or her face is turned. There is no clear view of her face."

"I never claimed to be a great photographer."

"So you took the pictures."

"Yeah, sure. Of all things, why care about the makeup?"

"Pictures were taken of her at the medical examiner's office. There are traces of heavy makeup on her hairline and on her lips and eyes."

"So?"

"According to the files, you were the first officer on scene. Is that true?"

"Yeah."

He watched the old man carefully. "Did you wipe the makeup from her face, Chief Knox?"

"Why would I do that?"

"You tell me. Why would you destroy evidence?"

230

He rubbed his chin covered in gray stubble. "Maybe I didn't want it getting around what she looked like. I knew more police were coming, and I'd hated the idea that it would get back to Roger and Adeline that their little girl died looking like a freak doll."

"Her face was made up to look like a doll?"

"Yeah, I guess that was what her face was supposed to look like. Nothing a parent needed to see."

Andrews sat back in the chair. "Do you remember talking to Diane Emery? She was a close friend of Kara's."

"If she was a friend, then I talked to her."

"She was found murdered days ago and dressed to look like a doll."

The old man's frown deepened, and his gaze dropped to his bent hands. For a long moment, he said nothing. "What are you saying?"

"That maybe you know a lot more about what happened to Kara Benson, but for whatever reason, you're hiding the truth."

Watery gray eyes met his. "Why would I do that? I spent years trying to find her killer."

"Or you spent years making sure no one else did." Andrews dangled the words as he would bait on a line. Never knew what you could catch with a statement or comment.

"That's a shitty thing to say. I worked for years on that case." He drained what remained in the cup by his chair. His brow knotted as he stared into the cup.

"The crime scene work was substandard."

"The day we found her, we were spread real thin. There'd been an arson fire in town, and one of my officers was burned trying to put it out. He ended up in the hospital with bad wounds. I wasn't really equipped to collect forensic evidence, but I was all we had. If any evidence was lost, misfiled, or compromised, you can lay it at my feet."

Andrews switched tactics. "Forgetting the evidence for a moment, what do you think happened to Kara Benson?"

Knox stared back into the empty mug. "Doesn't really matter what I think. It's what I could prove, and I couldn't pin the case on anyone."

"What are your theories?" He leaned in a fraction. "Every cop has theories. Whatever you say will remain confidential."

Knox pinched the bridge of his nose. "I'm all out of theories."

"You must have suspected someone, otherwise why would you give the files to Sharp?"

"He was the last in the family. Seemed fitting." The old man rose, stepped, stumbled, and then straightened himself. "Best you leave now, son. I'm not feeling so good."

"What are you hiding, Mr. Knox?"

"Not a damn thing."

"If Diane Emery was murdered by the same person that killed Kara, you are an accessory if you knew anything that would have solved Kara's case. You will not only have killed Diane, but you will be responsible for the death of another woman who is now missing. You remember Elena Hayes, don't you?"

"Elena is missing?"

"She is."

The pain in Knox's eyes was raw and brimming with regret. For a moment, it took Andrews aback because he saw the same eyes looking back at him in the mirror each morning when he shaved.

"What are you hiding, Chief Knox?"

"I gave you all my files."

Andrews understood how past mistakes often turned into festering wounds for anyone with a soul. "I'm an expert at hiding secrets, which makes me an expert at spotting yours."

Knox's lips flattened. He trembled as he raised his unshaven chin. "I don't have more information to share."

"Talk to me, Chief Knox."

"I'm not the chief anymore."

"Once a cop, always a cop."

"No. I stopped being a cop a long time ago." He pointed a finger at Andrews. "And the only one who needs to hear my sins is the Almighty himself." He opened the front door, letting in a cool gust of wind.

Andrews stared at the old man. Then taking a pen from his pocket and a slip of paper from a small notebook, he wrote down his number. "Call me if you change your mind."

He didn't accept the slip of paper. "I won't be calling."

Andrews laid the paper on a table stacked with bills and advertising flyers near the entryway before he walked to his car. The front door slammed hard. He turned and looked back at the house, certain Knox knew so much more than he was telling.

***

The fading scent of Tessa's jasmine soap still clung to Sharp's skin when his phone rang, cutting into the silence. Turning from his computer, he checked the phone's display: Vargas.

"Sharp," he said.

"You sound like anything but."

He pinched the bridge of his nose, in no mood for humor. "What do you have?"

"I finally received a call from Veronica Hayes, Elena's sister. I'd left her three voice mails since we started looking for Elena, but nothing. Veronica just returned from Mexico. Seems her beach house didn't have cell service. Anyway, Veronica insists it's not uncommon for Elena to turn her cell off when she's on vacation."

"That's not what Elena's office said."

"That's why I wanted to talk to Veronica in person."

"When?"

"An hour from now."

He checked his watch. "Text me the address, and I'll meet you there."

"Will do." She hung up and seconds later her text message arrived.

An hour later he pulled up in front of Veronica Hayes's Church Hill townhome. It was on a cobblestone street at the top of historic Libby Hill, one of the highest points in Richmond. Bright sun shone on the grassy now-vacant park near Hayes's house. Below, the James River meandered around a bend past the business center on the north bank, and on the south side, the industrial section. He looked upriver toward the Manchester Bridge, knowing Tessa's place was nearby.

The rev of an engine had him turning to find Vargas shoehorning a car into a parallel spot with only inches to spare on either end. She took one last gulp from a to-go cup and got out of the car, locking it behind her.

"Some view," she said, barely glancing toward the river.

"It is." He turned away.

"I've been thinking about Veronica's Mexican vacation. Can you imagine six days on a beach without your cell? Too much bliss to imagine."

"The sun is bad for you."

She laughed. "Since when do we worry about what's bad for us?"

"Maybe we should start."

She paused. "You're kidding, right?"

"No."

"Damn. What has gotten into you?"

"I'm fine."

She cocked her head. "It's Tessa."

He didn't speak.

She laughed. "How hard the mighty do fall."

Ignoring her, he climbed the brick steps of Hayes's town house. "What was Veronica's reaction when you spoke to her?"

"She's understandably upset."

He understood that kind of pain. He wondered if Veronica would handle it better than he had with Kara. "Let's hope she has information about Elena to share."

They walked up the wide brick steps past wrought iron pillars toward a black lacquered door with a tarnished door knocker. Vargas knocked.

Seconds passed, but they heard no sound. She knocked again and still no sound. She reached for her phone. "She said she'd be here."

Sharp leaned to the right and looked inside the floor-to-ceiling window. He saw a flicker of movement in a back room. "Someone's in there."

Vargas knocked again, and this time unsteady footsteps moved toward the door.

A fit and toned woman with long dark hair opened the door. In her late twenties, she bore a slight resemblance to her sister. Whereas Elena's face was angled and lean, Veronica's was round. She was attractive, but compared to her sister, would have been described as plain. She wore jeans and a sleeveless blouse that revealed a cuff tattoo on a honey-tanned right bicep.

"Ms. Hayes, we're with the police. I'm Julia Vargas. We spoke on the phone. And this gentleman is Agent Sharp, also with the Virginia State Police."

"Please, come inside."

Veronica guided them through the center hallway of the house to the back kitchen, which offered a panoramic view of the river. The kitchen had been renovated to include marble countertops, pendant lights, and professional-grade appliances. French doors opened out onto a deck. Prime real estate coupled with top-notch renovation equaled big money.

"I've just brewed a strong pot of coffee," Veronica said. "Can I get you a cup?"

"No, thank you," Sharp said.

Vargas shook her head.

"If you don't mind me having a cup? Jet lag is kicking my ass," Veronica said.

"Sure, go ahead," Vargas said.

"When's the last time you saw your sister?" Sharp's impatience clipped his tone.

She grabbed a white cup from the cupboard and filled it with coffee. Sipped. "Last week, before I went to Cabo. She looked fine."

"As I said on the phone, she's not answering her phone," Vargas said. "And she's not at her apartment."

"When you called, Agent Vargas, I got worried, so I've been calling her cell. She's not answering. But I never panic unless it's been more than a few days. Like I said, she's a free spirit."

"Her office is worried about her," Vargas said. "She was supposed to call in daily."

"Elena's boss is a workaholic who doesn't sleep. He panics if he can't reach her in five minutes. She probably turned off her phone to teach him a lesson. She asked for a raise, and he didn't give it to her."

"Her office manager thought she went to the beach. Does that sound right?" Sharp asked.

"She might have told them that, but she's likely at our parents' lake house. She knows she won't get a surprise visit from her boss if he doesn't know where she's staying. The house is about thirty minutes north of Richmond."

"When's the last time you were up there?" Sharp asked.

"It's been a while. Elena loved it, but I never liked the place."

"Why?" Sharp asked.

"There isn't much to do up there. No nightlife. Once you tanned for a day or two, there's not much else. And that whole area gives me the creeps."

"Why?" Vargas asked.

"A girl died up there when I was in high school. Elena and I are the ones who found her body."

Sharp stood still, barely breathing. "Is that the Benson girl?"

"Yes. Elena and I were out for a morning jog a few days after she vanished. We were the ones that found her."

"Tessa McGowan mentioned that. I wasn't sure she'd remembered correctly given her accident."

"Yeah, she was pretty messed up. But she's right."

"Tell me about that."

"I was a junior in high school and had joined the cross-country team. I needed to get my run in, and Elena said she'd go with me. We were about two miles from the cottage when we saw a shoe in the road. We stopped, and there was a smell." She inhaled as if remembering the scent. "We never went into the woods, but we could see her clearly from the road."

His gut twisted. "Where was she?"

"She was leaning against a tree. We knew Kara's parents were worried and had been searching for her. My sister recognized Kara's outfit. She was still wearing her red Halloween dress. We called the police right away."

"Do you remember who responded to the call?" Sharp asked.

"The police chief himself. He tried to look in control, like he could handle it, but when he came back out of the woods, he was pale and his hands were shaking."

"You've a good memory," Vargas said.

"One of those moments in life when time stops and the details sharpen," Veronica said.

"The police chief called for backup?" Sharp asked.

"I suppose. He was on the phone with someone, and he looked like he was arguing."

"Did you catch what he said?"

"No. Sorry. After he got off the phone, he told us to go home and he would talk to us later."

"Did he talk to you later?"

"Yeah. But it was after the funeral."

"Was that conversation two or three days after the funeral?"

"Three days."

"Did you notice any other details about the body?" Sharp asked.

"Yeah. She looked like a monster out of a horror show. Elena really freaked out. I guess it was the weird makeup. Why all the questions about that case?"

Sharp kept his voice calm. "She was wearing makeup?"

"Yeah. A lot of it. Very weird."

"What was weird about it?"

"She was made up like a doll. Elena said it didn't make sense. Kara had not looked like that when they were at the Halloween party."

Sharp pulled out the picture taken of the four girls. "Two of these girls are now dead. Kara and Diane."

"Diane Emery is dead?"

"Yes. And now we can't find Elena."

Veronica's face paled. "I'll drive up to the lake house and tell Elena myself to call you."

"Give me the address," Sharp said. "I'll go up there."

Veronica shook her head. "You're scaring me."

"You should be scared," Sharp said. "We need to find your sister."

After Veronica wrote down the address, Sharp left the house, needing to get outside and breathe fresh air. *A monster out of a horror show.* The words sucker-punched him.

Vargas caught up to him as walked down the steps. "Where are you going?" she asked in a hoarse whisper.

"I'm driving up to Elena's lake house right now. I'll keep you posted."

"Roger that."

As he slid behind the wheel, his phone rang. "Andrews."

"I visited Douglas Knox today."

"And?"

"He's hiding key information."

"I know. Elena Hayes's sister confirmed that Kara's face had been made up."

"Knox said if he did wipe makeup off your sister's face, it was to protect your stepfather's and mother's feelings. I don't believe him."

"I'm on my way toward the lake to try and find Elena. I'll talk to Knox."

***

Douglas Knox sat alone in his home. For the first time in years, he'd turned his chair toward the windows and stared out at the still waters of the lake. The full moon dripped light over water so peaceful and so serene. It would be easy to believe this was a place of goodness.

He glanced in his lap at the revolver. Lifting it, he clicked open the chamber and made sure it was fully loaded. He snapped it closed and cradled it close to his chest as he glanced at the note he'd written. The quickly scrawled words were paltry. *I'm sorry. I should have done more.*

The creak of floorboards had him turning. Death stood silhouetted in the hallway. He came more and more often these days. Knox had been afraid at first but not so much anymore.

"What are you doing here?" Knox asked.

"Came to check on you. You didn't look so good the other day. I worry about you."

Knox coughed. "I never look good. I'm dying."

Death knelt beside his chair and carefully took the gun and inspected it. "I heard."

Knox stared at Death, wishing he'd end it all for him now. To do what he didn't have the courage to do. "News travels fast."

"Small town."

"What do you want?"

Death opened the revolver's chamber, then clicked it closed. "What did you give Sharp?"

"I gave him the files I collected during my investigation of his sister's death."

"Why?"

Knox leaned closer, staring into Death's cold eyes. "The guy is smart. He'll figure out what happened to Kara."

Death rose, tucked the gun in his waistband, and sat beside Knox. He pulled a syringe from his coat pocket. Gently, he pushed up Knox's sleeve and searched for a vein.

"What are you doing?"

"You know what I'm doing. I'm giving you your freedom."

Knox's heart kicked up a notch as he thought about dying. He'd been too afraid to live all these years and oddly was now afraid of letting go.

Weak thin blue veins threaded up his arms, which Death poked and prodded. Finally, Death found one vein plump enough to work.

"I let you down," Knox said.

"You didn't."

Knox let his head drop back against his chair. "I tried to help you, but everything I did for you failed."

"Time to release all those thoughts."

He wanted release, but didn't have the courage to do it himself. He was tired. And ready to face whatever fate his maker had planned for him.

Death slid the needle into Knox's arm with such tenderness, he barely felt more than a slight pinch. Slowly, Death pushed the plunger until the warmth spread through his old body, giving him a temporary boost.

"Thank you," Knox said.

Death patted him on the arm. "We've known each other a long time. We've got to look out for each other."

Knox's vision blurred. And seconds later, he stopped breathing.

***

It took Sharp less than a half hour to reach the lakefront community north of Richmond. He showed his badge at the security entrance to the development and drove up to the lake house. It was a massive home full of windows and wide porches to take maximum advantage of the view. Roger once had a friend with a home on this lake, and he had brought Kara and his mother up here often. They'd loved it.

He parked in the circular driveway and walked along the brick path to the front door. Sharp knocked, but he didn't get an answer. He looked under the flowerpot for the key Veronica had mentioned. Inside the house, he flipped on the lights. The house was utterly still, and he sensed no one had been there for months. He did a systematic search of all the rooms, but he did not find any signs that Elena had been here. For a long moment he stood in silence, tapping his finger against his belt.

Back in his car, he called Vargas and confirmed there was no sign of Elena in the house. As he reached the main road, he turned toward Knox's house.

Time he and the old man had a chat.

He reached the small rancher lit by a single light in the front window. When he approached the front door, he knocked. He tried the doorbell. No sound in the house. "Mr. Knox."

Silence.

He tried the door and found it unlocked. He opened it. "Mr. Knox!"

The hair on the back of his neck rose. He clicked on a light and drew his weapon. Papers and magazines were stacked high in the hallway. There were dozens of pizza cartons. The place smelled of rot and mold.

He moved slowly, checking left and right as he reached the center room overlooking the lake.

The back of a worn recliner patched in several places with duct tape faced the water. The stacks around the chair had toppled, suggesting the chair had been recently moved.

The air in the room grew heavier, and the worry in the pit of his stomach gnawed like a rat. Bracing, he came around the recliner and found Knox slumped back, a .35 in his lap, clutched loosely in his right hand.

Knox lay in his chair, his jaw slack, his heavily lidded eyes staring blankly into the air. Sharp approached the man and touched fingers to his neck. There was no pulse, but his skin was still warm. He was dead. Next to his body on the cluttered nightstand was a scrawled note. It read, *I'm sorry. I should have done more.*

CHAPTER TWENTY

Sunday, October 9, 7:00 p.m.

Tessa arrived at the home of Douglas Knox along with Jerry in the medical examiner's van. The residence was lit up with flashing lights from three squad cars.

"This is a lot of cops," Jerry said.

Tessa grabbed her kit. "He was a chief of police at one time. Always strikes a nerve with cops when one of their own dies."

"Right."

Out of the van, Jerry unloaded the stretcher from the bay. Tessa set her kit in the center and pulled on latex gloves, and the two pushed the stretcher toward the front door, where a state police trooper stood.

Tessa held up her identification badge. "Medical examiner's office."

He glanced at the tag. "Go on in, Dr. McGowan."

One step in the front door and she realized it wouldn't be easy to get past all the stacks and clutter. "Tight fit."

"I've been through worse."

They edged the stretcher past the piles, at one point catching several stacks of newspapers with the back wheel. In the center room, she saw the forensic tech shooting pictures of a recliner facing the lake.

"Dr. McGowan." Dakota's voice cut through her thoughts, making her stand a little straighter.

She tucked a loose strand of hair behind her ear. "Agent. I understand this is a possible overdose."

His gaze held hers a beat. "No signs of trauma on the body, but there's a note beside it that reads, 'I'm sorry. I should have done more.'"

"Let's have a look." She moved around him toward the front of the recliner and hesitated a beat when she saw the note. Her gaze shifted to the man's right shirtsleeve. The button was unfastened, whereas the left cuff was hooked. Rigor mortis had yet to set in, indicating he'd been dead less than an hour or two.

She pushed up the sleeve and saw the small pinprick at the bend in his arm. "Did you find a syringe?"

"No."

"You checked behind him, in the seat cushions, and on the floor?"

"I did. Nothing."

"Let's have a look in his bedroom and medicine cabinet first," Jerry said. "We might find it there."

"I looked there," Dakota said. "But you might see something I missed."

When someone died, their home often gave clues to the cause of death. Drugs, high-fat foods, too many prescription meds, and alcohol were all predictors of death. It was a short list, but they made up 90 percent of the cases.

She wanted to find the syringe, which could prove he'd done this to himself.

In Knox's bedroom, they discovered the bed quilt was rumpled but made, and judging by its looks, hadn't been slept in for weeks. On the nightstand was a collection of pill bottles, including medications for his heart, diabetes, and his thyroid. Another set of pills helped him sleep.

"Guy was a walking pharmacy." She pulled out her pad from her kit and catalogued the medications.

"All this would support an overdose."

There were more prescription pills in the bathroom as well as a dozen over-the-counter cold and pain medications. In the kitchen she discovered a dozen frozen meals that had been cooked and their half-eaten containers tossed in the trash. Also in the trash were two large empty whiskey bottles. But no syringe.

"So what do you think?" The question came from Dakota, who stood at the kitchen door.

"I want to have a look at the body again," Tessa said.

She moved past him and stood in front of Knox. Again her gaze was drawn to the right arm. She touched the mark. "Every detail about this guy suggests he wasn't doing well. This needle mark is fresh. He could have injected himself, disposed of the needle, and sat back in his recliner to die." She straightened and studied the disheveled mess around him. "But why worry about being tidy at this stage? Why not just sit in his favorite recliner, inject, and let it randomly fall?"

"Do you think someone killed him?" Dakota asked.

"I don't know. But it bothers me we don't have a syringe. We'll have to run tox screens to see what's still in his body."

Dakota stood behind her, his body radiating energy. She looked at him. His jaw tensed, and his right hand was clenched at his side as he stared at the body. "Are you okay?"

"I'm fine." He nodded toward the door. "Outside. Please."

"Sure."

She followed, and when they were away from the house, he said, "I interviewed Veronica Hayes this afternoon, and she thought Elena was staying at her family lake house. She wasn't. Elena is still not answering her cell."

Tessa glanced around to make sure no one could hear her. "Do you think this killer has taken her?"

"Yes. Veronica said Kara was wearing heavy makeup. Knox told Andrews if he cleaned her face, it was to protect my mother and step-father." His abrupt cadence hinted at his frustration over compromised evidence at his sister's crime scene. "Veronica said he didn't call for backup right away and he was arguing with someone on the phone."

"Knox might have known who killed Kara?"

"That's exactly what I think. At Roger's funeral, I believe he had an attack of conscience." He shook his head. "Knox had been friends with Roger for years, and all that time he withheld critical information that could have solved Kara's case."

"Who would he be protecting?"

"I wish I knew. But he gave me those files for a reason. I'm convinced now the answer is buried in them. I'm seeing Andrews early in the morning."

"I can come along if it'll help."

"Not necessary."

"Dakota," Tessa said, dropping her voice. "If I can help, I will."

His gaze held hers. "If I need your help, I'll call."

***

Elena opened her eyes. Her mind pulled out of the hazy fog again, and she struggled free of the confusion muddling her thoughts and distorting past and present into an unrecognizable twist. Her blurred vision cleared. The room was windowless, but it was not the same room she'd been in before. A dim light in the corner cast a warm, soothing glow. At first she thought it was a hospital room, but then she saw the large mirror in the corner and the four-poster bed. She blinked and tried to raise her hands to her head. They were still fastened to the chair with large leather straps.

"What the hell?" Her voice sounded harsh, foreign. She breathed in and out, shaking off more of the heavy drugged haze from before.

How had she gotten here? It wasn't an accident. This wasn't a hospital. *Think, Elena. Think!*

Her mind tumbled back through the darkness, and she remembered the man. He was attractive and smiling. She'd seen him before. He'd been around her building weeks ago taking pictures. She'd thought he was another art student from the university taking photos of the train tracks running by her apartment building, which had once been a tobacco warehouse. When she'd seen him the second time, she'd noticed he wasn't carrying a camera. And he'd spoken to her. She'd smiled. And then there'd been the bite of electricity. Her mind swirled. Her legs tumbled.

Now as her gaze swept the room, she felt the steady burn of pain on her face. Panic flared hot in her belly. What the hell was he doing to her?

She twisted her hands in the straps, trying to work free. Her right hand was double-jointed, and the strap still had a little play in it. If she concentrated, she could push her thumb out of joint and pull her hand free. It had been a party trick as a kid. A sure way to make her mother pale and her friends watch in shock as she popped it in and out of its socket.

She closed her eyes. Tried to calm her racing heart. But the sleep swirled around her like a dark fog threatening to wash over her body. She drifted and nearly answered the siren's call when she caught herself.

"No! I can't sleep." She knew in her gut sleep meant death.

Drawing in a breath, she pushed her thumb against the leather strap as hard as she could. At first she felt no movement. So gritting her teeth, she pushed harder until the thumb slid out of the joint with a pop. Pain shot up her arm.

Wincing, she tugged against the strap. On the first pull the leather grabbed her hand and aggravated the pain in her thumb. Biting her lip, she yanked hard. Pain cut up her arm, but this time her hand slid free of the leather. She pressed her thumb against her thigh, shoving it back in place.

Wiggling her fingers, she quickly went to work on the second strap. She tugged at the leather and the silver buckle, scraping her fingernails against the metal. She heard a rip and a snap. Outside the door sounded the rattle of keys. Her heart jumped and she yanked madly on the strap, but it would not give.

Then the door opened, and in the light stood her captor. She couldn't see his face as he stared at her for a long moment.

"I can see you've been up to some mischief, haven't you, Harmony? I knew you'd be a hard one to control. That's why I didn't stray too far."

He came in the room, closing the door and locking it behind him. He set a tray of food on a table and came around the chair to reach for her free hand.

In a desperate attempt, she jerked her other hand hard, felt the stitching of her restraint stretch, and pulled free. Driven by adrenaline, she balled up her fist and drove it right into her tormentor's throat. The blow stunned him and forced a sharp intake of breath as he stepped back. The moment was long enough for her to scramble off the chair. She wobbled, turned, and ran for the door. It was locked. Frantically, she fumbled with the lock until it clicked open. A twist of the knob and the door opened. Relief collided with fear and the desperate need to run and get away.

Out in the hallway in the dark, she ran blindly, her heart jabbing so hard against her rib cage, she thought bone would crack.

"Harmony! No. This is dangerous. You need to rest and heal."

Her breathing came harder and faster, and she pulled at the bandages on her face, so desperate to have them off, her nails scraping her tender face. Wherever her fingers clawed, her skin burned. *God, what has he done to me?*

She spotted a door at the end of the hallway but stumbled to her knees before scrambling back to her feet. She closed the distance to the door. Trembling fingers wrapped around the knob. She twisted, and nearly wept when she discovered it was unlocked. She pushed it open. Cool air and a cloudless night sky greeted her. She stepped outside, gravel biting into her bare feet. She ran, unmindful of the pain. Ahead, she saw a stand of trees and thought desperately that if she could get to the woods, she could hide.

Behind her, she heard an anguished wail that forced her to glance over her shoulder. Footsteps followed and a flashlight clicked on.

"Harmony, don't leave me. Not yet. You aren't finished."

She didn't want to know what *finished* meant. Stones cut into her bare feet as she made her way toward the woods. Beyond the trees she saw lights. *God, someone help me!* She tripped and nearly fell before catching herself as she approached the stand of trees. Her heart pounded in her ears, her lungs ached, but she believed she would get free of this madman.

Just as she reached the first trees, strong arms grabbed her by the hand and yanked her back. She bumped backward against a hard chest as arms banded around her waist. He whirled her around and punched her in the gut, cutting off her air and silencing a scream.

He supported her sagging weight as he whispered, "This is very naughty of you, Harmony."

Tears stung her eyes as she tried to pry the iron hold open with her fingers. "No."

Shadows darkened his face. "You aren't going anywhere, Harmony."

Elena's fingers balled into a fist and she swung wildly, connecting with his nose. He grunted in pain.

He grabbed her wrists and twisted her arms painfully behind her back. "Don't make me hurt you. I don't like to hurt you." He dragged her several steps forward into the beam of moonlight and stared at her torn bandages and damaged skin. "You've ruined my work, you selfish little bitch."

She spit into his face. "What work? What have you done to me?"

Grabbing her chin, he turned her head from right to left. "What have you done to yourself? I've spent hours working on you. Days!"

She tried to break free and kick him. "Fuck you!"

His hands slid from her arms to her neck as he dragged her into the shadows. Strong fingers tightened around her delicate neck as he squeezed. She grabbed at his face, tried to push him away, but he tightened his hold. Her breath caught, and soon her lungs screamed for air.

Her vision blurred, and she became light-headed. "Stop. Let me go."

"You've made me angry, Harmony. You've been rude and ungrateful."

Her legs gave way, and he lowered her to the ground, squeezing harder with each whimper. "Please." She didn't recognize her voice. It sounded distant, lost, and desperate.

He straddled her, locking his knees around her ribs and sitting on her midsection. "Harmony, I was ready to give it all to you. But you're an ungrateful doll."

Those were the last words she heard.

CHAPTER
TWENTY-ONE

Monday, October 10, 8:00 a.m.

Sharp arrived at the office of Shield Security after fighting rush-hour traffic clogging I-95 between Richmond and Washington. He showed his identification to the guard at the front gate and then to a second guard inside the building. "They're expecting you, Agent Sharp. Take the elevator to the fifth floor."

"Thanks."

His heels clicked at a determined pace as he crossed the polished floor and punched the elevator button. The ride to the fifth floor took mere seconds. The doors opened to a frowning Garrett Andrews.

"You're late," Andrews said.

"Traffic."

"What do you have?"

"I want to hear everything you've learned from Knox's files and your interview with him. He died last night."

Andrews showed no expression. "How?"

"Looks like an overdose," Sharp said. "He left a note that said, 'I'm sorry. I should have done more.'"

"Interesting."

"Why?"

"As I mentioned, I asked him basic questions about your sister's investigation, and he wouldn't answer me," Andrews said. "He said the day she was found, he was short staffed because there'd been an arson incident that day. And as I told you, he also suggested he wiped her face clean before other officers arrived."

"Do you think he was protecting someone other than Roger and my mother?"

"Yes. I think he knew who killed your sister or at least who was responsible for her death, and he covered it up." Andrews absently rubbed the back of his hand. "According to my searches, Knox came to the area from Denver. He was married, divorced, and he has two daughters. He also had a son who drowned when the boy was twelve. Neither Knox's wife nor the daughters joined him when he moved to Virginia. After he served for ten years as police chief, the city council voted him out of office. Local newspapers reported he was furious at the ouster. He applied for his private investigator's license and for the next eight years did work ranging from insurance company fraud to cheating spouses. His biggest client was Roger Benson."

"Knox stayed close to Roger Benson, who lost a child while Knox was chief of police. Maybe he felt a bond with Roger because each lost a child."

"Maybe. Or maybe Knox wanted to keep a close eye on the investigation." Andrews opened the door to his lab and moved to his computer. "Odd that Kara, Diane, and now Knox died of overdoses. Maybe whoever he was protecting turned on him." He pressed several buttons, and the picture of Kara, Diane, Elena, and Tessa appeared on the large screen.

Andrews enlarged the image with the swipe of his finger. "As I said, Knox mentioned an arson case the day your sister was found. Said it was a confusing, chaotic day. In fact, I found evidence from that arson case in your sister's file."

"Papers get misfiled."

"I believe there's more to it than misfiling. I'd like you to get a copy of that arson case file. I don't think the papers were misfiled but put there intentionally. A trail of bread crumbs, if you like."

"Leading to?"

"Evidence. I want to see if evidence from your sister's case is in the arson file."

"Interesting."

"I believe Knox had a key piece of evidence and for whatever reason couldn't destroy it, so he hid it." He handed Sharp a printout listing six case files. "I'd also like to see these case files. They are arson cases that have occurred in your hometown area in the last twenty years."

"Why these?"

"I suspect our killer blows off steam lighting fires."

Sharp reached for his phone and within minutes located a contact in the town's police department. "I need these files pulled now." He rattled off the date Kara was found as well as the six other case files. "Look up the date. There will be an arson case that day. Call me back when you have the files, and I'll send a trooper to get them today." When the clerk on the other end hesitated and made an excuse about workloads, Sharp gripped his phone tighter. His tone was tight, ripe with anger. "I'm sending someone by today. Be ready." After a rushed promise to find the records, the clerk hung up. He texted Riley and informed her of the situation. She agreed to pick up and deliver the files to Andrews.

Sharp glanced at the image on the big screen. "Can you search for any other cases similar to Kara and Diane's and perhaps Elena's? If we are dealing with the same killer, I'd bet money he's been honing his skills on other women."

"Skilled tattooing takes practice," Andrews said. "Who knows, he might also have set a few fires around the times of other murders."

"Exactly."

"I'd also like you to consider exhumation."

"What?" Sharp said.

"I've been reading your updates on the Diane Richardson case. You said there was a doll found in the trash behind her apartment, and there was also a doll left at Elena Hayes's home."

"Right."

"There was no evidence of a doll found at Kara's crime scene."

Tension banded up Sharp's back. "Correct."

"I believe this killer has evolved considerably in the last dozen years. But as much as his skills have improved, I believe leaving the doll is a kind of signature for him that might have begun with your sister."

"You think he put something in her casket?"

"We won't know unless we exhume her body."

"Jesus, Andrews."

Andrews didn't speak.

"Let me think about it."

**

The modest funeral home was located on the south side of town a block from the railroad tracks and six blocks from Terrance Dillon's home. Sharp parked in the back of the lot and got out of his car.

Inside the funeral home, gentle music played over hidden speakers, which he supposed was intended to soothe the grieving. In an unseen room, wheels squeaked, and he imagined a casket being positioned. He thought about his sister. His mother. Roger.

Sharp shrugged his shoulders and tugged at the corners of his cuffs, already wishing he could leave this place. He hated the idea of digging up Kara's coffin, but he couldn't ignore Andrews's logic. If she held the key to catching this killer in her coffin, he'd start proceedings today.

He followed the carpeted hallway to the placard marked "Office." He knocked and found Norman DeLuca in a dark suit standing behind the receptionist desk, arranging name cards.

DeLuca looked up. "Agent Sharp. Good to see you. Still working on the Terrance Dillon case?"

"I'm looking into another case."

"How may I help you, Agent Sharp?"

He fished around for the right words. "I came about my sister, Kara."

"Kara Benson? She's not been with us for a long time."

Not with us. It sounded too polite. "I want to know about the final moments before her casket was sealed."

"What do you mean?"

"Who was there? Did anyone put any item in the casket with her?" He thought about the dolls left at Diane's and Elena's homes.

"It's been twelve years. I would have to check our files for any items inventoried."

"Can you do that now?"

DeLuca glanced at his watch. "I've new clients arriving soon, but I think I can do this." He motioned Sharp toward a computer, and he pressed a few keys before the name *Benson* came on the screen. "Her final clothing selection was a white lace dress. She wore a heart-shaped necklace and a bracelet with her name on it."

Both pieces were favorites of hers. He'd given Kara both the necklace and bracelet. "Anything else in the casket?"

"There was a doll."

"A doll?"

"Yes. I personally placed it beside her just before her funeral."

"Who gave it to you?"

"After your parents left, a young girl came into the viewing room and gave it to me. She said your mother wanted it left with your sister. The doll apparently had been Kara's."

No. That wasn't right. His sister wouldn't have wanted anything like that. "Who was the girl?"

"A friend of the family, I suppose. I didn't recognize her. I didn't question the girl. I hope I didn't offend your family," Mr. DeLuca said.

It was the killer's signature. He was likely at the funeral. "Do you have a list of the people who signed the guest book?"

"I have a scan of it in our computer files. Would you like a printout?"

"Yes."

More keys tapped. The printer hummed.

DeLuca inspected the pages, then handed them to Sharp.

"Never pleasant when a young one leaves us. We try to help, but it's never easy."

"Thank you."

"You didn't say why the doll mattered."

Because the fucking killer wanted it there. "I'm not sure it really does. Just struck me as odd."

"Why?"

"Kara wasn't a fan of dolls."

"Maybe she was, and you didn't know it."

Sharp meticulously tucked the pages in his notebook. "You might be right. Thank you again, Mr. DeLuca."

"Of course. Return any time you have a question."

On the way out, he glanced at the upcoming services and caught the name *Terrance Raymond Dillon*. "The Dillon funeral is going to be held here?"

"Tomorrow at ten."

Sharp moved to a side table and picked up a flyer. He stared at the paper, the feelings of regret and anger weighing heavy. "And the expenses were covered."

"It's all taken care of," he said.

"By who?"

"The community. A crowdfunding account was set up, and it grew quickly. What it doesn't cover, I will."

"Do you do that often?"

"Sometimes. Mrs. Jones is asking in lieu of flowers that donations be made to the Terrance Dillon scholarship fund at his high school."

"Good to know. Thank you."

"Will you be attending tomorrow?"

"I will."

"Would you like me to reserve a seat for you? It's going to be crowded."

"No." He forced a smile. "Thank you. I can fend for myself."

"See you tomorrow."

In his car, he called McLean, his one friend who'd attended Kara's funeral. McLean picked up on the second ring. "What's up?"

Sharp reached for his cigarettes. "You attended Kara's funeral."

Silence hung heavy between them. "I did."

Sharp cleared his throat. "Did you see her?"

"I didn't mean to, but yes, I saw her. I arrived late to the funeral home. The door to her viewing room was still open. I think Roger and your mother had just left."

"Was she holding a doll?"

"Man, I don't know. I could barely focus on her."

"Did you see anyone else around her?"

"I heard footsteps outside the door, so I left and went to stand in the back of the chapel."

"Okay. Thanks."

"Why you asking about this?"

"Just chasing a lead. We'll talk later."

"Yeah, sure. Anything you need."

Sharp hung up and immediately lit his cigarette.

He watched as a couple walked hand in hand into the funeral home. The woman was crying, and the man looked like he was barely holding up.

If the killer had attended Kara's funeral and had killed Dillon, there was a possibility he would attend this funeral as well.

***

Douglas Knox's autopsy took less than three hours. Dr. Kincaid performed the grim duty with Tessa assisting. There was no sign of external trauma to the body, other than the needle mark in his arm. Dr. Kincaid ordered a full tox screen.

"Let's have a look internally," Dr. Kincaid said.

Though the crime scene suggested this might have been murder, Tessa knew the medical examiner could not rule out natural causes.

Dr. Kincaid made a Y incision and soon had the old man's chest open. She removed the rib cage, and they got their first look at his heart. It was a colored muscle twice its normal size.

"He would have been dead within the year," Tessa said. "I'm not surprised, given all the heart medication in his medicine chest."

"It was a miracle he was able to function at all," Kincaid said. "I understand he left a note."

"Yes. All it said was, 'I'm sorry. I should have done more.'"

"Sorry for what?"

"He didn't say."

"What was the date of his last prescription?"

"He had a half-dozen prescriptions refilled two days ago."

"Fills his meds and then kills himself." She shook her head. "I've seen this before. He was screwing up his courage."

Dr. Kincaid examined Knox's vital organs, discovering several others were also close to failure.

They were just finishing the autopsy and closing up the body when Dakota arrived. His gaze raked over Tessa, and her skin prickled as energy snapped through her body.

"Agent Sharp," Dr. Kincaid said. "I'm ruling Douglas Knox's death undetermined until I get the tox screen back. Then I'll make a final determination."

Nodding, he approached the table. "When will that be?"

"A few weeks."

He glanced at the clock. "Do you have a heavy docket today?"

Kincaid stripped off her gloves as Jerry wheeled away the body. "Several hours to go, but Dr. McGowan is free."

"Good," he said, without giving Tessa a chance to comment. "Dr. Kincaid, there is a chance I may have to have my sister's body exhumed."

Tessa's throat tightened with emotion, and she didn't trust herself to speak. She understood the logic but knew it must be tearing Dakota up.

Dr. Kincaid nodded. "If you decide to proceed, Dr. McGowan and I will be on hand and will take good care of her."

"Thank you. I hope it's not necessary."

"Keep me posted," Dr. Kincaid said.

Tessa followed him into the hallway.

Sharp stopped a few feet past the doors and turned to her. "I'm headed back to Shield Security. I have a list from the funeral home detailing all the people at Kara's funeral. I've sent scans to Andrews at Shield, and he's already analyzed it. I'd like you to tag along. You were there. And you knew the players in town."

"And if I can't remember, I can call Holly. I just need to change."

"Right."

"Give me ten minutes."

He checked his watch. "I'll meet you in the lobby."

Fifteen minutes later Tessa stepped off the elevators and found Dakota pacing. "Sorry. Got a call from the lab. Had to take it."

"No problem. Are you hungry? Need to eat?"

"No."

"Let's go."

He was parked across the street, and she hurried to match his long strides. She slid into the passenger seat and snapped her seat belt in place.

His computer sat between them. In the backseat was a box filled with active investigation case files. It was neat and organized. She'd kidded him once about his organization in both his car and apartment. He'd attributed it to the marines, said he'd picked up habits he doubted he'd ever shake. The faint hint of cigarette smoke told her he was stressed.

When he settled behind the wheel, she was aware of the breadth of his shoulders. The cut of his jaw. The way his fingers wrapped around the gearshift when he put the car in drive and pulled out of the space.

"The funeral director said there was a doll in Kara's coffin."

She twisted in her seat and faced him. "Say again?"

"According to the funeral director, a little girl brought the doll to him and told him Kara's mother wanted it laid beside her."

"Why would this killer ask a child to give the doll to the funeral director?"

"The doll seems to be his calling card. The child was a way to deliver the doll without him being noticed."

"Why would the killer attend her funeral?"

"Killers go to funerals for a variety of reasons. Guilt, remorse, a perverse need to relive the murder. That's why I want to go over the list of those in attendance."

"Assuming the killer would have bothered to sign the register."

"If he showed, had the doll put in the casket, I'd bet money he couldn't resist signing the log and not even use an alias. He'd want a lasting memento of his presence."

"Jesus."

"Yeah." He tightened his grip on the steering wheel. "Andrews suggested an exhumation."

"God, Dakota."

They drove in silence as Dakota cut through traffic at speeds frightening to most people. She'd forgotten how fast he drove, but now as before, she didn't worry. He'd always maintained an utter sense of control.

"About what happened yesterday morning." She needed him to hear this. "If it happened again, I wouldn't be sorry." She settled back in her seat. "In fact, I'm planning on it happening again."

He glanced at her, the sunlight splashing across her face. "You don't know what you're saying."

For the first time in a year, she felt a sense of calm. "I know exactly what I'm saying."

He didn't utter a word for the final fifteen minutes of the drive. They pulled up to the front gate of Shield Security. Dakota showed both their identifications and told the guard they were meeting Garrett Andrews.

In the lobby, a large, muscled man was waiting for them. He wore black slacks and a black turtleneck that covered most of his neck and arms, but she saw the faint scarring on his left hand and on the left side of his neck. He'd been badly burned.

As he approached, Andrews's cool blue gaze didn't show a hint of welcome or emotion. "Agent Sharp. Dr. McGowan, correct?"

"Yes," she said, extending her hand.

Without hesitation, he accepted it in a firm grip.

"Welcome," he said.

She sensed he'd read a book on politeness and was ticking through bullet points. "Thank you, Mr. Andrews."

Andrews guided them toward a bank of elevators, and when they were inside, he pressed the top floor. The computer expert made no effort at small talk, and Dakota, who had never mastered the skill, didn't attempt it either.

When the doors opened, they followed Andrews along a carpeted hallway to a state-of-the-art computer lab. "I've cross-checked names of attendees you sent with a database," Andrews said.

"And?" Dakota asked.

"Two of the men had a prison record. Larceny, drugs, no charges involving sexual assault or any predictors suggesting an escalation to murder."

"Women are also capable of killing."

"Agreed," Andrews said. "So I had a look at anyone who might have had a mental-health issue."

"That kind of information is now classified by the HIPAA law. How can you access this?" Tessa asked.

Andrews stared blankly at her. "If it's connected to a computer, I can get to it."

Judging by the equipment in the room, she had no doubt he had the digital world at his fingertips. "Good to know," she said.

"What about people who were there and are now showing up during the course of this investigation?" Dakota asked.

"Diane, Elena, and I were there." Tessa scanned the list shown on the large display screen. "Stanford Madison was there."

"Madison?" Dakota said.

Andrews tapped computer keys. "I didn't see his name."

"He has a distinctive signature," Tessa said. "It's unreadable."

Andrews pressed more keys and blew up the list. "It must be this one."

She looked at the elaborate scroll swirling over what looked like mountain peaks. "That's it. It's how he signs his work. It's supposed to be an *S* and *M*."

"He was earning his master's in art at the school you attended, correct?" Andrews asked.

"Yes," Tessa said.

"Until a few days ago, Madison was preparing for an art show," Dakota said. "After I paid him a visit, he tossed all his work in the trash and vanished. I've got a BOLO out on him."

"Interesting," Andrews said.

"He also knew my sister, as well as Tessa and Diane," Dakota added.

"It sure shines a bright light on him, doesn't it?" Andrews said.

"The evidence pointing to Madison feels heavy-handed," Tessa said.

Andrews nodded. "If I wanted to frame someone, he would be the perfect choice."

"You think he's being framed?" Dakota challenged.

"I think it's important to keep an open mind and not get tunnel vision based on personal bias," Andrews countered.

"He's crawled under a rock and is planning his next move."

Andrews shrugged. "Give me his basic data. I'll search for him."

"How?" Tessa asked.

"Most of us leave a digital trail. If he has one, I'll find him."

"There have been no hits on his credit card," Dakota said.

Andrews absently rubbed the back of his hand. "Let me look. Anyone else you remember from the event that struck you as odd, Dr. McGowan?"

"I remember very little. I was still recovering after the accident and was moving slow," she said.

"Given Sharp's theory about the Dillon boy's connection to Diane Richardson's death, it's logical to assume the boy's killer would be present at his funeral. Will you be attending his funeral?" Andrews asked.

"Yes," Dakota said. "It's tomorrow at ten at DeLuca's Funeral Home."

"Send me the guest book as soon as the funeral is finished," Andrews said. "I want to cross-check."

"Assuming the killer signed the book before," Tessa said.

"He signed it," Dakota added. "This guy has displayed his work twice, and he wants credit for it. I'd bet money he derives satisfaction watching a roomful of people mourn the person he killed. It's his version of an art exhibit."

"That's so demented," Tessa said.

"No argument there," Dakota said.

"I've also scanned for crimes involving facial tattoos and women," Andrews said.

"Any hits?" Tessa asked.

"None yet," Andrews said. "But it's only been a few hours. I'll keep you posted."

He stared at Tessa a moment, then shifted topics. "I dug deeper into Knox's past since we last spoke. His son who drowned had a juvenile record. Knox did a good job of covering up his son's troubles, but I was able to access records. The kid liked to set fires."

"Fires," Dakota said. "What did the Knox kid set fire to?"

"Trash cans in his backyard. But what landed the kid in real trouble was a fire in his neighbor's backyard. Incinerated a toolshed filled with gasoline and the neighbor's dog. Caused quite an explosion. Knox paid the damages, lost the police report, and that was the end of the matter. The boy drowned a month later." Andrews handed Dakota a file. "A copy of the arson file."

"I won't ask how you got this," Dakota said.

"Wise."

Tessa and Dakota thanked Andrews and made their way back to the car. On the return trip, neither spoke. She thought about the two women she'd known who had died senselessly and knew Dakota well enough to know he was processing the case. When Dakota pulled up beside her car, she hesitated before getting out.

"It's what you do when you're quiet for long stretches," she said to him. "You're looking at the puzzle pieces."

"Yes."

"I always felt like I was intruding when you'd get quiet. I felt shut out."

He faced her. "You were always my anchor. I didn't have a right to expect that of you, but you reminded me there was more than the work."

"You have every right to expect that of me. I am your wife." She shook her head. "You always looked annoyed when I tried to speak to you. I thought I was doing something wrong."

A smile quirked the edges of his lips. "I've been told that I always look annoyed."

"You do." She smiled. "Though it does make you look kind of sexy."

His dark gaze held hers, but she didn't move toward him. Again, it was up to her to bridge the gap. Fine. She'd keep reaching out until he understood she wasn't going anywhere.

Unhooking her seat belt, she leaned in and kissed him on the lips. Watching her, he didn't pull away but didn't kiss her back. Why did he always make it so difficult? She leaned into the kiss and nipped his lip with her teeth. A growl rumbled in his chest, and he deepened the kiss as he wove his fingers into the curled strands of her hair. She could feel the emotions racing toward the surface as the kiss grew in intensity.

The car radio squawked and broke her concentration. As if sensing her thoughts, he said, "The job will always be there. There will always be puzzle pieces to assemble."

"I know. I can handle it."

He pulled his fingers from her hair. "I don't want you to handle it. You deserve better."

"I want you."

He straightened. "We couldn't hack it for an entire year."

"I've tried life with you and without you. I like it better with you."

He shook his head, and getting out of the car, walked around to her side. He opened the door. For a moment she didn't move, then she grabbed her purse and slid out. He stood stone straight. The shields were back in place.

She fished her keys from her purse and opened her car door with the click of a button. "I'm not giving up on you, Agent."

He closed his passenger door and turned toward her as she sat behind the wheel.

She lowered her window. "You think you're tough." Her smile wasn't bitter or sad, but knowing. "But I'm tougher. See you soon."

She started the engine, and as she pulled out of the parking space, she glanced in the rearview mirror. He hadn't moved. Good.

***

Sharp couldn't sit behind his desk after speaking with Tessa. He was jacked up with nervous energy and thoughts of her. If he let her back into his life and she left again, what the hell would he do? When his phone rang, he was grateful for the distraction. "Agent Sharp."

"Andrews. Your friend Madison has surfaced. He's back at his studio. Electricity usage has spiked."

"Not very creative."

"We're all creatures of habit."

"True."

"Keep me posted."

"Will do."

A coldness settled over the fire in his belly as he returned to the man's studio, where he could see light seeping out from a back room. "We're all creatures of habit," he muttered, repeating Andrews's words.

He parked and strode up to the side door. He banged his fist against the door, standing to the side as he waited. At first, silence, so he banged louder. Finally, there were footsteps.

The door snapped open to a disheveled Madison, who immediately tried to slam the door. Sharp blocked it with his foot. "We need to talk."

"I don't want to talk to you." The thick scent of bourbon wafted from Madison's breath. "Jesus, can't you give me a break? I'm in mourning here."

Madison rubbed long fingers over the thickening stubble on his chin. His shoulders slumped and he stepped aside, allowing Sharp to enter before walking back to the small room.

Sharp closed the door. "I've been looking for you."

"Why? You delivered your news. Leave me in peace."

"You lied to me. You told me you broke it off with Diane."

"I did."

"Then why were you stalking her?"

Anguish deepened the lines around his eyes. "I wasn't stalking her. I just wanted to talk to her. Tell her I was sorry."

"I watched the surveillance tapes from the camera next to Diane's front porch. You showed up at her house at least twice."

Madison rubbed his forehead with trembling fingers. "I was having second thoughts."

"Why'd you throw away all your paintings?"

He crumpled into a chair. "I couldn't look at her. Jesus, her eyes seemed to follow me. Haunted me. I couldn't take it. I kept thinking if I'd stayed with her, she'd still be alive."

"How long were you two together?"

"We met in college, but then lost touch. We met again two years ago at one of my art openings. She came to say hi. Said she recognized my name. We were together a couple of years. She was my muse. The woman gave me inspiration. But as my workload increased, she began to resent it. She started making demands on my time. I resented her getting in the way of my work, so I broke it off."

"But you moved to Richmond a couple of months ago. Why break up and then move to her city?"

"It didn't take long for me to realize the breakup was a mistake. Without her, I couldn't work. I wanted to make it right between us. I thought I could save our relationship."

"Her mother says Diane was the one that broke it off."

"Diane's mother didn't like the idea of me as a possible son-in-law in the first place. And then to have me break up with her daughter, well, she was embarrassed. But the old woman did her best to poison Diane against me. The harder I tried to win Diane back, the more she seemed to resent me."

"It must have been frustrating trying to apologize and then have her refuse you."

"I was so sure she'd take me back eventually. And when she didn't, I couldn't eat or sleep. It was terrible."

"Did her rejection make you angry?"

"Sure, it made me angry."

"Were you mad enough to kill her?"

Bloodshot eyes rose to Sharp. "God, no!"

Sharp scrolled through the images on his phone and showed the picture of Diane's face to him. "Someone did a number on her face. It's what an angry man might do to a woman who's rejected him."

Tears welled in his eyes. "Jesus, that's Diane?"

"It is."

Tears streamed along his face as he looked away. "I would never hurt her. Never."

"You've been in the city for the last two months. You had the opportunity."

"I couldn't have done that to her, and I wasn't here the entire two months. I was in Florida for two weeks."

"When?"

"I left about three weeks ago and only returned last week."

"You could have left her locked in a room with food and water."

"I wouldn't do that!" he shouted.

"What do you know about Kara Benson?" Sharp asked, shifting directions.

"Kara?" He slowly shook his head. "She and I went out a couple of times in college."

"Do you remember what happened to her?"

"She overdosed."

"Were you at her funeral?"

"Yeah. She was in one of my classes, and it was a small community."

"Do you remember the last time you saw Kara?"

Madison shook his head. "What does Kara have to do with Diane?"

He ignored the question. "When was the last time you saw Kara?"

"The night of the Halloween party. She was there with Diane and Tessa."

"I understand you caused a fight between Kara and Tessa?"

"I might have stirred it up between them, but it wasn't that big a deal."

"It was a big enough deal for Tessa to leave the party distracted enough to get hit by a car. It was enough of a big deal for Kara to leave the party alone and end up with the guy who fed her the pills that killed her."

"What the hell? I didn't have any connection to that. I was young and trying to hook up."

"Do you remember what Tessa, Elena, and Diane were wearing at the Halloween party?"

"Sure. Doll costumes."

"What did you think about the outfits?"

"I don't understand."

"Sure you do. How did they look to you?"

"Sexy as hell. Half the guys at the party couldn't stop looking at them."

Sharp flexed the fingers of his right hand. "Do you have a fetish for dolls?"

Madison rose, his gaze hardening with a survivor's glint. "Do you have any solid evidence connecting me to Diane's murder?"

"Not yet. But I'd like a DNA sample from you."

Madison shook his head. "Cops get DNA samples from suspects."

Sharp considered reaching for his cuffs but knew the instant he detained Madison, he'd have to read him his Miranda rights, and the whole dynamics of this interaction would change. "They also use DNA to weed out the innocent. I'm looking for a killer, and I need to keep my focus on the target."

"You mean me?"

"DNA will rule you out."

Madison balled up his fists. "I'm not some fucking monster!"

"I'm not arresting you. I'm asking you to come to the station with me and answer a few questions. I need help solving this case."

Madison shook his head. "I'll meet you downtown as soon as I get ahold of my attorney."

Sharp chewed on two or three choice words before nodding. "I'll wait while you call."

***

When Tessa didn't come home by seven as the Dollmaker had expected, he backtracked to her office, where he found her car. Her routine was still new and remained unpredictable, so it was important he kept a close eye on her so he could figure out her pattern. Watching and planning for his next doll offered him a thrill as tantalizing as the transformation process.

He sat for another thirty minutes, waiting and watching. To calm his nerves, he dug a small sketchbook from his glove box and sketched her face. At first he drew her as she was. Pretty, in an ordinary sort of way. And then he reimagined her new face on the opposite page. He made her face appear more round. He thinned and arched the brows. He stippled her cheeks with freckles. Transformed her lips into a heart shape. She would be so pretty. He was rock hard with anticipation.

When the office door opened and she exited, he closed the book and sat straighter. A breeze teased her hair as she walked toward her car. So beautiful. So sweet.

He reached for the handle of his door, wondering if he could make some kind of contact with her. He wouldn't take her now. He would just talk to her. Say hello. He was sure she wouldn't be afraid of him. Just then, a city police patrol car pulled up. She waved to the officer, who remained stationed near her car while she got into her vehicle and locked the door.

Annoyance bubbled before he chased it away. He could yield to frustration, or he could simply focus on the prize. He'd get his Serenity soon. Very soon.

CHAPTER
TWENTY-TWO

Tuesday, October 11, 9:30 a.m.

It had been a frustrating night with Madison. The man had lawyered up immediately and was released within the hour. Madison had refused to answer any questions or give DNA. However, Sharp had given him coffee in a paper cup, and when Madison left it behind, Sharp had collected it and sent it for testing. He'd know within a day or two if the DNA was a match.

Now Sharp stood outside the funeral home staring at the large collection of mourners. Terrance Raymond Dillon had been eighteen, but the loss of his life touched hundreds of people. Today's showing was far different than Roger's final send-off.

He watched countless mourners stream into the simple building. He didn't always make it to the funerals of his homicide victims, but when they were young, he did his best to attend. He was here searching for a killer, and he was also saying good-bye again to Kara.

As he stepped on the curb, he spotted Tessa. She wore her hair loose around her shoulders. *Dress-up hair,* as she'd once said. Her dress was simple and black, but it skimmed her slim body, reminding him of how much he enjoyed her shape. Dark heels, another rarity for her, made her long legs look even more beautiful. She stood with her hands tightly clasping her purse. Dark glasses covered her eyes.

"What are you doing here?" he asked.

"You said you were going to be here, and I wanted to come as well." She checked her watch. "I knew you'd be early."

He glanced around to make sure no one was listening and lowered his voice as he took her elbow in hand. "You used to lecture me about coming to these. Said it wasn't healthy."

"Well, now I'm not lecturing. Now I'm walking a mile in your shoes and am here to lend my powers of observation. I'm all eyes and ears, Agent Sharp."

"You don't need to be here."

Her smile was bright. "Well, let's go inside."

He muttered a curse.

"Who should I be looking for?" she asked, already scanning the crowd.

He guided her toward the door. "You don't look for anyone. That's my job."

"Today, it's also my job."

She'd never been one to argue, but when she dug in her heels, no amount of persuasion made her change course. She was back in his life. And like it or not, seemed determined to stay. "Focus on the funeral."

Tessa drew in a breath. "What was it you said? Killers return out of genuine grief, and some also want to savor the pain they've caused."

"Something like that." He pulled off his sunglasses. "I found Madison."

"Where?"

"He went back to his own place."

"Is he under arrest?"

"His attorney arrived about an hour after he did at the station. He's out now. But not before he accepted a cup of coffee and drank from it."

"You have his DNA?"

"I do."

"You should have results in days."

Sharp shook his head. "Looking forward to it."

They passed a thick hedge of shrubs and entered a vestibule carpeted in rich, soothing green. Organ music drifted from the main parlor already filled with several hundred people. At the front of the room was a polished cherry casket outfitted with shiny brass filigree and handles.

Sharp had made a donation to the online crowdfunding account for the funeral. Judging by the flowers and the other frills, many others had done the same. Beside the casket was an enlarged version of Terrance Dillon's senior high school picture, likely shot over the summer in anticipation that he would graduate next spring. Under a blue cap and gown, he grinned.

Tessa grew still as she stared at the photo. "He looks even younger in the picture than he did in my office."

"Yeah."

The organist began to play "Amazing Grace," and the audience stood to sing. Sharp and Tessa couldn't find a seat and ended up standing against the parlor's back wall. There were few hymnals left, but a woman sitting in front of Tessa handed over hers. Tessa nudged the book toward Sharp, and he accepted his half. She sang as he watched the group.

Tessa's voice was clear and bright; he had to focus hard on his job and not stare at her. He'd forgotten how angelic her voice sounded. She'd been shy about singing and often only sang when she thought she was alone.

The memorial ran longer than most. There were several people to eulogize the boy. His coach. An uncle. His pastor, kids from the high school, teachers, and friends. All spoke of a highly motivated and fun-loving kid who dreamed of college and his future. The one noticeable absence was Jimmy Dillon, who'd been denied permission to leave jail under guard to attend.

The last song ended and Tessa took the book, closing it softly and tucking it in a pew.

"Let's go outside. I want to watch them leave," he said.

Without thinking, he took her hand and guided her through the growing crowd of people. Her fingers wrapped around his, and he struggled to breathe. The more he touched her, the more he missed her. He found an alcove off to the left, just inside the main doors. They stood there and watched.

"Everyone looks so upset," Tessa said. "I know death is emotional. But I've grown used to dealing with the clinical side of it."

"This side is definitely messier."

A young girl hurried past them, her hands crushing tissues and trembling as tears streamed down her cheeks. The girl vanished into the ladies' room.

"I think I need to duck into the ladies' room. She looks upset."

"Good idea."

Tessa followed through the restroom door. As Sharp stood by the wall, he flexed his fingers. Almost pleading for something to happen. More mourners streamed out. Several young men about Terrance's age huddled in a group by the door. He recognized Ronnie and Garcia.

Sharp walked over to them. "Hey, fellas," he said. "Agent Sharp with the Virginia State Police."

"What are you doing here?" Ronnie said. "Doesn't make sense cops would be here."

"I want to find out who killed Terrance," he said simply. "Talk to the people who knew him."

"Ain't no one going to find out," Garcia said. "He was knifed in an alley. Shit happens."

Ronnie curled his fingers into fists. Light-colored eyes flamed with anger. "Fuck the *shit happens*, Garcia. Terrance was the real deal. He was a solid guy."

"I've only heard good things about the kid," Sharp said.

The young men looked from side to side as if they were embarrassed to be seen with Sharp.

"When's the last time you saw Terrance?" He often asked the same question twice. The truth was easy enough to recall, whereas lies weren't as easy to track.

"Friday night at the last game. He was all excited about seeing his girl," Ronnie said.

"You said before he didn't have a girlfriend," Sharp said.

"Nice going," Garcia said.

"Why does it matter now?" Ronnie countered. He looked at Sharp.

"We promised Terrance we wouldn't tell," Garcia said.

Ronnie shook his head. "We weren't supposed to tell when Terrance was alive. Now he's dead." He looked at Sharp. "Terrance got back together with his girlfriend, Stephanie. He didn't want his grandmother to know because she was so worried about him getting the scholarship."

Garcia shook his head. "Then the dumb bastard got himself killed. Ain't no reason for a guy to be in an alley in the city unless he's selling drugs."

"He was eighteen, Garcia," Sharp said. "When I was eighteen, I did a few stupid things. I'm lucky to be alive."

The boys didn't speak.

"Where's Stephanie?" Sharp asked.

"She just ran into the bathroom crying," Ronnie said.

"Thanks."

"You really want to find this killer?" Ronnie asked.

"More than anything," Sharp said.

Both boys nodded. As they filed out of the funeral home, he caught sight of Tessa, who stood with a young girl by the ladies' room. Her gaze locked on his, and she motioned for him to come over.

He weaved through the crowds. The girl beside Tessa was petite, not more than seventeen. She had sandy-brown hair skimming her shoulders. Pale skin made the flush in her cheeks all the brighter.

"Agent, this is Stephanie White. She and Terrance were dating."

The girl looked up at Sharp but didn't make eye contact with him. Tessa wrapped her arm around the girl's shoulder. "It's okay. I know he looks like he could bite, but he won't."

Sharp eased back a bit and did his best to smile.

Tessa shot him a look as if to point out he still didn't look approachable.

He cleared his throat. "I'm sorry for your loss, Stephanie. I really am."

"He was a good guy." Stephanie twisted a tissue in her hands until it was a tight spiral around her index finger.

"That's what everyone is saying." A sigh shuddered through him. "Stephanie, I'm here to get any kind of lead on the guy who stabbed Terrance, but I can't do it without your help."

She glanced up, her watery gaze so full of loss.

"I think Terrance made a delivery on Sunday night," Stephanie said. "He recognized someone he wasn't supposed to, and it got him killed."

Tessa tightened her hold on the girl and whispered in her ear. The tissue in her hands tore in half.

"He texted me. At first I didn't recognize the number. But he said it was Terrance."

"What did he say?"

"That his ride had arrived."

"What time was this?"

"Near midnight on Sunday night." She shook her head. "I texted him right back, but he didn't respond. I told him to leave. That whatever Jimmy had gotten him into was bad."

"You knew his father was in town?"

"Terrance told me Jimmy started writing him, but he made me swear not to tell his grandmother. Mrs. Jones hates Jimmy."

"What was his last text to you?"

"'White van here. Got to go.'"

White van. Like the vehicle cruising around Diane's town house.

"We never found any phone. Do you still have the text?"

"Yes." She dug the phone out of her purse and showed him the number.

Sharp wrote it down. "And he's never used this number before?"

"No." She lowered the phone back in her purse. "Terrance was a great guy. He wouldn't have hurt anyone."

Tessa handed her more tissues. "You did a great job, Stephanie."

He handed her a card and a pen. "Write your number on the back. When I find this killer, you'll be one of my first calls."

With a trembling hand she wrote out her information and handed it back. He gave her a fresh business card. "Call me if you think of anything else?"

She studied his name, her shoulders straightening with resolve. "I will."

Stephanie looked up at Tessa. "Thank you."

"You also have my number. Call if you need me."

Nodding, she walked toward the front door. When she was out of sight, Sharp said, "Thanks. I don't think she would have talked to me if not for you."

"Can you blame her?"

He glanced at her, not sure if she was annoyed or not. "I'll admit I'm not the most approachable."

Laughter sparked in her gaze, and then she sobered. "Given what you do on a day-to-day basis, it doesn't surprise me that you're so distant and angry. How do you do this year after year?"

"Someone has to give a shit. And I like what I do."

She intertwined her fingers with his again, sending ripples of energy shooting through him. "I really get that now."

"Do you?"

"Yeah."

Saying she understood the demands of the job was far different from living with it. They'd tried that once and failed.

"The inventory reports I read stated there was no phone in Terrance's belongings," Tessa said.

"I think the killer took it."

"You'll trace the number?"

"Andrews can, and with any luck it'll lead us to this guy."

***

The Dollmaker stood outside the church, watching the swarm of mourners who piled into their cars and lined up behind the long black hearse for the short trip to the cemetery.

He was surprised to see Serenity here. She didn't know Terrance, but when he saw her approach that cop, he knew she had come here for him. Tessa was a sweet, sweet woman and out of a deep sense of loyalty was trying to fix her life with this cop. But it wasn't fixable. They didn't belong together. She just didn't know it yet.

She belonged with him.

"Damn you, Harmony. You shouldn't have run. You shouldn't have been afraid. If you'd been patient, Serenity would have joined us, and the three of us could have been a family."

He blamed himself for Harmony's escape. For Terrance's death. Both deaths were examples of his overconfidence. He'd planned this all so well, but he'd not allowed for mistakes. And he'd made two serious ones.

But no more mistakes could be tolerated. With the cop asking questions about his dolls, he had no choice.

He had another doll to make.

***

When Sharp received the text from Andrews requesting a meeting, he agreed immediately. Andrews played his cards close to the chest. Sharp arrived at the Shield offices just before one in the afternoon. He flashed his badge at the two guard stations and rode the elevator to the fifth floor, where he was escorted to the computer lab. Andrews sat behind a collection of screens, each with different images. The man seemed lost in thought.

Sharp cleared his throat. "Andrews."

Andrews stared at a screen before finally turning around. "Let me buzz Bowman. He wants to hear my debrief."

"Sure."

Andrews dialed a number on his phone console, relayed Sharp's arrival, and replaced the receiver. "Bowman's on his way."

"I didn't realize he'd taken a personal interest in this case."

"Bowman and Shield both hate cold cases. I briefed them both on our earlier case discussion."

"So why am I here?"

"There's more data to consider."

Before he could ask, the door opened and Bowman crossed to shake Sharp's hand. His grip was firm and his gaze cutting and direct. "Thanks for coming, Agent Sharp."

"I should be the one thanking you for taking on the case," Sharp said.

"It's been a month since the Shark case closed. I've already got an itch to close another. Andrews, fill Agent Sharp in on what you've found."

"As you know, I planned to search all cold cases that might be linked to your sister's as well as Diane Richardson's case. I fed all the details into national and international databases." He reached for the clicker of the overhead projector.

Bowman shook his head. "We don't need to see Kara Benson's crime scene photos."

Sharp raised his chin. "Don't change your methods on my behalf."

Andrews reached for his clicker. "I'm going to show you the faces of three women found in three US cities over the last eight years. They were spread across the western part of the country and were prostitutes. Authorities weren't overly concerned about solving their cases. I also did a computer search of all the media outlets for murdered women made out to look like dolls."

Andrews clicked on the overhead. Sharp studied the screen. The women were all young, and each wore makeup resembling a doll as well as a wig. "One of the local media outlets in Denver quoted a detective's briefing. He called this killer the Dollmaker, as you have, for obvious reasons. I did some digging into the case files of the three women. As I said, one victim was in Denver, one in Salt Lake City, and the third in Colorado Springs. There's nearly no paperwork on the women's backgrounds or forensic data from the cases. Two of the three women weren't found for three weeks. These women lived on the margins. It took months for anyone to file missing persons reports on any of them."

Sharp moved closer to the screen. "Were there any suspects in any of the cases?"

"A local drug dealer in Denver came under scrutiny in one case," Andrews said. "He not only had his hand in prostitution and strip clubs, but he had an affinity for young girls. But he was cleared."

"Cleared or he hired a good attorney who got the charges dropped?"

"Good attorney who got the charges dropped. But this suspect was shot and killed last year in a nightclub fight."

"Were there any other similar murders matching this killer's MO?" Sharp asked.

"I checked the FBI database and didn't see any other crimes that matched the criteria. Doesn't mean they didn't occur."

"How did he keep them immobile?" Sharp asked.

"There were multiple needle marks on their arms. I think he dosed them often with heroin."

"He chose the most vulnerable, and he picked areas where he was less likely to be caught."

"What about victims before Kara?" Sharp asked.

"There were no similar cases that came up in my search engines predating her death."

"Do you think she was his first?"

"I would say so. I would guess seeing Kara with friends dressed up as dolls flipped a switch in the killer. Many aspects of her death suggest a lack of planning. But whatever payoff he got when he killed her has spurred him to kill more."

"He's a professional now," Bowman said. "He won't stop."

"He doesn't want to be caught," Sharp said. He thought about Madison's tears and shaky hands when he'd pressed him at the studio. Some killers were eaten up with remorse and left clues for the police, subconsciously hoping they'd be stopped. Not this guy. "But if this is the same killer, he's now choosing women who are going to be missed. Why the switch?"

"I'd say confidence," Bowman said. "A bigger stage for his exhibit."

"I believe this guy is local," Andrews said. "He thought he could make a drug buy in the city that would remain anonymous. Dumb luck lands him face-to-face with a local kid. Just as I believe dumb luck put your sister in his path twelve years ago."

Bowman cleared his throat. "What do you know about your sister's last days?"

"We spoke on the phone a couple of weeks before she went missing. It was during the first days of her freshman year. She talked a lot, but I only processed about a quarter of what she said. She was like that. Talked a mile a minute." How many times had he replayed that last conversation?

Andrews rolled a pencil over his fingers like a majorette would a baton. "Let's get back to the boy who was stabbed to death. Assuming he knew the killer and recognized him, who could he have seen? Did he know Stanford Madison?"

"I haven't come up with a connection yet," Sharp said. "I should have his DNA back tomorrow and will know if he's our guy or not."

"Riley Tatum dropped off the twelve-year-old arson file," Andrews said. "In it was a note indicating there were three DNA samples in the county's climate-controlled storage attached to the Kara Benson file. I'd like to test those."

Sharp considered what Andrews was suggesting. "Knox hid the DNA from Kara's case in the arson file. For whatever reason, he didn't destroy it."

"That's my theory. That's why the arson case report was mingled in with her case. Why Knox mentioned the case to you." Andrews folded his arms. "As I said, Knox's trail of bread crumbs could lead to the truth. Knox didn't want the killer revealed, but he wanted to hang on to the evidence just in case."

"Leverage. He wanted leverage against the killer," Sharp said.

"Knox made a point of giving you these files, which tells me he wanted the killer found," Bowman said.

"The timing explains the motive for killing himself," Andrews said. "The truth is coming out."

The words *I'm sorry* scrawled in Knox's final note rattled in Sharp's head.

"Who would he want to protect so badly?" Bowman asked.

"When Kara died, the man had no family in the area. His son was dead. Roger said Knox was isolated the last dozen years." Sharp shook his head. "Roger thought Knox's withdrawal from the world indicated he was troubled by Kara's death. Roger saw Knox as a kindred spirit."

"The Knox boy's case is bothering me," Andrews said. "I dug further. The boy's body was never found. A funeral was held for him, and there's a grave marker in Denver, but there's no body in the coffin."

"You think the kid is alive?" Sharp asked.

Andrews nodded. "It's a working theory at this point."

"So he creates a new identity for the kid."

"A man like him would know how to do it," Andrews said.

"All these years, that bastard was Roger's friend," Sharp growled.

"What better way to control any subsequent investigations into Kara's case than to do it yourself," Bowman said.

"Tessa is retesting the sample located in the official Kara Benson file," Sharp said.

"I'd wager the results won't be different from the last time," Andrews said. "It's the new samples that matter. The ones filed with the arson case."

"Get the sample to us," Bowman said. "We can move faster than the state, and we'll have an answer by the end of tomorrow."

Likely a court would not accept a DNA sample misfiled over a dozen years ago, but it could help to zero in on the target. Sharp would worry about making his case stick later. "Right. Thank you."

"If your sister's case and this new case are connected by DNA, then this would be the one place where the Dollmaker has repeated his kills," Andrews said. "By the way, those numbers you sent me for Terrance Dillon. Neither the burner or his personal cell is online, but if and when either does show up, I'll pinpoint it within minutes."

What had Knox said? *Keep an open mind.*

***

The registered letter was waiting for Sharp when he arrived home. It was from Roger's attorney. Tearing it open with his thumb, he unlocked the front door and nudged it open with his foot. He flipped on lights, dropped his keys on the kitchen counter, and shrugged off his coat. The letter was simple, direct. He was Roger's sole heir. What remained of the estate, namely the lake house, was his. "Shit. I don't want this."

He opened his refrigerator and pulled out a beer, twisting the top and taking a long pull. The doorbell rang. He set the beer aside and put his hand on his weapon, moving toward the door. A glance through the peephole. Tessa.

He closed his eyes, relieved and worried all at once. He snapped open the door. "What are you doing here?"

She held up a bag filled with Chinese food. "I brought food, which I'll trade only if you tell me how it went today at Shield." Smiling, she pushed past him and walked straight toward the kitchen, where she unpacked the cartons. "I want to know all about it."

"It's been a long day, Tessa. I'm not in the mood to talk."

"Déjà vu. I'm not buying it," she said, laughing.

His response had been the theme of their marriage. Her begging him to talk, him too spent to talk. Now she wasn't begging. "Yeah."

"Tell me about Shield, we'll eat, and when we're finished, I'll clean up and leave. You were never good at eating when you were working." She set her bag on the counter and slid off her jacket.

"You put protein bars in my jacket pocket. They tasted like cardboard."

She unpacked the small white boxes along with a couple of sodas. "But it kept you going. Just like letting off a little steam and talking will do the same."

He unfastened his cuffs and rolled up his sleeves. "Yeah."

She unpacked plastic forks and handed him one. "The beef is still your favorite, right?"

He accepted the carton. "Yes."

She unwrapped a fork. "Eat up."

She settled on a bar stool and dug her fork into a bucket of vegetables. For a moment, he didn't know what to say, so he ate.

Finally he said, "I just received a letter from Roger's attorney. Roger left me his lake house."

She jabbed her fork in the half-eaten dish and left it there. "Wow. That's got to feel weird."

"I don't want the house."

"Then sell it. Donate the money, if it makes you feel better. Set up a scholarship in Kara's name. But before you do any of that, remember that you were all Roger had left, and he wanted you to have what was his."

"Roger and I didn't get along."

"When it came to the big issues, you were more alike than different. When's the last time you saw the house?" She rose and moved toward him, taking his white carton and setting it aside.

"Twelve years ago," he said.

When he didn't say more, she asked, "Are you at least going to see the house again? There could be items inside you want to keep."

He looked at her, his gaze heavy with loss. "I don't know."

"I can go with you."

"Why?"

"Moral support. I'm not working tomorrow."

"You don't have to do that."

"There's a lot I don't have to do. But I do it anyway."

He rose up from the bar stool. She set her food aside and turned toward him. He laid his hands on her hips, pausing, waiting for her to move away. She held her ground.

"You can kiss me," she said. "I won't bite too much."

His frown deepening, he traced her collarbone with his thumb. "I do."

She laughed. "Just you try. I'm faster on my feet than you." She cupped his face with her hand, and the sensation was a cutting blend of pleasure and pain. She leaned in and kissed him on the lips.

He stood stock-still. "I assumed our last hookup was about pent-up emotions and hormones. What's this time about?"

"I want you. That's never changed."

"Why do you want me?"

"I love you."

He tilted his head, his eyes level on her. "Love wasn't enough the first time. And I'll never be easy."

"You're starting to sound like a broken record." She took his hand in hers. "I'm a little older and wiser now. I see your methods might not be easy, but your heart is in the right place." She kissed him again, and this time he placed his hands around her waist.

She closed her eyes and allowed him to taste her lips, to explore her mouth, to savor her. When he drew back, she moistened her lips and reached for the buttons of his shirt.

"This time it doesn't have to be so frantic," she said. "I want to enjoy this."

Nothing was fixed between them. The issues ran too deep. And knowing that didn't stop him from reaching for the tail of her shirt and pulling it over her head. He cupped her lace-covered breasts and kissed her again. He slowly undressed her.

They made it to the bedroom, but barely. By the time she dropped back onto his bed, he was pulling off his shirt and all but ripping his undershirt off. Shoes, socks, pants went in seconds. When she scooted up on the pillows, he was seconds behind her. And when she parted her legs, he drove into her, hoping this was slow enough for her.

She wrapped a leg around his waist and pushed her pelvis up, matching his downward thrusts. Her hands gripped his shoulders as she kissed him.

When he growled out his release, she quickly followed, and he collapsed on top of her, their sweat mingling between their naked bodies. He stroked her hair back from her face, staring, afraid to voice his feelings.

They'd made no promises. And that was good.

No matter how sweet it was now, he wouldn't kid himself about forever. Forever was a fantasy. But God help him if she tried to leave again. He would not make it nearly so easy for her.

CHAPTER
TWENTY-THREE

Wednesday, October 12, 7:30 a.m.

A local.

Keep an open mind.

The words had churned in Sharp's head most of the night. Tessa had lain curled against his side sleeping soundly while he stared at the ceiling, one hand wrapped around her, the other tucked under his head.

When Tessa awoke, her hand slid slyly to his erection. As she stroked him, the plaguing thoughts vanished, and he was lost in pure pleasure. She straddled him and her body hungrily enveloped him. She moved up and down, desire building until they both tipped over the edge as ecstasy washed over them.

Her body coated in a fine sheen of sweat, she ran her fingers over his chest, finally resting on the rapid beat of his heart. She leaned forward and kissed his lips.

He pulled her to his side and held her close. They lay in silence for a few minutes.

"I need a shower," she said. "Join me."

He smiled and cupped her buttocks.

They showered, dressed, and stopped at a local diner for breakfast.

"So what's the deal with McLean?" she asked. "No sign of him last night."

"His mother still has a house near where we grew up. He's likely up there."

"You've known him since high school. He knew Kara."

"He was like a big brother to her in a lot of ways."

"Did he ever meet Diane?"

"He must have. She and Kara were friends." *Keep an open mind.* "What are you suggesting?"

"He's charming and fun to be around, but how well do you know him?"

"I also served with him. I saw him save a lot of good men."

Keep an open mind.

"You're frowning. I'm not trying to make you angry. I'm just asking the question."

"Vargas asked the same questions about you."

"She's a smart agent. She's willing to look under every rock for this killer."

"It's not McLean."

"Okay."

He balled up his napkin and tossed it on the table. "Before we go to the lake house, I need to pick up DNA from the county sheriff's evidence locker and drop it at Shield."

"What DNA?"

"We found a reference in Kara's file suggesting there might have been more DNA found on her."

She shook her head. "I doubled-checked the files. There was only one sample."

"Knox indicated there's more filed under an arson case that occurred the day Kara was found."

"Interesting. Do you want me to test it?"

"Shield Security will do it."

"It likely won't be admissible."

"I'm not looking for admissible. I'm looking for evidence." He tossed a twenty on the table. "I called yesterday. The sample will be waiting."

"Then let's go."

It took less than an hour to get the samples and drop them at Shield Security before doubling back to Roger's tree-lined street. Now his. He didn't want the place. Didn't want any ties to this past, but until Kara's killer was found, he knew he'd hold on to the old house.

He parked in the driveway and studied the white clapboard house with the expansive front porch. A massive willow tree draped its long and lazy leaves. The gardens were filled with overgrown boxwoods that cast off an aroma he always associated with the old and titled families of Virginia. As he got out of his car, he looked toward the swing that creaked back and forth. Empty stone planters now sported only dirt and dried vines. The building that had once felt oppressive now only looked lost.

"Roger wasn't taking care of the place," Tessa said.

Digging the key from his pocket, he walked up the wide front steps, remembering the time he had sailed down them on an old mattress destined for the dump. Kara had snickered. His mother looked horrified, as if someone had seen and would report back to Roger. She'd always lived in fear Roger would see beyond her beauty to the frightened young girl who'd moved out of her parents' two-room house in search of love.

The steps creaked under their feet as they climbed to the porch. The old lock was rusted and stiff, but when he wiggled the key back and forth, the tumbler turned. The door begrudgingly swung open, letting in light that illuminated the dust dancing in the air.

He reached for the light switch, knowing from the attorney's letter the electricity was paid until the end of the year. The dusty chandelier came to life, casting a weak light that couldn't penetrate the dark, musty rooms. To his right was a large parlor, and to his left the formal dining room. Both sat bare now.

"Where's the furniture?" Tessa asked.

"Roger told me when I saw him in June that he'd sold off most of it. Said he was simplifying his life." Sharp hadn't thought much of it. Hell, he'd always wondered how one man could use all this space. Now as his footsteps echoed in the emptiness, he realized how much Roger had lost.

Sharp had lost a sister. Roger a child. Both should have understood the other's grief, but each was so wrapped up in misery, neither thought to reach out to the other.

Sharp climbed the center staircase, flipping on the upstairs lights as he moved. The carpet in the hallway had dulled, and the formerly colorful walls had faded.

With Tessa following silently, he paused at the first bedroom, which had been his. Turning the knob, he slowly opened the door to find it stripped bare.

He moved to the next room and hesitated.

"This was Kara's room," Tessa said. "I remember it."

"Yes." He turned the knob and switched on the light. The room remained furnished just as it had been the last time he'd seen her on the canopy bed, shooing him out so she could talk on the phone to one of her friends. Memories of that day flooded back.

"Dakota," she'd growled at him as she sat up. "Would you butt out?"

He'd lingered, knowing it pissed her off more. Even at twenty-six he enjoyed riling her temper. "I thought you wanted to go running."

"I do."

He tapped his finger on his watch. "Daylight's wasting."

"I'm not a marine. Just go away. I'm talking to my friend Tessa."

"You have five minutes."

She'd tossed a pillow at him, but she would be downstairs in five minutes. They'd run for five miles, and though he'd slowed his pace for her sake, she did a fair job of keeping up with him.

Roger had not altered any detail in the room. Not a pillow, a picture, or the placement of her pens and papers on her desk. It was a memorial to the kid they'd both loved very much.

As Tessa hovered at the threshold, he moved to Kara's desk and glanced at the notes she'd jotted over twelve years ago. He picked up a picture of the two of them taken on the dock at the local lake at sunset.

"Damn it." He set the photo down.

Tessa approached and picked up the picture. "I've never seen this one before."

"I never got a copy of the picture."

Methodically he went through the drawers in the room as he would a crime scene.

"You should keep the picture."

"It belongs here."

"No, it belongs with you."

He found a sketch pad in the drawer and thumbed through it. Most of the pictures were of landscapes. Sunsets. A bowl of fruit. No great artwork. And then toward the end he found the sketch of a doll. And next to the picture in Kara's handwriting were the words *Very funny*.

"Have a look at this," he said.

As she studied the image, a frown furrowed. "Someone she knew?"

"It had to be." His gaze raked the room. "It never made sense to me that she would get in a car or leave the party with someone she didn't know. She was too smart for that."

"I agree."

He searched the rest of the desk, but in the end, he found nothing that told him who would have killed his sister. His frustration growing, he saved the sketch pad for Andrews before slamming the drawer closed. "Let's get out of here."

He moved to take the picture from Tessa and place it back on the desk.

"You need to keep this," she said.

"I can't look at it every day, knowing I failed her."

She shook her head. "You didn't fail her. This will be a reminder that you'll figure this out."

"No."

"If you don't want it now, let me hold on to it until you're ready."

"Suit yourself." He turned from the room, moving quickly, needing fresh air.

She followed and found him on the front porch, where the morning sun would warm him and the fresh air wasn't tainted with musty scents that only reminded him of loss.

As they stood in silence, a dented old pickup truck pulled up in the circular driveway behind his car. A younger man dressed in jeans, a clean black T-shirt, and work boots got out of the truck.

Sharp moved down the porch steps. "Henry Jones, right? Terrance's cousin."

"That's right."

"What're you doing here, Mr. Jones?"

"Here to check out the property. My dad and I work with Mr. Benson's lawyer, Donna Conner. When a property is empty or needs tending, she calls us. The place yours now?"

Sharp glanced at the still, dark house. "I don't know. Just found out it's mine."

Henry slid a hand in his pocket and rattled change. "Lots of good memories in this house. My sister used to play with Roger's daughter."

The smallness of this community never failed to shock him. Tessa came to his side, and he took comfort having her close. "You knew Kara?"

"I did. Nice kid. A little spoiled, but nice." Henry shifted his stance. "You make any progress on Terrance's case?"

He never made promises to a family when it came to finding a killer. He had always stuck to that rule. But not now. He'd find this son of a bitch. "I'll find him."

Henry nodded. "Thank you."

Sharp and Tessa moved toward his car. He found himself irritated and pissed off for no other reason than this near stranger had been here when Kara had been laid to rest and he had not.

"You'll figure it out," Tessa said.

"You sound so sure."

"Damn straight."

He'd forgotten how she could steady him and pull him back from the darkness. He leaned over and kissed her. She responded immediately, grabbing his lapel and pulling him toward her. He wanted to find a quiet spot. Strip her. Be inside her. His phone buzzed with a text. At first, he ignored it, but the damn phone buzzed with a second text.

"I have to check this." The words traveled past his lips on a sigh.

She moistened her lips. "It's okay."

He checked his phone. The first text read: Homicide. The second was the address.

"I've got to go to work," he said to Tessa.

She squeezed his hand. "Drop me at your place and I'll grab my car."

"Thanks for being here."

"I wouldn't have missed it."

***

When Dakota dropped Tessa off at her car, she was sorry to let him go. It had been nice being with him, working beside him and being a part of his world.

She kissed him good-bye and savored the way he leaned into the kiss and cupped the side of her face with his hand. She could feel whatever indifference he'd been able to muster toward her was melting. She'd chipped away at his guard, but would it be enough for him to take a chance on them again? Being with him had exposed raw nerves of her own. She loved the man, and she didn't want to consider they wouldn't work out their marriage.

Before she could back out of her parking spot, a text from her office erased her good mood. Homicide. Jane Doe. You and Jerry are on point. She texted back: Sharp? And the response: Already notified.

She met up with Jerry in the office, and together they rode in the medical examiner's van. They arrived at the crime scene in Richmond's north side near an abandoned one-story office building. She tossed a quick glance to Jerry behind the steering wheel and slid out of the van. Neither had spoken a word on the drive, each lost in the worry that the killer Dakota was now calling the Dollmaker had claimed another victim.

A cool wind blew, and immediately her eyes swept the scene for Dakota.

She glanced toward the flap of yellow crime scene tape and spotted his broad shoulders as he knelt by the body. Despite the chill in the air, he'd taken off his suit jacket and rolled up his sleeves, exposing muscled forearms, his weapon, and his badge.

He leaned toward the victim, studying her face closely as if willing her to share her secrets. When he rose, he took a step back. He turned and his gaze captured hers, and he made no move to look away. Heat rose in her cheeks as she thought about last night with him. Tessa crossed the deserted lot toward him.

She stopped at the tape and looked toward Martin, who controlled the crime scene. "Dr. Tessa McGowan with the state medical examiner's office."

"You're getting to be a regular," Martin said.

Jerry moved beside her. "Let's have a look at the body."

She peered at the woman slumped by the green dumpster in the lot overgrown with trees. She wasn't dressed in special doll clothes. Instead, she wore what looked like hospital scrubs. Her face was wrapped in bandages that were partly ripped and torn.

Tessa pulled on gloves and stepped under the tape. She knelt and studied the victim. Fearing she'd compromise evidence, she couldn't peel back any of the bandages around the scalp and face. But she could see small patches of the woman's red and discolored face. There were also dark-purple marks on her neck and wrists. This woman's tattooing was in the healing stage.

Her head, eyebrows, and legs had also been shaved or waxed. In fact, like the other victim, the killer had removed all traces of hair from her body.

Tessa glanced at the victim's thumb and saw the swollen joint. She turned the hand over and found no other signs of trauma. Her wrist had been scraped raw. "My guess is she found a way to dislocate her thumb and pull free from her restraints." She looked at the other hand. "There are scrape marks on the other wrist as if she might have been clawing at the restraint. Somehow, she freed herself."

She felt a little out of sorts in the face of this horrific violence, but as Dakota approached, her calm returned. He'd seen so much more violence than she ever dreamed possible.

"Why did he strangle her?" he asked more to himself.

She studied the fingerprint bruises ringing the woman's neck. "The markings suggest he used his hands, not a wire or strap. Makes me think he wasn't planning on killing her."

"Not yet. Not this way."

"This kill wasn't controlled or planned." She pointed to the thumb and torn bandages. "She got free, somehow saw her face, and scratched at the bandages. In the process, she ruined his artwork. That made him furious." She pointed to the scratches on the victim's face below the eyes.

"If she's supposed to be a doll, she should be docile and quiet in his mind," Dakota said, slipping into the psyche of the killer. "He killed her quickly and dumped her here because to him she was trash."

"He took so much time posing the other one," she said. "But this one didn't deserve that kind of care."

"Diane was his masterpiece. This one was a castoff. A broken toy." Bitterness sharpened the words.

Tessa tilted up the victim's face. For a moment she felt a twinge of familiarity as she tried to look beyond the trauma. "Have you or Agent Vargas found Elena Hayes?"

Dakota shoved out a sigh. "No, we haven't. I've left her several voice-mail messages, and we've been by her apartment, where we did find a doll. I've had a BOLO out on her for a few days."

She wanted to peel off the layers of bandaging right now and prove to herself this was not Elena. But she stifled the urge, knowing to do so would risk evidence contamination. But back at the lab, unmasking this victim would be her top priority. "I think you've found her."

"You think this is Elena?" Dakota said.

"I'm not completely sure. It's been twelve years since I've seen her, and this woman is so covered and disfigured. But it could be."

"Run her prints as soon as you can," he said.

She looked at him, realizing how all these years of never really accepting the cause of Kara's death had not been off base. Knowing he'd carried this burden tore at her heart. "If this is Elena, she's the second of Kara's friends to die."

The lines around his eyes and mouth furrowed deeper. "Think about the picture taken of the four of you at the party, Tessa. Kara was far left, next Diane, then Elena, and you're on the end at the far right. If this is Elena, he's working his way across the photo."

The four of them were the target of a killer? Nearly impossible to grasp, but she trusted Dakota. "Jesus. Why us?"

"Hell if I know." His words were clipped with anger and frustration. "I'm going to tell the uniform to stick to you like glue now."

One thing to theorize but another to tie up patrol officers. "Most of my day is spent in the medical examiner's office or surrounded by cops. It doesn't feel right having some officer follow me around."

"I'm not arguing this point."

"I made it to Southeast Asia and survived the jungles without an issue. I can get by in Richmond."

"Your team in Vietnam also had security attached to your detail twenty-four/seven."

"How do you know?"

"I checked."

"You checked? With who?"

"I still have contacts."

He'd been checking up on her while she was away. "I'm touched."

He showed no hints of emotion. "You get a guard."

Easier to move a mountain when his expression hardened like this. "Sure. Fine."

As she turned to leave, he took her arm. His fingers clamped warm, gentle, and unyielding around her arm. "I'm not doing this to be a hard-ass. You have to see that we're dealing with someone that's clever and dangerous."

She lowered her gaze to his fingers. She liked his touch. Wished he could pull her into an embrace and tell her that this was all a horrible nightmare. "I understand."

***

Sharp and Vargas met Veronica Hayes at the medical examiner's office. She sat in the waiting room, her back straight, her hands gripping a handbag that likely cost more than he made in a month.

"Ms. Hayes," he said.

At the sound of his voice, Veronica rose and faced them. Three-inch heels put her at eye level with Sharp. Dark hair draped her shoulders, and a white blouse and a fitted pencil skirt showed off her trim frame. "Why am I here?"

Vargas ignored the question by asking, "Did Elena like dolls?"

The question caught Veronica off guard. "She's a little old for dolls, don't you think? Why do you ask?"

"We found one in her apartment when we searched the place," Sharp said.

Veronica squared her shoulders. "I don't know what you found, but it wasn't hers. Dolls are not her style."

"Did she mention seeing anyone recently that she might have crossed paths with in college?"

Veronica glanced at her phone. "No."

A local boy. "Anyone she might have seen recently?" Sharp asked.

Her brow wrinkled with a frown. "We were in a new restaurant near the Boulevard and Cary Street intersection. What was it called? I remember. Island View. There was a guy. He spoke with her as she was coming out of the ladies' room. They talked for several minutes. She didn't recognize him, but she said he knew her. She said it was a little weird not to recognize someone who remembered you so well."

"Do you have a name?" Sharp asked.

"No. I didn't ask and she didn't offer."

His phone buzzed with a text from Tessa. It read: `The body has been identified as Elena Hayes.` He texted back, `Understood.`

As he raised his gaze, he realized Veronica was watching him closely. "Ms. Hayes, I don't have good news."

Vargas tossed him a glance, her face hardening with understanding.

Tears sparkled in Veronica's eyes as she held up the phone. "We just need to give Elena more time to call back. She's on some beach soaking up the rays."

"We asked you here because we strongly suspected that the body of a woman brought in a couple of hours ago is your sister. Our office just confirmed this as true."

"You've made a mistake. How did she die?" Veronica challenged.

"The medical examiner will make the final call on that."

"The final call. How could you not know?" She took a step back, pressing her fingertips to her closed eyes. "This just makes no sense."

Vargas handed Veronica a tissue from a small packet she kept in her jacket pocket. "I know this is horrible, but we have to know as much as we can about this man who recognized her."

"Do you think it was this guy who hurt her?" she asked. "Would he be so bold?"

"Some killers find it exciting to hide in plain sight. Stalking their victims is also part of the thrill and the chase," Vargas said.

"Stalk?" Her voice cracked. "This is a nightmare."

In the moments after he'd been told about Kara's death, he'd felt gut punched and had been sick to his stomach. He'd been unable to process much as he went to his CO and told him. It had been weeks before the marines allowed him to leave the front line.

"I want to see this woman you keep talking about," Veronica said. "I need to prove you're making a mistake."

"Her face might not be what you're expecting," Sharp said.

A tear spilled and melted Veronica's well-made-up face. "I want to see this woman."

Sharp nodded. "Let me make a call." He moved away from the two and dialed Tessa's number. She answered on the second ring. "I have Veronica Hayes here. She wants to see her sister."

"Give us a couple of minutes and we'll get her ready for viewing. I'll come get you."

"Thanks."

Sharp returned to Vargas standing next to a defiant Veronica, who was impatiently tapping her foot. "Just a couple of minutes."

"You're wrong," Veronica said. "Very wrong."

"Would you be willing to meet with a police sketch artist?" Sharp said. "You might be able to create an image of this man you saw in the restaurant."

"It was a month ago, and I really only saw him in profile."

"It can't hurt," Vargas said.

Doors opened to Dr. Kincaid and Tessa dressed in scrubs. Dr. Kincaid introduced herself and Tessa to Veronica.

Veronica looked at Tessa. "I know you."

"I went to college with your sister."

"You lived in town, didn't you?"

"Yes."

"You've seen my sister?" Veronica asked.

"Yes."

"Is it her?"

"Yes," Tessa said.

"You're wrong," Veronica said. "How long has it been since you two saw each other? Twelve years?"

"If you'll follow me, Ms. Hayes," Dr. Kincaid interjected.

Shaking her head again, Veronica followed, her high heels clipping the tiled floor in firm taps. They entered an exam room. No instruments were on display, and the stainless-steel sinks glistened. In the center of the room was a gurney and on it a draped body.

Veronica stopped in her tracks, her body stiffening.

"Are you sure you want to do this?" Dr. Kincaid asked. "We made a positive identification from her fingerprints."

"I need to see her," Veronica said. Some of the conviction in her voice had vanished.

Dr. Kincaid moved to the head of the table. She hesitated only a moment before she peeled back the sheet. The bandages had been stripped from the face, making the healing tattoos appear all the more raw and angry.

Veronica didn't speak but stared at the face for a long time. "Shit. This cannot be happening. She was only thirty years old."

So was Diane. And Kara had only been eighteen.

"I'll meet with your police sketch artist," Veronica said. Her voice was raw with emotion. "I'll do whatever it takes."

***

He stood in his studio, a strong drink in his hand as he looked at the empty chair that was supposed to be holding his precious Harmony. He shouldn't have lost his temper with her. God, he'd put so much work into her and if he'd been careful and patient, he could have fixed the damage she'd created.

"Damn."

He missed her so much that he'd turned on her phone this morning and scrolled through her pictures. He'd read her sister's frantic texts. "It shouldn't be this way, Harmony."

Years ago, he'd acted rashly with his first doll. He'd been watching her for weeks and each night he burned to touch her and remake her into a sweet doll.

She'd been walking home, her body swaying. She was dizzy from her drink. A drink he'd spiked. He'd been ready to offer her help as she approached an intersection. And then the car had hit her.

He could still picture her body flying like a rag doll onto the hood of the car. A woman nearby screamed. People ran to her aid.

So he'd backed away, terrified. He couldn't be associated with this. Knox would find out. So he'd returned to the party, shaken and anxious. Then he'd seen the other doll.

Kara had been drunk. She walked erratically. She was defenseless. And it bothered him that someone else might take advantage. So he followed her.

He didn't dare touch her or come too close until she turned onto a darkened side street. It was providence. She was walking toward him. And when she tripped, just feet away from the van, he knew she was meant to be his.

"Kara," he said.

She struggled to right herself, swayed, and turned, smiling. "Hey, do I know you?"

"Yeah. I was at the party. We danced," he lied.

"We did?"

He hurried up to her as she shifted and caught her before she fell. "Are you okay?"

"I'm a little drunk," she said with a giggle.

"It's okay. You want me to take you home?"

"Would you? That would be great."

So trusting. He led her back to his van and opened the front passenger door for her. He helped her sit and fastened her seat belt. "Buckle up."

She giggled. "This is so nice of you. I'm more messed up than I thought."

"I know. But don't worry. I've got you."

He closed the door and rushed around to the driver's side. His body buzzed with excitement. As he turned on the engine, she melted into the seat with no hint of worry. Her head tipped back against the headrest, and her eyes closed.

So still. So perfect.

"Kara? You okay?"

"Yes," she said without opening her eyes. "I just need to rest my eyes."

"Sleep. It's fine. I've got you."

When he pulled up in front of his small house, she was still sleeping. He hustled around the front of the van, glancing around to make sure none of his neighbors' lights were on. He quietly opened her door, unbuckled her seat belt, and lifted her in his arms. She was so light. So small. Her head slumped against his shoulder, and he knew he was in love.

He carried her into the basement and laid her on a worn red sofa. He pulled up a chair and sat in front of the couch, admiring his future creation.

When she awoke, he was sorry to see her eyes flutter open. But he was ready with a soda laced with drugs.

"Where am I?" she asked, pushing into a sitting position. Worry sharpened her gaze.

"My place. You forgot to tell me where you lived."

"Oh. Sorry." She pushed her hair out of her eyes.

"Here, drink this. It'll settle your stomach."

"Thanks. I don't think I've ever drank that much." She sipped from the straw.

"It happens."

"Never to me before."

She sipped more, but within minutes her eyes were blinking slowly. He took the soda can before she dropped it.

"What's wrong with me?"

"Nothing. You're perfect."

And she was asleep again. "Such a perfect little doll."

He hadn't been able to resist making up her face. She was dressed like a doll, but her face was all wrong. When she awoke again, she was shocked to see her face. He had to force her to drink more of the soda this time. He was never proud that he'd had to restrain her, but this was his first doll. He was still learning all the nuances of his artwork. During the four days that he kept her, he didn't realize the acute effect of alcohol on the narcotic he was feeding her. He didn't mean to overdose her.

When she stopped breathing, he tried to revive her, but was unsuccessful. He kept her lifeless body a few more hours, then knew the time had come to bundle her in a blanket and give her back. When he put her in the back of his van and drove across town, he was terrified.

He passed the chief, who recognized him. But he smiled as he gripped the wheel.

His first doll had taught him many lessons. The first had been that makeup didn't last. When he'd seen her in her casket, he had been devastated to see her skin scrubbed clean. His art had been destroyed.

So he'd learned the art of tattooing. The next three women after her, the practice dolls, weren't nearly as special. They were cheap imitations of Kara. He'd used them to hone his skills.

His perfect doll was Diane, but he'd let her go too soon. And then Elena had slipped her restraints. And his temper had gotten the better of him.

But there was still Tessa, his Serenity. She was the sweetest of all the dolls. She deserved his best work and his love. And this time he would not let her slip from his grasp. They could have years of bliss together.

CHAPTER
TWENTY-FOUR

Thursday, October 13, 7:30 a.m.

The Elena Hayes autopsy was the first on the day's schedule, and Tessa knew she'd be assisting Dr. Kincaid. Veronica Hayes had visited the medical examiner's office yesterday, and it had been heart-wrenching as she'd stared at what was left of her sister's face. Veronica had reached out to Elena's arm but couldn't bring herself to touch her.

"What kind of sick bastard would do this to her?" Veronica had asked.

Even now as Tessa and Dr. Kincaid did their morning rounds, Veronica's words were never far.

"I said, are you ready to discuss this patient?" Dr. Kincaid asked.

Tessa looked up. "Yes. Yes, of course."

Dr. Kincaid opened a refrigerated door and glanced at the face of an attractive man who had been in the prime of his life until last night, when he'd gripped his chest after a meal of organic vegetables and free-range meat and dropped to the floor. He'd been an avid runner and had no history of smoking. "What about his family history?"

Tessa glanced at her notes. "He did have an uncle who had a heart attack at forty-five. The uncle survived. His wife said he's never complained of heart trouble."

"What kind of medicines was he taking?"

"His wife brought in a bottle of antacids. It was nearly empty."

"Why was he taking the antacids?"

"He was complaining of mild heartburn."

Dr. Kincaid shook her head. "That's the last of our cases. The detectives will be here in about twenty minutes. Jerry is getting their case prepped and on the table. Have you notified Douglas Knox's family about his death?"

"I was able to get the number of his oldest daughter, and I've put a call into her. I didn't leave a specific message other than to call me."

"Good. We need to know how to proceed with the body."

"Okay."

Dr. Kincaid studied her closely. "Are you okay, Dr. McGowan?"

The question caught her off guard. "Sure. Why wouldn't I be?"

"Because Sharp called me last night and told me that you also knew this victim. He's worried about you."

She rubbed the back of her neck. "He's assigned a cop to me twenty-four/seven."

"Why?"

"He thinks there's a pattern to these deaths, and I might be next."

Dr. Kincaid's gaze darkened. "Sharp doesn't scare easily. I agree with his caution."

Tessa smiled, hoping it hid her worry. Last night she'd barely slept. If she wasn't trying to draw connections between the two murdered women and herself, she was thinking about Dakota.

All this time she'd thought he'd been using the past to avoid the future, but God, it looked like he had been right to worry. On an instinctual level he'd known Kara had been murdered.

When she stepped into her office, Dakota was standing there, staring at a picture taken of her and a group of forensic doctors identifying bones in the jungle.

"You look happy in this picture," he said without turning. "You didn't smile much like that toward the end of us."

"I was happy at that moment. We found the soldier we'd been searching for. But I wasn't really happy, mostly because I knew you weren't happy and I didn't know how to fix it."

"It's selfish of me to withdraw," he said as he replaced the picture.

Tessa didn't speak as he turned and crossed to her.

"I was angry and frustrated, and the better it got between us the worse I felt. It was as if I didn't have the right to be happy because my sister was dead."

This was the first time she'd ever had a sense of what he felt. "If it had been reversed and you'd died, would you have wanted Kara to suffer alone?"

"No. Of course not."

"I can promise you, she'd not have wanted this for you. She adored you."

"I can't make any promises about our future until I catch this killer. I understand myself well enough to know I won't be much better of a person than I was a year ago."

"You don't know that."

"I do."

God, but she loved this man. She'd told him often enough when they'd first married, but he'd seemed to brush her words aside. Leaving for Southeast Asia had been a last-ditch effort to get him to react, and when he hadn't, she left. Now Tessa was back, trying to hold them together.

"God hates quitters, Agent Sharp."

That prompted a half smile.

She took his hands in hers, half expecting him to pull away, but he did not. "You've taken a lot of bad people off the streets. You've given so many families closure."

"What's the saying? The cobbler's wife has no shoes. He can do for others, but he can't do for himself or his family."

"You're getting closer to this killer, Dakota. You'll catch him."

"It's not coming together fast enough. Especially if you're next on his list."

"What about the boy who delivered the drugs? You're nearly certain the drugs came from Dr. Bailey's office." The clean scent of soap mingled with his scent, and for the first time in a while, no traces of cigarette smoke.

"The office manager is still not talking, but I'm going to press her hard today. She's coming back to the station with her attorney."

"You can be a pretty scary guy."

He traced his thumb over the back of her hand. His touch was so soft and gentle, it would be easy to convince herself he'd not touched her. "I don't want you to ever be scared of me."

She smiled. "I'm not."

"Good."

She squeezed his hand. "What about Veronica Hayes?"

"Veronica is working with the sketch artist, and we're expecting an image soon."

"Let's hope she remembers enough for a good sketch."

"Yeah."

Her office phone rang and she glanced at the display, annoyed. She pressed the speakerphone. "Dr. McGowan."

"Carol Knox is returning your call. Line two."

She glanced up at Dakota. "Thanks, Sarah." She ended that call and explained to him, "Carol Knox is the chief's daughter. His ex-wife died six years ago."

His demeanor chilled in a blink. "I'd like to talk to her."

"Sure." She picked up line two. "Ms. Knox, this is Dr. Tessa McGowan, with the Virginia Medical Examiner's Office."

"It's about my father, isn't it?" Her voice sounded sad, resigned.

"Yes, it is. I'm sorry to say he passed away yesterday."

"How?"

"We're still trying to determine that. Do you mind if I put you on speakerphone, Ms. Knox? I have Agent Dakota Sharp with the Virginia State Police with me, and he'd like to ask you some questions."

She hesitated. "Virginia police? Yeah, sure."

Tessa pressed the speakerphone. "Ms. Knox, can you hear me?"

"Yes, I can hear you."

"Ms. Knox. Agent Sharp."

"Yes, Agent Sharp," Ms. Knox said.

"Can you tell me about your late brother, Robert Knox?"

The line crackled with silence for a moment. "I don't understand. My brother, Robbie, died twenty years ago. He drowned."

"What can you tell me about Robbie?" Dakota asked. "I understand he was arrested on arson charges."

More heavy silence. "I don't see why you would care. But yes, Robbie was in trouble more than he wasn't. As he grew older, he became harder to handle. And when he set that shed on fire with the dog inside, it devastated my mother. She and Dad both tried to get him help, but they couldn't seem to reach him."

"How did he drown?"

"Dad took him out on a fishing trip. It was a rainy, cold day. About halfway through the day, Robbie fell overboard. Dad said the current caught him and pulled him under. They never found his body."

"Was there any kind of inquiry into the boy's death?"

"I suppose. I was about fifteen at the time, and my parents kept most of the details to themselves. I do know in the end it was ruled an accident. I remember there was an insurance payout, which Dad gave to Mom."

"And then your father moved east."

"I think the strain of losing a child was too much. They split up right after Robbie died." She sighed. "Dad was different after Robbie died. He withdrew from us completely."

"What was it like for you, losing your brother?" Dakota asked.

"Honestly, my sister and I were relieved. Toward the end with him around, we slept with our door locked. He scared us."

Dakota looked up at Tessa. "What did he do that was so frightening?"

"I'd wake up at night and he'd be standing over my bed." She went silent. "He would tell me I looked so peaceful when I was sleeping. I looked like a perfect little doll."

"A doll?"

"Mom tried to tell Dad that Robbie had problems, but Dad insisted he could control Robbie. That he would grow out of his fantasies. My parents fought a lot toward the end of their marriage." Again she grew silent. "Look, this isn't a subject I like talking about. Robbie tore our family apart."

"Do you have a picture of your brother?" Dakota pressed.

"I do somewhere. I would have to dig it out of storage."

"It's important I see it as soon as possible. Can you take a picture of it and text it to me?"

"Why do you care about my brother?"

"I have a theory that might be way off base, but I need to check it out. I'd like to see a picture of him. When I do, I'll let you know what I'm thinking."

A heavy silence drifted between them. "You think he's alive, don't you?"

"Why would you say that?"

Her breath hitched as she spoke, and she had to stop a moment before saying, "Mom thought she saw him once about eight years ago. She swore she saw him standing on a street corner."

"Did she speak to this person?"

"She called out to him, but then he turned and vanished into a crowd. She was troubled for days. We all were. I even went back to locking my bedroom door. But she never saw this guy again, and we figured it was just a guy who looked like him."

"I need that picture," Dakota said.

"I'll look for it right now," Ms. Knox said.

"Thank you."

"Carol," Tessa said. "Call me back later and we can discuss your father's remains."

"Right. Sure. Thanks." The line went dead.

"You really don't think that Robbie Knox is responsible for these deaths?" Tessa asked.

"I don't know."

Her phone buzzed again. Jerry was summoning her to the autopsy suite for the Elena Hayes case. "I need to go."

"Right."

Tessa hurried along the hallway, focused on Dakota's deliberate footsteps behind her. In the autopsy room, Jerry pulled the sheet from Elena's body as Dr. Kincaid watched. The outside world faded away.

Elena's face was red and bruised from extensive tattooing. Clearly, the Dollmaker had not finished his work when she'd escaped. Tessa glanced again at the thumb that was still swollen. "Jerry, what do the X-rays of her hand look like?"

He turned and flipped on the light of the X-ray board, which illuminated an image of Elena's right hand. "She's double-jointed. It would have hurt like hell for her to distort it like this, but my bet is she did it as a kid."

Tessa stared at the X-ray. "It was one of her party tricks. Used to creep everyone out."

Dr. Kincaid studied the top of the patient's head, which had been waxed bare. Her gaze roamed over the red skin on the face and then to the neck and the bruising there. "X-rays show a fractured windpipe and hyoid bone in her neck. Strangulation killed her." She examined the injection site on the patient's forearm. "There's no other blemish on her body, but we'll test for drugs and signs of sexual abuse. She doesn't appear as malnourished as the other one. He couldn't have held her longer than a few days maybe."

"He's not wasting any time getting to work," Dakota said.

Dakota's phone buzzed with a text. Frowning as he read, he said, "Andrews ran the DNA samples found on Kara, Dillon, and Richardson in his lab. The DNA found on all three victims matches. He's now trying to see if DNA was collected from the three murdered prostitutes."

"There are other victims?" Dr. Kincaid asked.

"Across the country. This guy hasn't been dormant the last twelve years. He's been honing his craft."

Dakota received another text. "Shit. DNA is also a match to Knox. This guy we're looking for is Knox's son."

**

Sharp entered the interview room where Dana Coggin and her attorney sat at a simple desk. He took the chair opposite them and pulled it around to the side of the desk. Right now he wasn't looking to antagonize Ms. Coggin. He needed her help finding this killer, and if he could make her believe they were on the same side, then so be it.

"Thank you for coming," Sharp said as he reached out his hand to the attorney.

Ms. Coggin didn't speak but shifted in her seat and glanced at her attorney, a lean gray-haired woman whose dark suit made her pale complexion look sallow. A thin strong hand shook his. "I'm Martha Wells."

"Good to meet you." He smiled at Ms. Coggin. "And I do appreciate both your help."

Dana sat straighter, tugging the edges of her coat nervously. "I don't know what I can do to help you."

Sharp opened his notepad case and clicked his pen. "I'm hoping you'll work with me. Today, I may not be too concerned about you selling drugs if you're willing to deal. Tell me about the man you were selling to."

Ms. Coggin opened her mouth to speak, but her attorney held up her hand. "I'm not sure how my client can help you."

He produced a smile that he hoped was friendly. He pulled out two photos and laid them both facedown on the table. "Dana," he said, ignoring the attorney. "Let me show you what we're up against." We. A united front.

She folded her arms and sat back, silent.

He flipped over the first image. It was Diane Richardson's Department of Motor Vehicles picture. "I'll grant you this wasn't the best picture taken of her. I've seen other pictures of her, and she was a stunning woman." He tapped his finger on the picture, waiting for her to look at the image. When she did, he reached for the other image but didn't turn it over right away. Both attorney and client were silent as they waited. Sharp flipped over the picture. It was Diane Richardson's autopsy photo.

The stark contrast caught both women by surprise.

He pulled out two more pictures. Elena Hayes before. And the grisly after shot.

Again, Sharp waited as the weight of the images took hold. "This killer was able to do this because he could keep her drugged for long stretches of time." He grimaced. "This face gives me nightmares."

Ms. Wells now seemed to fully understand the implications for her client. "And if my client could possibly help you, you'd consider a reduced charge?"

"Yes." As much as he hated to let this woman get away with her crimes, he had a bigger fish to catch, and he had no doubt if he were patient, he'd nail Ms. Coggin again. "Who is the buyer?" He made it sound nonthreatening. He didn't dare voice his contempt for the woman.

"I'm not a petty drug dealer," Ms. Coggin said.

Her attorney held up her hand, again silencing her. "She'll plead guilty to a misdemeanor possession charge. Can we agree on that?"

Sharp stared at Ms. Coggin for a moment before he shifted his attention to the attorney. "She has to tell me everything."

Ms. Wells nodded to her client. "Agreed?"

"Yes," Ms. Coggin said.

"Tell him what you told me."

The woman hesitated. "I used to date Jimmy Dillon when we were in high school. I hadn't seen him in a long time, and a month ago I saw him back in his favorite bar holding court." She shook her head, regret clear on her face.

"Go on."

She cleared her throat. "I knew why he'd gone to jail, and I was looking for someone who needed quick cash. It didn't take much convincing to get Jimmy to say yes."

Sharp didn't want to hear her backstory. If he didn't need her right now, he'd be talking to the commonwealth's attorney about maximum jail time. "Who was the buyer?"

"I never met the buyer in person. I got a call one night from a man, and he said he knew I might be someone who could help."

"How did he know that?"

"I don't know. I really don't."

"You've done this before?"

"A little."

"Who did you sell to?"

Ms. Coggin glanced at her attorney, who nodded. "The doctor treated a patient last year who also had cancer. The gentleman was having trouble sleeping. Dr. Bailey refused to prescribe any additional meds, believing the patient was exaggerating his situation. The patient then asked me if I could help. I knew what he needed, but I played dumb. He came back again for a follow-up visit, and this time he begged me for help. He said he'd pay top dollar. I told him it could be arranged, and then I visited his house with several vials of propofol. I showed his wife how to set up the IV. The man died of cancer six months later."

"Who was the man?"

"Eugene Radcliff. He lived in the area." She met his gaze.

"Did he use them to kill himself?" Sharp asked.

"No. He didn't want to die. He was trying to live long enough for his daughter's wedding." She shifted in her seat again. "I went by the house to get the extras, but his wife couldn't find the vials."

"And you believed her?"

"Yes. Mrs. Radcliff was really worried. She thought her husband might have resold some of the drugs to a third party. Mr. Radcliff was worried about paying for his daughter's wedding and leaving money for his wife. The woman was terrified she was going to jail if anyone found out."

"She say who the buyer was?"

"Her husband never told her."

"And then?"

"I got a call from this guy, who said he wanted more of what I'd sold to Radcliff."

"And you did what?"

"Nothing. I thought he was a cop. But he called again. And this time he offered a lot more money. I wasn't going to make the delivery and risk arrest, so I asked Jimmy."

"And Jimmy got his son."

"I suppose." Her slim white fingers twisted around the strap of her purse. "I never saw the buyer or met him directly. But I did see a white van parked outside my house recently. It gave me the creeps."

"What can you tell me about the van?"

"It was outside my house three nights in a row. I knew it was the buyer. I just knew it."

"Did you see the driver?"

"I couldn't see his face. He sat back, staying in the shadows."

"What about a license plate?" he challenged.

"I wrote down the license plate of the van. At least part of it. I couldn't see it all." She pulled a piece of paper from her pocket and put it on the table.

Sharp looked at the scrawled numbers and letters that were three short of a full license. Not a name. But a lead. Playing into her fear of this man, Sharp offered, "You're likely in danger until we catch this man. If you think of anything else, call me immediately."

He gave her his business card, moved out into the hallway, and called Andrews, giving him the partial license number. Andrews promised an answer within minutes.

***

Tessa kicked off her shoes as she entered her cousin's apartment. After twelve hours on her feet, she was exhausted. As she padded into the kitchen, the front doorbell rang. Checking her watch, she moved toward the door, carefully remembering Dakota's words of warning.

She glanced out the peephole and saw Veronica holding a bag. She opened the door.

"Veronica."

A brittle smile tugged at red lips. "I asked around and found out where you lived. I wanted to see you and talk to you about Elena."

"Dr. Kincaid gave you a full briefing, didn't she?"

"Yes, yes, she did. But it's not the same. I wanted to talk to someone who knew Elena. Please, can I come in?"

"I'm happy to meet with you in my office tomorrow. Now is really not a good time."

"I know this is out of the ordinary. But we knew each other a little as kids. Please, I need closure."

Tessa, against her better judgment, stepped aside. "Sure, come on in."

Veronica glanced around the apartment. "I found this bag on your front porch."

"Oh, thank you," she said, accepting it.

"Aren't you living with your cousin? How is she doing?"

"She's great." Tessa rolled her head, trying to release the tension.

Veronica looked around. "Is she here?"

"No, we have the place to ourselves."

"Good. It's hard enough to talk about this."

Tessa glanced toward the bag, but when Veronica began to cry, she set it aside.

"I was on the phone with Mom and Dad," Veronica said finally. "They're flying back from California right now."

"I'm so sorry."

She shook her head, wiping away a tear. "I'm trying to understand this. I'm trying to figure out why someone would be so full of hate that they'd do what they did to her face."

"I don't know, Veronica. This person is clearly sick."

"You know Elena was sorry she didn't visit with you after your accident."

Absently, Tessa rubbed her leg. "It was a long time ago."

"Does it still bother you?"

"Only when I'm tired and have been on my feet too long. For the most part, it's not too bad."

"How did you get hit by a car?"

"You didn't come here to talk about my accident."

"No, I didn't. I met with the police sketch artist, but I'm afraid I wasn't much help. It was basically the face of a thousand different men." She fiddled with a ring on her index finger. "I've been trying to remember if there were any super creeps that stood out when Elena was in college. There were always guys staring at her. She was so pretty. So perfect. But I can't place anyone in particular."

"I've been doing the same. I just don't remember anyone."

Veronica shook her head. Tears glistened. "This is all so surreal. You know I have an appointment with the funeral home tomorrow? Jesus. I never pictured this moment in my life, ever."

"No one ever does. I was overwhelmed when my mom died. There were so many details to think about. I don't think I could have gotten through it all without my aunt."

Veronica shoved out a sigh. "Look, I can see you're tired and need to put your feet up. You're the only one I can really talk to about this."

"It's okay." As Veronica turned toward the door, Tessa said, "You need to be careful. We still don't know the killer."

"I saw the cop parked out front of your house. Are you scared?"

"More angry than scared. I want this guy caught."

She opened the door. "Be careful."

"Right."

When Veronica left, Tessa locked her door and turned her attention to the bag. Inside, she found a simple brown box. Carefully, she removed it and pulled off the top to find a layer of white tissue. Peeling back the layers, she caught the glimpse of black hair and then a glass eye with a fixed stare. Her heart rammed against her ribs. It was a doll. "My God." She dashed to the front door, snapped it open without thinking, hoping she could catch Veronica. But when she opened the door, the man standing there stopped her midstep with the touch of a stun gun to her gut.

"Dr. McGowan?"

Gritting her teeth, she couldn't form words as she looked up at the man, knowing they'd met recently. Her body tingled, twitched, and burned from the effects of the stun gun as her legs crumbled. He lifted her, supporting her weight as he took her inside the apartment.

Before the door closed, she looked past him to the cop car. The cop's head was slumped forward. She opened her mouth to scream, but she couldn't draw in air to speak. The door closed. Finally, she muttered, "Don't do this."

He stood her upright and released her as he searched his pockets for something. All the while he watched as she staggered to an entry table for support, willing her legs to work.

Hands trembling, she reached for a vase, gripping the lip as she concentrated on lifting it. It felt as if she were lifting hundreds of pounds. Finally, she turned and hurled it at him.

The man easily deflected the missile with one arm as he held a syringe in the other. "There is no need to be afraid. I'm not here to hurt you. I'm here to transform you, my sweet little doll."

Screaming weakly, she turned to run, but her body still wouldn't perform. She tripped, and strong hands grabbed her.

"You are being naughty, little doll. You need to be still. You need to be silent."

He threw her to the ground, and the power of his thrust sent her tumbling to her hands and knees. She began to crawl. "No. I'm not a doll."

Easily he overtook her and pulled her hair, yanking her head back. "Why did you make me hurt you? I don't want to hurt you."

"Stop, please."

He pushed her flat against the floor and tugged her arms behind her, tying them tight at the wrists. "I know what I'm doing, little doll. Stop fighting me before you hurt yourself."

"Stop!" she hissed, barely able to form the word. Blurred vision and muscle spasms made it impossible for her to sit up.

He bound her feet and rolled her on her back. He pulled a clean handkerchief from his pocket and shoved it in her mouth. "This isn't fun for me. It breaks my heart to have to be so rough with you. But soon you'll be thanking me. I'll take care of you. Love you. You're my perfect Serenity doll."

Panic tore through her, a muffled scream escaping as he pressed her cheek against the floor.

She felt the prick of a needle in her arm and seconds later the warmth of some drug sliding into her. She blinked her eyes, terrified she'd fall asleep.

"You don't remember me, but I've been watching you for years." He smoothed his hand gently over her head. "Time and people have kept us apart, but now it's time for us to be together forever."

She shook her head, blinking again as her vision clouded.

"I've done this dozens of times before, though most of the people I spent my time with were far quieter. But don't worry, Serenity. I'm not here to kill you. We have so much living we can do together."

Tears welled in her eyes as she pictured the faces of Diane and Elena. As he pushed the syringe's plunger again, her head swirled and she thought about Dakota. Regrets. How much she loved him.

***

Sharp was driving north on I-95 when his phone dinged with a text from Ms. Knox. He opened the attachment to a picture of a young boy who couldn't be more than ten. Familiarity teased as he struggled to connect the dots. Then the phone rang. Andrews.

"Given the parameters, I've narrowed it to one man. Norman DeLuca lives near Terrance Dillon and he owns a business in town."

"Shit." DeLuca. The picture sent from Carol Knox was of a younger version of DeLuca. He forwarded the text to Andrews. "Just sent you an image of Knox's son taken when he was a boy."

There was only a brief hesitation. "DeLuca," Andrews said.

"He owns the damn funeral home. He likely knew Radcliff and his situation. Probably offered to buy the propofol from him. Big wedding for daughter coming up and leaving a widow. Money was too tempting. He's been around all their lives. He was at Roger's funeral. Terrance's funeral."

"And no doubt, your sister's. He'd been in town less than a year when your sister died, and he was working at the funeral home then."

"He put the doll in her casket."

"A very logical assumption. He never attended the college, but it's an open campus, and as a local, he could easily have been around them. He's only a few years older, so he wouldn't have stood out too much around the students."

"And the prostitutes killed in Colorado fit what his sister told me," Sharp said.

"Explain."

"Knox's ex-wife told her daughters she was certain she saw her son years ago. She lost the guy in the crowd. Really rattled the woman," Sharp said.

"I'm trying to connect the deaths to his credit card receipts. If he traveled, there'd be some kind of record. Given a little more time, I'm confident I can show a link." Keys clicked in the background. "And DeLuca's Funeral Home was a corporate sponsor of Terrance's football team. That's how the kid recognized him."

"I'll head to the funeral home now." Sharp drove toward DeLuca's.

He dialed Tessa's phone, and when it went to voice mail, he cursed. "Tessa, where the hell are you? I think I know who killed Kara, Diane, and Elena. Norman DeLuca. Tall, with dark hair and olive skin. Just stay the hell in your house or close to the cop assigned to you."

His next call was to the cop on duty. On the fourth ring he received a crisp, "Officer Smith."

"Where is Officer Baugh? He's supposed to be on duty in front of Tessa McGowan's house."

"Officer Baugh is being taken away in an ambulance. He was drugged. Still passed out cold."

"Where is Tessa McGowan?"

"Missing."

He floored the accelerator as he redialed Andrews. "Tessa is missing. What can you tell me about the funeral home?"

"I'm pulling building plans now. Bowman is with me, and he wants to talk to you."

Sharp barely registered. "Sure."

"Bowman here. I'm sending our newest man and putting him on an intercept course with you at DeLuca's."

"I don't need a new guy."

"It's McLean."

***

Tessa woke in stages. At first she was aware of a quiet shuffling around the room, then the strong smell of chemicals, and finally an aching pain in her side. Eyes closed, she tried to raise her hand to her head but couldn't lift her arms.

What was wrong with her? Was she still asleep? She thought back to when she was in the car accident and she couldn't move her legs. Fear sliced through her as she tried to convince herself that she was okay. But her legs didn't move. She didn't feel the prick of the doctor's probe on the bottom of her feet. Had she been in another accident?

Terrified of what she might discover when she awoke, she hesitated, praying it was a dream. But as tempting as sleep was, she knew this was real. Summoning her courage, she opened her eyes, wincing against the bright light. Again, she tried to raise her arms, but this time realized they were not paralyzed but strapped at her side. She was in a chair akin to what she'd have found in a dentist's office.

As her mind cleared, she focused on a stainless-steel table laid out with surgical instruments similar to the medical examiner's office.

"Good, you're awake." His voice was soft, soothing, and calm. "I didn't want to rush you. I thought you'd need the rest."

She stared for a moment, willing her mind to calm. "Let me go."

The man came around the side of her chair and smoothed his hand over her hair. "Certainly. All in due time."

"Why?"

His smile was so soft and pleasant. "Oh, don't look so upset, Serenity. You're with me now, and you are safe."

Panic clawed, making it hard to remain calm. "I'm not Serenity. I'm Dr. Tessa McGowan."

He shook his head. "Out there you may be, but in my world you're Serenity. My perfect doll."

"I'm not a doll. I'm a woman."

He stepped back from her. "If you keep scrunching up your face, those wrinkles will stick. Didn't your mother tell you that?"

"I know you from Terrance Dillon's funeral."

"I took care of him as well as Kara and Diane. They didn't send me Elena. I just found out they're going to cremate her, but then that's not such a terrible loss. She ruined her face, destroyed all my beautiful work."

Beautiful work. She struggled to remain calm. "She got away from you."

He stepped back, frowning. "Almost. Not quite. I'll be more careful with you."

She twisted her hands in the bindings. A part of her wanted to scream and rant, but she could already tell by his reaction to Elena that he didn't respond well to harsh tones. "I remember you," she lied as she struggled to place him.

"You do?" He took a step toward her.

She suppressed a flinch. "You were kind. It was a terrible time for me when my mother died."

"I knew you were upset. Like a broken little doll. I wanted to take you in my arms that day and tell you it would be all right, but I couldn't. There were too many people. But I kept up with you all these years."

"You spoke to me," she lied.

"I was there."

"Maybe we didn't speak, but our connection was so strong."

"Yes."

It was the utter calmness of his voice that made her want to scream. He was way past insane. And he was going to kill her if she didn't figure a way out of here.

DeLuca reached for the scissors. "This won't hurt."

Tessa tensed and tried to edge away. "Why are you changing me?"

He glanced at the shiny tip of the scissors. "Don't be scared. You see, I have to cut off your hair. That's the first step."

"Before you cut my hair," she said, quickly, "tell me about the dolls."

"The dolls?"

"The ones you've made. I saw Diane. The work on her face was so detailed. Fascinating. Elena ruined herself. I know that and can't judge you on that work. But I know you've been practicing on other girls."

He looked pleased as he gently stroked her face with the back of his hand. "They don't matter. Only you matter."

"Who were they?"

"Whores. Just whores."

***

"I have a hit on DeLuca's phone," Andrews said. "A rookie mistake to leave it on at a time like this."

Behind the wheel of his car, Sharp pushed the accelerator. "Where is it?"

Andrews tapped computer keys. "Very near the funeral home."

Sharp drove through a red light and raced down the center street, his lights flashing. When he turned the corner toward DeLuca's, he cut the lights and slowed as the brick funeral home came into view. "I don't see any activity outside."

Keys tapped in the background. "Is there a building across the street?" asked Andrews.

Sharp looked and confirmed the building.

More keys tapped. "The building has been vacant for over eighteen months, but DeLuca purchased it six months ago."

Sharp got out of his vehicle and drew his weapon.

As he moved toward the building, a Jeep rolled around the corner and parked behind him. McLean jumped out with practiced ease, his weapon drawn.

"McLean is here."

"Roger that."

Ending the call, Sharp glanced at McLean. "Tessa's inside. I'm not waiting."

McLean's face hardened with a resolve that Sharp hadn't seen since the battlefield. "Let's go."

***

Tessa flinched when DeLuca ran his fingers through the strands of her hair. His touch was gentle, but she knew his plans involved pain and destruction. "It really is pretty," he said. "And I'm tempted to keep it, but dolls don't have real hair."

"Some do." She struggled to keep her voice light and her racing heart calm. As he turned toward his instrument table, she glanced at her hand restraints and saw that the buckle on the left side was slightly askew. She thought about Elena's dislocated thumb and the marks on her wrist. She'd been in this same chair and found a way to free her hands. It was possible.

She twisted both her wrists as DeLuca studied a collection of scissors and razors. She didn't want him thinking about surgical tools.

"Why did you choose Kara first?" she asked.

"I didn't. I chose you first." He turned and smiled at her.

"I don't understand."

"I wanted you first. I slipped a sedative in your beer and was waiting for you to drink it. But you took only a couple of sips before you and Kara started to fight. You stormed off, and I followed you. I was afraid the drugs would take hold, and I didn't want you simply collapsing on the sidewalk."

She remembered being angry. And then dizzy. Distracted.

"I wanted to help you. I wanted us to get to know each other better. I was right behind you when you left. I saw you start to stagger as you stepped into the street. And then the car hit you. So many people were around you, I couldn't help you."

All these years, she thought she'd been distracted and stupid. "So you went back for Kara."

"I returned to the house just as she stumbled out the back door. She couldn't have gotten drunk that fast, and then I realized she must have picked up your cup."

"Did you speak to her?"

He touched the tip of the sharp scissors with his fingers as his eyes got a faraway look. "I walked behind her several blocks. I was mad at her at first. She'd messed up my plans. And then she tripped and fell in the ditch. She started to cry, and it broke my heart. I went to her. My little broken doll. And when I touched her, she looked up and reached out to me. When I took her hand, it was one of the sweetest moments of my life. She collapsed in my arms."

"That was kind of you." She struggled to keep her voice even as she remembered Kara's autopsy pictures.

He looked at her hopefully. "I was nice to Kara. I even had a name for her. It was Felicity. Even though she'd been bad, I was nice."

"What happened?"

"I carried her to my van. So sweet. She settled in, and I hurried around to turn on the engine and the heater. She looked so cold."

She wasn't found for another five days, but she'd been dead less than forty hours when discovered. "It must have been hard to let her go."

"At first I drove to her dorm and parked. But when I looked at her sleeping face, she looked so sweet. Tears came to my eyes."

"You couldn't just leave her for someone else, could you?"

He looked away and turned back toward his worktable. "No. I couldn't. So I took her back to my apartment. I laid her on one of the couches in the back and sat with her."

She twisted her hand in the left cuff and watched with growing desperation as the threads holding the strap together loosened. As he turned, she froze. "How long did she sleep?"

"Overnight."

"And when she woke up?"

"She was cranky. In such a bad little mood. And I realized then that I missed seeing her sleep. She was such an angel when she slept. I used to love to watch my sisters sleep. So peaceful."

"What did you do when she awoke?"

"I gave her a drugged soda."

"She was missing for several days."

"While she was sleeping, I cleaned her clothes. Applied makeup. I'm good with makeup."

"You prepare the bodies for funerals. Makeup is a part of that."

"It's not easy making the dead look alive. But I'm one of the best." He opened and closed the scissors quickly. "By the time she started to awake, she was perfect."

"And then you gave her a little bit more medicine to help her nerves."

"Not a lot. Just a little. She fell asleep, and I snuggled next to her on the bed."

"She was found dead."

"I fell asleep beside her, and when I woke up, she was awake and trying to leave me. She started screaming. Yelling. I hate yelling. I forced more drugs into her. She choked and gagged; she was so terrified. To this day, I regret losing my temper." He shook his head. "At first, when she went still, I was relieved. She was my perfect girl again. She lay so still in my arms. A real doll. I couldn't resist her. She was so beautiful. So I took her back to the bed. We laid together all day and the next night. Taking her virginity was beautiful."

Tessa tried to hide her revulsion. "Did you plan to overdose her?"

His face tightened with regret. "No. That was a terrible accident. I thought I was just settling her nerves with a few more pills. I loved her so much when she was quiet."

"When did you realize she was dead?"

"Early on the fourth morning. I panicked." He looked at her as if he needed her to understand. "I took her to the woods. But I didn't just dump her. I couldn't just discard her like trash. She meant so much to me. So I leaned her against a tree. I wanted to preserve her dignity."

"But that wasn't enough to make you feel better. You'd killed her, and nothing was going to make that right."

"I didn't want to hurt her."

If she could keep him talking, she might be able to reach him and make him see this was wrong. And if she couldn't reach him, then she was at least buying time. "You set the fire the morning she was found."

"I was feeling guilty. Lost. The fires calm me. They always have."

"Knox knew you'd set the fire, didn't he?"

"He'd been consumed with finding Kara, like everyone else in town. He never linked her to me."

"But the fire told him you were upset about something."

"Yes. I was trying to stay calm. Trying to be good. But Kara was dead, and I knew it would mean trouble."

"Did Knox confront you after Kara was found?"

"He came by the funeral home that night. He was upset and so angry. He was ready to arrest me when I broke down crying. I was so sorry. I didn't mean to hurt her. I told him she took the drugs on her own. It was all a terrible accident."

Tears welled in her eyes as she struggled to keep her voice calm. "And Diane, why did you change her?"

"You four were part of a set. I wanted her to be perfect forever. Like Kara, but better. You see, I can work for hours to make it perfect, but it can be destroyed with the swipe of a cloth. When the other funeral attendant and I picked Kara up from the medical examiner, she was clean. There were no traces of the pretty little doll I created. It was as if she never existed. It broke my heart to see my work washed away."

"So you saw to it that Diane's would never fade." She avoided the word *mutilate*, knowing she walked a razor-thin line with this killer. "The work you did on her was very detailed."

He nodded. "I've worked hard to perfect my craft. It was important that I get it exactly right."

"All that work, and you killed her. Was her overdose an accident as well?"

He closed his eyes, his face tightening with regret. "No. I am ashamed to say I was seduced by the stillness. I loved her so much when she allowed me to pose her and play with her."

"I don't understand." Her chest tightened as she tried not to imagine the last moments of Diane's life.

"A doll doesn't move," he said simply. "She merely is there for me. All of me. Unconditionally. She is all mine."

Every instinct in her body demanded she twist her hand in the strap. The muscles in her body begged her to rip her hands from the restraints and get free. She wanted to run to the door. Scream for help. But she couldn't surrender to impulse. Like Dakota, she had to lock away her fears until she could find the right moment to escape. "Who wasn't there for you?" She spoke softly, as if soothing a small child.

The question sharpened his gaze. "What are you saying? That my family didn't love me? My mother and father loved me. My sisters loved me. They just didn't know me."

"I know they loved you," she said shifting course. "But their not understanding you must have been so painful."

"I saw the fear in my sisters' eyes. They started locking their doors at night. I just wanted to watch them sleep. Do you know how much it hurt me when I discovered they were locking me out?"

"I spoke to your sister Carol to tell her about your father's death. She said your mother saw you eight years ago. Did you try to go home?"

"I wanted to see Mom. But when she looked at me, she was terrified. It broke my heart."

"That's when you killed the woman in Denver, right?"

He pressed his fingers to his temples. "Questions, questions. You sound like a doctor. A know-it-all."

"I don't know it all, but I want to. I want to understand you." She forced a smile that she prayed looked friendly. "I just want to be there for the real you. I mean, we are going to spend more time together."

He studied her, his gaze narrowing as he slowly shook his head. "No, you're trying to get into my head." He set aside the scissors and reached for a straight razor. "It's what women do. They twist your thoughts, and they confuse you. Say one thing. Do another. Dolls don't do that. They are what they are."

"I'm not like that." She feared that desperation was creeping into her tone.

"No, you are lying. My father used to say all the time how my mother would get in his head. She drove him crazy with her complaints about me: 'Robbie is staring at the girls again. Robbie stole more matches. There was a fire today.' But my father wouldn't listen to her. He was kind to me despite all her complaining. I loved her, and all she could do was talk about the bad things. I thought things had changed while I was away, but I saw for myself eight years ago she still hated me. A mother shouldn't hate her son."

"What were some of the good things you remember about your mother? There must be happy memories." She needed to keep him calm and talking.

Absently he studied the light gleaming on the scissors. "I loved my mother. I loved my sisters. I just wanted to be close to them. They didn't understand."

"Your mother loved you. You were her flesh and blood."

"She didn't. I know it. That's why I set the fires. I wanted to burn away the pain."

"The fires weren't your fault."

"Dad didn't like what I did, but he tried to understand. He kept telling me the anger would go away, so he was always covering up for me."

She hesitated before she said his real name. "It's okay, Robbie."

He tensed at the sound of his name. "No one's called me that in a long time."

"Did your father help you change your name?"

"He knew how it was done. He had a new name for me. He brought me to Virginia. Got me the job at the funeral home. It was all fine for a long time."

"Until Kara."

His grip tightened around the scissors. "She was an accident. I told you that."

And Knox had covered it up. "He figured out you killed Terrance."

"Yes."

"How?"

"Stupid and sloppy on my part. I didn't mean to hurt the boy. It was never part of the plan. Knox came by the funeral home early, and he saw my van. He looked in the back. He never really trusted me and was always checking up on me. He saw the boy."

"But he didn't tell."

"I begged him not to. I told him it wasn't my fault. He just stood there staring at me, and I thought he would. I thought that was it for me.

"But he just shook his head and left. When he showed up at Roger Benson's funeral, I thought he'd tell then. But he never did. He was too afraid."

"He must have loved you very much."

"I thought so."

But Knox sent his files to Agent Sharp. He knew Sharp would figure out the trail to the DNA evidence hidden in the old arson case.

"Why kill Terrance?" Her voice was a hoarse whisper.

"He saw my face. He said he wouldn't tell, but I couldn't take that risk. I had Destiny to think about." His eyes darkened. "I was truly sorry about his death." He looked at her, his eyes filled with anguish. "I tried to make his death quick. Painless."

The overhead lamp glinted off the blade. Fear twisted inside her. "Are you going to kill me?"

"Oh, no, Serenity," he rushed to say. "You aren't going to die. You'll be my masterpiece, and we'll be together for a very long time. Now that we know each other, you can keep calling me Robbie. I like the sound of my name when you say it."

He reached for a fistful of her hair and sheared it off with the scissors. He stood back for a moment holding the thick clump of hair like a trophy. "It must feel freeing to have all that gone."

The jagged edges of her hair brushed her cheeks. "Please don't do this, Robbie. You don't have to change me to make me love you."

A distant thud stopped his approach. Frowning, he paused for a moment and listened. She glanced toward the ceiling, praying it hadn't been the wind. *Please, Dakota, save me.*

Seconds passed, and when they heard no other sound, he gripped the scissors and cut another chunk of her hair.

She winced, knowing the loss of hair paled compared to what she was about to lose. Her face, her dignity, her life with Dakota. It was the idea of never seeing him again that made her most sad and angry.

He'd grabbed a third handful of hair and raised the scissors when a loud thump echoed from above. He fisted her hair tighter. Another bang crashed, followed by the sound of wood splintering.

"Robbie, they've found you," she said. "Robbie, please, you still have time to escape. Run while you can."

He clung to her hair an extra beat before he released it and glared at the door. "They have not found me. I made sure we were well hidden."

"Please, Robbie, run."

"Stop telling me what to do. Get out of my head." He was clearly agitated. "No one is going to take you away from me. No one." DeLuca patted her on the shoulder. "Don't go anywhere, I'll be right back."

"Where are you going?"

"To take care of any trespassers."

When he vanished through the door, she focused on the loose wristband. She twisted her hand, pulling and straining against the strap, feeling her skin bruise and scrape. The leather creaked and stretched, wanting to give way. She yanked harder as tears of frustration rolled down her cheeks.

She would not die in this room.

***

When the door splintered, Sharp stumbled inside but quickly steadied himself. He stared inside the dark warehouse space. The main level was vacant except for scattered boxes and trash that still remained from the last tenant. The windows were covered with white shades that had yellowed over time. In the center of the room were several pillars, and in the back, a door. Sharp reached for the light switch, but when he flipped it, nothing happened. He moved toward the door and found it locked with a dead bolt.

Sharp started to move when McLean laid his hand on his shoulder. "What?"

"Listen," McLean said.

They both stilled a beat, and somewhere below them the stairs creaked.

"He's here," McLean said. "And on the move."

Headlights swiped across the front of the building, and he saw the flash of blue lights. Through the broken door, he spotted a Virginia State Police cruiser. Riley rose out of the car and rushed into the building, her weapon drawn.

"More on the way," she said.

"There's a door inside that's locked," Sharp said.

She glanced at her cruiser and ran back to retrieve a tire iron. As she raced up to Sharp, she studied McLean. "Who are you?" Riley asked.

"Later," Sharp said, taking the tire iron.

The trio raced toward the door. Sharp drove the tire iron into the doorjamb and, using leverage, popped the door loose.

***

DeLuca heard the grind of metal against metal seconds before wood split. The house had been breached. A helpless rage rolled over him, and he pressed his fists to his temples. This wasn't right. This wasn't fair! No one had the right to come into his house and take what was his. He was just getting started with Serenity, and he was not going to let anyone take her from him. He'd waited too long. Planned and dreamed about their time together for too long.

The thud of footsteps creaked on the floor above him, and he knew they were coming for him. The urge to burn the building down around them all was strong. He ran back to a storage closet and unlocked it quickly. Inside was a canister of thermite, a metal powder he used to start his fires. If he spread the accelerant on the steps and set it ablaze, then that would buy him time to get out the back with his Serenity.

Simply thinking about the fire calmed his nerves and cleared his muddled thoughts. He wedged open the container and ran up the steps. He dumped it on the wooden staircase, which would be the perfect tinder for his blaze.

At the bottom of the stairs, he tossed the empty vessel aside and reached for a match in his pocket. Just as he struck it, the door at the top of the stairs slammed open.

He looked up into the face of Dakota Sharp, whose eyes burned like Lucifer's. He dropped the match and ran to get his Serenity. If he moved fast, he could grab his Serenity and escape out the back as the fires consumed Agent Sharp.

***

"Help!" Tessa shouted when she heard the crash upstairs. "Help!" The acrid scent of smoke drifted from somewhere above her. Her heart kicked hard in her chest. DeLuca had set a fire.

Tears pooled in Tessa's eyes as she pulled so hard on the strap that the skin on her hand bled. Instead of frustration, she yanked harder, hoping the blood would make her skin slick. She twisted and turned her wrist, unmindful of the pain.

As the scent of smoke grew heavier, footsteps thudded in the hall-way and she knew DeLuca was coming back. "I am not dying here today."

With a final, desperate pull, she jerked her hand free. Success chased fear as she focused her attention to the other strap. Her fingers trembling, she undid the buckle and she quickly swiped away the leather. She rolled and stumbled free of the chair, falling on her hands and knees. Even as her head spun from adrenaline, she scrambled to her feet. Footsteps thudded closer toward the door. She raced to the work-table and grabbed the scissors, gripping them in her blood-soaked hand.

The door banged open.

DeLuca stood in the doorway, his eyes wild with fury and panic. When he saw her standing, his dark eyes narrowed and he raced toward her.

She braced.

Gripped the scissors.

She held her ground, knowing if she ran, he'd catch her and it all might be over. She had to stand her ground. Wait for her moment to strike.

When he was only inches from her and reaching for her arm, she lunged.

DeLuca tried to sidestep the blow, but she was quick enough to jab the scissors in his forearm. As smoke began to roll in from the open doorway, he howled. He recovered quickly and sprang for her again. "I know you are afraid, Serenity, but I'm here to save you. The building is on fire. We only have a minute before this space fills with smoke."

He moved to grab her again as if his words were enough to soothe her, but she struck again, cutting his arm once more. He howled, all traces of worry vanishing in a flash of pain.

She raised the scissors to strike.

"Fucking bitch," he growled as he grabbed her wrist, suspending the scissors in midair. "I thought you were different."

"I'm not your goddamned doll, you twisted son of a bitch."

DeLuca looked hurt for a split second before he grabbed her hand and twisted so hard that bone snapped. Pain shot through her arm. He'd broken her wrist.

As the smoke crawled through the room, she thought about all the times Sharp had lectured her about self-defense. All the times she just wanted him to let the past go. Balling up fingers from her good hand, she drove it straight for his throat. He barely deflected the move and grabbed her by the neck. His fingers clamped into her like an iron vise, and the madness darkening his eyes told her he was seconds from crushing her windpipe.

She jabbed her knee up, aiming for his groin but striking his thigh. The blow was enough to make him grunt and ease up on her throat for an instant.

He slapped her hard across the face. Her thoughts scattered as the pain ricocheted through her skull. He raised his hand to strike again.

The door slammed open with such force, the hinges gave way. Through the smoke she saw Dakota. His eyes were dark and feral as he raised his weapon.

DeLuca grabbed Tessa and turned her around as he tightened his grip on her neck. Dakota had trained for years as a sniper, and though it had been a decade since he'd been in the military, he didn't hesitate to take a difficult shot. He fired twice.

Both bullets struck the side of DeLuca's head and burrowed through his brain. Blood and brain matter sprayed her face. Tessa flinched as she stared at Dakota, his gun still pointing at his target. For a moment she was afraid to move for fear Dakota would have to shoot again.

DeLuca's grip slackened, and he fell to his knees, his dead weight pulling her down with him. His weight pinned her to the floor, knocking the air from her lungs. She pushed against him, desperate to be free.

Dakota yanked him off Tessa, and weapon still drawn, quickly scanned the room for any other threats. McLean rushed the doorway with Riley.

Holstering his weapon, Dakota gathered her up in his arms. "Tessa?"

Her tears tumbled uncontrollably as her fingers gripped his arm. The iron hold she'd had on her fear slackened and gave way.

Sharp picked her up, and they all hurried toward the back exit that led outside to a set of concrete steps that rose to a back parking lot.

Outside, the cool fresh air brushed her face as the roar of the fire inside the building grew more ferocious.

Dakota wiped DeLuca's blood from her face. "Are you hurt?"

She shook her head as she stared at the blood now clinging to Dakota's palms. "Just my wrist."

He touched her shorn hair. "Are you sure? Tessa, you can tell me anything."

She hugged him carefully, guarding her injured wrist. "I'm okay. He was going to do terrible things, but you stopped him. You saved me."

His arms tightened into a steel band. "I thought I'd lost you."

"I'm here." She'd never stopped to think he'd been as terrified as she had been.

"And I'm not letting you go again. Ever."

She drew back and cupped his face in her hands. "I'm holding you to that."

His smile was more feral than relieved.

The building was alighted with flames as McLean stood guard and Riley ran to her cruiser to call for backup and fire crews.

She hugged him again, using his strength to steady the rush of emotions that threatened to overwhelm her. Finally, when she caught her breath, she looked up into eyes that glistened with tears. "He killed Kara."

Sharp cupped her face. "He actually admitted that?"

"Yes. He also killed Diane and Elena."

"Jesus." He pulled her into his arms again.

"I love you. I don't know if you want to give us a second chance or not, but I love you. It's all I thought about in there."

He threaded his fingers again through her hair, fisting the short pieces in his hand. "I've always loved you. Too much maybe. I'm never letting you go again."

She smiled. "Good."

EPILOGUE

Five weeks later

Sharp didn't bring flowers for his sister.

He wondered if that was a mistake as he knelt in front of his sister's fresh grave. He'd had her body exhumed, and they'd found the doll buried beside her. Tessa and Dr. Kincaid had been the ones to examine her and remove the doll cradled at her side before putting her back in the ground next to her parents.

"Kara, I thought about bringing flowers," he said. "I hear girls like them. But I never pictured you with an armload of daisies or roses."

He reached in his pocket and pulled out a deck of cards. "Remember how we used to play gin? God, I hated that game, but you loved it." Shit, the hours he'd sat listening to her prattle as they'd traded cards. He laid the deck on her grave. "Thought the cards were more fitting. Tessa told me she put a pack in your hands."

He brushed dead leaves aside. "I just wanted you to know we got him. He's dead. And if there's any justice, he's burning in hell now."

Norman DeLuca. He'd been there all along. Standing at the funeral of Kara. And then at Terrance's funeral, his eyes moist with what looked like genuine sadness and regret.

Sharp suspected DeLuca had said the truth when he told Tessa he'd not meant to kill Terrance. He'd not expected to see Terrance standing in that alley, and when the kid got a glimpse of his face, he really believed he had no choice. If the kid had talked, Diane would have been found and his secret, his creation, discovered.

A search of DeLuca's home found a box of grisly photos of all the women he'd killed. There'd been a few pictures of Elena during her transition. Her face was so raw and red and layered in tattoos. There had been multiple pictures of Diane before, during, and after her change. And the other women who fit the homicide reports of several prostitutes in the Denver area. Their files had been pulled, and a look at their autopsy photos showed that DeLuca hadn't perfected his gruesome skills. On these women, he'd not only practiced on their faces but on their backs and legs as well. One woman's entire chest and back were covered in permanent ink.

At the bottom of the box of pictures were images of Kara taken during the days she'd been missing before she was found dead. He'd applied and reapplied makeup to her several times and propped her in a chair, holding a doll. There was no telling if she was alive or heavily drugged during those grim photo sessions.

DeLuca's secrets had been peeled back layer by layer, photo by photo.

Sharp learned that DeLuca's identity had been stolen from a young infant who'd died in Alaska the same year Robbie Knox had been born. When Robbie Knox "died" and became DeLuca, his father put him into a mental hospital in Virginia, where he was treated for six years. By the time he moved to Virginia to live near his father, Robbie Knox had long been forgotten.

It still twisted Sharp's gut to know that DeLuca had held his sister for days. He woke up often in the night, unable to sleep, forced to pace and battle regrets. To know she might have been found if Knox hadn't been hiding his own secrets.

Sharp's only bit of solace was that she didn't realize what was happening due to the heavy sedation. Or, at least, that was the hope that kept him sane.

And, of course, Tessa was there to wrap her arms around him and coax him back to bed. When he didn't feel like talking, she didn't press; when he did, she sat and silently listened.

Sharp removed a flask from his pocket and held it up to Roger's gravestone. "I should have toasted you at your funeral. You were right all these years." He took a long swig, grimacing as the whiskey burned his throat. He turned to his mother's grave. "Mom, I did bring you a flower. I remember how you liked them." He laid a single rose on her grave. "Take care of them, Mom."

He rose, staring at the three headstones, taking some comfort in the fact that they were together.

When he turned, he saw Tessa leaning against his car. Her short hair was loose, now styled into a layered cut that suited her. The doctors had removed the cast from her wrist, and her bruises had healed.

She stared at him with such understanding and longing, it took his breath away. "You okay?"

Leaves rustled under his feet as he moved toward her. She opened her arms, and he stepped into the embrace. For a long moment, he simply breathed in her scent.

"Are you okay?" she repeated.

"I never felt I had the right to be okay," he said. "Kara was dead, and I just didn't deserve any happiness."

She tightened her hold. "Dakota, she wouldn't want that for you."

"I know. But I couldn't shake the feeling."

"And now?"

"I can finally say I'm okay. It's done." He raised his gaze and kissed her. She wrapped her arms around his neck and held him close.

He cupped her face in his hands, and when he broke the kiss, he felt a sense of renewal. She'd moved into his town house nearly three weeks ago, and he was getting used to accepting that he was not alone anymore.

"Let's go home," she said.

Sharp took her left hand in his and from his coat pocket removed a diamond ring. He slid it on her finger until it pushed against her wedding band. "Not the biggest in terms of carats, and I'm sure there are some rings that sparkle brighter, but—"

"But nothing," she said, snatching her hand back so she could admire the ring. "It is stunning."

Flickers of doubt shadowed his eyes. "You sure? I can get another."

"No," she said, hugging him. "No. It's perfect."

"I love you," he said, his voice rough with emotion as he held her tight.

She kissed him on the lips. "And I love you too, Agent Sharp."

"Marry me."

"We are married."

"Let's do it right this time. With friends. Make it a celebration."

She hugged him. "I'll marry you as many times as you ask, Dakota Sharp."

His lips broadened into a wide grin, and he kissed her again.

ABOUT THE AUTHOR

Photo © 2015 Studio FBJ

New York Times and *USA Today* bestselling novelist Mary Burton is the highly praised author of twenty-eight published romance and suspense novels and five novellas. She lives in Virginia with her husband and three miniature dachshunds.